D0278505

The
Leviathan

The Leviathan

Rosie Andrews

R A V E N BOOKS
LONDON · OXFORD · NEW YORK · NEW DELHI · SYDNEY

RAVEN BOOKS
Bloomsbury Publishing Plc
50 Bedford Square, London, WC1B 3DP, UK
29 Earlsfort Terrace, Dublin 2, Ireland

BLOOMSBURY, RAVEN BOOKS and the Raven Books logo
are trademarks of Bloomsbury Publishing Plc

First published in Great Britain 2022

A catalogue record for this book is available from the British Library

ISBN: HB: 978-1-5266-3733-8; TPB: 978-1-5266-3734-5; WATERSTONES SPECIAL
EDITION: 978-1-5266-5286-7; GOLDSBORO SPECIAL EDITION: 978-1-5266-5285-0;
EBOOK: 978-1-5266-3692-8; EPDF: 978-1-5266-3694-2

2 4 6 8 10 9 7 5 3 1

Typeset by Integra Software Services Pvt. Ltd.
Printed and bound in Great Britain by CPI Group (UK) Ltd, Croydon CR0 4YY

MIX
Paper from
responsible sources
FSC® C171272

To find out more about our authors and books visit www.bloomsbury.com
and sign up for our newsletters

To Hugh Rooney

Hell is truth seen too late.
    – Thomas Hobbes, *Leviathan* (1651)

Lay your hands on him; remember the battle –
you will not do it again! Behold, the hope of a man
is false; he is laid low even at the sight of him.
    – Job 41:1–34

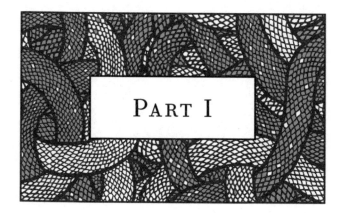

PART I

I

24th March 1703

A place far from the sea

S he is awake.
And I must remind myself of how it began.

The end of all things. It was a time of witches, it was a time of saints. A time when rabbits hunted foxes, when children came into the world without their heads, and kings lost theirs on the scaffold. The world was turned upside down, or so some said. *Weep, England, weep,* the broadsheets cried, and the poets and philosophers, fearing for their own necks, delayed their poems and philosophies, or incarcerated them in Latin and impenetrable Greek, to be exhumed at a more enlightened date.

Now, less than a hundred years after men and magic began to drift apart, we walk a new earth. We have become *reasonable*, and cleave to our certainties as once we cleaved to our kings. Now, the buried stories are dismissed as old wives' tales, exaggerations, falsehoods. But still they bubble through the cracks, clinging on, refusing to go down into the dark.

They develop strange qualities, words stored for too long. In the dim light of my small study, never bright enough now, I lay them down in honest black ink, but they are past their bloom. The candle wax runs low, but still they come, and my pen moves over the page as if of its own will.

But it was my intention to remember. I rise and cross to the bookcase, turning the key and opening the latticed door. The bookcase stands near the window, which I keep slightly open in spite of the cold. A draught comes through, sharp-toothed, carrying the chill of the late-winter's eve and, drifting from the books, the smells that have walked with me since childhood: vellum, hide glue, resin, cuttlefish bone scattered across gossamer-thin pages.

Yet it is not a book I draw from the shelves, but a calfskin wallet, from which I brush long-abandoned spider webs and a thick coating of dust. The wallet houses many separate pieces of parchment: letters, pamphlets, other trifles collected over the years. Here is a sketch of the armies at the Battle of Edgehill, here a recipe for cherry wine I had thought lost.

There. Hidden amongst all that ephemera, cast out of sight and memory, is the sought-for object. I put my hand upon it, linger for a moment, and my intention falters. Perhaps I am just an old fool who should know better than to rake up what is buried. But I carry it back to my desk.

The handwriting – my father's – is economical, his frugality echoing from the densely placed words. Not every word is readable: the inevitable result of repeat folding and unfolding, or of water damage, perhaps. It is testimony, a witnessing, dated *16th August 1628*. The witnesses were my father, and his kinsman, John Milton. This, then, was where it all began.

We were late. The Guldern *had been at sea five wretched months. We had lost the convoy weeks before. The waves and gales moved against us, so less experienced men moaned pitifully and emptied their bellies over the side of the ship. This was the Kattegat strait, off the coast of Anholt, Denmark, in late winter, with darkening skies, narrow and treacherous, full of reefs and sandbanks, shallow enough…*

In a little while, Mary comes. She leans in, reading. The worry lines between her silvered brows are deep, but as I glance down at her hand on my shoulder, the wrinkles and liver spots fade in the gloom. I know we are lucky – if not among the luckiest

— to have lived this long and in such relative bliss. I ask whether anything has changed since supper. No, she says, looking up at the ceiling; everything is just as it was. But the fine tremor in her hand, still resting on my shoulder, belies her words.

Brightly, she asks if I want more coal heaped upon the embers, but we can ill afford to run the fire high these days. Still, the room is chill. My breath clouds the candlelight and the cold creeps in beneath my breeches. I gather about my arthritic knees a woven blanket that once belonged to my father. Mary asks how long I plan to write. I lie, saying I might be another half an hour. She hates it when I strain my eyes and scolds me, so I tell her I am not straining, but exercising them, the better to see her beauty. She laughs, a sound as soft as down, and leaves, unhurried and deliberate as always, taking all certainty with her. Alone, I return to where I left the story.

...Now my steps were taken downhill, the ship was so tilted. Riches, treasure, plunder — all of a sudden they were will-o'-the-wisps, phantoms. There was something else here, something that breathed and whimpered, something still alive. I groped like a blind man. With my snaphance in my right hand, I took another pace forward.

I lean back, rubbing my eyes to sharpen the meandering edges of my sight. This is a distraction, only, from what I know I must do, and from the knowledge encamped in the pit of my stomach, which has squatted there since morning broke and Mary came down the stairs with cheeks as white as lamb's fleece beneath her flyaway hair, and said the words I have so long known I would hear:

She is awake.

2

27th December 1643

North Norfolk

Dearest brother,

My heart grew wings when I received your last letter. I had worn my knees down to the bones in beseeching God that you would not be harmed. The knowledge that you would be in the van of the fighting weighed upon me such that I cannot describe the turmoil of my thoughts! Mercifully, my prayers were answered, and knowing that you are safe is the greatest gift the Lord could bestow on our small family. It tells me we are truly blessed by God. Because of this, I know Parliament will prevail.

Yet, now the danger has passed — or so Father informs me in my ignorancy of these things — I must admit what I have not before; that all has not been well at home. I beg you to return to us as soon as you are able. Please do not delay for any *matter.*

I will not share the whole story now. It is long and will, I fear, seem unlikely to you, reading by daylight. But I write in the shadows, by candlelight, with my hands shaking — even now you will see the difficulty I have in forming these letters — because our home is under attack by a great and ungodly evil.

This wickedness surrounds the harlot Chrissa Moore. You will remember she appeared in April, without character or respectable family name. I swear to you, Thomas, the girl is drawing our father more and more into her corruptions. There are times when I think he is fascinated by her, when he does not hear me. I fear for his safety, and for his soul. He is quite unmanned. She is Babylon, brother – the abomination of the earth.

Exodus is clear: 'Thou shalt not suffer a witch to live.' As this is God's Word, so I must act. The matter can wait no longer. I hope by the time of your return our home will be restored to peace. However, if the witch is victorious over my small strength – should God not see fit to lend me more – she might find in you a doughtier enemy. Do not fail God, or me. Please come home as soon as ever you can.

May God bless the King always, and may the army under Cromwell succeed in freeing him from the papists' evil counsel.

God bless you.
Your loving sister,
Esther

I folded the letter and replaced it in my jerkin. I had only taken it out to remind myself of its contents, and found that, in the fading light, with my body rising and falling with the trotting of my horse, I regretted it, as I could barely read my sister's shuddering scrawl. I remembered all the occasions Esther had asked me for help with her letters and felt a keen twist of shame.

She was hysterical, obviously. It was natural enough, being sixteen, stuck on the farm all this time. A young woman, particularly one with her imagination and melancholic humours, needed friends, people to laugh with and balance her tendencies towards overanxious thinking. Our estate was too isolated, buried in its own shallow valley, surrounded by just a few hamlets. She had no mother to teach and guide her. Apart from Father, the others in the house were servants: this girl, Chrissa, whom I hadn't met, and Joan, our other maid. Joan was an honest, kind girl, but daft, as inconstant as a kid goat. I decided to speak to Father about finding some companion for my sister, someone her own age who might bring her out of herself.

Of Chrissa Moore I hardly thought at all. Though Father rarely took on new servants and, had I given it more attention, I might have found it surprising that he had hired a woman without a character, I was preoccupied by other matters. I was injured, carrying a wound unhealed since Newbury, and every stumble of the horse brought a lance of fresh pain near my groin, filling my mind with unwished-for images: the sawn-off shaft of my enemy's pike as it struck out with disembowelling force, my desperate twist away, the other man's frightened face, and then the moment of shock as the steel point pierced my inner thigh. I had killed my man, but paid the price for it.

It was getting on in the day and very cold. We were passing All Saints, near Scottow, and the sky was beginning to darken. The church's stone porch looked inviting, but would be locked against bandits. These were turbulent days. There was no shelter for us here. 'Come, Ben,' I said. The horse whinnied, seeming to know it would soon be time for a meal and a warm stable, but there were no taverns or alehouses nearby, and anyway, it did not seem worth the blow to my thinning purse of seeking lodgings for another night. Not so near my destination.

Instead, I rode on, anticipating my welcome. I saw in my mind's eye what I so hoped to see in truth: Father's face lifting at the sight of me, his large hands enfolding mine. He would say I had proved myself. Treat me as a man, not a boy.

It was Christmas. I had just missed the day itself, but still the house would be snug and merry, with a fire in the hearth, perhaps a pie from the turkey or the boar's head, whatever Father had been able to get hold of for a simple celebration of Christ's birth. There would be no plum puddings, no hobby horses, no kissing bush of holly and bay hung from the ceiling, as Father, though he maintained it was not our place to judge others who followed the old ways in their own homes, said such things were licentious. Still, there would be wintry tales, warmed wassail, and small gifts for Esther and me on New Year's Day; a pair of gloves or a printed prayer. In the evenings, Father would roast apples and read from Revelation in his deep, strong voice.

At those thoughts, something soared inside me, something strong enough to steal my breath: a deep, resurgent hope. A hope that, once home, I would be forgiven the missteps of the past – I didn't want to think of them, but there they sat, huddled traitorously in the corners of my mind – and all would be as it was before.

Most of all, I thought of peace, even if it could only be temporary. If my journeying had told me one thing, it was that this was a land in chaos. How few moments there had been, on the road north, when I had not looked over my shoulder for vagabonds, or known the exact position of my sword. How the wind from the west had sniped at me, laughing at the inadequacies of my cloak and hat. I longed to put down my burdens and sink into the comfort of my own bed, free of the grunts and farts of other men, forgetful of the guttural cries of battle, safe behind our whitewashed walls.

By then, my sister's letter lay unthought of inside my jerkin, though somewhere at the back of my mind was a vague intention to talk to her about it. I would find out what disagreements and jealousies had soured things between her and the Moore girl, reassure Esther, and remind her that she was the mistress of the house, with no need to enter into petty wars with the servants. Should this Chrissa turn out to be a troublemaker, she could easily be dismissed.

First, though, I would wash. A kettle of hot water, clean linens, too much peat charcoal on the rufous-hued fire. I wondered whether, if I spoke particularly sweetly to Esther, I could persuade her to sing. The memory of her high, sad voice releasing its song like a mistle thrush on some long-ago occasion – a birthday, or Christmas – was bitter-sweet, as I knew Father would frown upon the frivolity of music in these more holy days.

I gave the horse an encouraging pat on his hindquarters – *rest soon, my friend* – and straightened my hat. We rode on.

An hour later, I leant against the trunk of an ash tree. It was too dark to see the tree clearly, but I knew it was an ash, and which one; I was less than three miles from home.

Somewhere above my head was a branch as thick as a man's waist. From that branch, in the reign of fat King Henry, two men had dangled by their necks for a murder they had not committed, or so the legend went, and their dolorous spirits had often been reported moaning about the trunk. I'd never heard them. I was told there was a stone boasting the Devil's claw marks around here somewhere, too, and a healing well, but had never found those, either, though I had searched many times; more, I suppose, to prove to myself that they were just stories for the credulous, than for any other reason.

I squinted into the darkness. The night had been lively with stars, but thick clouds had now passed in front of the moon's face, and I wouldn't have seen a camel lumber by six inches from my nose. It had not been my intention to stop, knowing the road like the back of my own hand, but when Ben had stumbled on his forelegs and limped thereafter, I'd doubted myself. I so desperately wanted the comforts of home, but if the animal broke a bone, I would have to put him out of his misery and I liked this horse.

So I dismounted and turned Ben loose in the field, seeking shelter beneath my cloak and the thinning canopy of the ash. I would continue in daylight until I stood once more on my own acres.

I suppose I was feeling sorry for myself as I huddled in a fissure of the ancient trunk. Ben was happy enough cropping grass ten or so feet away, and there was nothing for me to do except close my eyes, but my wound throbbed, and as I dug sharp stones out from beneath my breeches and shifted my weight against the hardened bark, I knew sleep would not come easily. It made me think of the night before the last fight, at Newbury. After a long march, the King's forces had reached the town before us. When we halted for a few short hours of rest, we had sworn violently on realising the site of our camp: the flats along the banks of the river, without roofs or beds, and on short commons. The fear, though, had been worse than any material discomfort; a ravenous cold deep in my belly, a tremor afflicting my limbs as I listened to fifteen thousand men talking without surcease, all knowing that in the morning we would face the earth-shaking terror of a cavalry charge, and the hot smell of musket blasts, woven into the noise of war, a noise like the end of the world.

I shivered beneath the tree branches and turned over, shoving my knapsack under my head. It did not help to dwell on the battle. We hadn't won, nor had we lost, and now Essex's army was ensconced in London, while the King had retreated to Oxford, and what would come next, no man could say.

There was the future to think of. The war wouldn't – couldn't – last forever. Even if I survived, and whether King or Parliament emerged victorious, the outcome might be little concern of mine, as I had no intention of remaining in England to see it. In the months since the fighting broke out, I had seen men shed an ocean of blood in pursuit of their rights and prerogatives. How much of the money in his pocket a man could be forced to hand over to his King, whether the law should apply equally to a beggar or a lord, what beliefs a man or woman had the right to hold in their heart – all such things lay in the balance of this war. And in their desperation to be free, the religious reformers had chosen revolution.

But I was tired of it. All of it. Tired of men beating one another into the dirt as though they were slaughtering hogs. Tired of hearing bones shatter and seeing my fellows soil themselves, all because some men far from the battle believed God had a perfect foreknowledge of who was damned and who was saved, and some others didn't.

And there was more than one way to be free.

On that same night, before Newbury, Captain Jack Trelawney and I had swapped the names of our people. He was senior to me in the company, and a little older, but as raw recruits we had worked out we had grown up less than twenty miles apart, and become friends. Before the battle we exchanged our information solemnly, like strangers, though we felt more like brothers, having shared the same feet of earth and the same scurvy food for more than a year now. We did this in the unspoken understanding that, if the worst happened to one of us, the other would seek out those who must be told, and give as false an account of the last moments of the dead as might be needed to avoid a deeper grief.

When we had finished, Jack scratched his beard furiously. In the dim light of the campfire his pockmarked face looked different: more thoughtful. He said, 'When this is done… When this is done…' I had the sense that what he was going to say mattered, and waited. 'The New World, Tom,' he said, in a voice thick with something hopeful, something new. 'Virginia, Maryland, Connecticut. There are ships sailing every day from Plymouth. Or there were before the fighting. All you need is the price of your passage, and your sword. There's land, millions of acres of it, and no bugger to tell you what to do. They grow tobacco and get fat off the proceeds.'

America.

The thought of that massive continent, its green expanses, its clear waters, its unclimbed mountains and untrodden shores, danced before me like a chimera.

'Doesn't the land belong to anyone?' I said, doubtfully. The idea of a space so vast, and yet lawless and godless was terrifying, and intoxicating.

Jack shook his head. 'It's endless, I tell you. There to be settled. What do you say?'

Startled, I said, 'Me?'

'Why not? You've no wife or children. You're a useful man. You stink like the back end of a fox, and you're too pretty for my liking, but you're not scared of anything and you pay your way. How about if we meet after we de-enlist, and get berths on one of those boats I was talking about?'

'That's if we're both alive,' I said, and Jack gave a short laugh.

'Can't say I'm confident of that,' he said, dourly. 'But will you think on it?'

'I will.'

And I did. Somehow, through all that followed, the pain of my injury and the deflated feeling in the wake of killing another man, my initial apprehension dissolved, and I thought of nothing else; for what could frighten me after this? As for living, Jack survived the battle, but he would not be going to the New World. He had thought his tassets too heavy, had gone out to fight without them, and taken a sawn-off pike in his thigh. The wound had been a bad one, and the tax he had paid his King had been in the form of a leg, cut off on the Round Hill as Essex advanced. Generous to a fault, when I spoke to him, he insisted I should go alone, and leave all that was rotten behind me.

Now, I was determined to do it. I just needed to get through the war, earn enough money for my passage, and find a ship.

In the darkness, as if he heard my thoughts, Ben nickered uneasily.

In the morning, the horse nosed my face, as if to say, *Come.* I pushed away his velvet nostrils, feeling the blunt, browning teeth beneath my fingers. 'Get off, demon-breath.' Ben continued to stand over me like a nursemaid until I sat up, damp all over where the night's water had settled, rubbing my ice-cold limbs, breathing clouds of the frigid air. It was not quite light, but I had slept longer than I had intended.

Ben ate breakfast – the church's grass, probably theft – while I searched for a stream I remembered ran through these parts. When I heard its trickle behind the nave, I approached, then knelt and cupped the water in both palms, and drank, wincing as the cold hit the roof of my mouth; I had not real-ised my hands had become so numb. When my thirst was sated, I washed my face and hands, forcing myself to think kindly of these final miles as a postscript on the end of a long journey that, soon, I would be describing to my father.

There was something wrong with the picture in front of me.

I surveyed the fields on the south-west side of our farm. Other parts of Father's land were tenanted, but these fields contained the animals we raised ourselves. I scanned the landscape, taking in the russet palette of the near-frozen ground beset with the long shadows of trees, barely touched by a sun that had risen sulkily in the two hours since I had left Scottow, and which would rise no further today. I held Ben's bridle as I looked through a gap in the hedge, out across the open fields. My eyes saw the problem before my mind caught up.

It was late December. Father liked to put the ram to the ewes early. There ought to have been a mating dance in play: running, bleating, mounting, a ritual at once crude and sacred, as old as time. I half-expected to see Father cresting the low hill between the farmhouse and the road with his drooling mastiff, and a 'Hey-ho!' for his son.

Nothing moved. An uncertain breeze stirred my cloak and, from somewhere nearby, an owl emitted soft hoots. It was late for the bird to be abroad.

What was that I could see? The light was thin and reedy. I strained my eyes to make out something lying on the ground, several hundred yards off, something lumpen and white, and beside it, another, and, as my eyes refocused, another, on and on, like a congregation of fallen angels. I watched, held between fascination and horror as, from a tree behind me, the owl swooped on its pale prey, holding down the unmoving flesh with its strong talons, tearing at the woolly hide with its cruel, curved beak.

I am become a brother of jackals, a companion of owls.

I shook the words off, secured Ben's halter to the tree and crossed the ditch boundary into the field. I had to see.

The first sheep might have been sleeping. It was hunched at the shoulders, resting on its front legs with its back to me. But as I came around to the animal's head, I saw her tongue, black and engorged. A single blow fly, a fugitive of summer, crawled across her nose. Deep, bloody holes gaped in her head where the owl, or the buzzards before it, had begun to feast. Her eyes had gone. But she had not been dead long. No more than half a day, at a guess.

I walked on. The second sheep had been less lucky than the first. She had died on her side, exposing her soft belly. Thin entrails trailed like ribbons where, sick but still living, she had tried to crawl away from her attacker. I heard a roaring in my ears: a far-away echo of soldiers as they tore into one another like carrion.

I counted the animals as I passed them. By the time I reached the far side and began to think about going back to reclaim Ben,

I'd lost count. Somewhere north of seventy beasts had died in this field alone. They bore no signs of violence or struggle, no injuries other than those inflicted after death. It had to be disease. But I had never seen anything as virulent as this, or heard of it. These ewes looked as though they had been healthy as little as a day ago. And they were well-fed, well-kept animals, as my father's sheep had always been.

The thought of my father gave me a jolt. I turned, retracing my steps. He had to know about this, if he didn't already.

I reached Ben and freed him. I was half a mile from home if we followed the road, and I considered mounting, but the horse still limped. I decided against it, and pulled hard on the halter to hurry him.

We encountered nobody as we went along. The track was smooth and solid. Few carts or gigs were driven this way; the path led nowhere except to our house, a good-sized property my father had built himself upon his marriage to my mother, who lay in the churchyard west of here, having passed before the blessing of committing her to memory had been allowed me.

Soon, we came to the house. Separated from the surrounding fields by a tall hedge and an orchard of apple, plum and damson trees, it stood some way back from the track. Ben appeared to prefer the road. He was not a nappy animal, but now he baulked, planting his weight so I had to drag him up the rocky path to the front door. I didn't bother stabling him, and instead turned him loose into the paddock. I would take him in later, and get some attention for his injury.

Our arrival seemed to have gone unnoticed. The door remained closed, and moreover locked from the inside, which was unusual. I knocked. No servant came to admit me. I rapped again, and waited. I saw, frowning, that someone had carved a small chain of daisy heads into the wood near the floor. From the back of the house came the dog's bark. On the third knock, the door swung open, revealing wide blue eyes in a face as colourless as curds. Hovering behind the heavy oak frame, younger than her years and as slender as a reed, lacking in the womanliness one would usually recognise in a girl of sixteen summers, stood my sister. 'Esther,' I said, joyfully, then was startled as her face crumpled, and she threw herself out of the door and into my arms, weeping like a child half her age. I was shocked; she was young, and often emotional, as girls could be, I supposed, but I had never seen her like this. 'I'm here,' I said, stroking her hair. 'Where's Father? I must speak with him. The sheep...' I gathered from the upset in the house that the disaster in the fields was already known to them.

'Oh, Thomas!' Esther wailed. 'It's... I...' But she could hardly get the words out.

I cradled her head, awkwardly. 'Now, Esther, calm yourself. Come. Let's go inside and we can talk to Father about what to do, and everything will be well.'

Esther pulled away. She pressed her small fists into her eye sockets, pushing back her tears, and when she lowered her hands, seemed more like herself. 'No, brother,' she said. 'It's not the sheep. Another calamity. And much worse.'

3

Ill-wishing. Imps in the shapes of polecats and ferrets. Familiars that wind themselves, in circles of ever-increasing tightness and intimacy, about unwitting female legs at night, or creep into their beds. Satan conspiring with widows and spinsters to murder livestock. Come now, do any of us truly believe these things? Does any sensible person credit that a man might be swept away in a storm raised by an angered lover, or stricken by an apoplexy at the behest of a woman he has disdained? I have to say, I did not. I believed in the things I could touch: the fissured bark of sea-going oak, the comfort of a Welsh silver coin in my palm.

I did not know, then, that fear itself could take form, could become a tangible thing. That lesson lay ahead.

'And so, you see, the girl, Chrissa: she lies at the root of all these things. You do see?' Esther's voice brought me back to myself. I continued to gaze at my father, who lay supine in his bed, his face distorted like that of a lunatic I had once seen paraded through the streets of King's Lynn, dribbling, only half-aware of his surroundings.

It was impossible to believe that the man now staring at the bedchamber ceiling had been, when I had last seen him, just a year ago, hale and vigorous – and, although I didn't think of it just in this moment, furious with me. Now, he looked like a scarecrow that had had the stuffing beaten out of him. His mouth was loose and wet, blue-lipped, his right eye sagging visibly below the bridge of his nose. Esther had managed to communicate that this affliction had come upon him in the night, and that Joan had been sent to Walsham to seek a physician.

With my father's hand in mine, as limp as a dead rabbit kit, I felt a sudden onslaught of pain; my groin had begun to ache again when I had stepped over the threshold behind my sister. I masked it from her. I had to be the master of the house now, and care for Esther and my father. But how? Where would our income come from, if all the sheep were afflicted? Did we have any stock left, and what had happened to the animals I had seen in the fields? The weight of responsibility felt like pressing stones on my chest.

What could I say to Esther? *You do see?* she had said, so plaintively. I certainly did not see. She had been babbling since I had entered the house, words upon words, mostly about the serving girl, Chrissa Moore, and witchcraft, and compacts with the Devil. Another mention of 'ill-wishing' might explode my head like one of Fawkes's barrels.

I stood and tucked my father more closely into his blankets, patting down the edges so he remained warm and there was less chance of him rolling from the bed, for every so often his arms would thrash and flail as his mouth formed sad, meaningless sentences. I could do nothing else for him now. I was indescribably weary, sick to my stomach and in my heart. I hadn't eaten since breakfast the day before. 'Is there food in the house?' I asked. 'I must eat, and then we can talk.'

Esther stopped pacing the boards, straightened her wayward fair hair beneath her cap, then wiped her face. 'Of course,' she said. 'I will prepare food. You should rest. Sleep… I…'

'No.' I came around the side of the bed and put my arm across her shoulders. She felt like a bird. 'I'll get my own food. And

19

some for you, for you feel like you're going to snap. And then I want to hear it all – from the very start.'

'On the third day after she arrived, Joan told me, God's truth, that a child was born in the village and it had an enlarged head. It was all blue-veined, like there was something inside it. And then, when Chrissa had been here a week, and I knew – even then – there was something strange about her, she made bread. I told her the exact quantities. I was very precise. But it was so heavily salted it was like she had baked with seawater. So, I told her she had to make it again. I was very patient, and simply said the bread was inedible. And then Father took her side. He ate most of the loaf, in spite of having to wash the stuff down with half a pitcher of ale. He made no comment at all about the taste.'

Esther was looking at me expectantly. I cut another hunk of cheese. There were some puny apples in a bowl in the middle of the table, and I took one, polishing it against my shirt. She waited for me to say something.

'Go on,' I said, encouragingly, but was beginning to see where it might lead.

'I knew from the start that there was something disreputable about her. Something low. Even the way Father found her was odd – in the fields after the sun had gone down. It was obvious just from that. She was base. I wondered at first whether she had been dismissed from a previous post. Father forbade me to ask him anything else – he said I wasn't showing Christian charity – but my worry was growing that there was something of the Devil about her, Thomas. I had to know.'

I felt cold at her words. People here did not welcome talk of the Devil. If Esther had been loose-lipped with her claims about witchcraft, our reputation might not recover from it. Of equal concern was the thought that she might herself be accused – it had happened before, women casting blame on one another, then all taken beneath the wing of the same ill-flighted rumour. Esther might be too innocent to make this calculation, but I was not. 'What have you done?' I said, in horror and alarm.

'Nothing other than ask some questions!' she said, indignantly. 'I set Joan to the task. I charged her to ask – discreetly – about her people, who had employed her last, whether she had a good character. That's all.'

'And?'

'Nothing. Nobody knew her. *Nobody* Joan spoke with recognised the name "Chrissa Moore", or anybody answering to her description. But I had started to feel Joan might sympathise with Chrissa, might even be her confidante. It wouldn't surprise me if she lied.'

I doubted this. Joan Gedge was a pious girl, of tiny stature and mean intelligence. Once I had found her trying to roast a bird with the feathers still on. I honestly did not believe it would occur to her to scheme against her mistress. 'Why did you think that?' I asked, taking pains to speak gently, knowing she tended to clam up when distressed.

'Oh, it was…' She flailed. 'It's hard to explain.'

'All right. And then? Because it was months of Chrissa being here before you wrote that letter.' I didn't mean to sound so doubtful, so added, more carefully, 'What happened to cause you to write to me?'

She shifted uncomfortably in her seat, her cheeks glowing salmon pink. 'Well, it was difficult, brother. Father was obviously taken with her, but in all honesty, I didn't initially suspect anything was going to happen. Yes, I thought she might be lewd but I was embarrassed to take any further steps and admit – even to you – that there was such a person in our home. That I had not been able to protect Father. And the weeks passed and passed, the whole of the summer, and nothing very alarming happened. I had the constant feeling... a queer, black, turbulent feeling that something was wrong, but it was nothing solid.'

'When did that change?' I sounded like a lawyer, and flushed. Esther didn't seem to notice.

'It was just before I wrote my last letter.' Her voice had risen, and her eyes brimmed with more tears. She twisted the edge of the tablecloth between her fingers. Wrapped in the heavy woollen shawl passed down to her by our mother, she looked years younger than she was.

'You can tell me,' I said, coaxingly. I was expecting more of the same – tales of jealousy, salted bread and favouritism – and blamed myself. I should have kept in closer contact, tried to come home more often. If only I had not gone off to fight... If only I had not...

Esther continued. 'It was a fasting day. We had been to church, all three of us together. We walked down the lane. I could see the way she was drawing Father in, coquetting with him. He walked behind me, next to her, and I walked at a faster pace, in front. But then I turned and saw it: his hand on her arm. It was just for a moment. But Father! He would never look at a woman like that, not with Mother dead and in the ground. Never. I was so humiliated for him. She was low, not worthy of him. I walked on and didn't say anything. And neither did she, of course, although she knew I knew. She didn't even have the modesty to look ashamed.'

I weighed the different parts of this tale. It was true that our father had shown no interest in a second marriage. It seemed unlikely a man who had weathered raising two children without settling on some respectable widow would now decide he needed the convenience of a wife. Nor could I reconcile my knowledge of my father – as humble and God-fearing a man as any I knew – with Esther's report. And yet I knew – only too well – the temptations of the flesh, as Esther undoubtedly didn't. The thought of my father slaking some hidden lust on a servant girl discomforted me, but I couldn't dismiss it as a possibility. And it certainly did not speak to me of communion with the Devil.

Carefully, because I did not want to provoke her to tears again, I said, 'Are you certain that it's not just as simple as that? A flirtation, nothing more sinister?' Esther flinched at the word 'flirtation', and I was glad I had not chosen a stronger one.

She said, 'I'm not finished.' But she seemed unable to go on. Then she saw I had eaten all of my bread, and reached for the knife to cut more.

'Please – complete the tale,' I said.

The knife hovered before she put it down. Her movements were twitchy; whatever she was about to say, it made her ashamed. 'That night we all prayed together. Father led the reading, and it was clear, not for the first time,' she qualified, 'that Chrissa had a scanty knowledge of God's Word. Father asked the catechetical questions and the answers she gave were either too vague or just wrong. But he carried on and eventually we moved off to bed. Since she had been in the house, I had had trouble getting off to sleep. So when there were noises, I heard them and got up.'

I decided to stop her. Surely, we did not need to drink to the bottom of this barrel. 'I see. Don't worry, sister, I think I know what must have happened, and I don't deny it's shocking.'

I uttered an oath, so disappointed was I, but Esther turned on me in reproof. 'Thomas, you mustn't blaspheme. It was very shocking, but it isn't the end of the story.'

I apologised, and nodded so she would continue.

'I confronted her. I didn't want to – the shame nearly finished me – but for me to let such things go on under this roof and not... would have brought me as low as her. I went into her room. Father had gone to bed. I opened the door. She was standing in the window; your window. She was quite unclothed. The candle had been snuffed but the moon was coming through and I could see…' She stopped, and in the space created, I found my mind distracted by the image she had drawn.

Yet I noticed something else at this point. She could not meet my eyes. I was reminded of one of the few occasions she had deceived me. One morning, years ago, she had claimed Joan had spilled a pail, when she had dropped it herself. There had been no milk for butter, and Esther had come to me in tears, later, admitting her sin, begging me not to tell Father. I had dashed across the fields to our neighbours' house, asked for a bucket of milk and covered the accident up, but, at the moment of my asking her what had happened to the milk, the same evasiveness had dulled her eyes as now.

She went on. 'In any case, I told her to make herself decent and to leave. Immediately. And not return.' She was straight-backed, defensive, as if daring anyone to challenge her. Imagining the scene, the diminutive Esther discharging the older servant, I was surprised she had such outrage in her.

'And Father failed to object? And she didn't argue with you?' The disgrace of Esther's insinuations would prevent Chrissa Moore from securing employment anywhere else around here. She must have been furious.

Esther's tone became more uncertain. 'He did, at first. But she had little to say for herself. What could she say? And she did not deny her indecency; she packed her few things, and went.'

'And that was it?'

'No. The next day, the sheep started dying. Father didn't connect the two things at first – he thought it was some contagion and he separated the healthy ewes from the sick. But they died so fast. He would fence off fifty ewes, all of them well, and when we returned in the morning…' Esther looked into the middle distance. Her face held only despair. 'And on and on, until we had no choice – I had to tell. I had to make it known that she was ill-wishing us.'

'Who did you tell?'

'At first Constable Dillon.'

Dillon was the local constable. A good man.

Esther continued. 'And then Mr Hale.'

This was a different kettle of fish. Hale was the minister. During his weekly sermons, I'd often wished myself in possession of a broader hat to stave off showers of spittle, like a rain of fire and brimstone from the pulpit. If Hale was involved, the girl might be in genuine trouble.

Esther said, 'And Mr Hale called in John Rutherford.'

'The witchfinder?' Esther nodded. 'Did he come?'

'Immediately, and took her off from the village. He was very kind to me,' she said, seeing my frown.

I'd never met Rutherford, who acted on behalf of Christopher Manyon, the Justice of the Peace in Walsham. I knew Manyon fairly well, or had done at one time, through my father, but Rutherford I knew only by reputation. And that reputation was something of a puzzle. He was paid for his services, so he was no holy man, but he seemed to follow the local assizes, drawing out confessions from women accused of cursing their husbands, talking to familiars, dancing in the light of the full moon.

Esther had remained wide-eyed and ingenuous as she related her tale. She appeared to expect me to say something. But the one thing I wanted to say was the one thing I couldn't. That I, Thomas Treadwater, did not believe in witches. Or the Devil.

That I no longer believed in God.

I coughed. 'And then Father fell ill?'

Esther nodded. 'It was yesterday. He had been out with the men and the sheep, trying to treat as many as he could. He came back at sunset. I could see immediately that there was some devilry at work. His words came slowly. His eye... Well, you saw. And he complained of a feeling of ungodly dread. I felt it too,' she said, simply.

'But he was still walking, and talking? He was not...'

'Not as we see him now, no,' Esther confirmed. 'That came later. After dusk.'

'What time exactly?' My hands balled into fists.

'I... I don't know. But I was retiring to bed.'

I wanted to shout, break things, strike myself bloody. At about the time I had been passing Scottow's church, my father had still been conscious, within the grasp of help. When I had rested beneath the ash tree to safeguard the forelegs of a cheap horse, I might have pressed on in the dark, arrived home on foot, and been reunited with my father while he still possessed the power of speech.

Seeing my pain, Esther continued softly. 'But there was nothing anybody could have done, Thomas. It was so sudden. He fell from the bed on to the floor, as helpless as you see him this morning.'

'Don't,' I groaned, seizing the roots of my hair. 'Don't talk of him like that!'

Helpless. My father was the strongest man I knew. He could still lift a sheep across his back. He was not even very old.

'I'm sorry, brother,' she answered, meekly.

I realised I had shouted. Scared her. Clutching the table's edge, I said, 'No, it is not your fault. It's just that I can't think of... But now we await the physician,' I said, quietly, regaining control. 'You said you sent Joan first thing?'

'With the cockerel.'

Joan would be riding a distance of about three miles. On the mule over the hard mud of the lanes, it would take at least a couple of hours, then she had to secure the services of a medic, and even then, if one would come, it might be a day or more before the man turned up. But I did not think there was a better option. Even if I rode out myself to seek other help, there was no guarantee I would find it, and Father would want me to manage matters here first. We were a body without a head, now; a state without a sovereign. Did I have it in me to rise to the challenge?

'And so, Rutherford took…' I hesitated, feeling uncomfortable with the name of this woman I had never met ' …Chrissa Moore?'

'Yes. To the Walsham gaol.' She seemed to shudder. 'They're watching her.'

I knew why she shuddered. To Esther, to watch a witch – sit with her, interrogate her, hear her whispered confession at midnight – was to eschew the light of God, to seek out the Devil's shadow.

The tales told by the watchers were all around us, repeated in dark and gossipy corners: deprived of sleep and food, the exhausted servants, widows and non-attenders at church who were taken up by men like Rutherford all implicated themselves in the end. Each of us had heard of those entertaining dun spirits in their bedchambers, singing their psalms backwards, offering up their breasts to demons in the shape of three-legged dogs, or knew someone who had heard of them. In those long-ago days, these impious confessions lived just beneath the surface of our lives, most often out of sight, but ever present, ever rumoured. The knowledge that evil lived in and amongst us, close enough to touch, hidden behind smiles of mother, father, brother, sister, was too much for those who believed such things.

And sometimes, as I feared might happen now, the terror this engendered would accelerate like an ill-fated heart, and break out into horror.

4

But the Moore girl wasn't my responsibility. I had enough to manage. My first task was the sheep. Even if there was no connection with my father's ailment, I had to know what was killing them. I put aside the thought that if enough had died, or there was no improvement, we might have to mortgage the land. If we were lucky, we could restock, but replacement ewes at this time of year would be expensive.

I left Esther praying – it was all she seemed to wish to do, but I was relieved she had something to occupy her – then went to see Ben. I stabled him beside my father's mare, a steady grey named Temperance, who, due to her age, had narrowly escaped being commandeered by the army the previous year.

I supplied the horses with water and hay. Temperance recognised me, nuzzling my shoulder with her soft nose. I checked Ben all over, looking for the source of his injury. Not finding it, I resolved to ride Temperance over to Noah Litt's acres later on. Litt, our nearest neighbour, was a wonder with horses, and might do me a turn by examining Ben, though I would probably have to help with his accounts next Michaelmas in return. I would also need to check how much silver we had in the house in case I had to purchase medicine or call a farrier.

I leant against Ben's flanks. The warm, solid body offered a fleeting sense of peace, allowing me to forget, momentarily, about Father, Esther, the unabating pain of my injury. I closed my eyes and breathed steadily with the horse, feeling his ribcage rising and falling under the blanket, taking in the smell of new hay. He knew I was perturbed, and nickered. 'Don't worry,' I said. 'I'll get someone to see to you as soon as I can. A warm stable and good food to eat is an improvement on these last days, though, no?'

I saddled Temperance, adjusting the stirrups and buckles to fit, as I was shorter than Father, with more muscle. I had ridden her before and she was an easy horse, but we would need to take things slowly; she suffered from arthritis, and would get winded more quickly than her younger counterpart. Still, until Ben's lameness healed, riding him would make things worse. We would take things at a walk.

The ride quelled none of my fears. Father was well off, or had been, in terms of sheep stock. The part of the farm we didn't let was around fifty acres. But it wouldn't pay for itself. We relied on the sheep for wool to be sold at market to the weavers. The profits were low and, although Father was something near a gentleman, the work was hard and often physical, even with a small team of men to do the bulk of it. Now, since my father lay abed and nearly every sheep I saw was food for crows, I feared what would come to pass: mortgaging, or even losing the farm. What if I could do nothing to prevent it?

I completed my circuit, came back towards the house, and frowned to see a strange horse tied to the gatepost. She was a brown mare, three or four years old. Temperance shied away as we came close, the mare responded in kind, and I dismounted. Had the physician arrived? Surely not. Joan had been gone only a few hours. Physicians, clever as they might be, were never so reliable.

As I opened the back door, Guppy, my father's dog, slipped by into the garden with a yelp, almost tripping me. I cursed. Perhaps it was due to the exercise I had taken, but the house felt colder than I expected. I paused to remove my boots, wincing as I pulled the muscle in my upper thigh. It took several deep breaths for the searing to subside, long enough to hear the hum of a voice from the kitchen.

I have a good ear for voices. I remember them like some men remember faces, their idiosyncrasies, all the unexpected things about them. And I take more away from them than most. I can usually spot concealed fear. Men find it difficult to disguise frustration or sadness from me. Even back then, I was often surprised how easily I could discern truth from a lie; voices told me more about people than their words did. But I noticed nothing singular about this one other than its evenness and its maleness. It had the quality of a blank page. If it had been a meal, it would have been pottage. If a rock, soapstone.

There was no possibility it could be the doctor. Joan didn't have wings. Who else might have heard about our plight?

I walked into the kitchen.

The man occupying my father's seat had shoulder-length brown hair, a fair, almost womanly complexion, and a slightly squat nose. He was, I suppose, handsome, but as a turtle dove is handsome, rather than its showier relatives, the swan, or the peacock. As I entered, he ran his fingers over the parting of his hair, smoothing it, and repositioned his hat nearer his elbow. These were pedantic movements, as if he cared a great deal about the exact placement of things.

Get your carcass out of my father's chair.

I didn't say it. I wanted to. But the honour a man offered a guest reflected the honour he owed himself, or so my father had taught me.

On seeing me, the newcomer rose. He was of middling height, shorter than I was, but dwarfing Esther, whose head reached only to my shoulder.

'Good morning,' I said. 'I'm Thomas Treadwater.'

Esther, whose cheeks, for unknown reasons, had reddened like twin cherries against the paler canvas of her skin, was bringing ale. She said, 'Brother, this is Mr John Rutherford, assistant to Sir Christopher Manyon.'

I had no reason to dislike the Justice of the Peace, or to fear him, and in a wager on Manyon's good judgement would usually be inclined to place a shilling with the old man, but I wasn't certain I wanted to extend that trust to his young prodigy. Not yet. And Rutherford was young. I guessed only a year or so older than I was. He cultivated the aura of an older man, carrying himself like a schoolmaster or politician, but didn't quite pull off the trick.

'Welcome, sir,' I said, as Rutherford extended his arm. His hand was smooth and cool as petals. 'I trust you have been offered food?'

'Yes, indeed,' said Rutherford, gesturing to Esther, who was hovering near him with a jug. He waited for me to wave him back to his chair. Once seated, he looked satisfied as Esther poured a cup. He drank a mouthful only, dabbing the sides of his mouth with a spotless linen sleeve. He did not compliment the ale.

I wanted to know why he was here. What I guessed gave me no pleasure. I had much to be getting on with, and wanted as little to do as possible with this matter of witchcraft and women's jealousies, run as sour as curdled milk. I wished he could be back upon his mount, treading the gathering leaves towards town. But instead I had to be cordial. Silently, I damned gentlemanly tact and thought fondly of the coarseness of fighting men.

Rutherford did not state his business. It was left to me to begin. 'You may know I returned only recently from my duties with the army,' I said. Rutherford nodded. 'I have been long away, and have known little of the matter I suspect brings you here. The matter of Chrissa Moore. And,' I said, considering how he had arrived before me and been alone with Esther, 'I can only guess my sister has, by now, told you of my father's infirmity.'

'That is correct,' confirmed Rutherford. 'It was in the hope of speaking with your father that I came here today, but of course...' He seemed to grope for the appropriate words. 'My commiserations,' he said, finally. 'I hope for your father's swift recovery, with God.'

'Thank you. As my father's only son, I am now his proxy in all things. Whatever you wished to speak with him about, you may raise the matter with me.'

Rutherford's eyes for a moment rested on Esther, who observed the interaction in solemn silence. 'That may be,' said Rutherford. 'There is some news I can give you in the presence of your sister; other revelations I must share...' He shrugged. 'It might be better for us to speak alone, but I will leave that to your judgement. It is with your sister's innocence in mind that I speak.' Esther dropped her gaze modestly.

I should have appreciated his reticence for Esther's sake, but there was something prurient about the set of his mouth, something like pleasure in his words. He seemed to glory in my embarrassment. I think, looking back, that I would have enjoyed hurling him by his fine collar out of the back door. As things turned out, it might have been better if I had, but he had Manyon's authority to be here, and I didn't want to provoke trouble. 'Please,' I said. 'Share what you feel is appropriate with us both. We may speak alone afterwards. If necessary,' I added.

Rutherford drew himself up. He spoke as if what he said was established fact. 'The servant Chrissa Moore, birthplace unknown, is accused of unholy intimacies with the Fallen One. Specifically, it is recorded that she did conspire with Satan to bring down maladies upon livestock, and that she did, by way of corrupting his otherwise godly temper, seek to seduce your father, Richard Treadwater, with the aid of the Devil.'

I looked across the table at Esther. She had paled at this bald description of the situation, but nodded to me. I signalled Rutherford to go on. I wished he would hurry up.

Rutherford continued. 'The girl denies it, which is usual in these cases.' This was given a dismissive air; clearly, he had already decided on the question of guilt. 'Without a confession, it is likely she will face the assizes when they come through in the summer, and in the meantime, we will gather statements. Including yours,' he said to Esther, who nodded again. 'And any other evidence.'

'I'm sure my sister will be happy to assist in any way she can. But I will insist on being present for any witnessing. As she is a girl and a minor.'

Rutherford waved his hand. 'Certainly. But it is not for that purpose that I came today. The statement can and must wait until we have apprehended all the deviants.'

'All?' I said, confused. My stomach lurched. Surely, he could not be talking of *Esther?* My earlier fear returned, keen-bladed. The thing I had feared had happened. By accusing others, Esther had drawn the gaze of the witchfinder upon herself.

Rutherford took another sip of ale and made a general noise of confirmation as he swallowed, replacing the cup on the table. 'Those who commune with dark forces rarely do so alone. Even now, I am drawing in on those who assisted Moore in her practices. And this is where I believe you can help me, Miss Treadwater.' As he turned to Esther, there was something unctuous in his tone.

Esther, who had been staring down at her hands, looked up. 'I?' I had never seen her so apprehensive.

'Yes. I recall when I visited here with you last, before your father's unfortunate turn, you spoke of a girl you thought might be in sympathy with Moore. Another servant?'

I spoke with a half-clenched jaw. 'My sister has told you all—'

'On the contrary, Mr Treadwater,' interrupted Rutherford. The formal salutation rang false on his lips, as if I were being mocked. 'Your sister was visibly reluctant to tell me more, when last I was here, and there were hints, only, but it is vital that we know the absolute and entire truth. After all,' he continued, 'if the young lady of whom I speak is innocent of any unholy conspiracy, then she will have' – again, he dabbed at his mouth – 'nothing to fear.'

I glanced at Esther. This, then, was what she had been concealing from me. Not only had she implicated the Moore woman, but Joan, little Joan, who had been with us since the age of ten and never raised her voice in quarrel or her hand in temper to anyone. I flushed in shame. This was my fault. If only I had not left... But Rutherford was looking at me expectantly. I tried again. 'If you are talking of our servant, Joan Gedge, she is an employee in good standing here. There may be some error, but—'

'There is no error. We have already apprehended Goodwife Gedge—'

'Joan's *mother*? A middle-aged woman, a woman I have known since childhood...'

'A witch, sir!' Rutherford's voice, which had possessed such a malleable, silky texture, rang out harshly. 'A woman guilty of acts of *maleficia*. She was found with banned herbs, a knab of toads in the garden—'

'She's old. She does not keep up with the work of the garden and the toads multiply, as toads are wont to do,' I said, with a sarcasm that seemed lost on Rutherford. 'There is nothing at all—'

'Nevertheless, she is in our custody. As with the mother, soon too for the daughter, if I can only ask a few questions of—'

'No,' I said, flatly. Rutherford looked shocked, but then recovered himself and raised one thin eyebrow. He reached down by the side of the table and pulled up his knapsack.

'I have Manyon's mark here. It gives me the required authority. I have only to report to him and I am certain you know what the outcome will be.'

I am a man of a certain temper. In these later days, that temper is tamed; love, marriage, domesticity, though not children, have calmed it. But my instinct is towards battle where battle is needed, and on that day I contemplated putting my closed fist through Rutherford's throat.

Then I looked at the bag. Manyon was a powerful man, and if I went against him, I could find myself on the inside of a gaol cell. There would be nobody to manage the farm, or look after Father and Esther. As tempting as it was to deny Rutherford, I had to bury my anger. I swallowed. 'Very well,' I said. 'Please keep your questions short and to the point.'

Rutherford hid a smirk. 'Thank you. Justice Manyon will be gratified to hear of your co-operation.' He turned to Esther. 'Miss Treadwater, could you tell me what first raised the suspicions you mentioned, with regards to the girl, Joan Gedge?'

Esther twisted the fingers of her right hand in her left and fidgeted in her seat like a trapped rabbit. 'Well, I... I...'

Rutherford nodded encouragingly. 'You told me of her friendship with the witch – with Chrissa Moore?'

'Yes,' Esther said, hesitantly. 'They seemed to... Well, I can't say that Chrissa liked Joan. It wasn't quite like that. Chrissa was... You've seen her, I expect?'

'I've questioned her. What was the nature of their friendship? A close one?'

'I would say... Joan often said that she liked Chrissa, that she could see why... well, why men liked her.' Esther seemed to be dragging her words out of her own body.

'Chrissa Moore had male admirers?' Rutherford's voice was tight with disapproval.

'Oh yes,' Esther said, looking relieved, as though this were a far easier question. 'It was the way she walked, and held herself, as much as anything. I did not think she was modest.'

Rutherford's nostrils flared. 'No. It does not seem that she was. A terrible failing in a woman. Was the girl Joan modest?'

Esther nodded. 'Joan was ever so humble and mild. She always did just as I asked. Until…'

'Until the witch came?'

I snorted. 'Mr Rutherford, I must object. These are not my sister's words.' Watching Esther under Rutherford's attentions was like watching the dance of a puppet condemned to follow its master's convoluted twists and turns of thought. 'If this performance is to continue, I insist it takes place in Walsham, under Manyon's direct supervision. I insist, sir,' I said again, as Rutherford protested. 'I will bring my sister as soon as my father has been seen by the physician. Without delay.'

Rutherford could not argue with this. He nodded. Then, dashing my hope the interview might be over, he leant in close, so I could smell the ale on his breath and something that might have been lavender water. 'There is the other matter.' I remembered there had been something Rutherford wanted to speak about with me alone. I didn't think I was going to like it.

'Sister, would you remove to the parlour for a few moments?' I asked, careful to keep my mounting discomfort out of my voice. Esther rose, curtseyed to Rutherford, and left.

Now I could strip away the veneer of politeness. 'What is it?'

Rutherford coughed. 'Bear in mind that I was coming here to speak to Mr Treadwater, the senior, about this aspect of the business. I would not usually be at liberty to disclose…'

I squeezed my eyes shut. *Be patient.* 'Please, Mr Rutherford, if you could be as direct as possible, I would be grateful. I've much to do.'

Rutherford sat back, offended. 'Yes, well, unfortunately this will not be of much comfort to you, in that case. The witch—'

'The alleged witch.' As exhausted as I was, I couldn't let that pass.

Rutherford's face softened with a small, apologetic smile, as false as fool's gold. 'The *alleged* witch,' he conceded, 'claims to be carrying your father's bastard.'

5

'She lies.'

The words were out before I could stop them. My father, crippled and beloved, could not speak for himself, could not defend himself against these accusations, and before I was truly aware of it, I was pacing the kitchen, reddening and furious.

Rutherford was not disturbed by my discomfort in the slightest. He looked like he revelled in it, his eyes gleaming with excitement. 'Well, naturally, it is as yet to be ascertained whether—'

'She lies,' I insisted, my voice rising. I didn't stop to think whether Esther could hear. 'My father would never...' I trod upon the memory of Esther's tremulous words, and of the image they evoked: a woman, her face in shadow, her form unclothed in the moonlight.

Rutherford's answer carried the smoothness of false reassurance. 'Of course. Her testimony must be judged in the light of what we know: she is a corrupt woman, given to falsehoods, and Justice Manyon is sceptical of her claim, as, of course, am I.' He paused. 'And yet...' I looked at him sharply. 'Yet, we cannot *know*,' he said, his volume increasing to counter my automatic contradiction. 'Women, as Genesis so clearly illustrates, will naturally deceive men, but, as your sister was the only gentlewoman in the house, we will take *her* testimony at her word, and she, unfortunately, insists that there was indecorous contact between your father and the girl. If this has resulted in a child – not that she would deserve such a blessing – then the situation will be bad for the Treadwater name, as well as for the chances of bringing the witch to justice.'

I looked towards the parlour. The side of my body nearest the door felt chilled, as if the fire in the other room couldn't reach me. But the memory of Esther's stricken face as she told me of her fears about Father could. I was certain her words had come forth in honesty. Whether or not they were supported by a true knowledge of the facts was another question.

'I must see the girl, then,' I said, in the end. 'I must judge for myself the truth of her claim.' I took a deep breath. 'And – should her accusation against my father not be revealed immediately for the lie it is – I must assume responsibility for her, until the position becomes clearer with time.'

Rutherford shook his head. 'The girl is held in a cell. And she is dangerous. She is not to be seen.'

'I will see her,' I repeated. 'I insist upon it. Justice Manyon is a very old friend of my family and I am certain if I appeal to him…' I trailed off. Let him think about it, see that his interests aligned with my plan.

After a few moments' visible calculation, Rutherford shook his head again, but this time in reluctant admittance. 'I see no need to trouble a busy man. I am sure we can arrange it. For a few minutes, at least.'

'I must see Goodwife Gedge, also,' I said. 'As her daughter's employer, I must undertake for her fair treatment.'

'Very well,' Rutherford agreed, but did not look pleased.

I advanced. 'And there is no reason for my sister to know anything about this. She is distressed enough as it is.'

'She must accompany us to swear her statement.'

'Of course.'

'And one or other of you will be needed to identify the Gedge girl, if she has been apprehended by that point.'

I opened my mouth to object, but there was a hardness in his jaw, a truculence underlying all that politeness. I held back words of denial, knowing argument would merely serve as grist to the witchfinder's mill. Manyon was the more reasonable man. I felt sure that if I could see the magistrate and explain the strain Esther had been under, I would be listened to, and perhaps Joan and her mother could be kept out of this messy business.

Rutherford and I made an appointment to meet Manyon that afternoon in the foyer of the small courthouse in Walsham. Esther would be coming too. I walked with him to the bottom of the path, then watched as he retreated the way he had come.

Looking back on that first conversation with the witchfinder, I try not to analyse every decision I made, not to criticise every question I asked, or regret each I left out. But however I frame my choices, although I did not know it then, the damage had been done.

When I returned, Esther was kneeling on the hearthrug facing the low flames. She appeared deep in thought. I wanted to challenge her, ask her why she had not told me before Rutherford's arrival that Joan was implicated in this matter, but I feared to alienate her. We only had each other in the whole world, at least until Father recovered. How I hoped that would be soon.

'Esther,' I said. She did not turn. 'Esther.' She looked about her as if in surprise. I stopped by the fire. 'We have a journey we must undertake today.' I thought about how to break the news that she was to be questioned, but she spoke before I could continue.

'Of course. I understand that my statement will be required by the magistrate.' She sounded quite calm. 'I am ready to travel, once Father has been seen by the doctor.'

I couldn't promise this. I said, 'If Joan knows of your accusation against her mother, let alone herself, she will not return here, and perhaps she has not had opportunity to find a medic before being taken up.' Esther looked even paler, as if this consequence of her finger-pointing had not occurred to her. 'I think we will need to secure the services of a physician ourselves, in Walsham, or even Norwich. We'll leave at once, and take the cart. Do you know whether Father had ready money in the house?'

She didn't.

'I'll see what I can find.'

I remembered my father kept a strongbox under the bed, with the key usually kept in the study. Retrieving it, I went upstairs. I winced in pain as I knelt and rummaged below the bedframe, shrinking with shame. This felt like robbing him, as though he might wake, hear me, and cry out, 'Thief!' Few things had ever felt less natural than withdrawing the small stash of coin while Father lay above, helpless as a child. Along with the silver, I drew out an unwieldy bunch of keys of various sizes and ages, and noted, frowning, that I had not seen it before. We were missing no keys. But I had no time to think about it now, and replaced them in the strongbox with the remaining coin.

Before leaving, I stopped to drip some water into my father's mouth. I took one unresponsive hand in mine, willing him to understand. 'A day, no more, and we will return with help for you. My oath upon it.'

His eyes were like a room abandoned. I could not bear to look upon them, and turned away.

Father had named the mare Temperance, but as I fought to encourage her into the trap, I thought to rename her Obstinacy, or Petulance. It was unlike her; she was usually an amiable beast.

Esther stood by as I calmed the horse. She showed no impatience, but neither did she help. Ever fearful of large animals, she had never learnt to ride or to drive the cart. It was another area in which I now felt I'd been remiss.

In the years I had been down-country, first as a scholar, then a soldier, I had imagined Esther would move into womanhood in the manner of other girls, but, even before the war began, I had returned to Norfolk from beneath my tutor's watchful eye to the impression that my sister had stalled somehow. Her childhood anxieties – the dark, our father's health, the condition of her little herb garden – had shown no signs of receding. She seemed to be growing further away from me, and from the world. Then when I had joined the army, I had again harboured hopes of returning to find her, if not betrothed, at least flowering into the beauty her small, even features had always implied she would be. But she seemed more of a child than ever.

Once we were ready, I grabbed the handle on the side of the cart and pivoted into the driver's seat. As I twisted, pain streaked through my inner thigh. For a moment I was afraid my wound had reopened. I froze, glancing down at the injury. Esther noticed.

'Brother, you're hurt,' she said, and came quickly to my side. 'Why did you not say so? I would have prepared a poultice.'

'It's nothing,' I said, settling into the seat and pulling the rug about my back. 'Just a strained muscle from my ride.'

Esther accepted this explanation with a relieved smile. As she climbed up beside me and I flicked the reins, setting off, I thought about how to deliver my advice. We drove half a mile down the road before I came to the right words.

I began. 'Manyon is an astute man. He will brook no half-truths, or embellishments. You must listen with care and then be moderate in your speech. And pause before you answer.'

'For how long?'

I didn't allow any exasperation at this question to come to the surface. 'Merely for as long as you need,' I said, gently, flinching as the cartwheels ran over a pronounced dip in the track and the pain radiated again through my groin and thigh. 'What you say will be written down, and might be revisited in your testimony in court, should it come to that.'

Esther drew her blanket close about her knees. She looked fragile in the seat beside me, despite her heavy travelling cloak, with something delicate and breakable about her. Even in the daylight she was still pale, and I wondered whether she had been eating properly. I knew Manyon, if sufficiently spurred on by Rutherford, would press her closely, and feared she would not bear up under that scrutiny. Whilst that might mean relief for Joan and Goodwife Gedge, who, I had no doubt, had been taken up out of foolish superstition, it might have the unintended effect of leading Esther herself into trouble; what if they decided her complaint was malicious?

As we rumbled uphill, I turned my thoughts to the problem of Chrissa Moore. Her name stood in my mind for enigma, and for danger. I knew what most thought of unmarried women who found themselves with child. It was not that I agreed. More often than not, in my experience, whatever sin was involved was paid for in generous measure by the woman herself. I had seen them many times, thrown on the charity of the parish, pressured to hand their child over to a more 'godly' family. When very young, I had listened to men like Hale, to their preaching and condemnations, and I confess I thought the women wantons. But that was then. I had not understood how such things came to pass. As I grew, I noticed how many served in the houses of rich men, and left with swelling bellies. I pitied them.

But, in these particular circumstances, an illegitimate pregnancy could only mean shame and ridicule heaped on our name. Father's reputation would be trampled, and at exactly a time when he could not defend himself. And I would be responsible for an infant, a child whose mother might hang before it was weaned. There was not for one moment any question in my mind of turning my own half-brother or half-sister over to Hale to be raised by the parish.

But the mother herself… In truth, I imagined her as a venal creature. Perhaps she had passed by and seen a widower, a man of means, whose son was absent. She might even have pictured herself in my mother's seat.

I thought again of Esther's letter and its frequent errors. 'When Father is recovered and all this is behind us, I will help you with your writing,' I said, dipping my head to avoid a low branch and yanking on the reins to slow Temperance before she could pull us into another hole. 'There is much profit in reading, over and above the Good Book.' Even as I said this, knowing how I had rejected opportunities I had been given to study more deeply, I felt like a hypocrite. I did not wish to examine that feeling too closely. Neither did I add that I thought Esther's life too bare, without friends of her own age, or real interest in anything other than her catechism and our home. A proper facility with the printed word might help occupy her mind, and give her some escape from mundanity.

'Thank you, brother,' Esther said, primly. Then she fell silent as the cart continued its bumpy progress towards Walsham.

It was market day.

Having passed through many towns with the army and on my way back to Norfolk, I was familiar with the ways in which the war was changing them. Narrow, dirty streets that had once teemed with men seemed emptier wherever I went. Walsham was no different. The men had all gone to war. Many of the missing would never return. Their bodies would litter battle-fields, rot in copses and bloat in reed beds. And those that did return might not be whole. I thought again of my injury, how lucky I had been that it had not been a leg, or a hand. I thought of poor Jack. How easily it could have been me.

We were delayed by a short queue of other carts. My mind was only half on Manyon and Rutherford. I was trying to remember where in the town a proper physician – not an unlicensed quack applying the same impotent powder to every open wound – might be found. But I had been too long away. On my last visit here I'd been a boy, my eyes more open to the passing of a ripe maid than a short-sighted, grey-haired man of the universities. Any one of the townhouses built around the courthouse might belong to a country doctor; there was no signage. I would have to enquire, either in the marketplace or in the court itself, and hope to receive a recommendation.

'Let us alight here,' I said to Esther, worrying about the cost of the physician.

We reached the small courtroom, and I spotted a free horse ring. I secured Temperance, then chained the cartwheels to the ring as well, ignoring the protests of a fat merchant also trying to manoeuvre his packhorse into the space. I could not help but notice the low, barred windows of the gaol. These told those outside the fate of those within and, indeed, what awaited any person who threatened the peace and order of their community.

Esther was checking her appearance, straightening her skirt, which was wrinkled from the ride. I began to stop her, feeling she should not have to improve her looks for anyone, then thought it might be no bad thing if she looked like the respectable, godly girl she was. I reached out to smooth a curl of hair away, then rubbed her cheekbone with my knuckle, as I had done when she was younger. 'Don't concern yourself,' I said. 'The only thing needed here is the truth.' She smiled wanly.

In the courtroom foyer congregated the usual people living off, and under, the law: two attorneys, clad in black robes and avaricious expressions; a clerk, sharp-eyed, as thin as a cord; three shackled men, one picking his nose and looking nothing more than bored, one muttering prayers to the roof, the third with the watery eyes of a drunk. Two chubby goodwives in the corner, deep in gossip, looked with curiosity as we entered.

There was one further occupant of the big room. Rutherford was early. Indeed, I suspected he had come directly from our farmhouse. He wasted no time with pleasantries, saying only, 'Let's go straight up to the office. I want to get this business under way immediately.' Only then, as if realising his want of manners, did he turn to Esther and bow slightly, saying, 'Miss Treadwater.'

'Manyon is expecting us?' I asked.

'Yes, yes; he has cancelled several other appointments in order to see you.'

'Then we should go up,' I said.

But there was no need. A door opened on the other side of the entrance chamber and a tall, greying man in an expensive cloak and high Cordoban boots swept towards us with a warm energy. 'Thomas! Good to see you, boy!'

I went to shake Manyon's outstretched hand, and was surprised to find both my own enveloped in a firm, welcoming hold. I had not seen the older man for several years, and now judged him to be one of those who never seem to age a day, the beneficiary of a strong body, a generous diet and a naturally austere temper that had not allowed him to run to fat or drink, like many other men of means. He stood half a head taller than I did, or Rutherford, and made Esther look like a doll.

'It's good to see you too, sir,' I said. And it was. There was something comforting about a face from the time before the war, a friend of my father's, and, if I were honest, about an older man of my own sort; it made me feel someone else might take charge, remove the heavy yoke from my shoulders. I knew deep down that this was nonsense, a boy's wishful thinking, but felt it anyway.

Manyon's face was set in sympathy. 'I heard the news about your father this morning, from John here,' he said. 'A very great shame. We are old friends, Richard and I. In spite of some of his more enthusiastic interpretations of God's word, I always knew I could rely on him. Whatever I can do, just make it known to me.'

'Thank you, sir,' I said. 'We must seek the aid of a physician in the town, as well as helping in whatever way we can with this inquiry.'

'No need, my boy,' said Manyon. 'I will dispatch my own physician to Worstead this morning – I have already called him here for instruction. Your father will have the very best of attention.'

The desire to fall to my knees in gratitude embarrassed me, and I settled for extending my hand again, which Manyon shook. 'My thanks, sir. Ours,' I clarified, nodding to Esther, whose lower lip trembled.

'Do not speak of it,' said Manyon, with the ready urbanity of a man possessed of a full purse. He turned his eyes to Esther. 'So, this is the young mistress of the Treadwater household?' His manner, which had so far been that of a kindly uncle, long absent, became more appraising. I did not miss the slight hardening of his eyes as he looked upon Esther, searching, I assumed, for signs of hysteria, or deception.

'This is my sister, Esther,' I said.

'Of course. And you are ready for your statement to be transcribed?' Manyon asked her, his thick brows lowering.

'I am, sir,' Esther said. The squeak of a passing mouse might have been detected over her voice.

'Then let us retire to my office. I will have refreshments served and you can tell me all you know. You too, Thomas.'

'It's not much, I must warn you, sir,' I said, as Manyon guided us to the stairs, his hand on my right shoulder.

'I'm certain you will be able to cast some light on things,' he answered, confidently.

Not much, I said to him. As it turned out, I knew almost nothing at all.

6

Manyon's office was large and well furnished. On the walls were portraits of several men of his ilk; uncles and grand-fathers in varying fabrics and fashions, their high foreheads and beaky noses very like the magistrate's. There were other mounted paintings, and several framed maps. As Manyon drew up seats and poured malmsey wine, I examined a fine portolan chart that showed the Mediterranean and Black Seas in clear and accu-rate detail, but became vague as the mind of the artist wandered north, towards the icy and unknowable coasts of Scandinavia. It was a lovely object, done on canvas, like a painting.

Rutherford looked at ease. He accepted wine from Manyon and passed a cup to Esther, who shook her head with muttered thanks.

'We wait only upon my clerk,' Manyon said, glancing at the lantern clock. 'Mr Rutherford, would you be so kind as to discover what delays him?' The witchfinder nodded before retreating to the staircase.

Manyon studied the papers while I sipped my wine and Esther fretted, but before long, the magistrate looked up. 'I knew your mother, my dear,' he said, kindly, to Esther. 'She was a gentle woman, and a great beauty. She was darker than you, much more like to your brother, but – if I may say so before we begin – the daughter, as in many cases of two quite different types from the same stable, is every bit the equal of the mother.'

'I give you thanks,' said Esther, turning pink. She was unused to effusive praise.

Having softened her, Manyon continued. 'When Mr Rutherford and my clerk return, we will be ready to proceed. Do you know what to expect from a statement like the one you are to give today?' Esther shook her head. 'Have you ever given evidence before?' Again, she said she had not. Manyon nodded. 'Well, that speaks in your favour in a case like this, I suppose,' he said. 'It is not unknown for people to make repeat allegations, and, of course,' he said, sighing, 'the more often the boy cries wolf... Acts of *maleficium* are, in addition, notoriously difficult to prove, so it is essential that we test – carefully – the motivations of the complainant.' This brief speech confused me – I did not know whether to be relieved that Joan and her mother might be spared, or concerned at what I felt was a darker hint towards the possibility that Esther might have a grudge against the women. There was a warning in his words: *don't waste my time.*

Esther nodded. 'Of course.' But the magistrate's shift to a more serious tone had clearly unsettled her.

I intervened. 'Sir, if I might ask you, have any statements been collected from the accused women?' I called them 'statements' deliberately. I harboured a fear that Manyon might call them 'confessions' already, though Joan's mother had been in their custody only a few hours.

Manyon, who had been studying Esther, looked over. 'No,' he replied. 'We aim to have our evidence complete before any questioning takes place. We will send in the searchers, obviously, and each woman will undergo a physical assessment.'

'Of what type?' I said, suddenly discomforted as I thought of Joan, wherever she might be. It revolted me to think of someone removing her clothes in a dingy room while others prodded at her.

'Our midwife – who is well trained in these things – will look over the body of the accused, searching for certain signs, which might indicate communion with imps, familiars, spirits, or the

Devil,' said Manyon. 'It's a standard examination. And will be done respectfully.'

'And after that it is decided whether or not there is sufficient evidence to move to a trial?'

'Yes. Although it may take time, not just to collect the evidence, but to bring the case, depending on how much the assizes are disrupted by the war. It is not clear whether they will sit in Norwich this summer. Many Justices over the country are being forced to sit the trials themselves, and at their own expense, if their communities bring enough pressure to bear. And I should warn both of you, it is becoming rarer for juries to convict in cases of witchcraft.'

'Why is that?' I said, curious.

Manyon gave a cynical smile. 'Perhaps we are moving into more enlightened times,' he said, 'or perhaps people are becoming wiser to the many reasons such accusations are made. Not that I mean to impugn you, of course,' he said to Esther, swiftly. 'We consider each case carefully and on its merits.' He looked at the door, frowning. 'When we are empowered to do by prompt and diligent clerks, in any case.'

I cleared my throat, nervously. 'I should tell you, Magistrate, that I do know the Gedge family, mother and daughter, and I find it hard to believe—'

Manyon held up his hand. 'I must beg you to wait, Tom,' he said, looking round again. 'I am an old man, and my memory serves me little better than a sieve. Until we have the proper tools to write your words down, I would ask you to hold on to them. Now, where is that boy?'

Further seconds passed, and finally Manyon stood, an expression of stern displeasure on his face. Just as he started towards the door, it opened and Rutherford moved back into the room alone. 'Magistrate, unfortunately Timothy has been detained.' I assumed Timothy was the clerk. 'He ought not to be much longer, but, if you would permit, I would be happy to—'

'No,' Manyon barked. 'We must have the proper procedure followed. The clerk of the court writes the testimony. We will wait.' He turned to Esther. 'In the meantime, my dear, would you be kind enough to accompany Mr Rutherford to the cells and provide formal confirmation of Joan Gedge's identity?'

'Joan has been apprehended?' I said, surprised and concerned.

'Oh, yes. Constable Dillon is an efficient man. It was from the Gedge girl that we learnt of your father's malady, as she came to the town this morning, looking for a medic. Dillon took her straight away. Your mule,' he added, 'is in our stables here. You may collect it at any time.' I nodded, distracted by my conscience: Joan had been trying to help us, and now she was locked up. What could I do?

Rutherford had extended his arm to Esther, but before she could rise, I said, 'I will accompany my sister.'

'I would prefer to speak to you alone,' Manyon said. 'About the other matter.' I took this as a reference to Chrissa Moore's claim against my father. I hesitated. I had no desire to send Esther into a gaol on her own. But then, if I did not, I might not have a chance to bring Manyon round to my way of thinking, that my father could never be guilty of so sordid an act.

Esther rose. 'I will be fine, brother,' she said, a little shakily. Then, straightening her skirts, she added, 'It is a simple enough task, and Mr Rutherford will protect me, I am sure.' This was met by an ingratiating smile from the witchfinder, who held the door for Esther and bowed to us, before leaving the room after her.

Manyon was silent for a few seconds, then indicated to the flagon to ascertain whether I would take another cup. I wanted none, but nodded. As I had learnt as a soldier, sharing cups bred intimacy, and from there came knowledge.

As the magistrate poured, he inclined his head towards the door and spoke in a friendly tone. 'Your sister seems a young woman of quiet courage.'

I took back my cup, nodding. 'Yes. Esther is... what many people would describe as meek, but...'

Manyon sipped his wine, then said, '*Altissima quaeque flumina minimo sono labi.*'

Deep rivers flow quietly. I wondered whether Manyon was testing me. 'Yes, sir. When she was younger, around the time girls become cruel to one another, she sought friendship with some maids in the village – girls her age, from some of the better families. There was one girl in particular, a much bigger saddler's daughter, not too gentle, and Esther was afraid of her. She told me how the girl would mock her, call her a little mouse fart, and then pretend friendship with her immediately afterwards – you know how girls are.'

Manyon nodded, wincing. 'I have daughters,' he said. 'Excuse me: please continue.'

'On this one day, Esther came home weeping, with scratches down her face, and I asked her what had happened. She said they had been playing near the old oak on the common, and the girl had come upon a bird's nest fallen to the ground. There was one uncracked egg, and the older girl decided to smash it, to see whether there was a live chick. She thought it would amuse the others to torture it, or some such thing. Well, Esther would not have it. She stood over the egg and refused to move, and when the girl tried to shove her away, she fought her.' I swelled with pride at the memory of my small sister, a girl who wept if she could not remember her psalms and would not kill chickens for a meal, bearing her battle scars, clutching her rescued, speckled egg, her eyes brimful with tears as she recounted her tale.

She had been ashamed, I remembered, until I had taken her in my arms and told her what I felt she needed to hear: that it was

52

no sin to defend the helpless, and that God would see her deed and recognise it as His own.

'Did the egg hatch?' Manyon seemed genuinely interested. I thought it a skill, to appear fascinated when one was not.

'It did,' I said, recalling my surprise. 'It was a jackdaw. A clever thing. It fledged in our barn and then hung about for several years. I had to feed it.' I chuckled. 'Esther was too soft to forage for worms.'

'What became of it?'

'One day it flew away. We never saw it again. She was cut to the quick.'

'Would that all girls could be so feeling,' Manyon said, ruefully. He looked again towards the door. 'What do you think of Rutherford, by the by?'

I thought of Rutherford's pretty face and solicitous manner. I knew my own face tended to tell the story of my heart, so made a concerted effort to keep it neutral now, and shrugged. 'I do not think of him,' I said. 'I've had no dealings with him.'

Manyon's gaze became even more penetrating. 'You've changed,' he said. 'I remember a boy with a speaking countenance, one who would have answered that question with a looser tongue.' When I merely smiled, he continued. 'He is my nephew, you know. My wife's brother's son. Not my blood, but deserving of the opportunity I have given him as my assistant, if only through the call of family. He gets on well enough. A clever man. He was pious as a boy, I remember. Meant for the Church.'

'He isn't so pious now?'

Manyon took a sip of wine and raised an eyebrow. 'His experiences have, perhaps, removed the shine from the path of the Lord, but I believe he remains a servant of God. He has trodden a hard road. He married, as young men do. She was a beautiful girl, Anne. John was devoted to her.'

'Was?'

53

Manyon confirmed the inference with a nod. 'She swelled with child. The baby came. A boy. But the mother faded with childbed fever. Dead within the sennight.' He pushed the cup absently about in a small circle. 'And so, John gave the infant to a wet nurse, a woman of the Fens. It was the only thing he could have done. Yes,' he said, nodding to himself, 'the only thing. One does not stop to think that…' He glanced up at me.

Despite myself, I was caught up in the tale. 'Think what, sir?'

'That women can be capable of such things. I know the Good Book tells us. I know that the serpent came first to Eve, and that evil moved in her first, but still…'

'The woman hurt the child?' I asked, wincing inwardly. Rutherford was a preening fool but nobody deserved that.

'No. It died from simple neglect,' said Manyon, with professional brutality. 'She buried the corpse in the grounds of her cottage. But she continued collecting her fee from John for several months, with reports of the child as bonny and thriving. There were several others. When they were discovered it was thought John would lose his mind.'

I struggled to imagine Rutherford as a grieving father, but sympathised with him. The thought of entrusting a child to one of the rough-looking wet nurses I had seen on the streets of Norwich stirred anxiety in my stomach. It reminded me of Chrissa Moore, her claim, and what grief might come of it. 'A great shame,' I said, carefully. 'And such wickedness.' I felt more than this, but Manyon was playing on my finer feelings, and I preferred to show no susceptibility, at least until I knew what he wanted.

'Yes. But he throws himself into his work. And he is good at it. He saw the woman hanged for her venality, as was right.'

'A man should be skilled in his profession,' I said, in delicate agreement. I had seen both men and women hang, and we had all heard of burnings, though thankfully I'd never witnessed one. I questioned whether such dire measures were necessary to prevent crimes driven – for the most part – by need. I was unusual in that, I think.

'And what of you?' Manyon said, with more jocularity. 'You've fought for Parliament, but this skirmishing won't go on forever.'

'We can only hope, sir,' I said. 'I have seen enough of war to satisfy the most bloodthirsty stomach.'

Manyon nodded gravely. 'And yet you volunteered for the Bands?' The Trained Bands were the county militia. When Parliament had raised their colours against the King, I had signed up as a volunteer. It was not my choice. My reasons were not something I wanted to discuss with Manyon, and though I felt uncomfortable letting him think I had noble motivations, I nodded.

'I did, and until my colonel releases me, I will serve to the best of my ability. But I hope for an end to it. It's no way for men to live.'

Manyon agreed. 'By God's will. So, what comes after?'

'My father wished me trained in the law.'

Manyon heard the equivocation and frowned. 'But?'

'Entry to the Inns of Court would require study at one of the universities.'

'Surely that's no barrier for a young man of your intelligence?'

The magistrate was good at flattery. He would be most effective in politics, should he ever decide to leave the quiet life of a rural Justice and stand for office. 'Father sent me to a tutor to prepare me for the examinations,' I admitted, and Manyon's face lifted in recognition.

'Yes, I remember, now. Fellow in Buckinghamshire country? Christ's, Cambridge, wasn't he?'

'That's correct, sir.'

'And he let you down in some way?'

I coloured. This could not be further from the truth, but I had no wish to share the whole tale with the perspicacious magistrate. The shame I had brought on my family was mine to bear, but that did not mean I had to publicise it. Yet I could not lie. That would be worse, somehow, shame piled upon shame, now that my father was unable to upbraid me for it. 'The failure was my own,' I admitted, finally. 'Mr Milton was not to blame.' And yet, still, despite admitting responsibility for the breach between us, saying the man's name left a foul taste in my mouth. I moved on. 'And now, well, there are no longer the funds.'

Manyon said, 'It is good that you have the honour to speak of past faults so. Very well,' he said. 'Consider your plans. Tend to your father first, and look to your duties, but it may be that once the war is over, I can help you get on.'

'That is very kind, sir.'

Manyon waved his hand. 'It is no more than I ought to do, being an old friend of your father's.'

Mention of my father brought back a corrosive guilt: not only how I had left him defenceless in an empty house, or how near I had come to seeing him before he was struck down, but worse, of how – and how often – in the past, I had let down his trust. But it was not the time to think of that now.

'Speaking of your father…' The magistrate's face was mild. I waited, my nerves on edge. 'The matter of Chrissa Moore is one of some delicacy. I have not talked with her at length, but…' Perhaps he heard something on the stairs before I did, or perhaps the wording troubled him, because he trailed off. Before I could urge him on, Esther and Rutherford returned, accompanied, finally, by the clerk, a young man whose dull eyes and anxious manner spoke of an illicit visit to the tavern. Manyon regarded the clerk with irritation.

I glanced at Rutherford, discomforted by the confidences Manyon had shared. I, and every other person I had met, knew many who had lost children, although none in this exact circumstance. I was looking for evidence of his grief, something that might justify the unyielding nature he covered with all that politeness. Perhaps a bow in his shoulders, or a hint of melancholy in the set of his mouth. He did not notice my scrutiny, because he was watching Esther, his expression unreadable. It was not admiration, at least not overtly. It was almost wistful.

Following his gaze to Esther, I saw that she shook, her small hands clutching the front of her cloak against the cold. I rose, and paid for it in pain through my thigh, but moved towards her. 'Sister, are you well?'

'Yes,' she said. Her eyes had a red glare about them.

'Move to the fire,' I said, shepherding her. She came without complaint, standing in the crook of my arm and letting the flames warm her.

Rutherford sat and took up his cup again. 'The young lady identified Joan Gedge,' he reported to Manyon. 'And it is pleasing to see a young woman of such proper sensitivity and godliness. The cells have affected her, that's clear, but she has done her duty.'

I ignored him and spoke to Esther. 'You saw Joan?' She nodded. 'Was she well?'

When she answered, it was in a cowed whisper. 'She wouldn't say a word to me. I stood for such a long time and…' I spun her about and looked at her face, cursing my own clumsiness. Her face glistened with tears.

I looked round at the other men. 'I would see my sister home as soon as possible. I must ask that we move on to her statement.'

7

Esther's voice trembled. 'They took to sleeping together in one room, against my instructions. They carved symbols into the wood of the doors and windows, so that I feared to enter. Joan's room had evil smells, and when I questioned Joan about it, she told me she but brewed draughts to ward off illness, according to her mother's teachings. I would see them at night, burying things, I know not what, but I did not dare go out of the house, and in the morning, I could not find the sites of the things they had buried. They muttered curses whenever I passed. I suffered racking pains, in my head and beneath my ribs, and there were times when I could not remember what I had been doing, so muddled did they make me. And the weather was terrible — they called in storms of wind and lightning, though there were few clouds above us. Such was their pleasure, to torment me with things that made no sense.'

By the end of the tale, Manyon's frown had deepened. Esther had answered his many questions in her gentle way, and he had probed with further enquiries. I admired his ability to place his finger on the pulse of a point without seeming to press too hard. I believed I might have underestimated him before. Esther had not shamed herself in her answers. She had spoken tremulously, but with all the appearance of truth.

Yet still Manyon frowned, and I knew why.

Esther's account of Joan Gedge's conduct had been clear and, as far as I could see, honest. Her words carried the ring of self-belief. But there was nothing solid, no knife in the hand, so to speak, by which the magistrate might be able to justify holding Joan further.

I was relieved. Esther's impassioned account had given pause to my confidence that Joan was innocent of evil intent, but not really shaken it. Both girls, my sister and our young servant, were credulous, and I could easily see how Chrissa Moore might have come between them, setting one against the other. Now that influence was removed, I hoped Manyon would release Joan. It might not be that she could return to work for us – she would hardly wish to do so – but I thought about how I might compensate her, and what I might do for her mother.

Manyon had indicated to the clerk to stop scribing. He seemed deep in thought, his hands folded together beneath his chin. When he spoke, it was slow and careful. 'It appears to me,' he began, 'that there is not enough here against Joan Gedge or her mother – at least, not enough to hold them for trial.'

'They will be released?' Esther asked, quietly. Was she frightened of this prospect? I scanned her face, but she was looking at Manyon, and I couldn't see her eyes.

There came a long pause, then Manyon said, 'Not yet. The searchers still conduct their business at the Gedge house, and what your sister has said here today confirms what I have thought; we must conduct a similar search of your property.' I nodded. I had expected this. We had nothing to hide. The magistrate continued. 'There is also the interrogation of Chrissa Moore, which will take place this afternoon. Given the girl's lack of proper account of herself – where she comes from, whether there was intent on her part to draw your father on to… corruption – there seems to be a better *prima facie* case against her.'

'What has she said in her own defence?' I asked.

'Nothing,' said Manyon, brusquely. 'Not a word to anybody since she was taken up.'

'She was ever quiet,' said Esther, suddenly. We looked to her, and she seemed embarrassed to have spoken out of turn, but when we waited for her to go on, she added, with a touch of defiance, 'It was a disrespectful silence.'

Manyon sighed. 'Be that as it may, the girl cannot be compelled to speak in her current condition…'

'What condition?' Esther's face was half in shadow, turned away from me.

I thought about lying, but the tinderbox was alight. I spoke gently, taking her fingers in mine. 'The girl claims to be with child,' I said. Esther's hand stiffened. 'It's a shameful lie,' I reassured her. 'She seeks to avoid a trial, I'm certain.'

Esther began to weep. Manyon looked uncomfortable, but Rutherford gazed on, admiring. It was time to leave. I stood. 'My sister is distressed,' I said. 'I'll see her home, if that is all that is required?' When Manyon nodded, I remembered the offer of assistance with a medic for Father. 'My thanks, sir, for your offer of help in summoning your physician. I will cover the cost, of course.'

Manyon waved this away. 'I will send him as soon as he arrives. And with God's providence your father will soon be back to himself.' He turned to Rutherford. 'Would you see them out?'

Rutherford bowed to his master, who said, 'I will keep you informed, Tom. I hope this matter will soon run its course.'

I walked down the stairs, supporting my weight on the wooden rail, as Rutherford provided his arm to a still-sobbing Esther. Each descending step brought fresh pain. My wound was getting worse. I felt, now, every moment of my long journey and my profound lack of sleep. Ahead of me, Esther leant in towards Rutherford. He was solicitous, murmuring to her as they approached the main foyer. I couldn't hear what was said, however I strained my ears, nor believe what I was seeing;

could it be that she *liked* the toady little man? That Rutherford would like her, given her youth, malleability and piety, I could easily accept, but that the feeling was reciprocated? It was hard to credit, yet there Esther stood, tearless, as we reached the tiled floor of the courtroom.

'Mr Rutherford,' I said, standing up straighter. I did not want Esther to see I was in pain. 'I would have words with the girl now.'

Rutherford turned as if he had forgotten. 'The girl? Oh, the witch. I do not think you will get anything from her lips. I sat with her all night – she said nothing.'

'Nevertheless, I would speak with her. And with Goodwife Gedge, and Joan. As we agreed.'

The witchfinder hesitated. I knew he wanted to refuse, but after a brief glance at Esther, he nodded. 'I will speak with the constable,' he said. He disappeared through a stone archway leading to the cells below.

The delay was short. Rutherford returned within a minute or two and beckoned to me to follow. I left him standing and found Esther a space on a bench. 'Wait here,' I said.

She clung to my hand. 'Must you go?'

'You went. I thought you very courageous.'

'No,' she said, blushing. 'It was only my duty, and what I owed to God.'

'As this is mine. Mr Rutherford will stay with you and make sure you come to no harm. I'll not be long.'

———

The square grey tiles of the courtroom's public floor gave way to rough-hewn stone on the spiral leading down to the cells. I thought of Esther's tread on these steps, just minutes ago, imagining her trepidation as she passed out of the light. For a moment

I felt guilty I had not accompanied her, but I had to remember the positive impression I thought I had made on Manyon – with luck, the magistrate could help propel me into a profession, one which would help me to support Esther, if Father failed to recover. This was no small thing; in fact, losing this prospect could be disastrous. If the sheep continued to die, if our small collection of tenants went elsewhere, we would have no means to restock or feed ourselves, let alone pay for medicine for Father. Manyon's good opinion might be the difference between spending a winter in our own kitchen, and begging as paupers on the highway. No, I had made the right decision to cultivate that relationship, I decided.

The gaol did not concern me much. I was less innocent than Esther. Once, unknown to my father or sister, I had been taken up for drunkenness, and had seen the inside of the county gaol at Norwich. I did not remember the way down – I'd been much the worse for drink – but clearly recalled being brought back up, having parted with every penny in my possession to secure my release without charge. This chamber was deeper, older and narrower than the larger one at Norwich, but the stink was the same: unwashed humans, the reek of sewage where the waste of the town dripped down from the street above, the stench of the bowels of the earth. It made me long for the winter air of the farm, for the freshness of the wind off the sea. I groped the walls as I descended, trying not to give too much thought to the provenance of the mucus covering the ancient stones.

I reached the bottom stair. Someone, probably the constable, had lit candles at regular intervals on the wall, so the dank, draughty space was just visible. I peered ahead, getting my bearings. I found myself in a thin, elongated cellar, lined on one side by stone and on the other by several doors, each with a barred window just large enough to shove through a hunk of bread and a cup of water – all the people confined here would receive, and that if they were lucky. The smell of mildew and dung was joined by a waft of stale ale and vomit.

'Good, isn't it?'

I spun about, wondering how I had contrived not to notice being shadowed down the stairs by such a hulking brute of a man. The figure that now extended a hand towards me reminded me of a sand dune: tall, large across the shoulders, back and neck, ox-like in his appearance. But Constable Dillon bore a broad smile of recognition, despite the gruff voice, and I remembered that the man was surprisingly jovial for one whose job was so thankless.

Dillon's responsibility was simple: to lock up, detain and present to the courts the detritus of the parish – the poachers, drunks, hedge-damagers, prostitutes, and fathers of bastards. At the thought of the last, I felt another flush of anger towards the woman I had come down here to meet.

Dillon was a fair gaoler in comparison to many of his type. Those released from his custody very often sent him a barrel of apples at Michaelmas or a ham at Christmas, and spoke of his reasonableness and his mighty singing voice. Those who hanged said nothing much worse.

'Constable,' I said, shaking the meaty hand. 'It's good to see you, though I'm not sure what is "good" about this,' I added, aiming a nod at the squalid space beyond.

Dillon laughed, poking his head in beneath the low ceiling. 'This is a palace, lad, compared to some of the gaol-houses I've seen. Manyon had it put together – a good man, Manyon. Before he gave the funds for this, this cellar held nothing but ale and rats, and the prisoners were dumped in a hog sty on my land.'

Unbelievably, Dillon was not formally paid by the parish for his services as constable. He had his own tenancy to look after, and his position was technically unwaged. So, Dillon's adult son cultivated his fields while his father dealt with the vagabonds and beggars of Walsham. But Manyon was clever. He wanted none of the bribery, the petty corruptions that would arise from placing a man with empty pockets in charge of law enforcement within his parish. It was common knowledge that he paid Dillon himself.

Something grey streaked across our path. 'The rats are still here, then,' I said, watching as the creature scuttled off along the wall, disappearing into the dark.

'There'll be rats at the end of the world,' chuckled Dillon. 'What can I do for you, lad?'

'Mr Rutherford sent me down. He's given his permission for me to speak with the prisoner, Chrissa Moore, and to check on the Gedge women.'

Dillon paused, his face losing its open friendliness. 'Rutherford, eh?' I nodded, knowing the witchfinder had spoken to Dillon, and realising that Rutherford was held no higher in the constable's esteem than he was in my own. 'Does the magistrate know he's sent you down here?'

I liked Dillon and didn't want to lie to him. I said, 'He may be having that conversation now; I'm not sure. He was explicit in his own permissions, though.'

After another moment's thought, Dillon said, 'Good enough for me. Watch that one, though. Don't turn your back on her.'

'Which cell is she in? And the others?'

Dillon pointed down the corridor. 'The third one. The mother and daughter are in together, in the very far cell.'

I couldn't see to the end door. I requested the use of a candle and Dillon agreed. The small, bright flame was comforting. 'I'll be just a few minutes,' I said, 'but I do need to speak with the Moore woman privately.'

The older man looked uncomfortable again, but eventually he nodded and retreated up the stairs, his keys jangling at his waist.

Wishing I could follow Dillon back to the world above, I moved instead into the gloom.

The first two cells were hardly deeper than the length of a horse and considerably narrower than the span of a man's arms. Each contained more than one inmate. It was from the first cell that the stench of vomit emanated; two men, paralytic with drink, slumped against the walls. Neither stirred as I passed. The second cell was host to three others, again men, all sullen, hungry-looking creatures. One called out an obscenity as I walked by, perhaps mistaking me for Dillon. Another laughed.

Before I reached the third cell, I stopped still.

But the fearful, and unbelieving, and the abominable, and murderers, and whoremongers, and sorcerers, and idolaters, and all liars, shall have their part in the lake which burneth with fire and brimstone: which is the second death.

The words from Revelation came as clearly as if I had the Bible open in my hands. I heard them in my father's voice. I closed my eyes briefly, taking in the stink of shit and piss: the smells of the world. There were no sorcerers, no witches. No compacts with the Devil or familiar creatures suckling at nerveless teats. Only drunks and whores, whoremongers, and heretics, like me.

8

March 1703

A place far from the sea

My bedchamber overlooks a small walled garden, not grand enough to be called an orchard, planted with trees of apples, plums and greengages, like the ones that graced my boyhood home. The trees are bare of fruit or leaves today. They were put in during a lovely spring half a century ago, with Mary leaning on the rake and me taking mountains of flint stone out of the chalky soil. They back on to an empty sheep paddock, sloping upwards, and on either side endless fields, now just brimming with a hint of green, but in summer abundant with waves like a dry yellow sea.

I usually wake to birdsong, sweet and sharp. This morning, though, the birds have gone, and the silence outside delays the return of full awareness. The sun is almost up before I come to with a fierce gratitude to have left my dreams behind – I rarely dream, but of late the Furies pursue me through sleep, their wings beating like thunder, voices spiralling into a whirlwind of bestial shrieks; to what end, I do not know, but still they screech, taunting me.

I shake myself fully awake, tasting the relief lying flat offers my knees and back. It is a short-lived pleasure. I remember what I must do, and it gives me no solace. Not waking Mary is an art perfected over decades, and I roll evenly to my side of the bed, spreading my weight, trying not to cough. As I swing my bare feet a clenching pain drives deep into the centre of my chest. It greets me most mornings. For thirty seconds or so, I push my fist in vigorous circles against the skin, as the physicians have instructed me, though it does no good. The rubbing blanches my sternum, bleaching its autumnal red, branching scars to powder white. As the colour seeps back, I almost think they bleed.

Standing, I pull on my stockings and breeches, then my waist-coat, and put my feet in my bedroom slippers. I slip my hand into my pocket so the keys I carry with me at all times brush against my skin, and wrap my fingers about them. They antic-ipate me, like a handful of gunpowder, a tiny keg that at any moment might rip my hand to fleshy ribbons.

I pad over to the window and peer through, noting how far the wind has dropped. The mercury in the ash barometer on the ledge is high, and the sky, the benign blue of a dunnock's egg, is still flecked with white feathers. The trees stand so still they might be carved from stone. It did, as I expected, snow over-night, but only a little, so each branch and leaf is iced with a light dust like grated sugar. But the ground bears no ribbons of tiny footprints. There is no sign of any creature passing. The silence is sovereign.

'Thomas,' comes Mary's sleepy voice from the bed. She is cocooned in quilts and blankets, so all I see is her nightcap and the curve behind her knees, usually occupied by the cat, which, this morning, is nowhere nearby.

'Good morning, wife,' I say, returning to her side as fresh realisation dawns upon her, and her face moves from content-ment to deep unease. She sees I am decided, and stirs more quickly.

'Wait, and I will be with you,' she says, beginning to rise. 'Or perhaps wait until—'

I place my hands on her shoulders. 'No.' Then, as she remon-strates, 'No. I cannot have you in this. I must go alone. And it must be now – I have delayed long enough.'

She takes my hand. Her skin feels tepid, papery, as if the life is seeping out of her. I press her hand close to my chest. I want to keep her here, to protect her. 'You tremble,' I say. 'Have courage. All will be well.'

Even before I have finished, she is shaking her head. She possesses almost no hair on her brows now, and her left eye begins to cloud with cataracts, but still her anger is a sight. 'How can you say so? You know the danger, Thomas!'

'Look how far we have come together. Now is not the time to fail in your trust.' A certainty that might have been courage in the mouth of a younger man sounds wheedling to my ancient ears. And so, it seems, to hers.

'There is trust, and there is rank foolishness.' She is out of the bed now, pulling on her warm bedgown.

'Foolishness?'

Frustration whirls beneath her words. 'Foolishness is you going up there alone, when…' A pause. 'It's rash.'

'Let's have no more talk like this, dear heart,' I say, as robustly as I can manage. Then, more softly, 'I don't know what I will find. And I do not fear what I do not know. Nor should you.'

But this is a lie. Of course I fear what I do not know. What else is there to terrify us?

I cannot blame Mary for her anger, her doubt, even her resentment. Yet I must insist on being alone in this. There is no other choice.

I hold tightly to the keys, though the metal feels like a burning brand against my palm, and go downstairs. I have no appetite – my gullet convulses at the thought of food – but collect wine, bread and a cold breast of pigeon from the pantry. I light a fire and heat a bowl of onion soup, then place all on a board before kneeling to pray, asking that God not forsake me until my task is completed. I almost convince myself that I am heard. When finished, I rise awkwardly, releasing a laboured grunt. I add a lit candle to the tray, and move towards the stairs.

My hands shake as I walk, and my knees threaten collapse. It is the turn of the year, almost spring, but the house is held in the grip of a voracious cold as in the very dead of winter. I carry the tray up, passing the bedrooms, and come to the door at the end of the corridor. This door is kept locked, always.

I place the tray at my feet and insert the smaller of the keys in the lock. It turns with a click. As I open the door, for the briefest of moments, I smell the sea, taste the salt freshness of the ocean against my lips, and it comes back to me: the deafening cry of the wind over the waves and the clap of thunder, drawing ever closer. My ears are alert for the tiniest true sound. The cacophony fades. It is nothing but my fancy.

There are fourteen steps. No windows. At the top stands a second door of double-timbered oak, locked, and braced with a heavy plank. I built this, and know it will hold fast.

No sound drifts down from above. I retrieve the tray, and raise my foot. Then, without fully deciding to do so, I retract it.

Are you so afraid of the dark? The thought of my cowardice needles me, and I begin the climb.

I reach the last stair. The air feels whisper-thin, as if I have ascended miles, not mere feet, like a Virgil or an Odysseus, though moving in the wrong direction. The house below, with its hearth and scrawny cat licking its hindquarters beneath the kitchen table, might be another world.

I deposit the tray on the floor, taking care not to extinguish the candle, and haul the length of wood from its brackets as I have done thousands of times.

The door squeaks open. My shape blocks out the light from the candle, so the space ahead is muted and shadowed. My breath is harsh in my ears, my fear a gobbet of iron in my stomach. The sea smell is nearly unbearable now.

The attic is simply furnished and clean. On one side there is a bed, with a warm coverlet, a bureau of drawers, several rugs, and a washing station. A piss pot stands beneath the basin, empty. On the other side, not original to the house – I put it in myself – a small window allows in light and has a view of the fields beyond, and beneath this window is a wooden bench-seat. Its resident's face is set towards the window. Steel-grey hair, turning white at the roots, hangs loose and long, partly obscuring the unbleached linen nightgown beneath, almost reaching the shackles encircling the ankles.

I wait.

'Do you smell it?' The voice is gritty, the cost of long years of quiet. 'The sea?'

'No,' I say, finally. My voice cracks.

The figure turns to face me, the nightgown falling open at the throat, revealing pale skin criss-crossed by a pattern of faded lines, oxblood red, like a river and its tributaries. They reach as high as the left clavicle. 'Are we near?'

In the few moments before it is obvious I am not going to answer, I am aware of being assessed. I am the subject of a gaze. A short laugh is released like a weapon. 'The years lie upon you like treacheries, Thomas.' I do not contest the verdict. I am too much distracted, because I know this voice. It is the one I have feared. Something I have clung to crumbles inside me.

'I brought you food,' I say, finally, holding out the board.

A single brow goes up. 'You would break bread with me?'

I move several steps closer. 'I would feed you. You cannot feed yourself, at least not easily.'

The gaze shifts downwards to the shackles, the chain linking ankles to wrists. 'Then, by all means, we shall eat,' comes that wry voice again.

I lower myself to the bench, noting the smell of sweat, of unwashed flesh, of shed skin. A bowl and a few jugs of heated water is the limit of what I will be able to haul up the stairs myself, but I resolve to do it. Mary will take me to task and insist on doing it for me, but from now on, I vow, nobody but I will enter this room.

I lift the cup so that the wine might be reached, and wait. When the cup is half-emptied, I lower my hands and offer the bread, holding it steady as the small, white incisors tear off a chunk and chew in delicate bites. I continue to offer the bread until it is gone, then spoon white soup from the bowl. 'I remember you liked this, before,' I say, to no reply. With the food finished, I look upon closed lids of translucent flesh, webbed with veins of watchet blue, with barely a wrinkle to signal the passage of the years.

A sudden movement in the corner draws my attention. A flash of brown and pale blue; a lone jay, sheltering from the chill, having strayed down the chimney in error, perhaps. Or a hole in the thatch that will need to be mended. The jay scampers on spindly legs. It cannot find the way it came in, and flutters between the beams, cawing in panic. I sympathise, but cannot see any gap through which I might thrust its struggling form, even if I could catch it.

'This is a new world.' I hear these words and turn back, eager to see the expression accompanying them, but the same bland nothingness prevails.

'New, how?' I ask. 'What do you remember?' I scold myself for asking two questions, but the mistake does not cost me my answer.

'Smaller. Shrivelled.' The words are released quietly, not without contempt.

'How has it shrivelled?'

'Ideas. Beliefs. Faith.'

'How do you know?'

71

The jay lands by our feet and skitters away towards the bed. 'How does that creature know it must have the open skies? That this room, however sheltered, will be its death, such that it will break its wings to pulp against its walls?'

The bird, which was pecking at a floorboard, alights awkwardly. Then it rushes for the window, seeming to sense its near freedom. But it has not counted on the glass, and falls, squawking, back to the floor.

'I do not know,' I admit. Then, tentatively, 'What do you remember from before?'

But I can get no further answers for my pains.

When I look again, the jay is gone. I search for it, in the following days, and find its untouched remains languishing beneath the bureau.

I descend the stairs, fasten the door behind me and place the key in my pocket. Only once the door is locked do I rest my forehead against the wood and breathe. I stay there for several minutes, gentling the churning currents of my mind. But peace does not return. My heartbeat is out of kilter with the rest of me. Almost without realising it, I have been scratching myself. Across my chest and arms, my scars have come alive and seem to crawl across the surface of my body, producing a pernicious need to rub, to remove the skin like snake scale, just to be rid of them.

You will never be rid of them.

The words rise inside me. *Never. Never.*

I need Mary.

Downstairs, I call out to her. I go through the kitchen to the parlour and the study. She is not in the house and my greatcoat is missing from its hook.

The doorframe is wreathed in hard frost and ivy. Displaced shards of ice hit the ground like broken glass as I brush past, and my feet indent the thin dusting of snow. The ferocious cold is an unlikely ally; the air purges my lungs like fire.

'Mary!'

I pass the bare vegetable patch on my right and the pig in its sty on my left. Though the ground is hard, the straight rows and absence of straggling grasses sing of time lavished upon it. This is where Mary is so often to be found. She erects fences against rabbits and wears her fingers to calluses to create trellises, which, though melancholy now, at the end of winter, in the summer will hum with bees and perfumed blooms, the children of her heart.

The north-west gate leads to the trees I saw from my window this morning. The gate is stuck. As I push on the knotted slats, it resists, requiring my full weight to swing it. How I miss my old strength, the careless vigour of my arm! I'm weak, now. This rickety thing will outlast me.

In the orchard, my shadow flees before me, tree to tree. The shorn branches that usually whisper to one another, their lonely fingers reaching out for the comfort of touch, are caught in the silence. 'Mary?'

She huddles in my coat against the drystone wall, facing out and away. I see her shoulders are shaking before I am within twenty feet of her. 'Mary?' She is carrying something, cradling it.

When she turns, I see it in her hands: the little corpse, a tattered bundle of dove grey and brown, as stiff as dried leather. Her hands, their palms laced with the faint mottled scars of so long ago, are red and sore with the cold.

I move closer. 'What's happened?' I say, though I can see. She cannot get the words out. The cat was old, I tell myself. Sixteen years last winter. And slow, with blunted teeth, easy prey to a fox or badger.

'He h-hardly went outside,' she said, between halting breaths. 'Then last night I couldn't find him.'

I fumble for words. It has been so long since we were grieved. 'Let me bury him,' I say, finally.

She shakes her head, wiping the stream from her nose. 'The ground is too hard.'

'I'll manage.'

I take him from her hands. He is — was — an ancient, dringling thing, useless at ratting and not much better at controlling his bladder, and, like most good cats with adoring mistresses, he worshipped her, and reserved for me only a frosty disdain and an insolent swish of the tail.

I examine him all over as Mary watches, a strange, bright look in her eyes. He must have been out here all night. He is almost frozen solid, his grizzled fur beaded with snow. I run my hands through it, expecting torn flesh, broken bones, dried blood, but there is no mark anywhere. Death came quietly.

'Old age,' I say, cautiously. 'And the cold. It is a natural end.'

Mary spits. 'It's been less than a day. It blights all it touches. And it has always targeted those I love. What happens when it turns on you?'

I lay him on the ground. She waits another moment for my answer, but then stalks back inside. I nearly go after her, but search out my spade instead.

9

28th December 1643

North Norfolk

The shape occupying the cell was not a woman, at least not obviously, until I held up the candle to add detail to its outline. I saw dark hair and a dress that might once have been any colour, but now looked fallow brown. I saw no face, and realised that the woman had her back to me, and was sitting on a low bench which, presumably, had been placed there in deference to her claimed condition.

'Chrissa Moore?' My voice sounded hollow this deep into the cellar. She did not turn at her name. 'Miss Moore? My name is Thomas. Thomas Treadwater.' I might have imagined it, but knowledge of my name did not seem to dismay my listener – if anything, her spine lengthened rather than slumped. I waited, then said, 'I am here on behalf of my father, Richard Treadwater. And to discern the truth of your claim that…' I paused, almost unable to release the words. 'That my father has left you with child.' Still, she did not turn.

I hesitated. I did not want the men in the accompanying cells to have anything to repeat to the magistrate. Finally, keeping my voice so low that she was the only person who might hear, I said, 'I know you are no witch. There are those who believe in such things, but I am not among them. My sister is a sensitive girl. Whatever she reports will be based in truth – Esther is incapable of serious falsehoods – but that does not mean she has the correct understanding of the things she has seen.'

This produced a change, finally. The woman stood, and I saw for the first time how tall she was, how her hair fell down her back like tangled shadows. But still she did not look in my direction.

'The disappointment I feel,' I continued, 'isn't directed at my sister, but at my father; not because I believe the accusation you have made against him – I don't believe it for an instant – but because I never thought him such a fool as to put himself in the position where he might be so accused.'

Besides some incoherent murmuring from the cell that housed the drunks, the gaol was wrapped in a suffocating silence. The woman seemed disinclined to hear my words, or acknowledge me in any way, and I knew I had to press further, to provoke her, if I was going to get anything from her at all. I said, 'For my father to admit a whore to the house, on whatever pretext, was the act of a sick man, I am certain.'

At last, she turned, and I heard her intake of breath.

No, the sound came from my own lips. Esther had spoken of Chrissa Moore's male admirers, and I had imagined a dimpled wench, pretty and impudent, like the women who had followed the army. She was nothing of that sort. She cast off shadows as she stepped towards the light. In this world of goitred necks and pitted noses, few could boast such skin – white, as smooth as butter, throwing back the light like the surface of a pool of calm water. She had high cheekbones and a long, almost oval face, carrying an expression I could not read – she was frightened or angry, but I could not tell which. The light was dim, but there were depths to her eyes, and I imagined them flashing with fury or scorn.

But how could I admire her? I shook my head, exiling these thoughts. I was becoming as imaginative as Esther. She was a beautiful woman, it was true – far more so than I had expected – but she was no queen or great lady. She was locked up, at best a liar, at worst a literal whore, and the mother of a fatherless child.

When she spoke, her voice had the quality of torn lace: damaged, covering some refinement. 'You're Esther's brother?' I nodded. Her mouth crimped in suspicion, and she said, 'You don't look like it.'

'Nevertheless,' I said, 'it's what I am.' She didn't answer, and examined her feet, letting hair fall over her face. I was growing impatient but, having made this much progress, knew to wait.

'What do you mean, he's sick?' she said, at last.

I almost explained, but felt that same anger that had accompanied her stubborn disregard of my earlier words. In some way, I knew not how, my father's malady was her fault, and I had no intention of being a source of information for her. 'That is none of your concern,' I said, knowing I sounded haughty. 'What I need from you is the truth of the relations between you. You have claimed to have been intimate with him, and I need to know now how much truth there is in that claim.'

I heard the last thing I expected from her lips: a laugh. She was mocking me.

I flushed. 'Madam, I see nothing funny here. I charge you to answer me, on your honour.' It might have been the rush of blood through my veins, but my wound had begun to pulse and ache afresh. I was reminded of my own impotence, and mingled with that fury was something else – something uncomfortably close to envy, at the thought of my father's hands on warm, willing skin that shone in the candlelight like porcelain.

She had made a fool of me, and I hated her for it. As she turned about, I felt certain she wouldn't say another word and resolved to give her no more ammunition. Leaving her, I moved down the corridor, to the cell Dillon had said held Joan Gedge and her mother.

The odour further down the passage was even less pleasant than it had been nearer the stairs: musty, as though the rats had chosen this spot for their privy. Poor Joan, to be caught up in this nonsense and shoved in this dark hole, to be probed and questioned and accused. I determined again that I would do everything in my power to ensure her release.

Behind me, one of the drunks seemed to have come to life. He started thumping on the door of his cell, shouting, 'Dillon, get me a mug of water, will you? Or ale? And a lump of cheese? Dillon! Come here, man!' He sounded like he had been here before.

The constable, probably used to the sudden waking appetites of the layabouts he collected during his sweeps, did not appear, but the inebriated man continued to holler and bang as if his racket might have some effect other than to provoke his cellmate to quiet him with a well-aimed kick and a demand: 'Shut your fucking gob.'

I ignored the noise and approached the final cell. I counted nine paces. As I neared the door, I stopped and called out, 'Joan? Joan Gedge?' An answering draught caused my candle to flicker, and I guarded it with my hand, having no wish to be plunged into total darkness. The little flame barely warmed my palm. Behind me, the men proceeded to argue in the incoherent, time-honoured fashion of drunken fools, then came the sound of a scuffle, punctuated by a squeal from one of the two, and a grunt of satisfaction from the other. From somewhere nearby, drifting down through the ventilation gate, there came the bustle of the street: fishwives laughing and scolding, victuallers' patter, lawyers deep in discussion. But from the cell itself, nothing, no noise at all.

They were huddled together on the floor against the interior wall. I came close to the bars and said again, 'Joan?' The housemaid was curled in a ball, diminutive beside her mother, a large, robust woman, gone to fat. This difference between them was something of a running joke in the parish. I had heard them described as the fat goose and the famished goose. Goodwife

Gedge's bulk now shielded her daughter, so I could see her ample hips and stomach, but just inches of Joan's slight frame poking out. 'Goodwife Gedge?' I said, trying to stir the mother instead. She did not move.

I was more keenly aware than before of the smell: I had thought it was rodents' urine, but there was an unpleasant, herbaceous stink coming from the cell itself. I placed my free hand on the bars and rose up on my toes to get a better look.

They were asleep. I opened my mouth to call out to them but then closed it again. The warring prisoners were now making noise enough to drown out the trumpet call on the Last Day. Nobody could sleep through all this, unless deaf.

The cell was partially lit by light from the barred window. I saw Goodwife Gedge's round face, registered its pale and unnatural stillness, and felt the pull of fear, the same inexorable, run-or-die terror I had felt on the battlefield. I stepped back, said, 'Dillon!' I dropped my candle in my distress and it went out. I was entombed in the darkness. 'Dillon!'

Realising that my voice only added to the confused carnival of sounds produced by the scrapping occupants of the first cell, I retreated, breaking into a run as I went past Chrissa Moore, staying as near to the wall as I could. I passed the quarrelling men and came to the bottom of the stairs. The light near blinded me as I hurried up and round, my leg burning. I kept calling the constable's name until Dillon reappeared, his amiable expression replaced by one of alertness. 'What is it?'

'The Gedge women,' I said, my breath coming like bellows. 'I can't rouse them.'

The constable groped for his keys. 'Mind out of the way,' he said, and pushed past, his large feet surprisingly fleet on the stone stairs. Dillon seemed to see like a bat in the dark chamber but, without the candle, I had to grope the wall to save from tripping on the uneven floor. I heard the jangle of keys again as the constable opened the end door, and watched the great bulk of the man enter the cell.

I realised I was hanging back near the cell that held Chrissa Moore. As Dillon dragged the first unresponsive shape out into the passage, there was a sudden cry next to me, and in the barred square there appeared a lead-white, frightened face. She clung to the rails, the opposite of the regal figure that had laughed moments before. On impulse, I went closer, and I grasped at her fingers. They were as cold as the ice I cracked off the well chain each morning in the depths of winter. 'Woman, if you know anything of this, tell me the truth! What role have you played in this?'

'None. I am no witch,' she said, in a hoarse whisper. 'You had the right of it when you said that. And no whore.' She pressed her face nearer mine. 'But you were wrong in one thing: you give too little weight to the dark and chaotic powers of this world. Do not dismiss them so lightly!' With this ominous hint, she inched backwards. 'As for me, if you would know the truth about me, seek out Lucy Bennett, in Norwich. You will find her on Ramping Horse Lane, near St Stephen's, and she will vouch for me, in her way.'

I pushed this aside and, thinking again of my father, said, 'What of the child?'

At this, the raw feeling in her face subsided; it was like a drawing down of shutters, a mask replaced. She loosened her grip on my fingers and stepped further back, disappearing into the dark.

10

Outside the courthouse, the day had turned bitter, and it was spitting heavy hail. Looking through the window, it was hard to believe this was the same day I had arrived home. The cold, dry night spent beneath the ash tree felt like weeks ago, yet it had only been this morning that I had ridden up to our farmhouse, expecting to find peace.

Against the cold, Manyon offered a warmed, spiced wine and an extra cloak for Esther, who sat shaking beside me. I accepted the wine – Manyon must have seen my hands trembling as I took it – but after a few moments forgot I was holding it. I closed my eyes to banish the images that rushed up at me, but they had sunk their livid roots straight down into the deepest places of my mind. Death I had seen – eviscerated men holding in their guts, calling for their mothers, begging for the mercy of a sword thrust – but I had never seen anything as terrible as the deaths I saw that day.

Yet my conscience pinched me like a vice. What had taken place was unthinkable, but even as I laboured to force it from my mind, I fretted. It was getting late. We should have been on the road home by now. My thoughts returned again and again to my father – whether he knew anything of our presence or absence beyond shadows flitting in and out of his sight, whether he was afraid, wondering whether we would come back at all, or driven mad by thirst or hunger. Whether he knew I was sorry, so sorry…

The atmosphere in the small office was less collegiate than before. The magistrate seemed to have stepped back into his official role, and sat straight-faced behind his desk. For himself, Manyon took no wine. He had dismissed the hapless Timothy and was taking down information with his own hand, questioning Esther, me, Rutherford and Dillon in turn. I heard nothing out of place from any of the other witnesses, nothing that would provide satisfactory explanation of the deaths of Joan and Goodwife Gedge.

Both women had been dead when Dillon pulled them from the cell. The constable had undertaken a perfunctory examination; then, dissatisfied with what he could see, carried them up the spiral stairs. Even in my distress, I had marvelled at the man's strength as he shouldered the matronly form of Goodwife Gedge, then watched from the bottom of what felt like an abyss of sadness as he carried Joan. She seemed to weigh no more than a newborn lamb and her fawn-coloured hair dangled limply over his shoulder. He might have been carrying home a kill from the hunt.

Dillon had set both women down in a window annexe, as far from the public gaze as he could manage. But people still saw. The shocked cries from those loitering on the courthouse floor had not deterred him as he had pulled back their eyelids and checked their mouths and tongues for blackness or swelling. He had bent low and sniffed inside their dead mouths. They had a blue cast to their faces, but there were no other obvious signs to indicate the cause of death, at least as far as my untrained eye could tell. Dillon said they were still warm, so death must have occurred recently.

'Hemlock,' Dillon said now, in response to Manyon's enquiry.
'You're certain?'

'As eggs are eggs,' the constable answered, stolidly. 'The smell of the stuff is unlike anything else. Check for yourself, sir, if you're in any doubt that I have the right of it.'

'No,' said Manyon, absently. 'I'm sure you know your business, Constable. But how? How?' He drummed his fingers against the table. 'The Moore girl was locked up, in her cell, the whole time?'

Dillon nodded. 'She was brought in before the Gedge women and she's right there now. Not a shadow of a chance of her getting out.'

'And their cells were not adjacent to one another?'

Dillon shook his head.

'The women were searched when they were brought in?'

'Yes, sir,' the constable said, robustly.

Manyon had no further questions, so sent Dillon to call on the coroner. He scribbled a few further notes before sitting back, thoughtful, in his seat.

I offered Esther a handkerchief and she took it, gratefully. I sat, not knowing whether Manyon waited for me to say something. I had already decided to say nothing of Chrissa Moore's words in the gaol. Something about them — her talk of chaos, perhaps, which I feared more than anything — had discomforted me. I wanted nothing other than to take my sister and return to the farm and my father by the shortest road. The less I said now, I was certain, the more quickly we would be away from this place and its horrors.

To my surprise, Manyon nodded to Rutherford, who had been, until now, a silent observer. Rutherford leant forward in his seat towards Esther, and steepled his fingers. 'Miss Treadwater, if I might ask you some questions about your exchange with Joan Gedge and her mother...'

This bewildered me. 'You were there, Mr Rutherford — what can my sister tell you that you do not know first-hand?'

Rutherford's face contorted in an awkward expression, then he offered an ingratiating smile. 'That is true of the first few moments but, as your sister will testify, there was a short time when she was unaccompanied in the presence of the two women. A short time only,' he added, as if that made it better.

I stared at Rutherford, unsure whether to laugh or to leap up and box his head off. I spoke slowly, as if to a fool. 'You left my sister in that dungeon – alone?'

I felt the warmth of Esther's hand, and realised how tightly I had been gripping the carved arm of my seat. Her small fingers unfurled mine from the wood and held them. 'Please don't blame Mr Rutherford,' she said, gently. 'I asked him to let me pray with them, and to leave us – only for a few moments, as he says.'

Manyon had drawn forward. 'So, you were the last person with the two women? The last to see them living, I mean?' His voice was still smooth, but there was a new layer of doubt beneath the courtesy.

Esther nodded miserably. 'That's correct,' she said, pressing the cloth to her lips to contain a sob.

'Did you exchange a few words with them? Perhaps a prayer?' he suggested, with ready tact.

'No. That is, I spoke to them, and I prayed, but they made no answer.' At this, I started. Had they been affected by the poison already when Esther went down to see them? It had been so dark; it would have been easy for Esther to think she spoke to listening ears, when in truth the women were dead or dying there before her unseeing eyes? I relayed this grotesque thought to the magistrate, and he made a careful note.

Then, he said, 'And you handed them nothing?'

Her eyes widened. 'Nothing,' she said. 'I would not…' She stopped, looking to me for reassurance. I nodded. 'I would have nothing to hand them, and why would they take anything from me if I did? After all, I am the reason they are here… that they were here…' At these words, she broke down again, weeping helplessly. I patted her hand, feeling utterly useless.

Manyon spoke almost to himself. 'Very well. I can see no explanation for how the women took hold of the substance, but there seems no doubt that they administered it to themselves, or to one another, and it makes little sense that they would do so at the behest of the person whose testimony saw them incarcerated here. Unless…' He drummed his quill on the wooden desk, *rat tat tat*. We waited on his words with drawn breath. 'No,' he pronounced, finally, to my deepest relief. 'Mistress Treadwater is right in that.'

'Then my sister and I can leave?' I asked.

The magistrate paused a moment, then agreed. 'You may be needed again. If the examination of the Moore girl this afternoon yields anything further, or if it becomes plain that she is with child as she says, I may call on you. In the meantime, yes, you may go. And thank you, both, for your assistance.'

Rutherford stood to see us to the door. He placed his hand on my shirtsleeve, and I resisted the urge to pull away. 'The searchers will still need to examine the house,' he said. 'I will call on you tomorrow; in the meanwhile, the room Chrissa Moore slept in is not to be altered in any way.'

'Very well,' I said. 'I'll find another spot in which to sleep.' I tipped my hat at Rutherford. 'Until tomorrow, then.'

Before leaving town, I sought out a farrier for Ben. This gave me the small comfort that, if I had accomplished nothing more, I was at least attending to my duty to the horse.

My wound ached all the way home. Temperance was fractious, Esther silent, and my own mind was heavily preoccupied.

———

I tried again, holding Father's face off the mattress as I spooned a second lump of Esther's thickened oat pottage into his gaping mouth. The task nauseated me: the too-red, wet lips, the lolling tongue, the half-aware look in the one of his eyes that would open fully. Using the spoon, I attempted to push some of the food over the mound of his tongue and past his teeth, hoping he would swallow it, but it simply caused him to choke, and I ended up swabbing the regurgitated mess off his chin. Eventually, I gave up and sat for a few moments in silence.

I was still sweating, pain surging through me like a spear. Every joint and muscle ached. When I lowered my forehead to the back of my hand, it was clammy, but still I shivered, and my belly cramped tight and sour. An infection was setting in.

I sniffed at the pottage, a richer imitation of what I had eaten in the army. I could easily recall the taste: cabbage and onion, always past their best; meat juice if we were lucky, tough bits of sinew and heavy seasoning to disguise its origins if we weren't. The frequent slop had interfered with our stomachs, and we often joked it had been better on the way out than on the way in. I remembered how I had complained so hard even Jack Trelawney had tired of it, and told me, as an enlisted soldier, I was lucky I was fed better than a beggar, and blessed if I was paid at all.

'I hated you, Father,' I said, realising that my father wouldn't have known my train of thought even if he had been able to hear me. 'For such a long time, I hated you for sending me there.' I closed my eyes, conjuring up the mortification that had flooded my father's face as he waved Milton's final letter in front of me. 'I thought you so harsh.'

My father's voice had rung out with anger. 'Once again, you shame me in your inability to master yourself. You dishonour the name of Treadwater. I give you a choice: join the Bands, and defend Parliament and God against the King's ministers, thereby reclaiming something of our dignity and the values I taught you, or –' and here he held up his hand against my protests '– no longer call yourself my son.'

I had never seen the contents of Milton's letter, and never wanted to see them, but I could imagine well enough what was in it.

The last day I spent under Milton's tutelage in Chalfonte started in the dark hours of the morning. Waking, I heard the warbling of a treecreeper through the window, and toyed with rising from the bed and returning Elizabeth to her own chilly room before the servants began to light the fires and collect the chamber pots. But, as I envisioned cold draughts of winter air hitting my feet, the blanket being withdrawn, I drowsily dismissed the thought. What would a few more minutes hurt?

Beneath my hand, Elizabeth's slender thigh was as warm and soft as sable. Her leg encircled mine, and she slept peacefully. I, too, had slept, though not so well, constantly stirred by her unclothed limbs. I hadn't wanted to let her sleep at all, but to pull her atop me again, to draw her down so that her breasts touched my body and I might kiss her gentle mouth. While she dreamt, I lay restless and aflame, fondly imagining the little room at the top of my tutor's house as a haven, a place outside time, where the two of us might live out our years in halcyon bliss.

These things, we always think, when we are young.

My reverie was interrupted by the sound of booted feet striking wood, stair after stair taken in angry succession. My room was the topmost in the house, an attic, a tiny, cramped space with nowhere I might stash the rousing form of Elizabeth, who raised her head from my chest as I started upright and said, 'What is it, Tom?' I rolled, cat-like, from the bed and cast about beneath it for my breeches and boots. I found her nightdress bunched on the floor and threw it up to her.

'Quick, put it on!' I said, urgently. The door flew open, and a voice, stern and censorious, demanded she rise and dress herself. I started to speak in her defence, blundering, talking of marriage, but her uncle cut me dead and I desisted. We had made no such promises, in truth. I wasn't even certain she loved me. We had spoken of the future, but lightly, and she had skipped prettily to other subjects.

In some ways, this scene had been inevitable. I had known deep down we could not continue to escape detection as we kissed behind rose bushes and joined hands under the dinner table. Sooner or later, beneath Milton's irascible eye, we would have been discovered, and so we were. Perhaps I welcomed the chance to return home, even in disgrace. In any case, now each of us would have to look to our own reputation. But I couldn't escape the guilty thought that hers might turn out to be rather the more brittle of the two.

Now, over a year later, I continued my address to my father. 'I was in the wrong,' I said. 'I know that now. I let you down so badly and I have deserved all that has come after.' I watched my father's trembling lips, wishing my words might be heard, but knowing in my heart that I spoke aloud to myself. 'I was a foolish boy, but you look upon a man now,' I said. 'I will not fail you again.'

I thought of Elizabeth: returned to London in disgrace, dead of the plague just five months later, lying in disputed ground south of the River Thames. For many months, while on the march with the army, I had comforted myself with how I had done my duty and offered to marry her – an offer refused with accompanying venom by her uncle – and I had ached for her, but in truth, if I closed my eyes and tried – I did this now – to conjure her before me, I couldn't remember her face, only the vanishing impression of youth and sweetness. My regret, unlike my love, was deeper now, my abiding sense of my own error an indelible mark upon my conscience.

But back then, packed off to Norfolk with the command never to darken my tutor's door again, preceded by a letter to my father setting out the whole business, I nursed in my heart a cuckoo of misplaced rage, blaming Milton, blaming whichever of the servants had betrayed us, blaming even Elizabeth, for tempting me with her loveliness. I had marched on town after town and fought and killed, all the while believing myself to be the wronged one. Now, with Elizabeth gone, my father helpless, the farm probably ruined, I hung my head in abject shame, wondering how much pain might have been avoided, if only I had behaved with greater propriety, and thought of anybody except myself.

'Brother, the physician is here. In the parlour.' The door opened, and Esther's meek voice interrupted my thoughts; her news was infinitely more welcome than these memories. I rose wearily and placed the pottage on the trunk at the foot of the bed.

'We'll get help for you,' I said to my father, turning away.

I took the stairs slowly, feeling every contact with the wood as a searing jolt. I was light-headed, which did not surprise me; I had eaten little in recent days. As I reached for the rail to steady myself, my hand missed, I slipped; then, crashing down the stairs and only half-aware that I had fallen, I lost consciousness before I hit the bottom.

Once high, now fallen, chained forever within the circles of the world, yet within the boundless deep, it glides free, twisting in folds, never ceasing. To give liberty to its appetites, grown greater than the sulfuric cracks in which it is concealed, it labours without cessation, enduring plague and flood, locusts and salt, awaiting world's ending in ice and fire. Awake! Awake and arise. He who cast us down is abandoned. The colossal round of the world is discovered. The distant stars are mapped, christened, charted. The waves are parted. I am upon the wing, for Chaos reigns once again, and the march of time has begun anew.

As I was released from my dream-state, the pictures in my mind, of something turbulent and muscular, something that writhed and grew in the deepest of shadows, faded, and I was returned to the real world.

My mouth tasted like rotten eggs. I licked my lips, wincing as they cracked, and forced my eyes open. Desperately thirsty, I propped myself up, and recognised the stink of a poultice some-where on my lower body. I stretched out my leg, expecting to feel the familiar flood through the site of my wound, and felt a dull ache in reply, but that was all – the pain that had streaked through me like a hot poker was much relieved. How long had I been in bed? I strained to rise and fell back, weak, but no longer sweating or dizzy.

The room was dark, but moonlight pooled through the window. A rime of frost had grown against the pane, and tendrils of frozen water crept up the edges. I guessed it was the blackest part of the night, the witching hour, as far from midnight as it was from dawn, with not a soul moving anywhere. In this uncertain moment, I experienced an unsettled readiness, like being on the wrong end of a sword thrust, in that quarter-second before your enemy makes up his mind to move. My first impulse was to lie still, to conceal myself, if I could, from a threat I could not identify, that hadn't yet sliced into the silence around me.

But then it was not quite silent. There was something – faint and foreign – on the edge of my hearing. Forcing myself upright, I rubbed my face and eyes. As I drew my legs around and placed my feet on the floor, I tested how much weight I was able to put on the leg before the pain attacked again, and found I could stand easily. But I was wearing a nightgown, not the clothes in which I had last dressed myself. I touched my chin and felt rough, scratchy hair – at least three days of growth.

Where was the sound coming from?

I had no time to seek out a candle. I padded to the door. The upper floor was in darkness. The bedchamber doors were closed. But the noise came from Esther's room.

Feeling my way, conscious that it had been years since I had stumbled across the boards to my sister's room, I reached for the handle.

As I stepped into the room, adjusting my sight to the blackness, I realised the rumbling sound had been the scraping and thumping of Esther's bed against the bare boards. The convulsions of her body moved the bed, her back arched towards the ceiling, with her head and upper limbs thrashing. From her mouth were torn incomprehensible utterances, rapid and confused, hardly words at all, like the cries of tormented souls. I was terribly afraid, but resisted the urge to sink to my knees, remembering my promise to my father – *you look upon a man now* – and went forward. She had to be caught in the throes of some evil dream.

'Esther!' I cried. 'Wake, Esther!' I reached past the violence of her arms and shook her by the shoulders. Her feet kicked out and her torso pushed against mine with shocking force. I couldn't still her spasms. Long seconds passed. As I started to panic, her struggle abated, and she weakened in my arms. I couldn't see whether she had opened her eyes, but heard her voice. 'Brother, release me.' She still sounded only partly in the room, somnolent and groggy.

'By God, you frightened me,' I said, releasing her with a half-laugh. My heart still raced in my chest.

She came to a sitting position, and said, weakly, 'I am glad to see you well, Thomas.'

'How… How long has it been?'

'Four days.'

'Four days?' I repeated, stupidly. So it was New Year's Day.

'Yes. It was a blessing that the physician was already with us when you fell because he was able to clean and dress your wound straight away. Then he induced sleep with a tincture. You improved quickly, with proper attention to your leg.'

There was something wrong with her voice. Something forced and unnaturally calm. She didn't sound like Esther at all. I reached for her hand. It was cold. I said, 'What are you not telling me?'

The pause before her words was ages long. But she spoke steadily. 'After you fell, the physician examined Father. He concluded that the cause of his ailment was a sideration. I did not understand the entirety of what he said, but there seems to be no doubt that he was struck down by... by God.'

I felt a surge of irritation at the talk of Providence. 'That was the physician's diagnosis?' I said.

'Well, no. He called it an apoplexy. But...' Esther placed her hand over mine. 'With everything that has happened, I am finding it difficult to...' She took a deep breath. 'After the physician examined Father and left for the night, Father was smitten by a second, almighty attack. And this time he did not recover.'

I stared. I did not know how to ask the only question that mattered. 'Is he...?'

'Father died. The same night.'

With tears in my eyes, I squeezed her hand, lowered my head, and thought of the compendium of my losses. Elizabeth, my youth, my strength, now my father. Again, words came unbidden: *But put forth thine hand now, and touch all that he hath, and he will curse thee to thy face.*

II

Two weeks later, I brought Ben to a halt outside Norwich's Magdalen Gate, where we waited in a queue to enter the city. He pulled strongly on the reins, eager to get on, and I realised the horse was fully recovered. I was just a little further behind him. Though I had been confined to bed while my wound healed properly, sensation was returning every day, and now I was able to go about my work as before. The small rents had been collected and, to my great relief, no further animals had died. Slowly, as my leg improved, I began to ride the perimeter of the farm and take stock of how many sheep remained.

More reluctantly, I began to think about a return to the army. My colonel had sent the regiment home with instructions to travel back a sennight after the Epiphany. That feast had passed a week ago, but there were still matters here needing my attention. If I had to go, Esther could not be left. I was considering sending her to some of our people in Suffolk, distant cousins, though I knew little of them beyond their names. She wouldn't want to go, I was certain, but here she would be at risk of harm and, even if she stayed, a woman alone could not manage the farm.

That was another concern. The farm wasn't large, but Father had always been able to rely on hired labour. When I had returned it had been Christmas, and the men had been sent home to their families, just as I had from the army. But after the arrival of the witchfinder, the arrests, and what had taken place in the gaol, they had not come back. Though I had spoken to five or six other local men since, they had offered nothing but guarded suspicion. One had muttered darkly about the Gedge women and stalked off, the others had nodded along, saying they might report for a day's work, but none had come. Who could blame them? But these matters troubled me enormously. I did not know what my father would have done in my place.

They had buried my father while I slept. Nervously, Esther had told me of how John Rutherford, arriving to search the house – a search which revealed nothing new – had found her weeping in the company of her father's corpse, and me in a deep, drugged sleep. The witchfinder had paid the physician, ensured the death certificate was signed and funeral arrangements made. His actions had surprised me; I had not thought him so practical, nor so generous. Rutherford would be repaid every penny of his outlay – I would not be indebted to him – but I had to admit the assistance had come at the needful time. Still, I wondered what Rutherford might want in return.

The committal had been a hurried affair, with few spiritual preparations and little of the ordinary ritual. My father had had no chance to compose an epitaph. In the end, attendance was low. Rumours of witchcraft and bastardy spread quickly. Yet I comforted myself that of all the men I knew, my father was most ready for Heaven: humble, beneficent to the poor and careful of his soul. If he had hidden sins, they were well hidden indeed. Tentatively, I felt our name might recover, as people thought longer on his life and deeds.

But even so, this was the real world, where nobody could afford to take their reputation lightly. I had travelled to Norwich to protect my father's name and, if I could, discover the truth about Chrissa Moore. I needed to know where she was from, how she had come into my family's employ, whether she had contrived to destroy any other men, and what involvement she had had in the deaths of Joan and her mother at Walsham. Only then, with the tarnish rubbed off, could our name climb back to respectability, and we recover our credit.

But I didn't expect to find Lucy Bennett. I suspected the Moore woman had invented this advocate in hopes of further delaying a trial, or that Bennett, if she existed, lived a life of such depraved chaos that she would be difficult to pin down. Perhaps a whore, perhaps a procuress. But I had to try. Whatever I discovered, however incomplete, it might help me to cast doubt on the claims against my father.

I had sought out Manyon once more before deciding to ride to Norwich. I wanted to question Chrissa Moore further, see whether I might encourage her to speak to me again, as she had done in the gaol. Manyon, though every bit as hospitable as before, had been regretful. 'No, Tom,' he said, shaking his head. 'I cannot allow it. There have already been two deaths, which – even if I discount the allegation of witchcraft – I must place at the door of the Moore girl. And she will not be induced to speak, even were I to agree.'

'Not at all?'

'Not one word, either in her own defence or in confession. And the women's deaths have roused the town against her, understandably, as they are mourned by many. I am under pressure to disregard the normal procedures and apply more force in persuading her to speak. Not that I have bowed to such pressure, of course. Yet,' he had added, ominously.

Manyon had insisted the women's deaths were murders and not self-destruction, so Hale had agreed to bury Joan and Goodwife Gedge in the churchyard. It was only the magistrate's intervention that had prevented their corpses being hauled off to a crossroads and buried in a pit, pinned with stakes to prevent them wandering. For my part, I was less concerned about their return to this world than about their untimely exit. Their deaths weighed heavily on my mind. Two murders. Of people close to us. If Chrissa Moore were somehow responsible for their poisonings, she was dangerous beyond measure. But if the deaths were indeed self-murder, it spoke of their guilt, of ill-wishing, as Esther had feared. And in that case, Chrissa Moore might lose her life to a great injustice. That thought, though I kept pushing it aside, dogged me as I entered the city, persuading Ben along the cobbled road under the wall.

I had never been to London, and couldn't imagine the capital to be much greater than Norwich. I disliked towns and cities, preferring the rolling spaces of the countryside, but I admired the ambition of the Vikings, clergymen and merchants who had turned a small fortress-town into the second biggest trading centre in the nation. The city housed thousands of souls, some even said tens of thousands. Sitting on the winding River Wensum, it boasted twelve gatehouses and six bridges, and was encased on all sides by either its solid defensive wall or the bustling hum of the river. It was prosperous, with goods ranging from worsted wool to leather, ironwork, beer, pottery, candles and stockings and hats for its well-off inhabitants.

Yet there was much poverty. The great rebellion of Robert Kett nearly a century earlier had been driven by the enclosures of vast tracts of land, land which had fed the poor, for the grazing of rich men's animals, whose wool fed only the purses of their owners. And although it remained a tradition for a day in late August to be set aside as a holiday to commemorate the saving of the city from the plots and seditions of the rebels, I couldn't help but think it shameful that people should live in such debased conditions, and wondered, watching children walk barefoot in the wake of fat, well-wrapped merchants, not daring to beg a coin, which side I would have joined in that struggle. Here, I saw more varmints and vagrants than I had counted in any of the towns I had seen with the army.

Pausing, I offered a coin to a passing beggar, a small girl with mouse-tail hair and round eyes. I asked whether she might know of a Lucy Bennett, of Ramping Horse Lane, but she scampered away with her prize clutched tight in hand. I realised I was being too eager; the city was vast, I was in Norwich-Over-the-Water, and the urchins on the other side of the Fye Bridge would likely know more.

I remembered coming here with my father, who always told the same story – as if he had never told it before – of a woman suspected of witchcraft, forced by the townsfolk to recite the Lord's Prayer before being ducked off the side of the great, two-arched stone crossing. She had risen from the filthy water coughing and spluttering and cursing her captors, before taking an enormous breath and having the good sense to stay down long enough for them to decide she was innocent. My father had recited the tale with scorn, knowing the foolishness of the mob, knowing what damage they could do when riled.

I came away from the river into the city. The louring sky of recent weeks had retreated before a hard, still brightness, and as I rode I savoured the winter sun on my face. On my left the bobbled spire of the cathedral dominated the whole skyline. As I contemplated its huge nave and the width of its transepts, it seemed an impossible achievement. Its medieval builders must have harboured a great desire to impress upon their congregation the divinity of their task. But the soaring tower of expensive Caen stone impressed upon me nothing but the primacy of money in the body politic.

Next, I crossed into Tombland, moving slowly through the surging crowds, keeping my eyes trained on those nearby. There would be pickpockets, confidence tricksters, and still more beggars who doubled as pickpockets, and I kept a close watch on my purse down St Stephen's Lane, moving away from the market. Here were several taverns, including the Ramping

Horse. The road was lined with merchants' homes: substantial, two-storeyed, with tiled roofs, some opening on to courtyards behind. Those occupied by the rich traders were smart and clean, but others were dilapidated, with crumbling walls and missing tiles, and were carved up into shanty-like tenements, housing as many of the working poor as would fit inside the ramshackle walls. It was a strange mixture. I realised I had never paid it much attention when I had visited the city with my father. It was here, it seemed, that I needed to search for Lucy Bennett.

I looked about me. The passers-by were a motley crowd: merchants, men of the gentlemanly sort, some ragged boys kicking a bladder between them, on the verge of a row, and three young women – girls, really – who walked together, sending sidelong glances in my direction and giggling endlessly. They were dressed brightly, in the type of frippery that is less impressive on closer inspection. They might have been thirteen, fourteen at the most.

There was an apprentice lolling against a wall by a public water trough, watching the girls. He appeared bored, and canny. I approached him. 'I'm seeking a woman named Lucy Bennett,' I said. 'I was given this street as the address, but I don't know which house. Do you know anything of her?'

He leered at me. 'Looking for that sort of thing, are you? Wish I had your coin.' He spat a large gobbet of phlegm on the ground. I sighed and reached into my purse, withdrawing a groat; its recipient pocketed the money and gave the address I sought. I was surprised to be directed towards one of the better houses, a wide building no more than twenty years old, of timber and knapped flint, with its first floor overhanging the street below, and handsome glass windows. I nodded thanks to the grinning lout as I went towards the door, then struck with the heavy knocker.

After a wait of more than a minute, the door was half-opened by a grubby-looking scullery maid. She was thin, with a reddened, dripping nose, and I thought I would be ashamed to have such an obviously ill fed and unwell girl in my employ. Her condition, again, surprised me, for the outward appearance of the house was respectable. But I cleared my throat and began formally. 'My name is Thomas Treadwater, of Worstead. I seek an appointment with Mistress Lucy Bennett, as I am acquainted with a young woman I believe she knows: a woman called Chrissa Moore. I'd like to ask your mistress some questions about her, if she is amenable.'

The maid did not pull the door further ajar. Instead, she looked me up and down, then nodded curtly and said, 'I'll check.'

The apprentice was still watching, seeming amused by my cool reception. He whistled something merry and, when the girls reappeared from the alley, called out something cruder that made them laugh. They looked even younger close up, gathered together like a flock of tiny, brightly coloured birds. One of them dipped her shoulder to the ground, coming up with a stone which she tossed in his direction. 'Whores,' the lad shouted after them, and the girls called back violent insults of their own before running away, laughing.

I decided that, perhaps, after all, Esther had not been far wrong when she had judged Chrissa Moore's origins, and I was taken aback, for just a moment, by the disappointment that accompanied the thought. Why should I care what trade she plied?

Before I could scrutinise that question, the door opened again, and the servant gestured for me to come inside. 'No weapons,' she said. 'We lock them up here.' She had stopped beside a closet at the base of the stairs. I nodded and unbuckled my sword belt, watching as the weapon was placed under lock and key. Then the girl led me up the staircase, through two reception rooms on the first floor, and on into a larger room towards the back of the house.

I found myself in a room of contradictions. It was large and well furnished, with a table covered in sprigged silk and laden with sweet dishes. I noticed sugared apricots and rosemary, marchpane cakes and plums. There were several good chairs against the walls, two or three of them occupied by girls who, like those outside, looked better dressed and more advanced in years the further away one stood, and one rangy man, heavy-bearded, half-asleep. He was not wearing a uniform, but was still in possession of his sword, presumably for the benefit of any customer who might think of dodging his bill. There was an actual giltwood mirror – something I had never seen before – over the fireplace, but the room had simple rushes on the boarded floor, and was not often cleaned, by the look and musty smell of it. And despite the prosperous appearance of the woman occupying the seat before the table, the boy who sat at her feet looked thin and neglected, his skin pallid and his eyes, which fell on me as I entered the room, as dull and grey as week-old snow. He lowered them as I moved closer, and his hands fell to playing with a pendant around his neck; it had some small object on the end of the metal chain, but I could not see what as he turned it over and over between his scrawny fingers.

I bowed. The girls snickered. The woman at the table shooed them out with a single word and they fled, still giggling. I turned my attention to their mistress. This, then, was Lucy Bennett. She was monstrously fat, and draped in coloured fabrics of the better kind. The style was not particularly ordered, as if she had layered one bolt of cloth over another until she was covered, rather than bother to put on an actual dress, and, above the rainbow of silken flaps and folds, she had a coarse and pockmarked face. She did not rise to receive me, but I believed that, if she did stand, she would be as tall as I. For a moment I wondered whether I looked upon Chrissa's mother, but on closer examination, I saw that, beneath the flesh of her face, there was nothing of Chrissa's refined bone structure; her chin was non-existent, her nose disproportionate against her flabby cheeks, and her mouth ungenerous. Her eyes were hard where everything else about her was soft.

'Who might you be?' she said. Her voice, like her movements, was languorous and honeyed.

I had given my name at the door, but could be turned out at any moment and so spoke with more patience than I felt. 'My name is Thomas Treadwater, mistress. I was given your name and the location of your house by the woman Chrissa Moore, who wishes you to provide her with a… character, of sorts.' The explanation was weak, and I added, 'I am aiding the Walsham Justice, Christopher Manyon, in this matter.' It was a half-truth, but I hoped the mention of the magistrate might make her more receptive.

It seemed to have the desired effect. 'Manyon? I know the name,' she said, absently, but her grey eyes were sharp beneath their puffy lids. 'What news have you of Chrissa, then?'

'She worked for you?' I said, bluntly. The procuress raised her over-plucked eyebrows. I waited, unrepentant.

She reached out to the table, set to the side so she did not have to bend too far to pick up a sugared apricot. She placed the fruit into her mouth with obvious pleasure. At her feet, the silent boy watched the food go over his head and past her blackened front teeth.

She chewed unevenly, moving the food around her mouth in search of the best tooth with which to address it. Finally, she swallowed, then picked at one of her back molars and licked the resulting morsel from her finger before answering. 'Chrissa was never one of my girls in that way,' she said. 'Oh, the clients would have liked that. She would have earnt well, and for a long while – she was only eleven or so when she came to me. As lovely as the night, she was. Fresh.' She leant forward again and selected another fruit. 'But she would have none of it. Not her. I don't force my girls, you know,' she said, with pride. 'Not like some in my line of work. I offer them the choice: earn your keep on your back, or find another way to pay. Chrissa chose to use her other skills.' She shrugged, as if to say, such is the way of things.

I said, 'What skills were those, then?'

'Oh, this and that,' Lucy said, vaguely. 'We're a broad church under this roof. Plenty of things a person can do to get coin without opening their legs for it.'

Yes, like selling young girls to old men, I thought, revolted.

Lucy continued. 'I told her when she turned up, skinny as a pole and lugging this loiter-sack along with her,' she said, nodding to the boy at her feet, 'I'd only space for her, only room for those who could pay. She swore she could bring in enough for both of them. I'm not responsible for whatever she was doing — none of my concern. She would be out all hours. Still, she paid on time, and that's all that mattered to me.'

'And that went on for several years?'

After an uncertain sound I took as a 'yes', she chewed for a few more moments, then began again. 'Until earlier this year,' she said. 'She went as usual — and sometimes she might be gone for several days, so I didn't worry — but she didn't come back.'

'This was when?'

'Around Easter-time. Can't be exactly sure. I was just set to turf this lump out on to the street when a letter arrived from her, with her arrears, and a promise she'd send money again, regular, for the boy's board.'

'And did she?'

'Until a few weeks ago, she did,' Lucy acknowledged.

'What age is he?' I said, looking at the boy.

Carelessly, Lucy Bennett raised her eyes, as if trying to remember. 'Nine. Ten,' she said. 'He was but three or four when he came here.'

Ten summers old. I couldn't believe it. The boy was tiny. Shaggy black hair surrounded a round face. He had eyes of an odd shape and appearance, as though their maker had placed forefinger and thumb on either side and stretched. His expression was of the utmost innocence: superficially interested in me and my – relatively – fine clothes, but equally fascinated by a piece of muck he had found on the floor, which he now crumbled between his fingers. He reminded me of an idiot I had seen baited on the green at Ivinghoe when I had stopped there on my way home from Newbury.

I thought for a few moments, watching as the boy lost interest in his scrap of dirt and simply squatted on the floor, looking as though he had always been there.

'I have a proposition,' I said, finally. Lucy looked up with a gambler's curiosity and nodded for me to go on. 'I would like to take the boy off your hands. We are several workers short at my farm, and there are plenty of jobs to go around. We can put him to work in the kitchen.'

Lucy laughed unpleasantly, her large bosom heaving with private amusement. 'You'd like that, would you?' she cackled.

Not immediately understanding, I said, 'The boy needs to be provided for, and there is work to be done. And for fair pay.'

She continued to laugh as she eyed the boy. 'Him? Work?' Wiping a mirthful tear from her eye, she shook her head. 'No,' she said, with exaggerated regret. 'No. Henry might not be my own, and he might only be fed what his sister can afford...' She looked the skeletal child over from head to toe and shrugged. 'Perhaps a little less,' she acknowledged. 'But that doesn't mean I'm going to sell him to the first catamite who offers me a shilling for him. I'm a Christian woman.'

Now I received her meaning. 'God's blood, woman!' I said. 'Have you no decency? I want to help the boy, not... Not anything like you said. I know his sister – that is, I know where she is.'

At this, Henry's head rose from his chest. He stared at me and his round face showed a glimmer of agitation, but he said nothing.

Lucy seemed to be weighing this new information, considering whether it might be played to her advantage. 'Is that right? You might wish to tell her she missed her last payment for this creature.' I winced as her slippered foot jolted the boy's backside. The child barely reacted. 'But,' she continued, 'she'll not thank you, even if you do take him; she's as proud as a Pharisee, that one. Where did you say she was?'

'I didn't,' I said, shortly. 'But I can describe her for you.' I did so and it was easy. My waking moments since seeing Chrissa Moore had rarely been completely free of her face.

When I was finished, Lucy nodded slowly. 'That's her, all right,' she said. Her eyes gleamed with greed. 'Still, my duty as a Christian is to stick by my word and keep this boy in my house; unless, of course, you can undertake to pay me in Chrissa's stead, and compensate me, also, for the very small portion of her payments I take for his care.'

I suspected that was most of whatever Chrissa paid, and despised the old hag for her avarice. 'I will compensate you,' I said. 'The boy will come with me to my farm, and work, and perhaps in time,' I added, in a clearer voice, so that the boy understood, 'he will be reunited with his sister.' I hated myself for the hope I saw in the boy's eyes, a hope I had kindled for my own profit. Really, I thought in disgust, was I any better than she?

We haggled for some minutes over the exact amount, and then Lucy kicked Henry with her foot again. 'Get your things, boy,' she said. He scrambled to his feet and went to a filthy corner, from which he took a pathetic bundle of cloth and a stick. He disappeared for a few seconds into a side chamber, then returned, looking perfectly ready to leave.

'Does he have no shoes?' I asked, looking down at the boy's blue-tinged toes.

'Never needed them,' Lucy said, stoutly.

Shaking my head as I handed over the coin, I motioned to the boy to follow. He offered Lucy Bennett neither thanks nor farewell, and before long I had mounted him before me on Ben, and, thus laden, the horse picked his slow way through the centre of the city, back towards the Magdalen Gate.

12

We left the walls of Norwich behind, and the horse's hoofs squelched the wet earth and half-rotted reddish leaves. Above our heads, the blue of morning had given way to a blanket of single-hued grey.

'Can you read, boy?' I asked, after a few minutes' silence.

'No,' said Henry.

'Not the Bible, or your own name?' I was horrified, though I remembered when, at his age, reading had seemed a distraction from the real business of finding anthills and birds' nests.

'No,' he said, again.

Absently, I answered, 'That is something we shall try to remedy. A man should be able to read.'

'Yes,' said Henry, meekly.

'You'll call me "sir",' I said, in a stern voice I immediately disliked. More gently, I added, 'Or perhaps Mr Treadwater.'

'Yes, sir,' said the boy.

'But we shall stop for food first.' I felt Henry stiffen at the mention of eating, and steered Ben towards the edge of the road, to a bank hard-ridged with mud, near a water trough. I helped Henry down. 'First, we see to our animals,' I explained, as I allowed Ben a drink. 'A good horse is a tool, and we must guard our tools faithfully, that they may continue to serve us.' Henry nodded solemnly, but I was swayed by the boy's whey-coloured complexion, and gave him all the bread and cheese I had brought, watching as the food was consumed by a starving mouth. My eyes fell again on the pendant round his neck, and

I saw it was a tiny wooden sundial, ancient in appearance, with the gnomon wrought of tarnished metal, probably copper. It was well-worn, not very valuable, but unusual enough to fetch a few coins. I was surprised he had been able to hold on to it.

Why had I taken him? I examined my motivations, seeing little nobility in them. It was clear that Chrissa Moore had a deep attachment to her brother. Even once she had escaped the house of Lucy Bennett — and whatever she had done for money there — she had sent her earnings for Henry until her arrest. And she appeared to have cared for him for many years without other help — there seemed to be no parents or relatives. I had to admit, there were many who would have abandoned such a boy and sought a more comfortable position. Whatever her other faults, Chrissa's devotion to her brother was a thing to note.

And it might be a thing I could use. Henry being in my possession could loosen his sister's tongue, not with a confession, necessarily — it would not help the boy to see her hang for murder — but with a withdrawal of her claim against my father.

She would bleed soon, I thought, watching Henry chomp on the slightly-too-hard cheese, his eyes half-closed with pleasure. The moon had swelled, then waned from full to old since her arrest, and it could only be a week or so until her course spoke louder than words when it either came or did not. At that point, all would know that she did not stand with child. And perhaps Esther and I would be able to leave all this behind us.

What would I do with the boy then? I took a swig of water, thinking. Henry had made short work of the food, and was now prodding and pressing at his feet, as if my questioning of why they were bare had been his own first realisation of it.

Well, I would cross that bridge when I came to it. First, I would have to see to some of his needs. It was January. The wind bit hard as a jackal, and I would have to get the child some decent boots. I had some in the house that I had worn before manhood. They might do. 'Come,' I said. 'We still have some miles to go, and then I will introduce you to my sister.'

———

It was nearing dark by the time we reached the house. Henry had fallen asleep in the saddle. His head lolled on my chest, his frame limp and warm. As I felt him nodding off, I had reached behind for the spare saddle blanket and wrapped it around his front, so it was like carrying a market pig or a sheep before me.

I came down with care, pulling Henry from Ben's back, then put the child's weight across my shoulder, freeing up my hand to tie the horse. I felt my own tiredness as I did this, thinking of a hot meal and an early bed. For all of us. I would give no duties to Henry tonight, but would allow Esther to instruct him in the morning. Perhaps tonight I would question him further about—

No, better to let him sleep. Tomorrow there would be time to check his true understanding.

We went in at the back door. I breathed in, inhaling the smells of bread, the coal fire and lye soap. Someone had been washing.

As I manoeuvred Henry into the kitchen, I realised no candles or lamps had been lit, and the fire had been allowed to smoulder until it had gone out. The house was cold. I felt a brief, deep sadness as I saw Father's usual chair at the table, empty now, probably mine to occupy. But somehow I could not imagine lowering myself into the heavy oak seat, taking my father's place. Not yet.

'Esther?' I said. No answer came.

I deposited Henry in my father's chair with a cushion behind his head. The boy stirred but did not wake. I contemplated laying a fire to begin warming the kettle, but decided to seek

Esther first. I needed to explain the situation to her. I tucked the blanket more tightly around Henry and then added a rug. Finally, I left the kitchen again for the cold gloom of the yard, where I stabled Ben and saw to the animals.

I returned inside. 'Sister?' I raised my voice. Still no reply. Perhaps she was asleep. Yet it was early, and Esther was conscientious, never retiring to bed before her work was done.

I pulled off my boots and went through to the parlour. Opening the door, I saw her in a high-backed chair, face on to the flames. The fire needed stoking and more coal, but Esther sat unmoving before the dark orange glow that silhouetted her face and jaw. It was a more angular outline than I remembered, her baby fat replaced by a hardness I did not recognise. Briefly, without reason, I thought of her terrible dream and the ravings from her mouth on the night I had learnt of my father's death.

'Esther, I'm back.'

'I see you, brother,' she said, not turning to greet me.

'The fire needs building up again,' I said, feeling foolish, then relieved as she rose and knelt by the fender. 'Why were you sitting alone in the dark?' I asked. 'Were you thinking of Father?'

'Of myself.' She continued to dig in the hearth. Finally, once she had brought forth a crackling fire, she fell back on her heels. 'Sit with me,' she said, quietly, and again I had the feeling that something was new in Esther; the woman I spoke with was not the girl I had left.

I pulled up a chair and she returned to hers. 'So, what were you thinking of?' I asked.

'Of marriage. And children.'

I couldn't have been more surprised if she had said murder, or revealed she was considering becoming a travelling minstrel. 'What?' I said, stupidly.

'Marriage,' she repeated. 'Mine.'

I leant towards her. 'Do you think it might help if you decided to be more specific?'

The eyes turned upon me contained a new intelligence, a worldliness I had not suspected existed inside Esther. She smiled thinly. 'Sarcasm does not suit you,' she said. 'But yes, let me be more specific. I have received a proposal of marriage.'

I exhaled a hard, whistling breath. 'I see. Might I ask from whom?' But I knew.

'John Rutherford.'

'What? When?'

'This very morning.'

'What was Rutherford doing calling on you without me here?'

She gave a brittle laugh at my outrage. 'Be calm. I need no consent from you. And I have no father for him to approach.'

'He should have approached *me*,' I said, in anger. 'I'm your nearest male kinsman.'

She made a dismissive noise with her tongue. I had never heard such a sound from her before. 'Well, it's done now. I have accepted him.'

I turned away as a strong curse escaped me. There was amusement in Esther's voice as she said, 'As it is written in the Gospel of Mark, "All sins shall be forgiven the sons of men, and whatever blasphemies they utter."'

I pulled the chair closer. 'Esther, it's not too late. We can proceed on the basis that he should have approached me first. We can—'

'As in James, "Everyone should be quick to listen, slow to speak."'

'Then explain,' I said, puzzled, and not a little irritated, suspecting she was taunting me. It was out of character for her and I felt wrong-footed. 'For I am lost as to your reasoning. Do you like Mr Rutherford so very much?'

She shrugged. 'No more than other men.'

'Then why?'

Unexpectedly, Esther dashed her hand against the arm of the chair. 'I am alone here, Thomas.' When I tried to object, to tell her that she had me, that she would never be abandoned, she spoke above me, passionately. 'Yes, I am – quite alone. You will be recalled to the army in a matter of weeks – before Candlemas, if not sooner. You might not even come back. And that will leave me alone in this house, rattling about, with nobody to take care of me, without a future. John offers me a home, a position as his wife, the chance to have children and participate in the work of God by his side. Does it matter that I do not particularly love him above other men? Is that really so important?'

'Yes. Certainly, love is important.' I stood and paced before the fire, speaking clumsily in my agitation. 'Do you think I would ever let anything happen to you? Or want you to marry a man you did not care for?' I needed her to understand this, that marriage was more than a contract, and she was more than a helpmate, that it might be better to be alone than harnessed to another who could not love her. Eager to tell her, I reached for her, but she veered away. I clasped my hands behind the nape of my neck, groaning in frustration.

'I know you would never see me harmed,' she said. 'But I cannot stay here as your dependant forever. To be a wife, to bring children into the world, it is a godly thing. I have accepted him.' She spoke with finality. 'And there is nothing left but for you to give us your blessing.'

For long moments, I had no words, until eventually I sighed. Even to me, the noise sounded like defeat. 'Esther, I...'

But I could not finish whatever I had been about to say, even had I been able to give my words persuasive force, because Henry now opened the parlour door. His pale face peered round the frame. Esther turned back to me, a new enquiry in her gaze.

'This is Henry,' I said, shortly. 'He will be staying with us for the time being.'

'Here? In this house?' Esther took a step towards Henry, who shrank back as she moved.

'Yes,' I said. 'He can help with—'

'Yet *again* I am undermined in this house, in my sphere!' Esther snapped. 'If new servants are needed, it is *my* position to instruct them, not yours.'

I was alarmed – Esther had never spoken to me so angrily. 'Sister, recover yourself,' I said. 'I would not usually have done this but in this case—'

'There's always a case,' Esther said, wearily. 'Always a reason why what I want must come last. Why others are preferred before me.' She made to walk past me, and I moved to allow her, wondering how much of what she said was fair. Had I let her down, as she implied? Or did she mean somebody else… perhaps Father? I remembered how upset she had been by his apparent liking for the Moore girl. Was Esther's jealousy coming to the fore again?

Then Henry startled us both. His cry was like the shriek of a lamb as you cut into its throat. His eyes were fixed on Esther, and his face had turned even whiter; as Esther took another step forward, he turned tail and ran.

Esther stood as if struck. She made a slight movement, but I placed a hand on her arm. 'I'll get him,' I muttered. 'But we will be talking again about Rutherford,' I warned. 'Don't think anything is settled.'

I searched the house, reflecting on the stupidity of boys. What had frightened Henry so? He was not to be found in the kitchen, where his horse-smelling blanket and rug had been discarded on the floor; he was not cowering in the cupboard below the staircase, nor was he in any of the bedrooms. Sighing, I pulled my boots back on and lit a lamp. Esther was sitting by the fire as I went out.

He was not in the yard. He was not by the well. He was not in Esther's small herb garden or hiding behind the potting shed. I called his name, to no avail. I was cursing the cold and beginning to shiver by the time it occurred to me to search the stables.

'Henry?' Temperance was chewing ponderously, completely alone. The second stall was empty apart from some scurrying mice. Ben gave a whinny as I opened his stall, probably thinking he was being brought out for another ride. I rubbed his mane and said, 'Not tonight, boy. You've ridden far enough today. Now…' Stopping, I pushed the horse aside and saw what I had looked for.

'What are you doing here?' I asked.

Henry crouched in the straw. It was a dangerous place where Ben might easily have kicked out and struck him. But Ben did not seem to mind his presence, perhaps because Henry was huddled as quiet as the stable cat. His hands toyed with the wooden sundial on its chain, and I realised this object was important to him. 'Do you know how to use that?' I asked, and was rewarded with a wan nod. I said, 'I'll wager it's very complicated?'

'No. It's easy,' he said, finally, then added, 'My sister taught me.'

'Where did you get it?'

'It was my father's.' He kept his eyes on it, like it was a jewel, as if it comforted him.

'It's very fine.' With this small compliment, I squeezed past Ben's bulk, putting out my hand. 'Come here,' I said. Henry did not move. I shone the light nearer. He wasn't crying, but quaking with some visceral fear. 'There is nothing to be afraid of,' I promised. 'Come inside.' He shook his head vehemently. 'Come,' I said again, coaxing him with my hand as I might coax an injured animal. 'There's food, and a warm bed. It's cold here. And there are mice.'

The boy's voice was subdued. 'There was a snake.'

'Where?' I lowered the lamp, thinking I might see the mottled brown of an adder slithering to safety.

'Not here,' Henry said, miserably. 'In there.' He looked towards the house.

'There are no snakes inside, Henry,' I said. 'They're very frightened of people, aren't they, as we're so much bigger?'

He was shaking his head again. 'Big. It was big.'

My knees had begun to ache from the awkward position I had assumed at Ben's side. 'You had a bad dream,' I said, gently. 'You're tired and in a new place. It wasn't real. Come on, you can meet my sister and we can eat a meal together.'

But Henry moved backwards, pressing against the stable wall. 'Can't I stay here?' he whispered. His lower lip trembled.

'Not really. This is Ben's stall.'

'He doesn't mind,' said Henry. 'Please?'

I sighed, pulling myself back to standing on the other side of the horse. Whatever the boy thought he had seen, clearly he was terrified. But he could not sleep out here alone. Already the cold snipped at my nose and ears; it would be freezing tonight.

'All right,' I said. 'I'll tell you what I'll do: I'll go inside and get some soup and bread, and water from the well, and some blankets. And you can eat something and then sleep here. Will that make you feel better?'

An energetic nod followed.

'Right. Well, you sit here and don't go anywhere. I'll be back in a few minutes.'

Of course, Henry could not actually sleep in the stable. I would wait until he had eaten, drunk, and dropped to sleep with exhaustion, then I would move him into one of the upstairs rooms. By the morning, surely, amidst new surroundings and in the daylight, whatever had frightened him would be a distant memory.

I started back to the house.

That night, having been transferred over my shoulder, Henry slept in his new master's old bed. I would now take my father's, and put new linen on it before falling into a deep and troubled sleep, in which colossal snakes pursued me through giltwood frames, and the chain of a wooden sundial about my neck grew to monstrous proportions, until it choked off my breath.

I was becoming accustomed to bad dreams.

13

'So, she does not bleed?' I said, pausing the flow of my pen. 'Not yet,' Manyon said. 'But it cannot be long.'

'And no marks or teats have been found anywhere upon her form?'

'None. But,' the magistrate said, with the air of one delivering an important caveat, 'they have been known to conceal them in places where they are less easy to find than they might be on... more cursory examination. Write that down,' he added, and I did so, trying not to think about such concealed places.

We were in Manyon's office, three days after my return from Norwich, and much had changed. I had come first thing, not only to enquire after Chrissa Moore and whether there had been developments in the investigation, but to remonstrate with Manyon about Rutherford. I felt strongly that the witchfinder had overstepped his bounds with Esther. I expected Manyon to reprimand him strongly, and the betrothal to be swept beneath the carpet. But I had been taken aback by the magistrate's response.

Manyon's expression as I had described Rutherford's presumption had been nondescript. Yet as I had shared my concerns about Esther's youth, her vulnerability at this time, so soon after her father's death and given the circumstances of that death, he had begun to nod more sympathetically. 'Yes, I see that you have reason to be affronted,' he said. 'In your shoes I might feel similarly. But what does your sister say? She's keen on the match?'

'She says she is,' I admitted. 'But her judgement…'

'Has never been a matter of concern to you in the past,' Manyon reminded me. 'She is a good, modest girl. And Rutherford – whilst I concur that he has been rash – is a man of means and reputation. If he has acted precipitately, I can only say in his defence that it speaks well of his regard for your sister.'

So, Rutherford had got here first, I thought. Manyon's rebuttal was too smooth, too practised.

'He has acted disgracefully,' I insisted. 'I cannot see how his conduct speaks well of him at all. A man who approaches a woman like a thief is not a man I want tied to my family.'

Manyon was packing the bowl of his pipe. He had offered me a spare, but I had declined. Manyon performed this act as he did others: thoughtfully and with precision. It took him more than a minute. In the end, he said, 'But you understand that, through the tie to Rutherford, and through your sister, you will also be tying yourself to *my* family?'

I flushed. I had not forgotten that Rutherford was Manyon's nephew by marriage, but in my anger had spoken without thought, and now I had offended Manyon, whose family had its roots – before his grandfather had bought up swathes of property in the Worstead area – in Norwich haberdashery. He was no better than the Treadwaters, even if he had a great deal more money. I said, carefully, 'A connection which would be an honour, sir, in any other circumstances. But that is an aside to the point here, I'm afraid.'

'Is it?' Manyon's eyes narrowed beneath his bushy brows. 'The marriage might not be to your liking, and I understand that, but it might yet prove to be to your advantage.'

'In what way?'

'Do you recall the matter of my incompetent assistant, Timothy – a slapdash young man I have, recently, had reason to dismiss?'

'Yes, sir.'

'Well, it *had* been my intention to sponsor Timothy. A year or so as my assistant, followed by my funding to attend Cambridge, and my preferment in the law. An offer I am now inclined to make to you. I would also be willing to write to the army, where I have certain influential acquaintances, ensuring your release from your commitments there.'

The inference was clear. I rose to standing. 'I thank you, sir, but my sister is not for sale, and the implication contrariwise dishonours us both, and her more.' I was barely keeping my anger in check.

Manyon's face coloured, but to my surprise, he laughed, then stood and reached for my hand, which, once granted, he shook vigorously. 'Oh, well said, my boy! Very well said!' he said, continuing to shake. 'But, please, do sit down; you have misinterpreted me entirely – my fault, of course – but do sit.'

Not at all sure that I had, I returned to my seat. Manyon took a deep pull on his pipe, then waved his hand through the smoke in an elaborate circle, almost as if dismissing his previous comments. 'I should have made myself clearer. I think you are exactly the sort of young man I need working for me here, and allied to my family in general. Whether or not your sister marries my nephew – and you must trust that she will, since she has already accepted him, and she is of age – I would like to make that offer to you. I need coming men as my partners in the law, and I will need a candidate, eventually, to take my place in this very role. I think that person might be you, regardless of your sister's marriage.

'But,' he went on, 'I also think the marriage itself is sound, in and of itself. Take the two positions in turn: one, your sister does not marry Rutherford, or two, she does so. In the first position, your sister loses a match with a man of proven ability, of a faith with her, able to father a child – and John is a man with a strong natural desire to sire a family, given his bereavements – with a fine future, and with a true fondness for her. Yes, you are right to say that John should have come to you first but – and again, this is only in my opinion – he is young, and the young can be passionate in pursuit of the things they want.' I nodded in reluctant acknowledgement of this, remembering my own foolishness and impulsivity, with Elizabeth. Yet I found it difficult to entertain the notion of Rutherford as an impassioned lover.

Manyon continued. 'In the second case, your sister marries a young man to whom she has no objection; indeed, a man she has already accepted – if you will excuse my pointing it out – in contravention of your wishes, showing her determination to have him. She gains a secure home of her own, but close by her brother, and a husband who, as far as I can tell, is deeply enamoured of her. In time, perhaps a family. She will be a helpmate to him, he will be a protector to her. And she avoids what we both know she fears: being left alone and unwed, should the worst come to the worst, and you do not return from the wars.'

I was frustrated, knowing there was a kernel in what he said, knowing my own objection to the marriage was rooted in a somewhat unreasonable dislike of Rutherford. In truth, I had no firm footing for my aversion. I was being proud. Manyon looked at me as he pulled on his pipe, waiting.

'My father respected you, sir,' I said, eventually. 'I would like to apologise for my rash words. I accept you meant Esther no disrespect.'

'Thank you, Tom. What is your feeling on the marriage now that you have considered both sides of the question?'

It took a few moments to wrestle down my objections, but eventually I conceded. 'I will leave the matter to my sister's judgement. If she is determined to have him, I'll not stand in her way.'

Manyon gave a satisfied wink. 'Very good. And now, to the other matter. Do you think you could see yourself working here, at my side?'

It was a tempting offer, but I frowned. 'I cannot see how I could accept, sir, though I am pleased you would consider me capable,' I said, truthfully. 'My father is so recently gone, and there is much to oversee on the farm.'

'It's only a matter of seeing how it works out. You would be free to return to the farm at any point.'

'And you would write to my colonel?' Although he would be under no obligation to release me, the colonel might be swayed by a man of Manyon's influence.

'Who is he?'

'Colonel Bethel, sir.'

'Not Valentine Bethel?'

'The same, sir.'

'Well, then there is no obstacle!' Manyon said, with a confident smile. 'Bethel is a man of sense. His father and mine were good friends. He'll take my letter, and you will be your own man before the end of the month. Can I count on you?'

I didn't know what to say, and stumbled over my thanks. I did not deserve such kindness, such a chance. I accepted, and although at the back of my mind I knew I would – at some point – have to decide whether to make my life here, in England, or strike out for America, the thought of home, of having the liberty and funds to care for Esther, perhaps even see her children grown, wrapped itself about me like a warm, familiar blanket. The feeling that I now realised had dogged my steps since I had first seen Father lying stricken in his bed, of being suspended in mid-air, just about to fall, was receding.

There seemed no reason not to begin immediately. Manyon wanted to record details of a number of cases, including two of horse-stealing, several of receiving or selling stolen goods and one of scolding. It was my job to take dictation, recording the names and outcomes of the cases, witnesses and decisions, including whether or not to advance a case to the quarterly sessions, and the punishments meted out.

Throughout, I was light-headed with the knowledge that I would not be going back into the army. My pen quivered as I took down Manyon's words. I remembered, vividly, how writing had been such a chore at Milton's house, how I had cursed every hour of scrubbing black ink from my hands, yearning for manlier pursuits. I had been a fool. How could wading knee-deep in blood, shit and mud be preferable to this? I shook my head, holding the pen with something like reverence.

I was good at writing, too. Although it sounds boastful now, I am old enough to allow myself a small boast; I was a natural scholar, with a precise hand, a facility with languages and a memory both deep and broad. By the end of the first hour of work, Manyon was impressed.

'You're as quick as I hoped,' he said, rubbing his eyes in the lamplight. 'I'm too old to write as well as you. What was the name of the fellow who taught you, again?'

'My father taught me my letters, but my education was taken on by a man called John Milton.'

'Ah, yes. I recall the name, now, vaguely. Is he a man of reputation?'

'Not really,' I answered. 'He's a talented scholar, and something of a polemicist; a reformer, and anti-prelatical, if you understand.' Manyon nodded; there were many such men, now. 'He's particularly skilled in Latin and Greek.'

'How did you end up going to him?'

'He's kin to my father's family. A second cousin of my father's, in fact.'

Manyon's inquisitiveness seemed satisfied. 'I see. Well, perhaps in time the fellow will make a reputation for himself.'

'Perhaps.' It seemed unlikely I would hear of it. I had little desire ever to see my old tutor again, and was quite sure he would share my sentiments.

Manyon sat up straighter, an indication he wished to return to business that I was beginning to recognise. 'Let's move on to the allegations against the Moore girl, and whether or not to add the charges of the deaths of Joan and Goodwife Gedge.' He looked tired as he said this, as if the subject had been troubling him.

'Are you inclined to do so?'

'No,' said Manyon. 'I think the evidence insufficient. In spite of what I told the Reverend Hale, the case for self-destruction is stronger.'

And yet he had not dismissed the charges against Chrissa. It seemed unlike Manyon, somehow – indecisive. 'But?'

'As I said to you before, there is pressure from the community. Nobody wishes to consider that the women perpetrated the act themselves. Some wealthy men have bent my ear sideways on the subject. The Gedges were very popular, and the widespread account is now that Moore slipped them the hemlock by magical means, perhaps with the help of a familiar, a cat or some such creature.' He pressed his fingers to the bony bridge of his nose, closing his eyes briefly.

'But that's surely nonsense,' I said, too quickly, then wondered why.

'Many a nonsense has been hawked about many a marketplace as truth,' Manyon said, wearily, 'to the detriment of many a more educated soul.' I could not argue with that.

Manyon went on. 'But I suspect you are right in this case, although we cannot dismiss it as impossible. John sat up with her in the cells for three full nights after the Gedge women died, trying to draw out any familiar that might come to her, without success.'

I said nothing about familiars, nor the wisdom of hunting cats, ferrets and toads in the middle of the night, in the hope of catching them in conversation. Still, I could not help a shiver at the thought of Rutherford's midnight vigils in the gaol, sitting, perhaps, on a stool outside Chrissa's cell, enveloped by the recent history of that place, eyes squinting in the darkness for diabolical creatures. How had he gone about his work? Was he something like a priest, offering his ear, transcribing the confessions and confidences of his prisoners? Or more like a torturer, dragging incriminating words from them, complete with flecks of spittle and rabid curses? It did not seem like an honourable position, to me.

'And she still refuses to speak?' I asked, in the end.

'Correct. I am fast reaching the point where more forceful measures may need to be employed.'

'There can be no torture, surely?' I said, curious, again, about the little hiccough that rose in my stomach at the thought of it.

'Narrowly defined, no. Since the Long Parliament took up its seat, we are not officially required – or permitted – to torture under the law. And yet, if we send the girl to the assizes without having employed such methods as depriving her of sleep, or walking her, well, they will send back criticism of our laxity and they might even dismiss the case for lack of evidence.'

'So, a confession might be obtained merely by denying her sleep?' My voice could not hide my doubt. It sounded so unlikely, when I had suffered through so many nights of broken slumber with the army. Now, of course, I know what a lack of sleep can do, how it fevers the mind and saps the body of strength. I would not wish it upon my worst enemy.

Manyon gave a brisk nod. 'You would be surprised how effective such a simple device can prove, when the nights begin to add up. It drains the will like you would not believe.'

'But she cannot be subjected to rough treatment whilst she maintains that she carries my father's child,' I said, feeling less ambivalent about defending an unborn baby.

'That is so,' said Manyon. 'But the question of her pregnancy cannot stand in doubt much longer.'

I asked, with some delicacy, because, although I had to know, it seemed no legitimate concern of mine, whether Chrissa had bled, and took down the relevant notes, blushing a little. When I had finished, Manyon sat back. 'And what of the boy you took from the whorehouse?'

I frowned. I had not mentioned the boy to Manyon, and worked to cover my surprise. Henry's presence must have been disclosed by Rutherford, who had visited the farm two days previously, following Esther's revelation of his proposal. He had arrived with smiles, but I met him coldly and invited him into the kitchen, where I told him he was not to call on Esther again until the question of their betrothal was resolved to my own satisfaction, citing my sister's reputation as the reason. Rutherford asked what it would take to settle the matter, and I said I would give it thought. Having argued the point to a civil truce, we parted, but not before Rutherford saw Henry scampering about the garden, chasing a pigeon.

'You have acquired a new servant?' he asked, adjusting the bags on the sides of his horse, and looking at the boy's distinctive face with open curiosity. Was he seeing some resemblance between Henry and his sister? It was there, in a shared colouring and face shape, but was made less apparent by the years between them.

'Yes,' I said, shortly. I had given him no further details, and how Rutherford – and now Manyon – had ascertained where Henry had come from, was a mystery.

Manyon now awaited my response, but I needed to be careful. I did not know what he already knew, and could not afford to be caught in a lie. 'He's Chrissa Moore's brother,' I admitted. 'I travelled to Norwich to discover what I could about the woman's antecedents, and that led me to the house of a procuress who confirmed that the Moore woman had lodged with her. But,' I said, again not knowing why I took pains to point it out, 'not that she had whored for her. I still can't be sure how she made her living.'

Manyon raised his eyebrows. 'Go on,' he said.

'There's not much more to say. I felt sorry for the boy – the vile creature running the place kept him half-starved – and brought him back to the farm partly for his benefit, and partly, I admit, to see what I could glean from him about his sister.'

'And did you? Get any further, that is?'

I shook my head. 'The boy is a simple idiot. He knows nothing.'

Manyon grunted. 'Keep him close to your chest. Don't let him leave the farm – too many people in the town resent his sister.'

'He's not going anywhere,' I agreed.

'Oh, and on a different note,' said Manyon, rummaging across his desk for a scrap of paper, on which he scribbled quickly. 'An invitation.'

'For me?' I took it with a twinge of anxiety. It had been so long since I'd been invited anywhere.

'Yes. Do you know Welmet Huxley?'

'I've heard of him. He's a reformer, isn't he?'

'Yes, his great-grandfather was one of the first true Dissenters in the country, and the sons and grandsons followed him on. This is his address.'

The chit had details of a house several miles from Worstead, but I recognised it: a substantial property belonging to an estate on the road to King's Lynn. I had a vague thought that the owner had interests in shipping. 'He's asked me there?' I said, surprised, pocketing the paper.

'Correct. A meal, tomorrow evening, with a bed for the night. Huxley likes to dine with up-and-coming men, and sometimes feels obligated to do the same with old carbuncles like me. He's a friend.'

'Thank you, sir,' I said, already worrying about what I had to wear to the house of a rich man. Still, I wanted to go. It had been years since I had had an excellent meal in fine company. I could see, already, how Manyon might open up other such opportunities for me, to make connections and start building back my reputation, and could not help a dart of excitement.

Then Manyon said, 'Rutherford will be there, too.'

'Oh,' I said, with less enthusiasm. Manyon could not suppress a smile.

A peacemaker, then.

Later, as I rode the short distance back to the farm, I contemplated why I had lied to Manyon. Henry was not clever, it was true, but he was not the abject fool I had described. He played the part well, but events of the previous days had cast doubt on the performance.

Esther had not concealed her bitterness about Henry's presence, particularly once I had explained who he was and how I had come to find him, the morning after I brought him back. 'Why would you go there, Thomas?' she had said. 'It's a disgrace.'

I, still nursing my resentment about Rutherford, and thinking only of how I could scupper the match, responded briefly. 'I can't really explain it.'

'And I am certainly at a loss to do so!' she said, stabbing at her embroidery with her needle as if she wished to do herself an injury. I, struggling with whether I owed her an apology, left her to her work and went to find Henry.

He was back in the stable.

I eased Ben outside. The horse fretted in the cold air. After covering him with a blanket, I returned to the stable, and lowered myself down to the straw. The lamp lit up the boy's pinched, hungry expression. 'Henry, I need you to come with me inside the house. There is much work to do. I brought you here on the understanding that you would work for us, and that I would pay you. Do you remember?'

Henry nodded, but didn't move. 'Can't I just work here?' he asked.

'In the stables?' Another nod. I considered for a moment, then shrugged. 'There are jobs to be done here,' I admitted. 'Ben and Temperance take a lot of looking after. Have you worked with horses before?'

'No, sir, but I can learn.'

'That is the idea,' I said. 'Not just for you to be here to earn a wage, but to learn as well. And for that, you need to be inside the house, at least sometimes.'

When the boy shook his head, I was reminded of Chrissa's intransigence. I felt, somehow, though I would never do it, that I might drag Henry inside and beat him bloody and yet, when next I saw him, he would be crouched here behind Ben, quiet and still as a hunted hare.

'You lived inside at Lucy Bennett's house,' I said. 'What's different here?'

'Dunno,' came the low, miserable voice again. 'Sir. I just don't want to be in there.'

It was so cold I could not tell whether the fog was mist off the ground or our breath. 'Do you know how cold it's going to get out here when the sun goes down?'

Henry nodded.

'And so, you know I can't let you sleep out here. Not unless I want to defrost you in the morning. But I can agree this: if you stay outdoors during the day, for now, just for today, and watch the horses, then as long as you agree to come indoors at sunset, you may go straight to your bed and come out as soon as you wake again in the morning. Have we made a bargain?'

Again, the acquiescent little nod. Then his voice seemed to become even smaller. 'Will there be men visiting? Like at Lucy's?'

I had a thought to put my arm about the boy's shoulders, but held back. Who knew what the lad had seen in that scurrilous place, or what might have been done to him? 'Never,' I said, as firmly as I could manage. 'This is not that sort of house.'

Henry seemed to weigh this information. Then, looking up, his eyes glinting with a new curiosity, he said, 'What sort of house is it?'

So, the boy was not such a fool as he appeared. 'A respectable one,' I said, getting to my feet. 'Now, come to the back door and I'll give you food. You have a long day of work ahead of you.'

It was of that glint in Henry's eyes that I thought now, tugging at Ben's reins to avoid a wagon on the road. Was he more like his sister than I had counted on, more calculating? He seemed honest enough. Two days after his arrival, I shared bread with him in the stable, instructing him in how to feed and water the horses, and how to muck out the stalls; while he ate and worked, I took the opportunity to ask him questions about his sister. He seemed happy to tell what he knew.

'What do you remember of your life with your sister before you went to Lucy Bennett's?' I asked.

'Nothing,' came the answer, brief and definite, as Henry forked over a feeble heft of dirty straw. 'I was yet a babe, sir.'

'But your family hails from Norfolk?'

'I don't really know. My sister never said.' He didn't have the local accent.

'When did you last see your sister?'

Henry's half-frown seemed sincere. 'I can't be sure. Weeks? Months, it might be.'

I thought carefully about the wording of my next question. I wanted to avoid the boy's awareness that he was being interrogated, and therefore did not want to say 'your sister' again, but 'Chrissa' felt strange, too intimate, in my mouth, so I did not say that either. 'Are you very fond of her?'

Henry said, fervently, 'Oh, yes, sir. She is so good to me.'

'She sent money for your keep?' At this, Henry nodded, cheerfully munching his breakfast as he worked. 'And did you have... duties, in return for your stay at Lucy Bennett's house, like you do here?'

Henry pondered for a moment. 'Sort of,' he said, eventually. 'Not like my sister, or the girls there.'

'What sort of duties were yours, then?' I asked, keeping my voice light, mere chatter to go alongside the meal and the work.

'Serving, mostly,' he answered. 'Sometimes I was called upon to sing.'

'You sing well?'

Henry guffawed, a donkeyish, endearing sound that answered my question well enough. 'No, sir – like a crow! Just like a crow!' He kept laughing at his own jest. I could not help but chuckle a little, too.

'Why have you sing, then?' I said, once we had stopped laughing.

Now serious, Henry said, 'I think they liked to mock me, some of the men who came to visit the girls. Or to hoof me with their feet if my singing got too bad.'

'That was very wrong of them,' I said, sincerely. Henry nodded in solemn agreement. 'Did your sister sing, too?' He shook his head, but seemed less willing to speak than he had been. 'She had other duties?'

'Some. Not like the other girls, though. She'd go out at night, and when she came back, she had coin.'

'I see. But that stopped a few months ago, when she stopped coming in person and began to send money?'

'Yes, sir.'

'A lot of money?'

'No. Lucy always complained it was short.'

'Right.' *Enough for now.* I stood up and, almost without thinking, ruffled the boy's hair. 'Don't forget Ben's saddle cloth, like I showed you. I'll come back to check it at the quarter hour.'

Now, nearing home from Walsham, I thought ahead to the following evening: dinner at the Huxley house. Although I had been pleased at the prospect when sitting in Manyon's comfortable study, now I felt a tightening of guilt at leaving Esther, if only for an evening, so soon after Father's passing. Aside from anything else, it made her responsible for Henry, and Henry was unpredictable in his fears. I would have to have words with the boy before I went, instructing him not to bother Esther; but I thought there was little danger – he had not been within twenty feet of her since his arrival. He disappeared like a shadow whenever she came into a room.

But it was important that I went to the dinner. Manyon had clearly spoken well of me to Huxley, and to snub the invitation would mean loss of face, both with my new employer and a man who held sway with other powerful ears. If I wanted a career in the county of my birth, and I thought I might, I would have to go.

Of course, it was a transparent effort to bring me together with Rutherford. Yet I saw the sense of it. If the witchfinder was to be my brother-in-law, I would need to find common ground with him, and a meal in company was as good a way as any. I wished it had been a few days later, though – I would have preferred to be at home, poring over my father's papers, mending fences with Esther, shutting out the world. But it was not to be. Instead, dinner with John Rutherford; I sighed.

14

When I left for the meal, Esther was reciting from her catechism in the kitchen, her back straight against her chair, her hands open to admit the presence of God.

What will become of the righteous?

They shall be taken to Heaven.

What is Heaven?

A glorious and happy place, where the righteous shall be forever with the Lord.

What is Hell?

A place of dreadful and endless torment.

I did not disturb her. She had been no more than civil, in any case, since she had announced her intention to wed Rutherford, and I had not quite brought myself to admit my change of heart, if that was what it was. Once or twice I had approached her, but something dissuaded me from speaking. Interrupting her prayer wouldn't cause her to look any more kindly on me. I promised myself I would talk to her tomorrow.

The surroundings for the meal were opulent, but even knowing Welmet Huxley was hot on the heel of godly works, the food was scantier than I had expected. Having consumed the last mouthful of my mutton – still as tough a slice of meat as any I have chewed – I sat back, thinking about making conversation to stifle the continued growling of my stomach.

To my left was Huxley. He was probably the thinnest person I had ever seen, to the extent that it was disconcerting to watch him push his measly serving of meat and potatoes around his plate, as if the act of putting a knife to it might bring down the Devil himself to congratulate him upon his gluttony. His lovage soup had been sent back to the kitchen barely touched. I wondered whether the man was sick with some concealed inner pain. He grimaced and cleared his throat frequently, and, when he bothered to speak at all, spoke snappishly to his wife, a drab girl some years younger than her husband. They did not look content with life.

Huxley was undoubtedly rich. It had taken twenty minutes to ride from the gates to the stables. I passed acres of woods, landscaped gardens in which swans wintered on an ornamental lake, and a huge orchard. Huxley Hall itself was quite new, with an elegant façade of stone and glass. It had three wings, each with its own chimneys, though only one spiralled with smoke. On arrival I was shown into a big lamp-lit hall with stained-glass windows depicting, in an oddly beautiful manner, the bleak landscape of the Fens. There were no Judgement Day scenes here, no Old Testament figures carrying tablets or saints and their insignia. The builder of this house was a Puritan, like my father, but I knew my father would have had to bite his tongue at this ostentation. He would have praised the industry that brought such wealth, but the money itself, I thought, he would rather have seen gracing the bellies of the poor. And I? I was not certain what I thought yet. There was nothing wrong with a man earning his way in the world, but perhaps I thought he should do so with his own hands, and had yet to grapple with what he should do with the rewards. I suppose I was still young enough to envy Huxley's wealth, and the liberties I believed it offered.

After a wait of several minutes, a footman emerged and invited me to remove my cloak. I felt a pang of shame as I handed it over, revealing my shabby clothing below. The footman bade me follow, and we progressed through a windowed gallery densely lined with portraits, standing alongside white marble statues of serious-looking men, and women of angelic beauty. The centrepiece was a merchant ship in an unusual glass case, exquisitely rendered in oak, canvas and gold leaf, the model itself as long as I am tall. I would have liked to examine this more closely, but Huxley's man set a brisk pace, showing me through to the library. This room was huge, with at least seven or eight times the shelving as in my father's study, but where Father's few shelves heaved with the books and pamphlets he liked to read, here not all the shelves were full; Huxley was a new man, after all.

Manyon was already in the library holding a delicate crystal glass of fortified wine, engaged in conversation with a tall, austere-looking man who turned when my arrival was announced. The man came forward from the shadow of the shelves to nod formally and introduce himself as Welmet Huxley. I gave my name in kind, noting that Huxley's jacket and shirt were not particularly better than my own, and there was even a frayed cuff in sight. This made me feel better, although I thought it odd, in amongst all these luxuries, that a man would dress himself so poorly for guests.

'I knew your father by reputation,' said Huxley. 'It was on his account that I asked Manyon here to extend you an invitation.'

I bowed, but not too low. However deep my host's coffers, my father had taught me that all men were the same, each and all made in the image of God. I believed at least the first part. 'I am honoured that you would think of me. And it is a pleasure to see your home, and its beautiful grounds.'

Huxley shook his head as if to dismiss the compliment. 'A man must settle somewhere,' he said. 'This place is as good as any other.'

Manyon supped his wine and laughed. 'You're a modest man, Welmet,' he said. 'This house is as fine as any I have seen in Norfolk.'

'A terrible vanity,' Huxley conceded. 'And one I regret, somewhat, now that war threatens. At such times, a man might be better advised to hold his resources in coin, no?'

'You believe the King might prevail?' Manyon asked, and I groaned inwardly at the talk of politics so early in the evening, when it would almost certainly be the dominant topic once the pipes and brandy bowls came out.

I listened politely as we waited for Rutherford's arrival, but when there was a gap in the conversation, I took the opportunity to escape it by asking Huxley's permission to see the library more closely, and was granted leave. I scoured the shelves, surprised by how many names I recognised, having thought I had forgotten more than I had retained from my education. I noted bound works by Calvin and Erasmus alongside an army of pamphlets and tracts in meticulously labelled order: the names of writers like the pilloried, earless William Prynne and the Five Dissenting Brethren stood next to – to my surprise – that of John Milton, his lying beneath a fresh-looking document entitled *The Doctrine and Discipline of Divorce*.

I felt sure some of these writers had been exiled and their works banned, and that it was only the longevity of Parliament's seat, and the war itself, that allowed Huxley to be so bold as to store them in plain sight. He had to be very confident of a victory for the Parliamentary forces, or he would be advised to be more circumspect.

Behind me, Huxley and Manyon spoke in low voices; not quite whispers, but beneath the level of proper hearing. I heard the name Chrissa Moore, and remembered what Manyon had said about wealthy men of the community bending his ear.

Manyon was now seated opposite me at the wide oak table in the dining room. The magistrate was next to Goodwife Huxley, and engaged her in charming trivialities as they ate. The young woman answered, but briefly, allowing him as much space as he liked to talk, and Manyon made the most of it. His ability to discourse on things which might be of interest to a young woman – fabrics, poetry, botany and music – impressed me, as I had little knowledge of those things myself, but it drew no favour from his taciturn hostess. Nor did she pay attention to her husband. I felt sorry for Goodwife Huxley – a more miserably married girl bound to a greying old man, I had not seen. I thought again of Rutherford and Esther, wondering if their union would answer better than I had allowed, and resolved to apologise to her. It was, after all, her choice; who else's?

But Rutherford had not arrived at all. In the library, Manyon grew visibly embarrassed by the rudeness of his assistant's absence, and I hoped not to be marked out by any offence received by Huxley. Eventually, Manyon suggested Rutherford might have been taken ill. Huxley sniffed and said, sourly, 'Let us hope not. In these chaotic days, we cannot afford to lose such a soldier of God's works. Come, let us eat.' We went through to the dining room.

The meal was a sombre, slow affair, not worth the ride of more than an hour. As the meat course concluded, Manyon sank back into his seat. He looked ready for sleep, but perked up at the mention of the sweet. But Huxley looked sharp and wakeful.

'So, Manyon, what progress in the case of this witch?' Huxley asked, dabbling his digits in an exquisite silver fingerbowl to remove the mutton residue. I copied him, although the mutton had been so dry, I doubted it was necessary.

Manyon looked sidelong at me. His gaze seemed to hold a warning, if I was reading him correctly, to let him take the initiative. He need not have worried. I had no intention of stepping into the fray.

Steepling his fingers, the magistrate frowned as a servant refilled his glass. 'The position is a difficult one, as you must know.'

'Oh?' Huxley dried his fingers on the tablecloth and then peered at Manyon, who sipped from his glass and complimented the wine before answering.

'The girl has been incarcerated for over a fortnight, now. She has claimed – or she did at the time of her arrest – to be with child. I would thank you to keep that to yourself, by the way. And although all necessary measures have been taken to investigate her person, including a bodily examination, a search for familiars, a search of her personal effects, as well as several efforts to interrogate her and induce her to speak in her own defence, no further evidence has been forthcoming of any diabolical communion at all. Only' – and here he nodded to me – 'the tragic death of Richard Treadwater, and the clear evidence given by young Esther Treadwater, stand in the way of my releasing the girl—'

'But there were other deaths,' Huxley broke in. 'Surely it can be assumed that the deaths of Goodwife Gedge and her daughter, so closely connected with Chrissa Moore and so near her at the time of their demises, are attributable to her deviousness and devilish compacts?'

'It's possible,' said Manyon, warily. 'But assumption is not my habit.'

Huxley snorted. 'More than possible, I should say. I've seen those cells – I paid towards them, so I should know.

'There is no way Dillon was involved, and you've assured me they could not have secreted hemlock on their persons. The only explanation is diabolical assistance, a familiar of some sort, transitioning the stuff from one place to another. Come, now; it's clear the girl must be made to talk, using any means necessary. You know this as well as I. For all our sakes, when the assizes resume, this must have been dealt with by the book, or else we will all look foolish. Which is why,' he said, looking at the empty chair pulled up for Rutherford, 'I wished your assistant to be here, so he could relate the detail of the interrogations he has conducted with the Moore girl.'

'I will certainly be reprimanding him,' Manyon asserted, then caveated, 'should he be unable to furnish me with a good explanation of his absence tonight. But as to his interrogations, I fear nothing of note would be revealed. The girl stands as silent as the Tarpeian Rock. Surely, none of us wishes to see a public spectacle, ending in failure?'

Huxley nodded to his wife, who stood with a melancholy whisper of her skirts and left the room. Just moments later, a servant brought in a layered dish of sugared fruit, leaving it uncovered in the centre of the table. I stared at the fragile crust of sugar on orange peel and skinless plums, and found my mouth watering. I looked away, embarrassed, but Huxley encouraged me to take a slice. I placed one of the delicacies in my mouth. My tongue was overwhelmed by the sweetness of the crystals and tartness of the orange.

As I swallowed, Huxley continued. 'But there is a way, is there not, to lean on her without creating a spectacle?' His face was fox-like in the candlelight. His eyes fell on me and I felt the rapacious intelligence behind them. 'I am of the understanding that her young brother, a simpleton, has ended up in your care, Mr Treadwater?'

I almost choked as the peel passed down my throat, and took a sip of wine to regain control. Manyon and Huxley looked at me expectantly. I hesitated. So, this was why I was here. To play the

Judas, to part with Henry so that the boy could be used against his sister. What did they intend to do with him? Threaten him? Hurt him? With so few aware of the boy's existence and no family to object, the obstacles to Henry coming to harm were flimsy.

I met Manyon's eyes, trying to gauge what my new master wanted, but the magistrate sat well back in shadow, his shoulders relaxed and his face unreadable.

I glanced at Huxley, who had not touched the sweet food with any more enthusiasm than he had the savoury, but just stared at me from below his vertiginous forehead. I wondered what I was supposed to see in Huxley, a man of contradictory habits, who ate meat like a pauper and sweets like a king, who had constructed a house to rival those of the great men whose extravagance his Puritan faith decried, but wore torn cloth to dinner. Was I to recognise a man of God in him?

I thought of Henry and his simple, honest face, its expression frequently elevated by joy and crumpled with fear. I had not thought to assume responsibility for a helpless, friendless little boy. But I knew, also, where my own interest lay: unequivocally, in co-operating with men like Manyon and Huxley, because in their gift lay the preferments and privileges that would see Esther and me getting on in society, or not.

And, finally, I allowed into my mind the image of Chrissa Moore, whose face and form I had tried so hard to banish. The sweetness that still sat in my mouth from the sugared fruit tasted cheap now, in comparison to the memory of the richness of her voice and the depth of her wine-dark eyes. I blushed, and cast out the thought.

When I spoke, I tried to adopt Father's voice, channelling the calmness and sense of justice I remembered from my childhood. 'That is true, sir. The boy has been taken into my household, with an offer of work and board.' It wasn't difficult to sound certain; I knew in my bones that this was what my father would have done.

Huxley sensed a change, and his own voice hardened. 'With what reason? Surely, he's a beggar, and owns no loyalty from you?'

I took care with my words. 'You are correct, sir. I owe the boy no loyalty. One would be more correct to say he owes it to me, since I have taken him under my protection, and that of my name.'

Huxley leant in, probing. 'Young man, he is a mere servant, and his sister brought about your father's death. Surely, if the issue is the honour people might attach to your name, you are bound to see her come to justice. For your father's sake, if for no other reason?'

'I admit that my decision might seem odd to some observers but, for my father's sake,' I said, slowly, controlling the rise of anger at Huxley's presumption of what my father would have thought, 'I am bound by my word.'

My host's eyes narrowed, thinking, perhaps, that I spoke in jest. Then, as he saw I meant it, his expression tightened in hostility. Opposite, Manyon let out a bark of a laugh, breaking the tension. He said, 'I told you! Didn't I tell you? You've more hope of flying from that window than of persuading this young man to break his promise. A thing I admire about you, Tom,' he added, taking another glug of his wine. 'A stalwart!' He was still laughing.

Huxley was considerably less amused. 'You realise that the magistrate has the authority to send in the constable and simply take him, don't you?' He left out the implication: *if I tell him to do so.*

I nodded in admission. 'Magistrate Manyon has the undoubted authority to arrest the lad on a legitimate charge. There is none, as far as I am aware.'

Huxley didn't break his stare. The air seemed thick and the room too hot.

Manyon smoothed over the moment, still chuckling. 'The boy is quite right. Ah, I suppose there are limits even to the powers of magistrates. But there are more ways to kill a dog than by hanging, so to speak. We'll find a solution. Come, Welmet! Allow me to sample the tastes of your sweet table and then, if you will be so kind as to show me where I might sleep, I will retire to bed, where I shall dream of more enjoyable things. We will talk more of this on the morrow.'

Later, as a servant advanced up the stairs before us, the glow of a candle illuminating the way, Manyon turned to me, shaking his head, still half-amused. 'You do realise, don't you, that in the absence of another way to placate Huxley and his friends, the girl will now have to be walked? You left me no choice. And all to protect that mudlark child.'

Thinking of what lay ahead for Chrissa, knowing I bore some responsibility for it, I nodded.

At least Henry would be safe for now. She would thank me for that, at least.

15

Snow had gathered in pregnant clouds to the east, and the first flurries began to fall as Manyon and I parted ways at Walsham. The magistrate, if he was annoyed by the events of the previous night, didn't show it, and shook my hand heartily. 'You'll be expected today in the afternoon,' he said. 'The business of trying to prise open the jaws of that tight-lipped creature awaits us.'

His words reminded me: I was part of this, now. Aligned with the magistrate, and with more zealous men like Rutherford and Huxley, men who would scorch their own ground barren in their quest to root out Satan. How far would they go? How far would I go along with them?

The snow was bucketing down by the time I forded the river on to our land. Ben didn't like it, and was fractious. As we mounted the grassy bank to the road, he pulled against the wind that drove the swirling flakes into our faces. He was a young horse; perhaps he had not seen snow before. But I was thinking of easier days, endlessly white, with Esther and I bundled tight against the chill. As Father took us to church we would beg to stop along the way and he, before the reforming zeal truly came to him and he began to frown upon interruptions to the journey to God, would agree. The handfuls of feather-light, new-fallen snow turned my fingers blue as I pelted Esther with soft spheres, then we allied to build snowmen with outsized heads and misshapen, twiggy scarves. I remembered, though it could have been a different year, how Father once rested his capotain on the snowman's head and forgot to retrieve it, so he arrived bare-headed at church. The congregation had stared, but Father had never given much weight to what others thought, only to the call of his own conscience. In full hearing of the reverend, he said, 'God is forging a new Heaven, and a new Earth, and these are more important things than hats.'

He wished the snowman luck of it.

Returning to my current problems, I delayed thought of the afternoon. I knew what was coming, and didn't want to dwell on it. Instead, my mind wandered to Rutherford, who would surely be the right hand of the magistrate in this. Why hadn't he attended the dinner at Huxley's? My lip twitched in a smile; perhaps Rutherford had eaten there before and knew he would sleep on a half-full stomach. Still, it did not show him in a good light. I decided I had to speak to him, if only to reinforce our imminent family connection. I couldn't have his faults reflecting on Esther, if their marriage went ahead. I realised, with surprise, that I had started to think of the union as something that would probably happen, and felt guilt that I had failed to speak to my sister of it.

By now the weather had me tightly in its clutches. There was little wind beneath the weeping mantle of grey cloud, and the snow fell like a curtain. My cloak, boots and hat offered thin protection against a mournful cold that took residence in my marrow. Snowflakes mingled with tears plucked from my eyes by the biting air, and together they hardened into crystals on my cheeks. A raw-boned leveret caught out too far from its nest, half-buried beneath a light drapery of white, was an unwelcome sight as I approached the gate.

I was surprised to see no spiral of smoke from the chimney. No lights either. I drew Ben to a halt and made to start up the path, but the horse whinnied and dragged his hoofs, so I had to dig in my spurs. Still, even with as much force as I wished to exert, he refused. 'Come on, boy,' I muttered. 'Too cold for this, isn't it?' Finally, Ben acquiesced, and we rode up towards the house. I noted again the darkness at the windows and, as we drew closer, that they were all open. My thoughts turned to intruders. There were soldiers and vagrants enough on the roads for that. 'God's teeth,' I muttered, knowing I never should have left.

But the path was a pristine, undisturbed white. No thieving feet had trodden here. And what sort of intruder opened the windows? Even as I dismounted and reached for the hilt of my sword, I felt there was something more amiss. A thief would have entered, taken what was valuable – not much – and fled, not occupied the building he had just fleeced.

I did not call out to Esther or Henry. If there was someone inside who had no right to be here, I had no intention of alerting them to my presence. I walked with the cautious step of a soldier sent often out in scouting parties; I had always been able to tread noiselessly. I was tense, but kept my muscles loose and ready – men lose their lives because, wound by their nerves to tightness, they jump back in fright when they ought to strike out.

I crept through into the kitchen. The hearth stood cold, with no sign a fire had been lit that morning. The expected smells of warmed bread, smoke and lye were quite absent. In their place was a faint odour of stale ash, salt and, underlying that, something else I did not recognise, something foul, like the remnants of a bird half-chewed by the stable cat that once I had found beneath the kitchen table.

I almost didn't see Esther. She was in Father's chair. She sat in the shadow of its tall back, motionless, like a figure in a painting. Her pale hair was loose around her face and shone against the drabness of her dress. She wore no coif.

'Esther,' I said. 'Why are you sitting in the—' Her expression stopped me dead as I came about the chair and faced her. It was flat and leeched, somehow callous. Not like my sister at all.

When she spoke, it was in a brittle, clear voice. 'A baptised child lives in Kent, who will become learned. He will become the keeper of a great trove of knowledge, and will configure such debates as whether the shapes of bones found in the earth were brought there by flood, earthquake or God. He will explore the hidden affinities of the external world with the world of His creation, and from the rocks at the base of this island, his friends will draw a great bone, elephantine in its proportions, and petrified, and at first he will think it the remains of a great war beast of the Empire of the Romans, and then he will conclude that it is the thigh bone of a giant – man or woman – that has lain there since the beginning of time.

'But he will be tricked, ignorant as all men are; the learned ones, too. Two hundred years from now, they will exhume the jawbone of a great lizard, and name it, and set it on display so that men may marvel at it, but still they will live in the darkness of want of knowledge. And then a time will come when there is no darkness, and all will live in ceaseless, unblinking light. Do you think they will like that, Thomas?'

I couldn't speak. I stared. Esther's face was like chalk, my name on her lips a foreign thing. As the words ran from her like an undammed stream, her face moved with an animation I had never seen in her, her eyes settled on me so directly that I wanted to move back, to escape, quickly, into the open air. She was everything unknown and unknowable: the blurred face at the window, the whisper of a breath in an empty room, the dawning realisation of a world beyond the one we know.

'And later, much later – in the puny minds of men – when the monsters that live in the sea have disappeared from your maps, will come a time of reckoning. Like the times that have come before. And before. And will come again. A time when the gods sleep. A time of formless ashes. No sun, no fires, no earthquakes.

A time of Judas. A time of Cain. An endless winter. And they will rise again, from fathomless waters.'

'Esther, stop! Stop talking!'

She stopped. She was relaxed in the chair, her palms resting lightly on the arms. I moved forward, sinking to one knee by her side and taking up her hand. I gasped to feel her icy skin. *How long has she been sitting here?* 'Sister, what is this nonsense? Why do you sit here in the cold, with no fire to warm you? Are you ill?'

I could not process the words she had uttered. It was as if she had been speaking in tongues.

I stood and began to close the windows, but even as I did so, Esther rose to open them again. She was beside me, pulling at the frame, and our mingled breath clouded the glass as we wrestled. 'What are you doing?' I cried. 'This… this is madness!' I seized her arm, hardly knowing myself, just wanting to stop her, and pulled her back to her seat. She didn't struggle, and instead laughed; a high, maniacal sound. I resisted the urge to shake her, to silence her. I drew back, but still she laughed.

'Why are you laughing? Do you need a doctor?'

'Oh, a physician would make a pretty addition to this picture,' she said, still cackling.

I looked about the room, realising it had not been cleaned, and food lay in dishes from the previous night: half-eaten meat and oily, stagnant gravy. 'Can I get you anything?' I said, helplessly. 'Have you eaten?'

'I have eaten much,' she said, her laughter abating, although one further giggle escaped her, like a hiccough.

The gnawing feeling deep in my stomach intensified. I could not ignore what every part of my body was screaming: *leave, move away from her.* A visceral need to put distance between us was swelling inside me.

'This…' I could not say it, but the words drummed on the inside of my skull: *This is not Esther.*

My sister's sweet features hadn't changed. Her eyes were just as blue, her chin as pointed, her lips formed the same bow they always had.

But it was not Esther.

Thoughts whipped through my mind in chaotic flurries. Esther's letter, its voice desperate and lost. My father dead, his reputation hanging by a thread. Chrissa Moore, her other-worldly face turned up to mine from behind the bars of her cell. Henry running away, his steps dogged by a terror I had not understood. And Joan Gedge and her mother, curled together in poisonous, untimely death.

I was unable to turn from Esther. She met my eyes calmly. My sister's usual expression – uncertain, seeking approval – was absent. I quailed, knowing I looked on something I did not understand. When I spoke, I almost whispered. 'Where is she?' When no answer came, my voice rose as I said again, 'Where is she?'

'There is no "where",' Esther – or what was not Esther – said, again in that terrible composed voice.

I was shaking. To hear her speak of herself in that way was the most horrible thing I had ever known. I tried to form another question, but my mouth would not say the words. *What are you?*

My thoughts were turning back to the words of the letter in which she had first written of Chrissa Moore: *a great and ungodly evil.*

There is no such thing as evil.

Not-Esther was watching with keen eyes. I was reminded of the way I had once examined things collected from pools by the sea, when my father had taken us to wade in the shallow water off Snettisham Beach: baby sea scorpions, shore crabs and dog whelks. She was looking at me with *interest*. As if I were something she might study.

'Where is the boy? Where's Henry?'

'He is the son of nine mothers. He is known by many names. He protects against the wind. His horn is aloft. He saw me. Where is he?' The voice was sing-song, each bit of each obscure word rising and falling in discordant musicality.

'Stop it!' I wanted my father. I wanted to run. 'Stay here,' I said, uselessly, and saw Esther's lips part in another laugh.

I was mired in doubt and fear, but had to find Henry.

There was a snake, he had said. What had he meant?

I hesitated in the doorway. She was no longer staring in my direction. Instead, she looked ahead, at the wall, or at nothing. I wondered what she could be seeing. Where was Esther if her form was occupied by someone – something – else? Where had she gone?

I knew what I had to do. In the hall there was a large oak chest of useful things: boots, hats, thick-bristled brushes for removing dirt from the stone floor. And rope. I staggered towards the chest, fumbling with the catch. I dug, desperately. It was here somewhere. It had to be here. I found it right at the bottom and dragged it out, letting its coils burn my hands in my haste. Then I baulked. The thought of restraining her, of pinioning her slender arms, was beyond anything I had done as a soldier. It was unthinkable.

It's not her. The voice inside was quiet but insistent. *Esther is somewhere else.*

Was she dead? I stood with the rope between my hands and a cry rose in my throat. She could not be gone. I had lost too much. Mother, father, and now...

I shook myself. I had to fight now, fight for Esther. But I was so afraid. Every step towards her was harder than the most savage battle charge.

'Sister,' I said, approaching her seat, finding myself once more the subject of her gaze – she saw the rope but did not move – and wanting more than I had ever wanted anything to be far away. 'I do this for your safety.'

She did not resist. If anything, she seemed amused, and watched as I tied figure-of-eight knots, securing her forearms to the solid arms of the chair. It was anathema to me to touch her skin, though she did nothing in response.

When finished, I stood back, half-expecting her to vanish the knots. She spoke again instead. 'The first man you killed, the shock was such that you lost control of your functions.' I started, remembering. 'You kicked your man down, and he dropped his sword. You kept kicking him until he did not rise again. You had lost your own sword, and you picked up his, a Prussian-made blade with a fish-skin grip, which was not originally his either. It belonged to his officer, who had died earlier in the battle from a flintlock shot to the face. His nose came off, leaving a bloody hole. Your man, though, was not an officer, but you thought he was because of the sword. You bungled the first blow, striking at his breastplate, then ran him through at the armpit. As you withdrew the stolen blade, blood sprayed from the wound, and some of it struck your face. It tasted like copper in your mouth. And the hot piss ran down your legs. Does not the Lord go out before you?'

I lurched to the side and emptied my stomach, my sparse breakfast biting like hot vinegar at my throat. As I wiped the reeking bile from my mouth, her laughter sounded in my ears again. I stood, and stumbled from the room on shaky legs.

Outside, I called Henry. The snow was falling even more heavily now, and Ben was stomping and whinnying in the freezing air. The horse had tugged at his rope hard enough to almost dislodge the hook from the wall, and when I reached him, he was trembling from withers to flanks. 'Hush, boy,' I said, smoothing my hand over the side of his nose. 'I'll get you in.' He neighed violently, pulling harder. His eyes rolled white in his head. I hauled, he resisted; then, finally, hearing my oaths, he yielded.

I continued to call Henry as I led Ben round to the stables. I was comforted by the horse's presence and his warmth, and as I rubbed down the thin layer of snow that had accumulated on his coat, I pressed my face into the coarse brown mane. 'I wish I could stay here with you, boy,' I whispered.

I looked about the stables for Henry, but saw no unkempt mop of dark hair poking out of the straw. I thought through other places Henry might be, but in this weather... He would not have gone to the house on any account, so if he were not in the stables, the next place to check was the small shed where Father had once nursed plants ready to put them to the soil, and where Esther now kept some of her potted herbs. The thought of her conscientious hands potting and pruning the delicate plants was unbearable as I walked across the garden.

'Henry!' I called. 'Henry, come out!'

I realised the shed was locked. I had never known Father lock it before. It was in poor condition, with a wooden roof partly stripped to allow in the light, set well back from the road, hardly a target for thieves. I peered inside. 'Henry?' I shouted before realising, with another stab of worry, that the lock would have prevented him taking shelter here. I nearly turned to leave, but my attention fell on the far wall. I shielded my eyes against the snow again and squinted through the window. The plant was growing in a large clay pot. It had clusters of small, segmented leaves, like carrot tops, but bigger. I hadn't seen it in the garden before, and couldn't account for the nagging feeling at my core that said I should inspect it more closely.

I took a loose stone from the edge of the vegetable patch and smashed it against the lock five or six times until it broke. I levered the door open, ducking to enter the cramped space beneath the half-roof, then crouched close to the plant, examining the tiny leaves and the smooth, hairless stems with their darkish purple spots. I rubbed the leaves, put my fingers to my nose. The smell was musky, like urine. I stood, too quickly, thumping my head on wood, ignoring the pain, and backed out, breaking into a run to reach the pond. I plunged my hands through the icy sludge developing on the surface, into the numbing cold of the water below.

The poison that had killed Joan Gedge and her mother was here. Had clearly been growing here for several months. How could that be? I withdrew my burning hands from the water and rubbed them against my thighs. The plant had to be Esther's. Which made everything I had assumed since receiving her plaintive letter the result of a deception, a deception designed to make me believe Chrissa Moore was responsible for my father's death, and those of the two Gedge women, when in truth...

I recoiled.

Esther had killed Joan and her mother. In those minutes she had stood alone in the gaol cell, praying, remonstrating with the two women, what, in truth, had she whispered to them? How had that terrible voice I had just heard manifested itself, and to what effect? It was grotesque to think of her funnelling the leaves or seeds of the deadly plant through the bars, exhorting the women to chew, to swallow, watching as their hearts slowed and paralysis set in. An acid taste surged in my stomach, rising to the edges of my tongue.

And Father. Though I still could not be sure what had happened to induce his apoplexy, whether or not he had seen what I had now seen in Esther, it was clear Father was no victim of witches, nor of serving women and their ill-wishes. Chrissa Moore had been maligned. Had she seen the truth of what was happening? Perhaps she had spoken out about it. At least now, her arrest made more sense.

I cursed myself for my words to her in the dingy gaol. I, who had prided myself on my cleverness and worldliness, had been taken in by first appearances, gulled like a simpleton. I, thinking myself sophisticated, with my rejection of superstition and even of God Himself, now looked into the abyss of my lack of faith, and shuddered.

My thoughts were turbulent, tethered only by the knowledge that I had to act. Yet I remained crouched by the pond, staring into the water. Minutes passed, and still I could not summon the will to move. My teeth chattered. I had lost most of the feeling in my fingers.

It was then that I saw it: a head, poking out from beneath the guelder hedge separating the garden from the paddocks, and a tousle of ragged black hair attached to a small, unmoving frame. I skirted the pond, then fell to my knees on the other side.

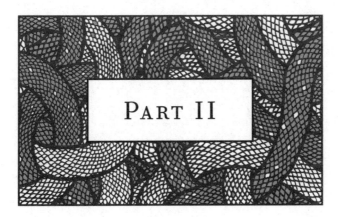

PART II

16

April 1703

A place far from the sea

Days pass, then weeks, and a stillness settles over us. The winds slumber. What air there is is thin, cold and bright, as though something pulls at the fabric of the world. The subtle dance from winter to spring seems delayed; buds do not peek from the soil, the birds have not returned from their migrations. When once or twice I have passed our boundary for supplies, I have felt like a ghost in an unrecognisable land, moving through small hamlets, encountering no beggars, hearing only the noise of closing doors and mothers scolding cowed children inside. Even the deer flee from me.

On one occasion, just as the sun begins to fall, I am returning from the vegetable garden when a tinker with his jangling cart drives a donkey up the track. He is the first person I have seen for a month besides Mary. I approach the cart, examining my visitor. He is squint-eyed, sun-burnt, heavy-bearded, and the cart groans under the weight of the dross he lugs about with him, from baskets of sulphurous eggs to torn leathers to broken-down pocket watches; anything, in short, that he might have acquired through barter, beggary or theft.

I spy bottles filled with dark, doubtful liquids, and two filthy, crudely carved puppets with tangled strings, presumably for entertaining the children of those whose silver he wishes to pocket. He asks for the lady of the house. For a fraction of a second, seeing his missing teeth and the deep-scored wrinkles of his face, I think, *he is so old*, before realising he might be twenty years younger than I; it is hard to tell through the dirt of the road. I tell him we need no pots or pans, and think, though I do not say it, none of his rancid cheeses. Yet I would pay him for news. And, though it pains me to say it, a few moments of his company. I offer the exchange.

He thinks on it with a choleric frown, chewing on a piece of dried meat like a cow at the cud. It takes him longer than I expect – perhaps a slow thinker, or perhaps he has questions about why a man of the gentle classes, even one falling on hard times such as myself, would pay him to stand on his land and pass the time of day. Eventually, though, he nods.

I realise I have almost lost the art of talking to those I do not know. I stutter. 'What news of the villages?'

'Bad, most,' comes the laconic reply.

'Any good?'

'Less.'

'Have there been any happenings you would call unusual?'

This brings another long moment of reflection, during which he scans the house and me. The donkey brays, and the curiosity in its master's eyes sharpens to a wily suspicion. 'I see your meaning, mister. Some things be all up and the wrong way about. An almoner got trampled Monday Hocktide.' He nods wisely, conspiratorially. 'And nestlings in the old loft at St Lawrence's ate the hen.'

Yes. Up and the wrong way about. My companion eyes me closely. He is not used to being listened to by men like me; rather, he expects to be shooed and abused, and chased off. That I do not do these things seems to give him no comfort. There is something he does not like about this place – I see it in his pinprick eyes. Soon he is asking for his sixpence, and soon after that, ambling off down the track again. 'Tell the lady I'll have those herbs for her next I call,' he mumbles, over his shoulder, as he departs. I almost call after him, to check what Mary has asked him to procure, as she grows almost everything we need, but he rattles away and the moment is gone.

Mary avoids me, too, more and more as the days get warmer. She keeps to her bedroom, or the garden if it is fine. When forced into my company, she talks without stopping about inconsequential things: the fruit trees, a shelf in the buttery that is bowing, a cracked trencher. This outpouring does not stop until I withdraw, either to my study or upstairs, to the attic. When she is not talking, she bites her nails down to the bloody quick, then purges the resulting wounds with rosemary. It is alien to feel such distance from her, like one of my limbs has decided to go its own way and depart from the rest. But I do not know how to close the breach. Well, that is not strictly true. What she wants, I know very well, but I cannot give it to her.

I try to read to Esther every day. I vary the themes, aspiring to Dryden and Greville, resorting more often to Pepys, but, remembering my sister's simple piety and love of her Bible, inevitably, God creeps in, in one form or another. Today, it is Milton, not *Paradise Lost*, but *Regained*.

My lengthy reading seems not to bother the creature I have always thought of as Not-Esther – an inadequate name, but since it refuses to name itself, I have had to improvise. In my mind, over these many years, I have given it many names, but it answers to none.

But Esther... my silent and unwitting charge these last six decades, I cling fervently to the belief that she is still there. That her essence, her soul, whatever constitutes *her*, survived the chaos that overtook us in those days. It is a frail hope, a foolish old man's dream, I know, but it is all I have.

Today, it talks of war. Not of its pity, but of its glory.

'Tsaritsyn. Volgograd. Stalingrad. Over a million souls. A peerless battle in the memory of man. They were reduced to the level of primitives. Many of them ate human flesh, because, when all was said and done, they did not want to die. They did not want to sink into the deeps below the deeps. And who can blame them for that?'

Yesterday it was copulation; specifically, of animals and man. This is typical. It is a creature of spiteful enjoyments, of cryptic divinations, and of lies. It is a storyteller, first and foremost. I cannot know how much of what it says bears weight, so I do my best to ignore it all. On this occasion, though, I sigh, and look over the top of the book. 'The reading would go more quickly, dare I say, if you did not maintain a constant commentary.'

For the first time, it sounds tired. 'The reading would go more quickly were it to be overseen by an arthritic gibbon. But we cannot always have what we want.'

'Indeed.' I lower my eyes back to the page. I prefer sarcasm to its other contributions.

'But I do not dislike you reading, in point of fact,' it goes on. 'It passes the time, such as time is.' Then, slyly, as I try to find my place, it adds, 'Esther likes it.'

The words achieve their desired effect. I put aside the book, looking closely at her face – I still think of it as her face, in spite of the creature's long occupation. Several moments go by while I try to form the question. Finally, I say, 'Is she still in there?' The gesture the creature makes is almost a shrug, but could be a nod. 'My sister lives?' I lean forward. It has been over a month since it regained its consciousness, after sixty years of what I can only describe as hibernation: eating, passing waste, sleeping, but never looking, hearing or speaking. But this is the first time since its return that it has deigned to share anything other than macabre drivel. 'Can I speak to Esther?'

'She is too far away,' it says, with desultory regret.

'Where?'

'Where are any of us?'

'No more riddles, demon. Where is she?'

It sighs. 'In here, somewhere. I am aware of her and she of me, but she cannot come to the surface while I inhabit this shell. Yet nor can I leave her. And as I cannot leave this…' it looked down at Esther's withered form '…wreck of a body, I suppose we are stuck with one another. And you, too,' it says, with something like a laugh.

My breath is tight in my chest, hidebound, as if someone sits on me. This is more information than I have had from a lifetime of questions. 'Why can't you leave her body?'

'She will not allow it.'

I sit back, stunned, but then press forward; while the creature feels inclined to speak, I must elicit as much from it as I can. 'How does she prevent it?' The pain radiates through my chest. I must not agitate myself. I breathe in deeply.

'She has some influence, some small, residual force,' it says. 'I must admit I do not understand it fully. But it is the same strength that prevents me from harming you. She is vigilant, and stronger than I had anticipated when first I entered her.'

I am thinking, furiously. There are things I have inferred – guessed – of course, from my first encounters with the creature, such as how it came to inhabit my sister, and where it came from. But there are things I still do not know for certain. 'Then why did you possess her, if you could not leave?'

'Why did the first woman take the apple? Why did she sink her teeth into its flesh?'

'Curiosity,' I say. 'A thirst for knowledge. And, although she knew it was forbidden, she did not know the price of disobedience. Her temptation was too strong.' But it does not respond. It hums a sailor's ditty as I say, 'What could have tempted you?'

The humming continues, and I realise I will not receive another hint. Instead, I say, out of my own curiosity, 'What has kept you asleep for all this time?'

'All of what time?'

I shake my head. Of course. Foolish. To this creature, a year, even a century, might pass like the dying breath of a sparrow. It does not matter. 'Well, why have you woken now? What has prompted it?'

'Your death,' it says. 'It comes swiftly now.'

The brutality of this statement does not torment me. The creature lies, but not about this. I swim in muddying tides. I feel the weakening in my limbs and bones that comes with old age. My time draws short. My concern is for what will happen after.

'And with my death? What will happen to her, and to you?'

'You will act before that.'

'How will I act?'

It begins to hum again, closing its eyes, shutting me out.

Outside, though I do not know it, the wind has begun to rise.

17

January 1644

North Norfolk

I rubbed Henry's cheeks as hard as I could, then did the same to my hands, generating more heat, gathering the boy up and trying to warm him. He had been curled in a ball beneath the lower branches of the hedge, and some of the juice of the shrub's red berries had rubbed off in his dark hair like blood. He had almost managed to conceal himself, but I lugged him out and carried him back around the pond to the stables.

'Guppy! Here, boy!' The mastiff was bounding about in the yard, marvelling at the inch or so of snow that had now fallen, but as I called he came on in great, loping strides. He forced his bulk in next to us, and I pressed Henry between my own body and the dog's chest. Guppy licked his face.

Henry lived. His breaths were shallow but regular. I shook him and he began to come around. As he regained awareness, he quivered like a field mouse.

How long had he been alone out here, and what had driven him even from the stables? I shivered to imagine his fear. The boy had seen what I had not, from the very moment I had brought him into the house. I cursed myself. It would have been better to leave him where he was, whores and all, rather than bring him to this Bedlam.

'Where is…' He was trying to say something. I leant in close to hear as he tried again. 'Where is… Mary?'

'What?' Was he delirious?

But Henry was coming back to himself. 'Where is Mary?'

'Who are you speaking of, Henry?'

'Mary. My sister.'

The crowd waited. The snow, having clothed the spire of St Nicholas's, in whose shadow most of the villagers had gathered to see justice done, had stopped, but the temperature was dropping still further as the day waned. Reverend Hale had drummed up a whole cross section of society here: clothiers, servants of great men like Huxley, the local barber-surgeon, tenant farmers and carpenters, maids and old men, all circling the green, wrapped in their warmest blankets, eager for the proceedings to begin.

Hale was like his name: beefy, red-faced, nearly as large as Dillon. The minister watched from his place beside Manyon and Huxley as the constable emerged from the gaol, bringing Chrissa Moore – or Mary – out into the light. As Mary came closer, Hale stared, and muttered below his breath about the dangers of iniquitous women. I was surprised he didn't cross himself.

On the other side of Hale stood Welmet Huxley. Hale had brought a flask of warmed wine to share, though Huxley declined it. One might have mistaken the three for old schoolfriends drawing together again after an absence of years, to watch a revel or a play. By virtue of my position as Manyon's assistant and because of the continued – and unexplained – absence of John Rutherford, who might have usurped me, I was nearest out of all the onlookers, and heard their exchange as Dillon deposited his silent charge on her knees. I tried to give the appearance of not listening by bending to correct the fit of my boot.

'She still defies us, then?' Hale said. His tone was that of a disappointed father, but excitement shimmered behind it.

Manyon affirmed with a grunt. 'Like all her abominable kind,' Hale continued. 'She has not spoken a word since she was arrested?'

'Not quite a complete silence, reverend. There was her claim to be with child if you recall. Yet there, we make progress. There is one thing we know now that we did not know yesterday.'

'Which is?'

'The girl is not pregnant.'

I lifted my head to look at the prisoner, on her knees in several inches of snow with her hands shackled before her, and was surprised to find her returning my gaze. She shook with the cold, and was filthy, her long black hair matted against her skull. Even so, the villagers whispered of her beauty, and some mothers muttered, 'Shame! Let her up.' Others vented their spite: *witch, bedswerver, Devil's doxy.*

Her beauty had worked against her. I had been unwilling to believe her a witch because I had not believed such powers existed, but had been ready to believe her a whore. Had she been thicker of limb, her nose not so straight, her eyes half as bright, perhaps I might have found it easier to withhold judgement. I might have arrived more quickly at the truth.

But I could not look back at a road untravelled. However blind I had been, I had to set my sights on the path ahead, and go now where it led.

I had left Henry in the stables, bundled in rugs, coats and cloaks. He had continued to shake and cry, but when pressed would not speak of the night he had passed alone, or why he had hidden beneath the hedge. Imagination filled some of the gaps. I winced at the thought of the creature's voice in the child's ear. Henry had been too wise for it, ironically. He had done what the Gedge women and my father had not; he had run.

I had left Esther still secured to her chair. Before going, I had prepared a white soup for her, and she had smiled amenably as

I spooned it into her mouth. She had spoken, but I preferred to forget her words.

I had had little choice but to come. Manyon had expected me, but that was not the problem; I could have made some excuse – illness, accident, violence. No, that was not the reason I was here. I was here because the woman being pulled to her feet by Dillon was the only person who knew the truth about what had happened in my home. She knew, and I had to know.

The obvious course of action – go to Manyon and Hale and anyone else who would listen, with the truth – I had considered only fleetingly. Anyone who saw Esther in the condition she was in now would want her dead. They would feign efforts to expel the spirit, and then imprison, hang or burn her. I would not allow that. Esther's only chance was for me to pretend everything was normal, and learn what I could. The problem was, I had no idea what I was going to do.

Manyon and Hale were still talking.

' …when a woman holds no penitence for her lewdness and her destructions, she leaves us no other choice. She might have avoided this, had she been more willing to surrender herself to the law, and to God's good mercy.' Hale's deep-set eyes were fixed on Mary, as I had to keep reminding myself to call her.

I had got no sense from Henry on the subject of his sister's name. He had only insisted, in tearful but firm repetitions, that he had no sister called Chrissa, and the sister who had taken such kind care of him at Lucy Bennett's house was Mary. 'Mary Moore?' I asked him, sternly, and the child had nodded.

It was starting. Manyon technically outranked Hale, but it was Hale who signalled to Dillon, who picked his ash cudgel off the ground. The constable looked reluctant, and I was not surprised. Dillon was a good man, and what he was about today was not God's work. The crowd watched as he spoke quietly in

Mary's ear until, to my surprise, she nodded obligingly enough, then he spun her about so her back was to him, and dug the cudgel into the base of her spine. She took three or four stiff steps forward. Beneath the long folds of her mudflat-brown dress she wore no shoes, and her feet were bruised and scabbed from the rough floor of her cell, already turning red as they trod the new snow.

Huxley's voice cut through the murmurs of the waiting crowd. '…the multitudinous ways in which the servants of the Adversary can deceive us. The secret conjurations, the nourishment of Satan's imps and fiendish minions, and from their very own bodies, as if it is not sin enough to allow the Devil into their bedchambers to start with. The cases I saw in Ipswich were sufficient to make your hair stand up on end. It must not be allowed to happen here.

'It is a relief, of course, that the Gedge women took their own lives although, certainly, they will burn for it. All this yelping about murder might fool the saddle-geese in the village, but it does not fool me. They were all equally guilty. At least now we have only this loathsome thing to manage. And we will drive the truth from her.'

'We will indeed,' said Manyon, watching as Dillon continued to propel Mary with regular jabs to her back and hips. This seemed unnecessary, for the girl walked steadily enough. It surprised me to see her so compliant. I had thought Dillon would have to drag her from her cell and beat her about the head.

Hale now leant in to Manyon, and spoke so that I had to strain to hear. 'You talked with her of her brother?'

'I did,' said Manyon, and I felt the magistrate's eyes on me. 'She knows where he resides.'

That explained Mary's expression when she saw me.

'But she did not agree to the proposal?' asked Hale.

'She didn't utter a word,' Manyon said, equably. 'But in any case, as Huxley here will testify, along with my assistant, who is trying so hard to appear not to be listening, it is not in my power to send the lad back to that den of thieves. He is not in my care, but that of Mr Treadwater, here.'

Ordinarily, I would have been embarrassed to be caught eavesdropping, but today it barely registered. I shook my head. 'Apologies, sir.'

'Not at all,' Manyon said. 'How is little Henry?'

My tongue formed some unremarkable lie, but its movement was halted by another thought, one that had first taken form when Manyon revealed that he knew I had taken Henry from Lucy Bennett's house: *how did Manyon know Henry's name?* 'He's well,' I said, cautiously. 'Doing some work with the horses.'

The events of the morning had made my brain slow. I felt enveloped in fog. *He has walled up my way, so that I cannot pass, and he has set darkness upon my paths.* The darkness was deeper than when I had been faithless.

I mused on this for a moment. Was I not still faithless? After all, God had not presented Himself. No dove had alighted, no warlike spears had split the clouds. The existence of evil, I feared, did little to confirm the existence of good. I shook my head to dispel such abstract thoughts; this was not the time.

The minutes passed into an hour, and still Mary walked broad circles on the green. The constable occasionally shoved her, but his actions seemed oddly lacklustre. The watching crowd, having begun by calling insults, with several of the younger boys picking up sods of frozen earth and snow to throw at her, now tired of the scene, which lacked the visceral spectacle of a hanging or a flogging, or the intrigue of a ducking, in favour of grumbling about the cold. But Dillon kept the pace of the walking quick, and soon Mary began to tire, her step less certain, slowing frequently enough to receive rough instructions from the constable to move faster. Then, as she rounded the corner nearest the spire, she collapsed.

Dillon reached down with his cudgel to prod her to her feet, and I moved forward to help her, but Manyon held out his arm. 'Wait!' he said. 'Get her up, Dillon. Walk on.' Still holding me back, he said, 'I ask that you trust me,' in a voice so low it had to be designed for my hearing only.

What was Manyon doing?

The trial continued. Dillon, who by now was suffering from the cold himself, his teeth chattering, the cudgel held in chilblained hands, was becoming irritable. He growled more than once at Mary. 'Talk, girl,' he said. 'Confess whatever crimes you are guilty of, and we can put an end to this.' But Mary said nothing.

Darkness could not be more than an hour away. Still, Mary walked on.

When she fell for the second time, Dillon pulled her up again. She looked to be nearly unconscious, her face slack. I saw Henry in my mind's eye, and thought there was more resemblance to Mary now the pride of her natural expression seemed stripped back. I shuddered to see her halting steps. I began to feel I had no choice but to intervene, and tell the magistrate what I knew. No man's good conscience could see this continue. But I wrestled with how to do it without endangering Esther, and could not see a way forward.

The crowd was melting away. The oncoming dark, ushered in by the arrival of blacker clouds signalling another wash of snow, had driven many of them to their firesides already, and even Huxley began to mutter about calling for his horse. As the throng thinned, I started to see the course of Manyon's thinking.

By the time Mary fell for the third and final time, there were but a few men and women left to see what Manyon did. He conferred briefly with Hale, then stepped forward. 'Enough, for now,' he said, authoritatively. 'Night draws on. Return to your homes. We can continue this tomorrow, should the girl not be inclined to speak when we return her to her cell.'

The remaining few, who for some time had looked restless and hungry, seemed satisfied as they sloped off towards their cottages. The reverend shook hands with the magistrate, then secured his cloak about his thick middle before returning to the church. Huxley and Manyon were talking as I hurried to Mary's side and knelt by her slumped form, then nodded to Dillon, who had also bent to retrieve his prisoner. I said, 'Go, man. Warm yourself by the tavern fire with an ale or two. I'll see the girl inside.'

Dillon shook my hand robustly. 'You're a good lad,' he said. 'Here, take these.' His fingers, clumsy and frost-bitten, fumbled the great bunch of keys as he handed them over. 'I wouldn't usually but… I think my balls are about to fall from my body.'

I pocketed the keys with a laugh, then removed my own cloak, using it to cover Mary. I pulled her up and, impulsively, lifted her off her feet. She weighed less than I had expected. I looked down at her face, expecting the same tinge of blue in her skin and slow return to consciousness I had watched that morning in her brother. But her eyes were open. Her body was warm against mine, and she met my gaze directly.

I had no idea what to say. I remembered my last words to her with shame, and this, with something else alongside it, rendered me speechless.

But Mary wasn't speechless, and was far from the end of her strength. Her hand gripped my wrist. She said, 'Do you have my little brother?'

'He's safe,' I answered, and then felt guilty, because it wasn't exactly true. 'We need to speak.'

'Soon,' she said.

Manyon was behind me. Huxley had hurried away on his horse before the second deluge of snow, and a devious smile now played on the magistrate's face. 'Come – let's get inside before we all freeze.'

'I feel I've missed something here, magistrate,' I said, still holding Mary.

'Put me down,' she snapped, pushing me away. 'I have no need of a donkey and can walk perfectly well myself.'

I did so.

'Men like Huxley and Hale will never be satisfied until they have had their pound of flesh,' said Manyon, leaning forward to pour wine in two small glasses, and beaming with the pleasure of having tricked his apprentice. 'I was satisfied there was not enough evidence to convict this girl,' he added, gesturing to Mary, who sat on my right with her knees huddled against her chest. 'But I was *also* certain that between John, that madman Huxley and the buffoon Hale, sooner or later, a means to wring a confession from her would be found.' He handed one glass to Mary and one to me. 'So, I went down to the cells myself. Didn't I, Chrissa?'

Mary nodded. She accepted the wine but did not sip it.

The mention of Rutherford was itching at me – where was the witchfinder? – but I had other, more important questions. 'I see, sir,' I said, in a tone of filial respect.

'And we came to an agreement, Chrissa and I. Put on a show, play up to the crowd some, and pretend to be in more discomfort than she truly was. For that is all they want, these simple people: to see her broken, to have their sense of the proper order of things restored. And with that done, we will hold her for a short time longer and then quietly release her, on the pretext that the testing we put her to yielded nothing.'

Mary sat like marble, keeping her eyes downcast. She still did not touch the wine.

'And when will that be?' I asked. When Manyon looked up sharply, I added, 'Her brother grows anxious for her, and I am sure both will wish to return to Norwich, or to wherever they have people.' I felt clumsy, fearing she would be angry I had spoken for her. Not knowing how to address her, I said, 'Is that correct, Mistress Moore?'

The look she turned on me was complex. 'My only wish,' she said, in that strange, torn voice, 'is to be reunited with my brother. Where we go from here is of lesser concern.'

Smoothly, Manyon said, 'In due course, my dear. In due course. Now, given the exertions of the afternoon and the situation we find ourselves in, I would like to offer you some more comfortable accommodation. Perhaps a room in my own—'

Mary interrupted. 'My cell is comfortable enough, given the short duration of my expected stay there.'

Manyon, with a ruffled cough, said, 'It must be as you see fit. But stay as long as you wish in order to recover yourself. I can have food brought and warmer clothes…'

Mary hesitated. I could see she wanted to accept, could only imagine how hungry and cold she had to be. Eventually, she shook her head. 'I need nothing,' she said.

Manyon stiffened at a second rejection of his hospitality. 'Very well. I will return you to your cell.'

I saw a chance, and said, 'I would be grateful for something in my stomach, too, sir. Shall I return Mistress Moore and call for some food to be sent up at the same time?'

Manyon stood, placing down his wine, and said, 'No, no, boy, I will do the honours myself. I'll call for Dillon.' He left the room, looking only slightly less pleased with himself than when he had entered.

We were alone. I turned to her, intending to tell her everything, but she spoke first. 'Henry cannot stay a moment longer in that house. I must beg you—'

I stopped her entreaty with one word: 'Mary.'

She stared.

'That is your true name, is it not?'

She gave no answer.

'Mary, I know. I know all about it. Or at least, something of it. You have been very afraid for him?'

After a long moment, she nodded, and then tears came to her eyes, but she blinked them back.

I said, 'Don't cry. He's safe, or he is for now. My sister can't harm him. What was my sister... My God.' But there was no time. 'Listen to me. Why did the magistrate want to help you? And how did he know your brother's name? Did you tell him?'

She shook her head. 'I told him nothing, other than that your father...' For the first time, she could not meet my eyes.

This was of desperate importance, and I could not quite admit why, even to myself. 'My father never touched you?'

She lifted her gaze. 'Your father was kindness itself to me. A rare man, and he never laid one finger on me.'

A pressing weight fell away from me at these words. Even as I thought of Esther, and what I would have to face, the relief of knowing my father had not shamed himself, that his name was safe, nourished and sustained me. 'How did—'

Too late. The door swung open and I sat back. Dillon had returned, puce from the sudden heat of a fire and what I presumed was a flagon of very strong ale. He beckoned to Mary. 'Come, lass.'

Mary stood, grimacing with pain. In the morning, her skin would be black and blue. She was dirty and unkempt, dressed like the lowest of serving girls, and still the single most beautiful thing I had ever seen. And then she was gone.

'Manyon's in the jakes,' Dillon said, over his shoulder.

As soon as Dillon closed the door, I rose. I had minutes at most. I began to shuffle through the magistrate's papers, opening one heavy desk drawer at a time. The light was dim, and I did not know what I was looking for. I discarded memoranda, warrants and summonses, records of fines paid and defaulted upon; none of this explained Manyon's sudden change of heart about Mary's fate.

I came to the bottom drawer. Here were some more personal things: bills for satins, quiddanies and quinces, perhaps for Manyon's daughters; a small collection of tiny portraits of young girls I took to be those daughters; and stacks of letters. With these I took more care, looking at the signatures, glancing often at the door and rehearsing excuses in case Manyon returned, not knowing how I would extricate myself if he caught me. But my search was in vain; most of the letters were complaints, or petitions begging for clemency, rather than truly of a personal nature. There was nothing here to give life to my suspicions. Perhaps, anyway, those suspicions were the product of an overtired, frightened mind, which grew wary of everyone and everything.

Yet there was something...

He had been some time. I poked my head out of the door and cocked an ear over the polished banister, down the twisting staircase. The usual milling crowd had gone, yet I could hear people. First Manyon – clearly finished with his bladder – his voice hissing, too quiet, and then another, feminine, still honeyed, but perturbed. I recognised it immediately and ducked quickly to crouch with my face to the bars.

'...what you said a week ago, Magistrate, so why might I believe it now?' More mumbling came from Manyon, then the other said, 'She is a source of considerable income to me, and unless—'

'The girl *will* be returned,' came Manyon's voice, a little more dominant. 'You have my word. I'd thank you not to question it.'

A mocking laugh followed. 'A fine fool I'd be, if I took payment in words after all these years!' Then there was a clinking sound and a satisfied grunt, with low, angry words from Manyon before the swish of a heavy cloak on the tiled floor, and waddling footsteps as she departed.

I had no time for thought. His booted feet sounded on the stairs. Darting into the office, I picked up my coat, baldric and sword, then retreated behind his desk, tripping over legal books and a stray box of candles. I fumbled with the spring catch and eyed the casement; could I squeeze through? I had mere seconds.

I opened the window and, looking out and around, saw nobody. I lowered my sword first, letting it go six feet from the ground, then flung my coat after it, gritting my teeth to inch my shoulders and back through the small opening. I held the snow-speckled frame and walked my feet down the wall. The brick was treacherous, and the drop cost me a painful half-roll in the thickening snow. As I rose to my feet, I put my back to the wall, looked up, and saw an arm protrude to close the window. Good. He would know I was absent, but no more than that.

I stood in the building's shadow. Just ahead of me, the dark was studded with distant lights. Manyon's guest had just left. On a night like this, with snow falling and a fugitive moon, beclouded, she could not be taking a sedan chair back to Norwich – and I could not imagine her riding. No, she had to have a room. But which way? I searched my memory. There were two inns, both offering dining and lodging for travellers; one, the Rose and Crown, lay east of the market cross and was far the superior of the other. Thinking of her flamboyant bolts of cloth and sugared comfits, I almost turned that way, but then

I remembered the filthy rushes on the floor and her eyes like twin beads of enamel-glass, and I realised Lucy Bennett would always be more at home among the sharp, acquisitive men who might take rooms at the Black Swan. I turned west.

I moved swiftly down the middle of the path, where the snow was thinner, using the footsteps of others as my guide. On either side, people hunkered in their shopfront houses, and bright pith-lights gleamed behind shuttered windows. I turned off the main street. Ahead, just three or four hundred yards down this rugged track rendered flush by the snow lay the tavern. Somewhere in between was my quarry. I was certain I was gaining on her.

But the road seemed to go on forever. Peering at a shadow, I reached for my sword, stumbled on a jutting stone and repressed a cry; yet the shadow was nothing, just a flicker of the moon departing an alley. I scanned the lane, glancing at windows and thatches, and my gaze just alighted on a cumbersome shape skulking towards the tavern's back gate. I began to run, aware of the risks of falling or being heard, but knowing I had to catch her. She stopped. No knock sounded. She reached out to push the gate, letting it swing shut as she went through, and I arrived in time to prevent it closing with my gloved hand. I followed, almost on the tips of my toes.

Bathed in the soft back light of the tavern, I heard the merry lilt of a lute over the hum of conversation, which muffled the sound of the gate closing behind me. To my left, a tall pile of barrels shaded the cellar windows, and on the right a beaten ribbon of packed snow and cobbled stone showed the winding way to the bar door. She seemed to have vanished. I took a cautious step. Perhaps I had been a few seconds longer than I had thought and she had gone inside…

A low and hacking cough came from my rear. I spun on my heel and caught a glimpse of a rounded shape behind the snow-mounded barrels, not ten feet away. I nearly moved forward, but felt abruptly menaced; more often than not, when you corner a dangerous creature, you end up bitten. So I said, 'I see you, madam. Come out.' I waited. 'I'm not here to hurt you. Just to talk.'

After a few seconds, a well-wrapped Lucy Bennett emerged, her arm extended. She held a stiletto dagger in her right hand, and her needle-sharp eyes widened in recognition when she saw who had followed her. 'You,' she said. 'I heard you trip. You might have caught me, if you hadn't.'

I did not say that I had caught her now. I did not need to. I had my right hand on the hilt of my sword. Her dagger was bravado; her hand shook, the tip wavered. 'You were at the courthouse,' I said. 'Manyon gave you money. Why?'

'What if I told you he's my uncle, and it's my birthday?' For the first time, I heard a note of something foreign in her voice. It might have been German.

'You want M— Chrissa Moore returned to your house, and he won't release her,' I said, almost thinking aloud, 'and nor should he, to you; but why would he hand over coin?'

She said nothing. But her gaze flicked to the space over my right shoulder, and I turned, too late. The blow came to the back of my right knee, heavy-booted and efficient, and I collapsed in the snow like a tumbled hedgepig. I rolled and saw the second kick coming in towards my face, and caught it on my arms. Had it not been for my leather doublet, it might have broken a bone. I scrambled backwards, trying to catch sight of my assailant, clawing at snow and sharp pebbles. Finally I got up with my back to the flinted tavern wall, snatching at my sword belt, but he rushed me before I could draw, and I found myself locked in a rough stinking embrace, all meaty breath and thatched beard.

His fist struck my underjaw, then more blows rained down like boulders on my kidneys and upper body. He grunted as he tried to trip me, and I realised, like me, he was flailing for his weapon. In the respite from the attack, I drove my knee hard into his groin, then cracked my forehead against his so that the bone exploded with pain. He fell back with a cry, but it did not prevent him unsheathing his blade. It drew the tavern light and glowed back at me like a flame. I produced my own sword and prepared to fight.

My enemy was as thick as an oak tree, muffled in wool and leather so I could not see his face. But he was quick. He had to have been a soldier, though I thought he was too old to be fighting this war. A father, perhaps, of a man by whose side I had fought, or who I had killed. Sometimes age was no disadvantage. My sword arm smarted with the pain of my lesson, having rushed towards my target and underestimated her. I would not make the same mistake again.

But to my surprise, he did not come on. Instead, he looked to his mistress, who appeared to be mulling over her move from the shadows. She glanced behind her at the tavern, and I knew her calculation: if I ended this night splayed on a carpet of blood-drenched snow, questions would be asked, a hue and cry raised. Her name might be known to the landlord, and certainly Manyon knew she was here – even if it was not in his interest to admit it, he might wreak revenge in some other way if his own apprentice was killed. Finally, she spoke. 'Leave him, Will.'

Will, close enough to be within reach of my blade, relaxed his, and shrugged. He took two steps back, but I kept my weapon high as they watched me. I might still die here tonight.

'You thought I was stupid enough to walk these streets without protection?' said Lucy, a sneer in her voice. 'You thought you could follow a woman like me, and do what?'

I coughed and wiped my mouth. There was blood in my spittle. I thought a tooth wobbled. 'Just talk, madam. As I said.'

'Like before? I remember you had quite a bit to say for yourself.'

'I asked you little enough,' I reminded her. 'But things have changed. A woman's life is on the line.'

She took a step nearer. 'And you believe you are owed answers from me?'

'Not owed,' I said. 'But I would have them, nevertheless.'

She almost cooed, 'Look, Will, he's a knight in armour, fighting injustice wherever he finds it. He thinks he's in love. Chrissa's soft quim has addled his mind, more like.' Her companion laughed, and her idling voice hardened. 'Get yourself home, boy, before I change mine.'

Behind us, the tavern music had slowed to a sweeter air. For a moment, I saw her differently, this fat, hardened woman, and imagined what had led her here. 'How old were you?' I asked.

'What?'

'When men first ill-treated you?' She laughed again, but it was an uncertain sound. 'Were they soldiers?'

Her companion was impatient. He had not put away his sword, and now he stiffened his arm again. 'Let's be done with him,' he said, straightforwardly. In his voice, I heard the echo of a hundred soldiers I had known. He would slit my throat, dump me in some godforsaken pond, and return to his dinner with a buoyant appetite.

'Go, Treadwater,' she said. 'Give her up. She's not worth your trouble anyway.'

'What did they do to you?' When she didn't answer, I gambled. 'I've seen it, you see. What soldiers do to women. What they turn them into. I think you were in Bohemia. But your mother, I think she was English.'

'What if she was?'

'Did they kill her?'

'Spitted her like a roasting pig,' she said, indifferently. 'But what is that to you?'

'And turned you into a whore,' I said. 'But when I asked you about Chrissa, and you could have said she took your clients, you didn't.'

'So?'

'You told the truth.'

'Suppose I did?'

'So you might as well tell it now.'

'Ha!' Her mirth was hard-edged. 'You don't lack cheek, boy.'

'No. I lack information.'

'Will you pay for it?'

'I have no money.' This was true. I had left the house without coin.

There was a long pause. The music from the tavern had stopped, and the snow had slowed to an odd, light tickle. Lucy said to her man, 'Will, go on in. Order ale.'

'But…' He looked at me doubtfully.

'I pay you, don't I? Go.'

Grumbling, Will went around the side of the tavern. We were alone. She seemed to know I was no threat, and paced unevenly, her bulk blocking the low moon from view. She moved back and forth, and once or twice muttered to herself. 'Use Huxley,' she said, eventually.

My mind spun frantically. 'To bring pressure to bear on Manyon?'

'That's the one.'

'He's not part of it?'

'Wouldn't know his cock from a sundial. He's a believer, that one. And Manyon needs him – or needs his patronage, anyway. Now,' she said, 'piss off. That's all you'll get from me.'

I moved forward, close enough to look her in the face. Uncertainty shifted there, competing with a subtle satisfaction. 'Thank you,' I said.

'Just let me not see you in Norwich again,' came the reply. 'If I do, I'll cut your face off and use your balls for earbobs.'

I believed it, and nodded, then took my leave. My journey back to the courthouse was thoughtful. Outside the silent building, I scooped snow from the wall into my mouth, spitting it, pink-tinged, on the ground, and straightened my clothing. I didn't bother wiping my boots, and walked sopping wet across the flagstone floor and up the staircase.

Manyon was in his office. 'Where have you been?' he said, but he did not sound irritated. There was still wine on the table; a high, merry fire in the grate. His mood was tolerant, equable.

'Walking,' I said. 'We were standing so long at the green, I needed to stretch my legs.'

He indicated my feet. 'Soaking wet,' he said. 'You should take them off, bring the feeling back. I'll do the same.' He began to tug at the leather tops of his own expensive boots.

'Thank you,' I said, but did not copy him. I did not expect to be here much longer. 'I was wondering, sir, whether you had heard from John Rutherford.'

'No, damn him. There's a mountain of work to do here and yet the boy is absent. Do you know,' he continued, placing one foot atop his knee and beginning to massage the toes, 'that they made the first shoes thousands of years ago – thousands – and yet they still have found no reliable way to make the things waterproof?'

I hesitated no more than a moment. 'I did wonder, sir, whether your leniency towards Mistress Moore was a result of your loyalty to John Rutherford, as your nephew.'

'You might have to draw that line for me,' Manyon said, absently, continuing to press at the soles.

'Well, his choice has fallen upon my sister, and any scandal relating to my father would therefore reflect on him and, by extension, upon you.'

'Come now,' said Manyon. 'I hardly think people would—'

'But then I realised it wasn't that at all.'

'No?' By now, Manyon had detected something new in my tone, and was no longer rubbing his feet through his stockings. He eyed me keenly, over lowered brows. 'Then what was it?'

I cleared my throat. 'She knew you, didn't she?'

He offered me a glass. I shook my head. 'Who knew me?' he said, curiously, before lifting his glass to his lips.

I nearly answered 'Mary', but said, 'Chrissa.'

His forehead moved quizzically. 'Eh? Naturally, she knew me; I'm well known enough.'

'I mean she knew you by sight. From Ramping Horse Lane. Where you visited, and where, I'm sure, the young – the very young – ladies have many colourful memories of your presence.'

He sputtered, and rose to his feet. 'What?'

'You were a customer. Not hers – I suspect, from those pictures I saw in your drawers, she was too old for you anyway. You prefer a more delicate type.'

Manyon's mouth tightened. 'So, it's slander, is it? I never thought it of the son of Richard Treadwater.'

I sloughed off his anger like water. 'Call it what you will. How do you explain it?'

For the first time, Manyon's voice rose. 'I do *not* explain it! How dare you! I am a Justice of this realm and—'

'And if the aldermen of Norwich find that you have been frequenting a house of such dissolute reputation, that's all you will ever be,' I said, brutally. 'And Mistress Moore threatened you with that, didn't she? You would have liked to send her back to that cesspit directly, but she made it known to you that she recognised your face, and would by no means be silent about it, whether you sent her back to Lucy Bennett's, or to the assizes. And you were caught between the Devil and the deep blue sea. You could do nothing: neither proceed to prosecution, nor vindicate her publicly and see her released.

'So, you waited. You waited until it was clear that she was not carrying my father's child, confronted her with that lie, and came to a treacherous bargain, one you never had any intention of fulfilling. Am I correct?'

Manyon's natural tendency towards calculation had reasserted itself, and he was calm. He said, 'What if you are?'

'Then your fine words about releasing the girl are just that, aren't they? Words. You have no intention of letting her out, now or later.'

How much of it was bluff? Some. I was almost certain I was right. Almost. I did not have a single shred of proof, though, and if Manyon gauged this – and there was every chance he might – I would have the grass cut from under me swiftly enough. As it was, I was acutely aware that I was firing the bridge that connected me to Manyon, and to the safe future he represented. If I were lucky, I would walk away from this a free man. If not, as he had hinted with his mention of slander, I might find myself as Mary's neighbour in the cells.

Manyon did not reply straight away. He regarded me from beneath his furrowed brow, reflecting. In the end, he simply said, 'What do you want?'

'The immediate release of Mistress Moore, who is an innocent woman. Your word that you will bring no charges against her. And the fulfilment of your promise that you will see me released from the army. That is all.'

Manyon considered. 'And for those small favours, you will desist with these venomous rumours?' I nodded. He drummed his fingers on the desk. 'And yet,' he continued, with a touch more confidence, 'you have no proof. The testimony of whores, you will appreciate, is a rather tarnished currency, even in these turbulent days.'

'True, but it would make an interesting tale in the taverns. I know every innkeeper from here to Cambridge, and I tell as good a story as the next man. And,' I finished, carefully, 'Welmet

Huxley knows me, now. Thanks to you. He will hear my version of things, and whether he believes you or me, well, we will soon find out.' I waited. With my chin jutting pugnaciously, I probably looked far more confident than I felt.

He eyed me steadily, his mouth twisting in contempt and disbelief. 'You would lose my patronage, and gain custody of a whore?'

My fists tightened below the desk. I said, 'She is no whore.'

After a moment longer, Manyon sighed and his frame relaxed. 'Very well. But do not think to come to me when next you need assistance, boy. You have used up your credit with me. And woe betide that girl if she crosses me again. Make sure she knows it.'

18

The world had become still and silent and, at some point, as I carried Manyon's reluctantly scrawled signature down to the gaol, the clouds had cleared. A low moon lit the way before the horse over the powdered white ground. The fields to either side went on and on, endless and empty, and above in the black, bright-starred sky, late-hunting gulls called out their searching cries as they soared towards the sea. The world might have been made this night, so clean and fresh did it smell and taste.

With Mary's shape before me in the saddle, I felt a strange measure of peace. She had spoken little since Dillon had released her, even when I had related my own story. She seemed used to her own thoughts, her own company. Perhaps that quality had served her well in the gaol. Now she swayed steadily with the horse's movements, her thin dress covered by my cloak. As we passed trees and ditches, all blanketed by snow, still she said nothing. I admired her seemingly endless capacity for silence.

We turned south at White Horse Common. I thought about continuing east for another mile or so and stopping at Rutherford's property, finding out what had befallen the man, but the thought of Esther drove me on. I wished myself home already. The journey was taking twice the time because the horse carried two, and the snow was deeper now.

'I would welcome your story,' I said, eventually, as we followed the river's course away from Walsham, towards the sea. 'All has been confusion since I returned to my home, and truth would pierce the mists.'

Tension entered her back and shoulders. Then, she spoke in a low voice. 'The tale is one I scarce believe myself. I hardly think you will credit it.'

Her mistrust was entirely fair. I had not valorised myself with my earlier conduct towards her. I said, 'Have I not shown you otherwise, through my actions? I have been a disbelieving fool; but now is the time for credulity, I think.'

'Very well,' she said. 'Where would you like me to begin?' Her tone remained clipped and wary. Despite the openness of her words, she did not trust me.

'At the beginning. Your beginning. Where are you truly from?'

'London. My father was a freeman of the Blacksmiths' Company. He made tower clocks. He was a skilled smith. When I was born and when I was younger, my family lived well.'

'What was his name?'

'Edward Moore. We lived in Southwark. I remember the bullbaiting, the dogs taking the bull by the nose and clinging on until… Well, you know how that goes. I hated that. But I don't remember much more. We left when I was nine or so, and moved out beyond Clerkenwell, because my father feared the plague. He was right to fear it. He took ill the following year, and so did my mother. Both were gone within days. Henry was a babe in arms. I was a child. My father… well, he left little of worth; he gambled away most of his property. That sundial, the one Henry carries about with him, only escaped being sold because he had given it me for my birthday. I was ten.'

Her matter-of-fact tone hid pain. 'How did you live?' I asked.

For a moment, when Mary had mentioned the plague and its terrible cost, I had remembered Elizabeth. With a stab of melancholy, I realised it was as I had thought before – I could no longer bring her face to mind. What I'd believed to be love had turned out to be no more than infatuation. Nearly all had suffered under the pestilence. Not only the dead. Families were scattered, decimated, whole villages abandoned. The bonds that had glued together close kin and neighbours were disintegrated. Mary's words brought an understanding of how she had inherited her chaotic life, not chosen it, and a rush of hot shame for having leapt to the conclusions I had.

'I begged,' Mary said, simply, in answer to my question. 'I held on to Henry and I begged. For a while, that served a purpose. But he got bigger, people's sympathy waned, the trickle of money grew thin, and suggestions as to how I should feed him became less palatable.' She shrugged. 'So I developed other skills.'

'What skills?'

She was quiet for a few moments, perhaps deciding how honest to be. 'My father taught me a great deal about iron, and balance wheels and the complex mechanisms that make them strike. I found that I was able to turn that knowledge to a different purpose.'

That was another surprise. 'What purpose?'

'I became a picklock.' When I, astounded, did not reply, she laughed. 'Yes, I was a thief. London would not do for my trade. It was too busy. I would have been caught in an instant. So, Henry and I moved about, and I sought the houses of gentry and the richer sort of farmer – houses like your own. Eventually, I came to Norwich. I looked for accommodation, but it was difficult, with Henry in tow. Then Lucy offered us a roof.

'She wanted something from me, of course, in return, but I would not part my legs for the scurvy men she called customers. I told her what I could do, that my price for half of my income was her care of Henry, that she would keep him from harm when I was away, and when I returned that we would have bed and board there. I offered her an invented name in the hope that, one day, Henry and I could leave, and go back to our lives without the stain of her house on us.'

'She kept to her bargain?'

'Mostly. She was constantly telling me how "her men", as she called them, had made offers for me. How a "clean" girl would satisfy men like that lecherous fool Manyon, who found their desires impossible to repress but feared the pox, or the French disease. But I was not to be her plaything, or theirs. I saw the potions and tinctures forced upon the other girls, to try to cover the damage. I saw the babies born sick and dying early, and I would have none of it.'

'You preferred, instead, to steal from others?' I spoke mildly, trying to keep the sting of judgement from my words.

'Preferred?' she repeated, with a harder laugh. 'Preferred creeping into the houses of the rich, silencing their guard dogs with meat and false affection, running from night watchmen who happened upon an open door? The risk of hanging? Yes. Yes, I preferred it to the stinking embrace of man upon man, and an early, beggarly death. Who wouldn't? Hold your hand before you judge me. Besides, I wanted something else. A different life for Henry, and I was saving for it. I was quite willing to put down my picklock, but I needed enough to support him first.'

Even then, she had a unique ability to make me feel small, though she has used it rarely enough over the years. I coloured. 'I apologise, Mary. Your choices are your business.'

'No, they are also yours,' she said. 'It was because I planned to rob your home that I ended up living in it.'

'Ah. This is where my father comes into the story.' My voice broke slightly. I felt her shift in the saddle, as if aware of the keen edge of my grief.

'Yes. He caught me.'

'What?'

'My usual way of going about it, so to speak, was to wait until the whole house slept. Men retire early in these times, so it was simple enough to take a position in the grounds and wait for dark. Your father had a good strong lock on the back door to the house, but one of my keys fitted well enough.'

'You do it with different keys? I've always wondered how picklocks manage their tricks.'

She shrugged. 'Oh, there is scarcely a trick to it. There are only so many designs for locks. Carry enough keys with you, it's nearly guaranteed one of them will fit. The skill is in the stealth. Well, I entered the house and searched the downstairs, and found little of value, except a strongbox key. And many keep a strongbox beneath their beds. It was a risk. But I had come a long way. Too far to turn back.'

I remembered the keys beneath Father's bed. I had not known at the time what they were for. Now another piece of the puzzle aligned.

I said, 'It's hard to believe you can enter a man's bedroom without him noticing.'

'It's not hard at all. If a man snores loudly enough, he usually sleeps deeply.'

'But you did wake my father?'

'No. My mistake was to think him in bed to begin with. I realised as soon as I went in that he was not there, and tried to get out, but he caught me.'

'What did he do?'

She paused. 'This part shames me. More than the rest.'

'Why?'

'Your father knew I would hang if he delivered me to the constable. And so, he did not. Instead, he lit lamps, heated cider, gave me bread from his own table, and he sat down and talked to me of the goodness of God, and the place of everything in existence in His creation.' Her voice wavered with these words, and I was hardly less affected. A hot lump rose in my throat. Pressure built, then tears came unbounded. I tried to hold them in, but she turned in the saddle to see me sniffing. I apologised again. 'He was the kindest man I ever met,' she said, softly. 'Of course you miss him.'

'What happened then?' I said, staring ahead at the crescent moon, finding something to focus on that was not an absence, or a fear.

'He offered me honest work, and a place to stay. I refused at first, not believing anybody could make such an offer without other motive, but again he spoke of service, service to God's Word and will. He said God loved me. He said there was a reason he had acquired a thirst and risen from his bed that night, and found me, and if I did not stay, then perhaps I would be working against God's plan for me. So I accepted.'

'But you left Henry at Lucy Bennett's?'

'I could not presume upon your father's kindness further. He had already been so good to me. He paid me a fair wage. He said nothing to anybody, not even your sister, of the circumstances in which he took me on. I could not ask him to take Henry as well. I sent my wage to Lucy, and saved a tiny amount, hoping, at some point, to reclaim him, and find somewhere decent together.'

Finally, I could ask, 'And what of Esther?'

'It's hard to…'

'We must have truth now,' I said, simply.

Mary nodded. 'Yes, I see that. She did me no wrong, not at first. I could see she was unhappy with my presence; that was natural enough, I suppose. She was worried for her father, worried I had somehow gulled him, and I think she was confused. She asked questions, and I said I'd travelled from London to look for work, which was true, in one way. But I don't think she believed me. And your father's regard for me made her very jealous.'

'She was cruel to you, then?' I thought of the monstrous voice – indeed, the thought of it had hardly left my head since hearing it – and wondered whether Mary had had to listen to it, too.

Carefully, weighing her words, Mary said, 'I wouldn't say that. She was quiet, very pious, exactly as your father had described her to me. But I began to feel that all was not as it should have been.'

'Why not?'

'Little things. She spied on me. I often felt that she was watching me at my rest. She was vigilant; yet, sometimes, when I spoke with her, she would seem to be elsewhere, miles and miles away. I would ask a question about the day's work and she would appear not to have heard me. When I entered her room to clean, there was a smell, like you get inside a shell. I could find no source for it. And the dog would go nowhere near her, nor the horses. Joan avoided her, too, if she could.'

'Did Joan tell you why?'

'Not straight away. She was very shy. But eventually, she told me Esther – though she had not always felt this way about her – made her feel cold. That she made her think about all the bad things she had done. She told me to visit her at night, when she slept, and I would see things.'

'What things?'

'She would say no more. She only told me to watch her. And so I did. I could move about the house without being heard, you see, so I opened her door and... Excuse me, I...'

'And what?'

She took a deep breath. 'You must have the truth now. Too much has passed... I opened her door, and found her in the grip of some sort of fit. Words escaped her that I did not understand, in a language I do not know. And noises as if from the pit of Hell itself.'

I'd heard such sounds, had denied them to myself, preferring to believe my sister only dreamt. 'Did you go to my father?'

'How could I?' she asked, with gentle scorn.

'I understand.' Mary had been taken in out of Richard Treadwater's charity. She could not begin throwing accusations at his daughter. 'Still, I would have thought Joan would have told her mother, or someone. Or my father. Surely, someone could have…'

'She was that afraid. We both were. It's perhaps a hard thing for you to appreciate: the difference between someone making a claim against women like me, or Joan – poor women, who can't defend themselves – and when the person is of your station in life. Nobody would have believed us.'

'I can't argue with that,' I said, grimly.

'We knew we had to make our own defences. So we buried blessings in the four corners of the orchard. We carved daisy chains at the bottoms of the doorframes, where they might not be noticed.'

'Charms against witches?'

'Yes.'

I sighed. 'I fear they were useless. She is no witch. The malignancy that possesses her has some other origin. But go on.'

'I wanted to protect your father, as he had protected me. I started to spend more time with him. I admit I played on his fondness for me, allowing him to see me almost as another daughter. I stayed by his side always, to ensure nothing of her evil could affect him. But I think I erred. Esther's feelings began to turn to hatred.'

'What did she do?'

'She began to shadow me about the house, always in my wake. She accused me of taking little trinkets she kept in her room. One day, she called me "witch", and I knew trouble was coming. I told Joan to play along, pretend to believe the claims against me.

Joan could not afford to lose her position. She was a simple girl – it would be easier for her to make out that I had led her astray.'

'And then they came for you,' I said. She nodded. 'Was my father still well?'

'Yes. When they came to take me, he argued with Esther. He said her accusations were made from spite, that she must withdraw them, or he would hold her to have shamed him before the whole community. She was devastated. I honestly believe...' Mary paused, as if trying to work out exactly what she thought. 'I honestly believe she had no idea that what she was saying was not true.'

'Did you tell this story to Manyon, at the gaol?'

'No,' she said, definitely. 'Nothing good could come of telling people what I had seen, or what I had done. They would say we were all witches together. And I could not afford for anyone to scrutinise my past. My hope was to outlast Esther's claim, that it would come apart through lack of proof.'

'As it did, in the end. But not before you had to suffer through Manyon's duplicity. I'm sorry for it.' Thinking of her bruised skin and tortured feet, I had to resist the temptation to tighten my arms around her.

Her voice throbbed with disdain as she said, 'Him? He's a purse-bothering little thorough-cough.'

Then I was laughing, suddenly, inappropriately. Realising how long it had been since I had felt mirth, I said, 'I suspect you didn't use such wealthy language in front of my father!'

She giggled, quietly. 'No – no, I did not.' Then she said, more seriously, 'But I don't think Manyon will be our main problem, now.'

'We might have to fear his vengeance,' I said, forgetting levity. 'And besides, the problems of my family are not yours. Where will you go?'

Her shoulders sagged. 'I don't know.'

I hesitated before speaking, not daring to hope she would agree. 'If you can bear it, you and Henry, you may stay on as long as you have a mind to.'

'Let us get there first,' she said. 'And then we will see.'

But what would we see? As we forded the river, the elusive peace that had arrived in Mary's presence took wing again and fled. Each yard we covered took us further from one defeated menace, but nearer another, one much greater, with everything about it veiled in uncertainty.

19

Even as we passed through the gate and I helped her dismount on the pathway before the house, Mary demanded to be taken to her brother. 'I want to see him right away,' she said.

'Wait,' I counselled. 'It's pitch-dark, and you're barefoot and freezing. Let me get a light, and see what I can find for your feet.' I eyed the house uneasily as I spoke. I dreaded going in, but it had to be done. The snow was not deep, and both of us knew the way even in the dark, but I was beginning to worry Mary would suffer frostbite.

'I'll come in,' she said. She was — and remains — a woman of sound courage. I agreed, gratefully.

In the dark shade of the building, as I unlocked the door, I looked up at Esther's room. I was just able to make out her window. Nothing moved, at least nothing I could see. But I knew she was there. It was not my vision that told me those malignant eyes were on me. I felt it in my soul.

Inside the house, agitation scudded through my stomach, my legs, my veins. My body seemed to have been hoarding fear, only to release it, howling, as soon as I crossed the threshold. It was only Mary's stoical presence by my side that prevented me running back out into the cold.

We found lights, and a pair of old patten shoes behind the back door. I plundered the chest in the hall again and came up with a man's waistcoat that, although it would not make her really warm, might keep off the worst of the chill. As I searched, she shifted at the bottom of the staircase, craning her neck to see the landing. 'She's up there?' she asked, and I heard fear in her voice, matching my own.

'I locked her in her room,' I said. 'With a key.'

'What about the window?'

'There was no time,' I answered, troubled. 'But I'll have to do something, otherwise...'

Mary was looking hard at me. 'She could get out?' I nodded, bleakly. 'What would she do?'

I closed the chest. 'I don't know. I can't be certain what the creature is capable of. But I think... I think if she is allowed her freedom, before I can find someone – something – that might bring her back to herself... I believe more people will die.'

'It's horrible,' Mary said, disbelievingly. 'I've never heard of anything like this.'

'Nor I,' I said, passing her the shoes and waistcoat. We went back out into the snow, and the vice-like tension in my gut lessened slightly. I could breathe again.

Henry was sleeping, curled up in the straw in the stables, when his sister found him. She did not speak, but her fingers grazed his hair, and when he woke, for several minutes he cried on her shoulder, saying he had thought her return a dream. 'I'm no dream,' she said, holding him close. 'And I won't leave you again. Ever.'

'Are we to go back to Norwich, now?' Henry asked.

But Mary glanced at me, her eyes hooded and doubtful. 'I don't know, Henry,' she said. 'There is much to decide.'

Henry's expression was guilty as he looked up. 'Mr Treadwater has been very kind to me. I wouldn't want to leave, except...' Mary appeared helpless, torn in two. She said nothing, and simply rubbed his hands between her own, avoiding his gaze.

I cleared my throat. 'You're welcome to stay on here, as I said. More than welcome.' This was true. I desperately wanted her to say she would, so great was my fear of being alone with Esther, with that voice. 'But...'

I didn't know if it was best for Henry to remain here. I decided it was not my decision to make. He was not my brother. Their prospects, I had to admit, were not favourable. Where would they go if they left? It was the dead of winter. Even now, armies were marauding across the heart of England. Though she could return to Norwich, and I would escort her there safely if she wished it, Lucy Bennett's house was little better than a poxy midden, not a place a small boy should be brought up, or where a woman would be safe, even if the procuress could be persuaded to take her back. Yet Mary would find no work or refuge in Walsham either. Too many people here feared and hated her now, and she had made powerful enemies; the magistrate, Hale, and especially Huxley, might find other grounds to arrest her if she came to their attention again. Manyon's last words had made that clear.

Before I could suggest that we talked out of Henry's hearing, Mary turned back to her brother. 'We'll stay, for now,' she said, soothingly. 'But I will think of what to do next. Don't be afraid. I'm here now, and nothing is going to happen to you.' She gave him a reassuring smile and he rested his head on her shoulder. It was like watching a mother cat settle her kitten, as she allowed him to curve into her, sheltering him beneath her chin.

I gave them their privacy, leaving them the lantern, and returned to the house, following the wayward curves of our footprints across the garden.

In the days that followed, without Father to manage the finances and tenants, and without Esther to take care of the household matters – the chickens, the vegetable plot, the greenhouse, the cooking and the cleaning – I realised how privileged I had been, and how many things a young man of good family might take for granted. The list of tasks that now dominated my thoughts was long.

Before anything else, my task was to keep Esther secure. It should have been a relief that she didn't struggle against her captivity in any physical way. But it wasn't. It felt like the edge of battle, knowing my enemy would strike, but not how, or when.

Her eyes followed me each day as I entered with food and drink. She ate the food and watched impassively as I emptied the chamber pot. It was Mary's idea for me to muffle my ears with a scarf, so I would not hear the creature's poisoned tongue. We took other measures, removing the means to light candles and anything that might be used as a weapon. On the first day after my return from Walsham, I climbed a ladder outside the house and nailed thickset boards across the window. It felt abysmally cruel as I hammered the iron-wrought pegs deep into the stone-work, but I could not take the chance of them loosening. When I had done, the boards created a solid lattice over the shutters, and withstood my strongest efforts to dislodge them, from inside and out.

Unobtrusively, in the days following her arrival, Mary began to assist me. She was not a servant any more, exactly, and although I was beginning to wonder in what light I should see her, she avoided discussions of the longer term. She willingly shouldered any work that needed to be done, but she had what Father would have called egalitarian ideas, as she divided the work of preparing a meal between the three of us on the second day, and then, on the third, looked over my shoulder at the accounts, asking questions and offering ideas. I liked it.

It was late evening in the week after Mary's release, and we were in my father's study. I supposed it was my study now, but I could not think of it as such. It was too soon. In just a few short weeks, my whole life had changed, and although the little room and its library looked the same, with the same fire in the grate, the same sturdy lintel over the door, nothing was as it had been.

Earlier, the three of us, I, Henry and Mary, had made food together, and now we sat about the desk eating salted fish and stored potatoes, drinking small beer. It felt like a confederacy, a tiny conspiracy. At any moment, I joked, I expected to hear the rat-tat on the front door of the King's men, come to remove us to the Tower.

'How did your mother die?' Mary asked. She could be blunt, more so than any woman I have ever met, but I found I did not mind.

'In childbed. I was young, and I do not remember it.'

'She was dark like you,' Mary said, nodding to the wall behind, where a portrait was hung of my mother, painted when she was a young bride.

It was a sombre painting, and I had never liked it, preferring my many imaginings of a more joyful girl. My mother wore a simple fallow dress and white collar, with her black hair scraped high off her long neck. She had dark eyes. Her nose was short and rounded, her lips pressed together in a line. She might have been pretty in life, but she was not pretty in this picture. She looked kind, though, and I think they had been happy together. I supposed she did look like me. It was true that I had inherited my colouring from both my father and my mother, whereas Esther had none of my looks. When we were younger, I had joked that she was a Saxon, my Saxon sister.

The fire was not drawing properly and the room was webbed with smoke. I opened a window and moved a stack of books away from the heat.

Mary looked about the small library. 'Your father kept all his papers here?'

I nodded. I would need to sort through the documents in Father's desk at some point. So far I had avoided the task, baulking at the thought of putting things to one side as rubbish, or coming across some treasured, unimportant thing that could not fail to move me. 'Yes. I've been meaning to go through some of it.'

'Why not make a start now?' she said. 'Henry and I can clear these things away.'

'There's no need.' I did not want her to attend on me.

Her voice was firm. 'We'll do our part. Besides, the task might distract you.' She didn't name the reason, but both of us looked towards the ceiling.

I agreed. I was reluctant to begin, but she was right. It had to be done.

Henry watched with curiosity as I produced a key and unlocked the drawers of my father's desk one by one, taking out parchments and ledgers, letters and pamphlets. Each item had a place, with everything arranged by type and then chronology. I thought fondly of the many nights Father had spent here, curating and studying, reading tracts from the Continent sent to him by friends in more radical towns. For a moment, as my hand closed around a history of the Hellenistic philosophies, I remembered his enthusiasm – his passion – for all types of knowledge, and felt a twist of mortification at how little value I had placed upon it myself. Then, pulling at the next drawer, I realised it was stuck and began to wiggle it about, trying to dislodge whatever was causing the bother.

Mary cleared the dishes, handing the bread to Henry. 'Take this through, Henry,' she said. 'Let's allow Mr Treadwater a bit of peace.'

'Henry can call me Thomas,' I said, stretching towards the back of the drawer and grabbing on to something jammed in a crack in its base. I tugged on it. 'I'd like it if you would, too.' I dragged the paper into the light.

'Thomas, then,' said Mary. I looked up, and saw the shadow of a smile. I had not seen her wear such an expression before, and wondered at its loveliness. It took the cares from her face.

'Don't feel you have to stay in the kitchen,' I said, looking away at the paper, so I did not stare. 'Use the parlour if it's more comfortable.'

The paper, a little crumpled from the drawer, was five or six separate pieces of parchment, unfolded, all covered in Father's tight, neat hand. I put the pages under the candle and squinted down at them. Mary and Henry were about to leave the room, but stopped when I, having begun reading, said, 'Wait.'

Mary stood in the doorway with Henry behind her, until I beckoned to them again. 'I think I have something, but...'

As was my habit, I had gone straight to the end of the document, checking for a name or clue as to exactly what I had in hand. There it was – my father's signature and, just above, a short summation: *Taken down by my hand on 16th August in the year of Our Lord 1628, in the presence of Johannes Janssen, previously of the sea-going vessel the* Guldern, *and also my kinsman, John Milton.*

I felt a sudden tightness in my chest. Milton. My tutor. The man whose resentment had sent me to war.

I returned to the head of the first page, and read what followed.

We were late. The *Guldern* had been at sea five wretched months. We had lost the convoy weeks before. The waves and gales moved against us, so less experienced men moaned pitifully and emptied their bellies over the side of the ship. This was the Kattegat strait, off the coast of Anholt, Denmark, in late winter, with darkening skies, narrow and treacherous, full of reefs and sandbanks, shallow enough that we winced like boys every time the helmsman dragged on the whipstaff, and I prayed to St David, for my sins. I beg your pardon, knowing you folk round here don't hold with that but... that's the truth, and there it is.

We had to put in, or as near to the island as we could. There were coves where we could wait out the storm, but too close, we all knew, and we would flounder, and our flooded bones would join their fellows on the seabed. It was a near thing in the end. The captain, a massive blubbering fellow, called us dogs, we called him the son of a whore, and he called on us to 'Pull! Pull!' I closed my eyes and thought of my Lysbeth, her freckled face, my promise to return, her dimpled flesh...

I looked up. 'Perhaps it is better, after all, if Henry does not read this,' I said.

'I won't be left alone,' Henry insisted, horror flooding his face.

'No, brother,' said Mary. 'I'll take you to the kitchen, and Thomas may come to find us when he is ready.' She closed the study door behind them.

I bent my neck to the ceiling. There, again: her slow, pacing walk, the pressure of her heels on the floorboards amplified to an agonising moan, playing on my nerves until they shredded.

I looked back down at the page.

We were going to wait, said the skipper, but some muttered about silver guilders, and others, like me – I'm a poor man, and there's no word in the Bible I know of against trying to change that – of goods: silk, spices and wine. God's will, but the doomed ship could've been carrying untold treasures. The law of salvage allowed for... But the skipper broke through. No man was to leave the *Guldern*. Any who tried would be had up for mutiny, keelhauled, then broken on the wheel, then his right hand would be separated from his body, and then he'd hang. Bastard meant it, as well.

We anchored. The storm hit before dark. The sea rocked us, the timbers complained. The men were crammed in stinking quarters, open-eyed and sour-bellied. Those that needed to shit over the bowsprit had to wait, so the gun deck hummed with a pestilential stink worse than normal. A lad of eighteen, with kinking red hair and droopy eyes, talked of ill-omens, saying he'd seen an albatross in the wake of the ship. A hulking German next to us growled (I understood him – my mother was from Saxony): 'There are no albatross in the Kattegat, or the Skagerrak, or the whole of the Baltic Sea. And anyway, they're lucky. Idiot carrot top.' Several men laughed, me along with them. The boy was quiet then. But we all thought of bad auguries. Couldn't help it, in that place. There was something about it that had us all in a lather – lying together like mangy goats in the dark, thinking of grizzly things. But some thought of money as well.

Those nearest heard me say it, and I'll tell no lie of it now; that ship was going down, probably with a fortune in goods. My friends and me decided it was worth the risk. If the skipper meant what he said – and we thought the villain more likely to board it in the morning with his cronies and take what he could himself – we would bend his neck, otherwise he might be persuaded to take a fair share and keep his mouth shut. If we had to, we could nab the officers and seal them in their cabins, perhaps sail our own longboat to Grenaa, and win passage to Hamburg, or London. It would mean leaving Lysbeth, but I would be rich, so there would be other wenches, and so far I had been with the Company four years, and all I had to show for it were fewer teeth than when I started, and smellier wind. All night, in whispers beneath the gale, I drummed up support.

But in the morning the sky had cleared, and the ship was still afloat. And now the skipper had changed his mind. We were to board, seize goods, rescue any survivors, and load them on the *Guldern*. He repeated: any man hiding even a grain of rice would be in irons until port. I wasn't scared of him. I was well muscled, and better-fed then than you see me now, despite the puny ship rations.

We were twelve: the skipper, his mate, the bastard owner – he wasn't going to miss the chance to line his pockets – and the rest of us common men, from five or six different places – Poland, Germany, Scandinavia, Russia. We couldn't all understand each other, but it was colder than the Devil's ice-house, so no one wanted to talk. I noticed the German from the night before, and the red-headed lad. The skipper gave orders – goods first, men later. He gave snaphance guns to those who could use them, and that meant me. The rest had cudgels. We took grappling hooks and ropes.

Boarding her was easy. We used the hooks to attach ropes and knock up a ladder. Then we scaled up to the main deck. We looked about, seeing how much water the vessel had taken on. Working out how long she had left.

I've never thought of myself as a brave man, nor am I going to try to convince you gentlemen otherwise now, but I confess I was greedy, so I stepped forward when most were still standing against the gunwale. I moved into a silence deeper than anything I had known, thicker than in church. The others held back. Even the skipper seemed spooked. But he gathered his courage – he had to – saying the crew must have got off. It didn't calm our jitters. 'Search the ship,' he ordered. Pointing to me and the redhead, he said, 'You two, the stern decks.'

The stink was the first thing. The boy lingered behind, so I went first, down to the aft cabin. There was a mewling as soon as the door opened: a cat – a mangy, skeletal thing – shot from under a table out on to the deck. I heard it squeal as someone kicked it away. Otherwise, the cabin was full of furs and cushions and rugs, and expensive instruments. But I got a whiff of something noxious and over-ripe, like meat left out in the sun. It wasn't bilge – it was decay.

The table was occupied. Two men slumped in their chairs. One had his chin squatting on his chest, but the other stared at me out of a pockmarked face. They had wrapped themselves in the thickest furs I'd ever seen – they looked like trappers waiting to get off and fill their chests with bear skins. It was queer. The ship was holed, but they should've had a chance. Were they dead before the ship was wrecked? Were they sore diseased, with some invisible plague?

Behind me, the lad was gagging. He pulled on my sleeve, muttering something about evil miasmas. I ignored him. There was something… The cabin had a door at the back that was closed, and I felt I needed to open that door. Then came the cry, high-pitched and keening. I moved further in and the boy let go of my sleeve. He clamped a hand over his mouth against disease and ill-providence. He snivelled that I was mad, then he ran.

I passed the bodies. They were not the first I'd seen. There were no injuries on their faces, and I guessed them to have been dead at least a day, not more than two. Perhaps, like I'd thought, they'd succumbed to plague or some other evil, but their skin was smooth like marble, without scabs or lesions, or marks from the cat's teeth. I ignored the temptation to rifle through their pockets. There was such a thing as poking fate.

The noise got louder. I wondered whether another cat might be trapped back there. As I stepped forward, I stumbled, because the ship was dipping on the port side. Everything shifted, bodies and instruments crashed to the floor and the table slid the span of a man's arms across the cabin. The corpses hit the deck and skidded towards me. I regained my footing and pushed on the door, opening it on to a black, cold space. The smell here was different — urine, I thought. But the noise had stopped.

Now my steps were taken downhill, the ship was so tilted. Riches, treasure, plunder — all of a sudden they were will-o'-the-wisps, phantoms. There was something else here, something that breathed and whimpered, something still alive. I groped like a blind man. With my snaphance in my right hand, I took another step.

'Johannes! Where are you?' It was the skipper.

'Light!' I called. 'Bring a light in here!'

'We're getting off. This thing is full of the dead. Get out and...' His sentence tailed off as cries rose up again in the blackness around us. 'What's that?' He came in the door, and his light revealed the corners of the room. There were no furnishings or furs — just bare wooden walls and, in a basket with two handles, close to the hull, an infant.

It had pulled itself up against the sides, so I could just see its fuzzy-topped head and fat hands clutching the wicker, and hear the noises from its mouth. I don't know much about babies, being the youngest surviving son of my mother, but I guessed it to be less than eight months old.

I put the paper down and pictured the scene. A child, alone in the dark with only the dead for company, breathing air redolent with the scent of decay, so cold it must have threatened to freeze its small body solid. How had it survived? What had killed its mother?

Not all my questions had answers in the cramped lines, but I read on, and ten minutes later sat back again, rubbing sore eyes. An unbelievable tale. A testimony to madness. It was difficult to believe Father had thought it worth writing down, or of doing so in the presence of a witness. Let alone a witness like Milton, who was hardly going to believe such a story any more than I did myself. Yet, still, my father was no fool. If he had thought this worth recording and keeping, there was a purpose to it. And I felt it deep down in my stomach; somehow, it was relevant. I just had to find out how.

I went back to the point at which the account became fantastical. I pored over the words again. One way or another, I had to make head or tail of this puzzle.

It reached for me. The boards were shifting beneath my feet – I had to get out. But I couldn't leave the mite there. I grabbed it. Its fingers closed round my hands and it clawed at my neck and face. It wasn't crying, just sticking to me like a limpet.

Then something rocked us, struck us off the starboard side and under the keel. I nearly fell, but just managed to hold my footing. The ship was going down.

There came a noise like a scraping along the underside of the boat, then something splitting apart. I clung to the doorframe with one arm, and the child and the gun with the other. Through the doors there was panic. The ship was leaning heavily, and the men had begun to slew and tumble down the deck. The skipper had drawn, and was aiming at something beyond the gunwale on the listing side, though I couldn't see what, but he lost his footing and, although he was able to grab the mast, the weapon fell into the sea.

The other men cursed and clawed the deck for anything to hold. I kept to the side, holding the gun ports and rigging, edging my way towards the ladder and the pilot boat. When I skidded, I lunged for the foremast and wrapped my legs around it. Another mighty blow hit the ship and I nearly came loose; my gun was gone, but I was able to unbutton my jerkin and shove the infant inside as it thrashed and screamed.

I saw poor carrot top lose his grip. He cried 'Mercy!' as he went over the side. The owner, both arms still wrapped round the mainmast, might have reached out to grab him but didn't. Instead, he and the skipper abandoned their mast, letting themselves slide towards the ladder. They were getting off. I was going with them.

Then… My good fellows, I'm just a sailor, and one who has had a cup too much to drink. You might not be set to believe anything I say that I saw, but I tell you by my troth that I did. And it was then that I saw it.

It reared up twenty or more feet from the water: a huge head, like a rattlesnake's, but hundreds of times more massive, with a blackbeard mane. Most of its body was green, but here and there, in patches, it was mulberry. It was red and bruised where it had struck the ship. Clingfish and urchins gathered on its skin, and some parts of it bled. I dared not look to its eyes, but saw its mouth gape as it thrashed, aiming its maw at the mast. If I screamed, I am not ashamed to admit it. I watched as the great, mindless leviathan, dredged from the deep places of the world, wrapped the coils of its upper body about the forecastle, and as it fell, and crashed, it uttered a nightmare sound I never wish to hear again. The impact dislodged me. I fell from the deck with the infant, over the gunwale, into the sea.

The shock nearly took me. Now you see me starving, these last months of my life given to keeping this child alive, but then I was strong. I kicked my way to the surface and came up near the rowboat. I don't know how, but I scrambled over her side. The child had swallowed water and I shook and hit it until it choked it up. It was screaming. The German was in the water. I pulled him aboard, and as the ship floundered, we each took an oar. We watched the ship as we rowed.

The demon's coils tightened. It used its bulk to crush the forecastle, squeezing bit by bit until the whole thing cracked like kindling. How big it was, I couldn't say. Some of its length stuck out of the water, but whether all, I don't know. Its jaws ground out a diabolical sound as it smashed up the deck. As we rowed for our lives, it broke the ship in two, and half of it sank with the monster beneath the waves. The rest followed within minutes.

The child watched, too. She did not cry.

My head ached. I read again the short declaration at the bottom of the page, saw my father's name, and that of my old tutor, and it ached more.

Sea beasts. Foundlings. What was this about? Why had Father written this story down in the first place, let alone kept it all these years?

I checked the year. 1628. The account – if not the events of the account, which I could not believe were real – was just under sixteen years old.

She.

She did not cry.

Esther.

Esther was just over sixteen years old.

How I wished I could have my father seated before me, if only for a few moments, to share his mind with me, to illuminate these shadowy corners of the past. But the ferryman turns not from his course, nor the world back upon itself. We were alone.

And of course, it had to be, could be no other way, in a world this topsy-turvy, that the one man who might have answers to offer would be the one with the least reason to give them: John Milton.

20

'What do you remember about your youth?' I asked.
I had not secured her to the chair again. I hated to see how the rope chafed her skin, leaving angry red welts that had now faded to purple. Esther didn't seem to mind whether she was bound or not. I suspected it was a small matter to whatever consciousness now held sway inside her. Her eyes were shut, and she gave no sign she had even heard my question. The evening light played pink upon her cheeks. She did not seem tired; but I was so exhausted I questioned whether I was in a dream, thinking I might wake up on the eve of Newbury, terrified of battle, but with an enemy I could fight.

I said, 'I remember little of your babyhood. I have clearer memories of you as a girl of five or six, but before that... Is there anything you can tell me? Anything that does not seem to you as it should have been?'

This was useless. It was the third time of asking, but it felt like talking to a statue. Nothing I said, if addressed to Esther and not to the *thing* inside her, seemed to have any effect at all.

Yet I did not wish to talk to *it*. Its words were lies. Its voice was a claxon sounding damnation. To engage it was to fall.

I thought of the events of the day just passed. I had woken early, knowing a neglected errand awaited me, and could not be left longer. Once the usual jobs of the morning were completed, I mounted Ben and took my leave of Mary and Henry. After explaining the importance of what I had to do, I chose an eastward path, riding into the sun. The journey over the fields on the hard-ridged soil felt like a release. There were raptors on the wing over the hedgerows, the fleeing tails of rabbits in the distance, and a wide pale sky above, with the clouds barely stirring.

I traced a route through Honing, where John Rutherford's small house stood near the blacksmith's forge. I knocked on the door and waited. When no answer came, I walked around to the back and found the door unlocked. After hesitating a few moments, I entered, calling Rutherford's name.

Several hours later, I picked my weary way back across the fields. I knew now why Rutherford had not attended the dinner at Huxley's, why he had been absent from Mary's ordeal outside St Nicholas's. I wished I could hand back the knowledge, for it was a poisoned chalice.

Before I reached home, I stopped at the church.

This was not our church. My father preferred the bigger congregation of Walsham, and he detected here, he had said, a whiff of the old ways, something left over from the corrupt days of monks and pardoners. It might have been something to do with rumours of a tiny priest's hole, a storm shelter carved into the thick walls of the squat, square tower. I had always loved the idea of this secret feature, and, as a child, often imagined myself having the run of it, laying my head beneath its whispering stones. Not that I was ever allowed to.

As I approached the little, walled graveyard, I reflected that I had always preferred it to the elegance of the greater churches at Worstead and Walsham. It was little to do with holiness. I liked the quiet, the peace.

The church was never heated, and the plain, colourless panes allowed in only a partial light, overshadowed by the ancient quatrefoils. I felt a chill as I opened the door, but it was nothing compared to the cold which had already set in my bones since visiting Honing. I came to my knees before the table in the tiny

Lady Chapel. There was no statue of the Virgin, now, of course. According to my father, there had been a lavish side altar in the days of his grandfather, but that had long been replaced by a simple communion table, its inscription carved in gold on green, speaking of its purpose: a place at which all could partake in the Body and the Blood of Christ.

I had never felt spiritual, not though my father had told me we were blessed by God, not though Esther had tried to persuade me, and not though Milton had done his best to extract some proper sentiment from me through means of rote repetition and hour upon hour of Bible study, until the words lived of their own accord in my head, whether I wanted them there or not. The mysteries of the service had eluded me. Occasionally, I had wondered whether I would have felt differently, had I been born a century earlier, hearing on Sundays, through the rood screen, the melodious chanting in Latin, the whispered appeals to the community of saints, and pleas to the Virgin for her compassion, giving access to the mercy of God. I did not think so.

But now, as I knelt before the wooden table and closed my eyes, inexplicably, my burden lightened. I was able to lift my shoulders a little higher, to chase away some of the stiffness in my limbs. I knew there was a prayer to Mary that some Catholics still liked to recite in secret, a prayer of expiation, but I did not know all of the words. Instead, I allowed the pristine solitude of this place to wash over me, cleansing me. I felt the weight of sin leave me and strength flow in, from I knew not where.

I left the church with knowledge of what I had to do.

With the events of the day behind me, sitting before my sister, I said, 'I'm sorry, Esther. I have failed you. Failed to keep you safe. I am the architect of my own sorrows, and now of yours.' I stood to leave.

'You have seen,' Not-Esther said. 'And you are afraid.'

I stopped, turning, and closed my eyes, tried to shut out the image that leapt in, but it was indelible, as I had known it would be. John Rutherford had hung from the rafters of his own cottage, his jaw and neck swollen, his skin purple, with his eyes protruding from his disfigured face. His tongue had rested like a greyish slug against his bottom lip and, at some point in that macabre dance, he had kicked off his shoes. His bare feet and lower legs were black where his blood had succumbed to the earth's force, then pooled inside him so they had the look of cuts of flyblown meat.

'I am afraid,' I admitted. 'How did you persuade him to such an act?'

'I spoke of his son to him. His plaintive cries for milk. The shape of his distended stomach, the grotesque parody of his knees, so large against his tiny body. The terror in his eyes as his face began to turn yellow. The piteous noise as he gnawed in hunger on his fists. It was not difficult. The man's grief was like a heavy cloak he could never take off, woven of the very finest threads.'

I wanted to hit her, to shake the voice out of her, do anything to silence her.

My revulsion seemed to possess me, as the creature had possessed her, until I thought I might erupt in violence; and still the voice would not relent. 'How did it feel, to bury him with your own hands, to hide the work of mine?'

It's not Esther. It's not.

I left the room.

My plan relied upon protecting Mary and Henry. I could not leave them alone for as long as would be needed, not unless I could find a way to quiet the creature's malice.

'We can't lock her up forever,' I said.

'No,' Mary agreed. She was frowning, pacing the kitchen with folded arms. She started a sentence, then withdrew, tapped her fingers on her elbow, and just slightly closed her eyes.

'What?' I asked.

'Nothing.'

But it was something. 'What were you thinking?'

She came to sit beside me, pouring herself ale. 'What if we could find something – some drug – that would make her sleep? That would silence it? Then you could…' She thought again. 'You could go to Chalfonte, find Mr Milton, and discover what you could, and I could stay here and watch her. We wouldn't have to restrain her then, just keep the door locked.'

'You would do that?' I asked, startled.

She nodded. 'It's not only that your father helped me.' She lowered her gaze, her cheeks reddening. 'That matters, and I will always be grateful, but in truth, Henry and I have nowhere else to go.'

So we searched the little potting shed together, and sniffed, rubbed or tasted every plant, identifying each – foxglove, bryony, henbane, aloe vera, quince – and investigating the contents of every bottle. Esther had been diligent in labelling her pots and concoctions, and my father's books on botany helped when we needed further knowledge of the effects of a particular plant.

'Here,' Mary said, hefting aside a pot of parsley and showing me a wad of paper on a damp shelf.

'That's Esther's,' I said. 'Her recipes.'

We took it back into the house and thumbed through the pages. In it, Esther had carefully recorded the names of the plants she knew and loved, but it took time to read her wayward scribble. Eventually, we found a recipe marked *dwale*. I quailed when I saw the ingredients – alongside harmless things like sow bile, vinegar and lettuce there stood more ominous names: hemlock juice, henbane, the white poppy.

'Look,' Mary said, poring over the page. 'It says to mix this with wine, induce her to drink, then when we want her to wake, revive her with vinegar and salt. It gives the quantities. This should make her sleep.'

'Or kill her. I can't give this to her,' I said, in despair.

Mary clutched the book, conflict written all over her face. In the end, she put it down in her calm, slow way. 'She is your sister. I cannot tell you what to do in this.'

In the garden, Henry chased Guppy and allowed himself to be chased by the mastiff in turn. He beamed as they tumbled together on the drifted snow. I said, 'Can you tell me what you would do, if it were Henry?'

Mary looked away. 'Would you believe me, if I said so?'

'I would believe you if you said so,' I said, steadily.

She was biting her thumbnail, but stopped. 'I think I would do it. Even given the danger, the risk of someone finding her like this… You've said yourself, if she is discovered, they will burn her. And now the danger is even greater, given Rutherford's fate. She will be accused of his death if he is found.'

Bleakly, I said, 'Rutherford will not be found.'

I had not liked Rutherford. He had been priggish and vain, but to lay him on his back in a shallow grave and heap clumps of earth over his clumsily wrapped body had been one of the hardest things I had ever done. I had wept for Rutherford, lying, not where he belonged, with his Maker in consecrated ground, beside the family he had lost, but in an unblessed ditch in a copse of oak and birch trees.

And I had wept for Esther. Esther, who had saved the jackdaw's egg, because she could not bear the pain of helpless things. How I had wept for her.

Mary said, warily, 'Even if he is not found, Esther is far from being above suspicion. They were known to be acquainted, and now four people have died or disappeared around her. I understand your reluctance — God knows, I fear the drug as you do — but to keep her close and silent while we seek answers elsewhere? It may be the only way to save her.'

I ran my eyes over the smooth oval of her face, first searchingly; then, without meaning to, admiringly. Despite all she had suffered, I did not believe Mary held any grudge against Esther.

I realised that she could see me staring. 'Mary, I...'

She blushed and stood. It was enough to silence me. 'I will see to the fire,' she said. 'It's becoming cold.'

21

It took several days to get the mixture right. There were one or two ingredients we didn't have, but in the end, we produced a tincture that roughly matched the recipe. Esther did not struggle against the drug. I offered it to her as wine, and she drank it down peaceably enough. For several long minutes, it appeared that it had not worked. Then, the voice slowed to a listless crawl.

It began, 'The old Egyptians worshipped Apep as the embodiment of chaos. Apep, the world encircler, was the mortal enemy of Ra, the God of the Sun, but because Ra exceeded Apep in power and overcame him, Apep had to hide from him. But he could not be vanquished entirely. Every night, having laid low beneath the horizon, he would attack the ship of the Sun God, attempting to trap his rival in his coils, never submitting in his quest to regain his power. His worshippers believed him responsible for storms, earthquakes and the vanishing of the sun behind the moon.'

I was used to its interminable storytelling. I had gone elsewhere. When my sister's shoulders began to sag and her face relaxed into a stupor, the face in my mind was Mary's. Soon, Esther's mouth, still mumbling tales of serpent gods and chaos demons, could not form the words. Moments after, I caught her head as it sank towards her chest. She slept.

I lifted her, going past the window towards the bed. My heart was full of anguish as I thought of the difference between Esther – who weighed as little as Henry – and Rutherford, whose corpse had been almost too much to manage. She was so slight a breath of air could carry her off. It was disturbing to think that, if what I suspected held true, her body now housed two consciousnesses, while Rutherford's had been reduced back to the flesh, the soul inside dissipated; who could know to where?

I placed her carefully back up against her pillows, and pulled the bed closer to the window, wondering whether it was foolish to think she might appreciate the light. When she was tightly tucked, as if she were five or six years old and waiting for a cup of milk, I lowered myself to sit beside her and stroked the flaxen hair out of her eyes. I began to recite her catechism.

How do you know that you have a soul?
Because the Bible tells me so.
In what condition did God make Adam and Eve?
He made them holy and happy.
What is a covenant?
An agreement between two or more persons.
What covenant did God make with Adam?
The covenant of works.
What was Adam bound to do by the covenant of works?
To obey God perfectly.
What did God promise in the covenant of works?
To reward Adam with life if he obeyed him.
What did God threaten in the covenant of works?
To punish Adam with death if he disobeyed.
Did Adam keep the covenant of works?
No; he sinned against God.
What is sin?
Sin is any want of conformity unto, or transgression of, the law of God.
What is meant by want of conformity?
Not being or doing what God requires.
What is meant by transgression?

Doing what God forbids.
What was the sin of our first parents?
Eating the forbidden fruit.
Who tempted them to this sin?
The Devil tempted Eve, and she gave the fruit to Adam.

At a noise in the open doorway, I stopped and, turning, saw Mary. She had rounded the top of the stairs and was listening to the recitation. She waited with her arms folded across her chest until I had finished.

'Do you like the catechism?' I asked as she poked her head through the door.

'My family was not very religious,' she answered, shrugging. 'We went to church, of course, but I think Father observed the forms of it rather than the substance. And then when he and Mother were gone there was less opportunity. I believed in God, but imperfectly,' she finished.

I nodded, understanding. 'Here it was very different. After my mother died, my father took solace in religion. He became more and more devout. Esther was always of one mind with him about it, but I...' I tapped my fingers together, struggling to find the right words, knowing I was prising open a part of myself, exposing it in a way I had always believed – and sworn – I could never do. 'It was always too certain for me. Too absolutist. And my father did his best to be patient, but it was a sore disappointment to him, I fear. My doubt tortured him.'

Mary looked at me for a long moment, her gaze level and calm. There was no judgement in it. 'Faith in God is a personal thing,' she said. 'A matter of conscience. We do not perform it for others. Even those we love.'

I said, eagerly, 'That's it. Exactly that. It was so real for him, but for me it felt like acting. I despised myself for it. And sometimes I even despised him. He always... He was so desperate for me to see it his way. I think that's why he sent me to Mr

Milton. He thought he – Milton – could succeed where he had failed.'

'As if any young man ever changed his mind to please his elders,' she said, with a wry smile.

'It was a profligate waste of time, berating me and forcing me to recite ideas I didn't accept,' I said, bitterly.

'Was that why you left Mr Milton? He couldn't change your mind?'

I shook my head. 'What, then?' she asked. I didn't want to tell her. The shame was still tight-knotted inside me, holding my words hostage. But then I remembered how I had demanded her secrets as we rode home from the gaol. I could not ask for truth from her and keep my own sins hidden. Slowly, the whole sordid tale came forth. Elizabeth, and Milton's anger. My return home. Elizabeth's death. How I had known, on some level, when I took her to my bed, what I was doing. How it had been a means to an end for me, though I would have denied it at the time. And how Elizabeth – although my fondness for her had been real enough – had paid the price.

'I could not be more ashamed,' I confessed. 'I dread facing him.'

I expected her to tell me it would all be fine, that there was some ingenious other way, one we would work out together. She stared down at the floor for several seconds, tapping her slippered foot against the threshold. Then she met my eyes. 'Yes,' she said. 'I can understand why he was furious with you. You did wrong.' This brought a fresh flood of shame.

'I can't... I can't go to him,' I said. 'There must be another way. There has to be.' Even as I spoke, I hated my own cowardice. But I craved an escape. An easier road.

'I don't think there is,' Mary said, in a harder voice. 'Sometimes there is just one way. And is it not time to forgive yourself for the mistakes of the past? If Mr Milton doesn't do the same and isn't willing to help, in that case, he'll say no, won't he? But that's all. Is that not a risk you are prepared to take – for Esther?' Her eyes were still without judgement, but without false witness, either; she held nothing back. *This you must do*, her expression said.

What was it I had said to my father, just a few weeks ago? *You look upon a man now. I will not fail you again.* My emotions wrestled one another, then I broke the difficult silence with the only answer there was. 'Of course.'

Mary smiled thinly. She glanced towards Esther. 'Does she sleep?'

'Yes.'

She crept in, looking down. 'She's so small. Like a doll. How is her breathing?'

We checked. It was steady, her chest rising and falling rhythmically. Mary came to the foot of the bed and sat down. She looked exhausted; her skin was almost translucent, but with deep purple circles beneath her eyes. I saw how much worry she had been hiding, how well she had masked it. 'Are you well?' I asked.

'I've been less tired,' she said, 'but yes, she sleeps, and I am well.' She paused, then said, in a more subdued voice, 'I... I wonder whether this is a relief for her – for Esther, I mean. Or whether...'

'Whether it is worse? To be trapped inside her own head, with that?' She had voiced my own fear. She nodded. 'I don't know. I can only hope that she is in a more peaceful place.'

It was cold in the room, as it always was now. But the cold had an empty quality, as though it resulted from the air being sucked out. Mary wrapped her arms about her middle. 'What do you think it is? The creature.'

I thought of its unnatural knowledge of things within and without, of future and past, and of the cruelties in which it seemed to revel. 'I believe it to be some sort of elemental force. A demon? A demi-god? Or something that thinks it is.'

'Not the Devil?' As she said it, her voice quivered. For a people so preoccupied, how rarely we named him.

There was a time when I would have said – to her, if nobody else – that I did not believe in the Devil, but now I could only shrug. 'I don't know.'

'But it's evil, whatever it is.' She sounded definite.

I paused. 'I don't know. I think it's angry. I think it's trapped.'

'It sounds as though you pity it.'

'You don't?'

She shook her head. 'Perhaps I need to find it within myself, somewhere, to do so, but no, I don't pity it. I pity us.'

I finally found the courage to say it. 'But this is not your fight. You could take Henry and go. I would not see you penniless; there is no need for you to stay here if you do not wish to. You could leave.'

'Yes,' she said, and dread yawned in my stomach. 'I could. But I will not.'

'Why do you stay?' I asked, smoothing the linen around Esther, though it did not need it. I hardly dared look at her.

But she had risen, and she took three steps towards me. Her hand reached for mine where it lay on the bed, and closed about it. Her eyes were lowered. Her touch warmed me. We waited, and watched.

I travelled swiftly, lightly, not wishing to risk the horse, but with no alternative. Every day I was away from the house put Mary and Henry – and Esther – deeper in danger.

I could not afford to be stopped, or questioned by outliers from some over-zealous army post about my reasons for travelling at this strange time of year. Keeping to the least used roads, those that were slow and winding, rocky and pitted with holes, or popular with bandits and thieves, I kept my sword close, and slept, shivering, in thickets and hedgerows. I kept Manyon's letter close to my breast, with its seal and permissions, knowing it might not be enough if a curious officer wanted to know why I, able-bodied and of fighting age, was not with one army or another, or worse, thought me a Royalist spy.

I was lucky. The weather held. I progressed beneath a clear sky and slept without freezing, or just about. At the end of the fourth day, I approached Chalfonte from the north, thirsty and hungry.

There was every risk the master of the house would be absent. The violent tumults of these times had scattered men like crop seeds. Perhaps Milton had egressed for the Continent, or London, like so many others.

Again, I was lucky. When the door swung to, it revealed a face I recognised, and an expression that said its owner remembered me, too. It belonged to a woman, large of body, small of eyes, red in the face, with neat grey hair under a spotless white coif. Her disdain on seeing me made her cheeks ruddier. I was embarrassed, which had a similar effect on mine.

I spoke with false confidence. 'Goodwife Bern,' I said. 'It's good to see you again.' She looked me up and down, noting my dishevelled appearance and stained travelling clothes. I was certain I stank, and wished I didn't, as this woman, Milton's housekeeper and cook, had never liked me even when washed. I could not blame her. In the three years of my residence in Chalfonte, I had stolen her pies, flouted her curfews and mocked her unceasingly behind her back. Then, when that back was turned, I had shamed the whole household. I saw those days so differently now, and was regretful that I had no time to make amends. I said, 'Is the master at home?'

'He's here,' she said, unwillingly.

'Would you announce me, please?' I asked, when she did not welcome me inside.

With obvious reluctance, closing the door behind her, she retreated into the house. I leant against the doorframe, allowing it to take my weight, then straightened as the door came ajar again. 'He'll not see you,' she said. Was that pity I detected in her face?

I allowed my eyes to close, weighing the words that might move him. Then I said, 'Tell him... Tell him Richard Treadwater is dead, and I come on God's business. Please.'

She seemed as if she would refuse, but then sighed. 'You'd better come in,' she said. 'Go through to the kitchen. I'll talk to him, but you know what he's like.'

I was weak with relief. 'Thank you,' I said, berating myself for each and every time I had made the life of this good woman more difficult.

She laughed to herself. 'Don't thank me yet, lad. You may yet find yourself turfed out on your backside. He has no time for fools.'

The kitchen was as ordered and meticulous as I remembered. Pewter pottingers, wooden trenchers, copper skimmers, metal mugs and tankards hung in their places, everything dusted and well purposed. The floor was spick and span, without a cobweb or stray ball of fluff on the trestles of the oak table where Goodwife Bern now employed her substantial upper arms to beat a series of lamb chops into submission, each meaty blow hastening a puff of flour into the air and causing me to cough.

'He's writing,' she said, pausing to traumatise another chop. 'You know how that goes.'

I did. I remembered how days would go by without Milton emerging from his library. Every so often the bell would ring and Goodwife Bern or one of the other servants would scurry in to see whether food or drink were required, and from time to time, when our tutor was too impatient to bide the delay, the door would open a crack and we two or three scholars would hear him call for ink or candles. 'The leopard does not change his spots,' I said.

Goodwife Bern shook her head slightly. 'I don't know about that. He married last year.'

'He took a wife?'

'You could say that. A girl, really. But she's gone.'

For a moment, I thought the housekeeper alluded to grief. 'She passed away?'

'No. Just gone.'

'Gone where?'

The big woman shrugged again. 'Back to her people. He's been like a bear with a sore head ever since.'

I did not remark that this was no change, as far as I was concerned.

'What did he say?' I asked now. 'When you told him of my father?'

She lifted her broad shoulders, liberally sprinkling flour. 'Something about grass and a shrinking flower – I wasn't paying attention.'

I spoke under my breath: '*The grass withers, the flower fades, but the word of God will stand forever.*' When my listener frowned in confusion, I said, 'It's from Isaiah.'

'Hmm. If you say so,' Goodwife Bern said, pummelling the final chop. 'Do you want more ale? Or bread and cheese?'

'No ale, thank you. It was as much as I needed. But I would thank you for some bread. The travails of the road lie heavy on me. Would you mind if I took a basin outside and washed?'

'Help yourself,' she said. 'You know where everything is.' She seemed bemused, and I wondered whether I had changed so very much.

The water in the barrel was covered by a thin layer of ice, which I broke. I splashed my face and neck. Standing in the cold shadow to the west of the house, my thoughts travelled once more to the past and I could almost imagine myself to be eighteen again. But where my time here had been felt as a torture, an imprisonment before the liberty of true manhood, I felt it now as a release. Here, if I kept my eyes closed and imagined nothing, I might banish thoughts of monsters.

But not for long. Just as I cupped my hands to my mouth and took in water, a low cough alerted me to a new arrival. I swallowed, shook the water from my hands, and turned.

I had been caught unawares by my old master, who now watched me from ten or so feet away. Milton was a short man, and ascetically thin. It had been whispered among his pupils that he had acquired the nickname 'The Lady of Christ's' during his time at Cambridge, and none of us had expressed surprise. He looked much younger than his true age. He had not been quite a contemporary of my father – there were five or so years between them – but they might have been father and son, where years were concerned, although not in looks.

Where Richard Treadwater had been dark, with stern features unless he happened to smile, everything about Milton was fair in its palette and moderate in its shape. The light grey that now streaked his hair did not stand out against its natural acorn colour. His brows did not announce themselves and, beneath them, his irises were neither this shade nor that. You could have mistaken him for a weakling, if not for something in the eyes that could cut through like a spear thrust, giving the shadow, the hint of the mind within. Except that it was equally likely he would look at you, and yet not seem to be looking at all; to me,

Milton had always seemed to be someone whose inner world was just as real as the true world was to the rest of us.

I had imagined this scene again and again, and had thought of sinking to my knees to ask Milton's pardon, but now the gesture seemed ridiculous. I feared being laughed at and then, as Goodwife Bern had predicted, thrown out on my behind.

'My father is dead,' I blurted.

His eyes regarded me with emotions I could not read.

'And there is this,' I said, reaching inside and extracting the papers I had carried with me all the way from Norfolk. Milton frowned as I held them out. He did not take them. Instead, he moved in the opposite direction along the path, to a bench situated beneath the high laurel hedge that divided us from the rose garden. He seemed to move more stiffly than before, the inevitable result of two years of war and political argument. He sank down on the bench, then hit it once with the palm of his hand, resignedly. It was an invitation.

I followed. Milton rummaged in his pocket and brought forth a pair of wire-framed spectacles. He balanced them on the bridge of his beaky nose and held out his hand for the paper, which I passed over wordlessly. As Milton read, for what seemed an eternity I listened to the chacking of a pair of fieldfare thrushes in the evergreen branches, and the occasional small noises of recognition from my companion.

When he reached the final page, Milton removed his spectacles again. For a few moments, his sight seemed fixed on the stark curves of the rose bushes. Finally, he said, 'I wonder that your father didn't throw this away. But he always did keep things overlong. He was sentimental, in that way.'

'Yes,' I said, restrainedly. It hurt so much to be near someone who had known him before me, and perhaps better. It reminded me that there were hidden histories I would never know, stories I would never hear.

Milton still seemed to be deciding whether to speak more fully. In the end, he said, 'I grieve with you.' I nodded, looking away. Milton waited until I had mastered myself, and then lifted the parchment slightly, saying, 'What purpose does this hold?'

'I was rather hoping you could tell me.'

22

The flames wavered before Milton's eyes as he looked towards the hearth. He kept the papers on his knee and every so often drew deeply from a pipe of fragrant tobacco. Even when he spoke, he did not break his gaze from the flickering fire. With a great woollen blanket wrapped about his shoulders, he looked like a prophet, or a sorcerer.

He said, 'You did have a sister named Esther. She was born to your mother in 1626, and the lying-in was long. Your father told me the child became stuck in the birthing channel, and not only was she born dead, the effort killed your mother.

'It was not long after that, in 1628, that I stayed with your family during a sojourn from Christ's. There was plague in the city – a constant threat – and my father thought a trip to Norfolk would be beneficial for my health. Your father and I were distant kinsmen, though he was somewhat older, but we had enjoyed one another's company in the past and I was not unwilling to go. He was so recently widowed that I thought he might value my companionship in those weeks. He seemed to, and I found time for writing and a measure of peace, after the frenetic pace of the university. I say a measure of peace, for any household with such a storm-cloud of a boy in it will always have some inclement days. You were missing your mother, and would not talk of it, not even to God. I counselled your father to be patient; grief wanes, be it ever so keen, and the sun's warm rays are felt again in time.

'During this particular week, your father had business in King's Lynn. I went along. You were left with a nursemaid. It

227

was not a trip for pleasure, but rather an opportunity to source timber for the farm. It involved an overnight stay and then early trawls through yards to view the wood and barter with the dealers. I was, in truth, fatigued, and wished I had remained in the house.

'There was great poverty around those parts. Poverty in the midst of affluence, as the town itself was fat with wealth, but many of the men who haunted its streets were sick, disabled by war, or made weak by hunger. It was disheartening to the soul to see these half-starved creatures limping along, begging for the meanest crust of bread, in a nation where so many lived as kings. Your father felt it, too. We talked of it as we walked, of a greater Commonwealth, the country we one day envisaged, where all would share in the bounty of God, with power vested in the ablest, not the most mighty, and all souls ruled by reason, not by one man's whims, dragged ever forward by the twin horses of vanity and insatiable greed. It was a hope we allowed ourselves: a vision. A glorious image of a time when the power of tyrants over ordinary men would be as a rumour on the wind – a speck, only, in the history of a godlier kingdom.

'Perhaps it was the tone of that discussion that dictated what happened next. We neared the sea, where the Ouse flowed into the Wash. The sun was yet low, though it was midsummer. Along the road we passed vagrants and adventurers, and many men we believed to be sailors, all hungry for work and bread. And though it was not within your father's power, or for that matter mine, to assist them all, we each drew deeply from our purses to alleviate the want we saw there. We wished we could do more. It was not until your father halted, placing his hand upon my chest to stop me, that I realised how strongly he felt about the sight before us.

'A man held a child close to his chest. Girl or boy, it was impossible to tell. Its hair was matted and very fair. It was hard to believe the child and the man might be related – he was dark, his face ravaged by wind, salt and water, and the face of the small creature that clung to him, mewling, was as pale as angels' wings. Your father stopped near him, gave him a coin for the child and bent down to question him. He asked whether the infant was his, and at first the man did not understand. Then your father spoke to him in French, and he replied that it was a foundling. But he spoke with so much weariness and fear that we were suspicious.

'He did not seem to be one of those who used an infant to gain more income from gullible strangers and live high as a result of their charity, passing the poor thing about his friends so they too could win the sympathies of rich widows and clerics; he was thin, his wrists and ankles mere bones covered by shrivelled flaps of skin. His eyes were dull, and those of the child, which did not cry, no brighter. He seemed to have no expectation of being helped.

'Your father suggested we proceed to an inn. Drawn to greater sympathy, perhaps, by his own recent grief, he wanted to hear the man's story and was willing to delay his business. He promised him ale, bread and cheese, fresh milk for the child. And the man came. And there, requisitioning the paper and quill I always carried in case inspiration came to me, your father took down these words.'

Milton unfolded the paper again, seeming to look at and then beyond it to the fire, as if his meticulously ordered, capacious mind might conjure in the flames the physical forms of the four: the starved sailor, the silent child, the poet, the father.

He sighed. 'It was an entertaining tale. But I cannot say I set much store by it. The smell of strong wine was on him, once we entered the closer quarters of the tavern, and his hands shook from the deprivation of it.' He waved the paper. 'Is there some truth here? Perhaps. I had my doubts about the heroic feats he

spoke of. I wondered whether there might be a whore somewhere, or a sister, the mother of the poor infant. Yet it did not
anger me, if the whole thing was invention. He had to eat.'
Milton shrugged, gave a mild smile. 'I live, by and large, on the
same skill, after all.'

I could not contain my questions any longer. 'My father took
the child in?'

Milton nodded. 'She was a girl. He named her Esther, too,
which, in the Persian or Greek languages, speaks of a star. And
he took her home, to be your sister.' He lifted the sheaf of parchment. 'This account stands as a record of Janssen's story, and of
your father's kindness.'

My hands were tight around my cup, so tight the knuckles had
turned white. 'But she's not my sister.'

'No, indeed.'

'And we do not know how she came into the world, who her
parents were, or...'

Milton looked up sharply, almost as if he heard the unspoken
part of my sentence: *or what*.

'No, but it seems likely Esther was born of a passenger on
the ship boarded by the men of the *Guldern*,' he said. 'While
there are superstitions concerned with having women aboard
such vessels, it is not unheard of. Necessity dictates that women
travel, just as men do.'

'But with such a small child? And according to the sailor
Janssen, she was found alone with two men. Both dead – and
none who can say how.'

Milton shrugged. 'Plague is not uncommon aboard ships. If
the woman died, her body would have been thrown overboard,
along with those of any other victims. Ungodly to deny her a
Christian burial, perhaps, but not unusual. It does not require
much imagination to see how the child was orphaned. No,' he
said. 'If the story Janssen told had any truth in it, and I set aside,

of course, its preposterous conclusion, for which I blame the drink, it lies in the fact that he found the child, and saved her, and – a decision which, of course, originates somewhere in the design of God – decided to feed her, and starved himself to do it. A worthy deed, I think.'

Milton's reference to the plague had unsettled me, making me think, somewhere beneath the images of foundlings and drunken sailors that crowded my mind, of Elizabeth. I toyed with the fringe on the cushion on my seat, and brooded.

Milton waited quietly in the half-light for some time, his eyes still moving over the paper. After a while, he said, 'What truly brings you here, Thomas?'

The tale spilled from me. As I spoke, Milton sat, rapt, no longer looking at the fire, his gaze boring into me instead. His expression showed all the appropriate signs of sympathy when I spoke of my father, but he could not disguise the gleam of enthralment that came into his eyes when I told the rest: Chrissa Moore, the Gedge women, Esther, Rutherford, and finally, Not-Esther.

I once again had the impression that my old tutor was a man unlike others. He did not unconsciously cross himself – as even the most reformed men were still wont to do – or solicit blessings when I spoke of Not-Esther's diabolical mutterings, of the preternatural knowledge owned by the creature, or even of its white-hot malice. He leant forward, hands folded over his lips, hungry for every morsel. He seemed inclined to interrupt at regular intervals, but restrained himself.

When I reached the end of the story, I felt parched and drained, like over-exerted soil. I sat back in my seat and stared at the ceiling, resting my throat from talk, and heard Milton murmur that the tale was fascinating.

I looked back at the older man. 'I am confused, sir,' I said. 'You sound almost entertained by this devilish mess.'

231

'You have me there,' he said, in a voice as soft as silk. 'I am caught in blasphemy. It has always been my weakness: a novel story, well constructed. I must congratulate you on the telling.'

Now, it was my turn to lean forward. 'Then perhaps it is a weakness we can use. Your knowledge of such tales, I mean. Have you ever heard of such a thing before? This sort of – possession? And what can Janssen's tale have to do with this? It cannot be coincidence.'

'Stories of a soul taken over by a spirit or demonic entity could not be more common in the present day,' Milton said. 'But before the papists and monks became aware of the potential for profit, through exorcisms and the like, they were rare. There's the account in the Gospel of Mark of the spirit brought out of the boy by Christ, but of course that spirit was mute – a mere animal presence, not an articulate consciousness such as that which you describe. Such dumb creatures undoubtedly exist, and are said to bring on bestial fits, ravings, attempted self-murder and so on, but any suggestion that they might be prophetic...'

'But also in Mark,' I argued, 'an impure spirit recognised the divinity of Jesus, did it not, demonstrating some knowledge beyond what it could have known? Some preternatural understanding?'

'Yes,' said Milton. 'But what you describe in this Not-Esther... the sophistication of its dialogue with you... I have heard of nothing similar, outside the realm of papist, superstitious nonsense.'

'And what of Janssen's story? You called it preposterous, yet what is there in this whole saga that is not? Have you heard of such a thing before? Such a monster?'

Milton hesitated. He smoothed strands of fair hair away from his high forehead. 'In the annals of make-belief, only,' he admitted. 'But yes, such things are known.'

'Tell me.'

'Accounts of sea monsters are as old as accounts themselves,' he said. 'Aristotle described serpents large enough to devour oxen, and leave their bones by the shore.'

'But that supposes they are close enough to the shore to catch an ox,' I said, dourly, and Milton nodded.

'Aristotle does not give us much to go on,' he continued. 'But there seems to be some resemblance between what Janssen describes – a horse-like head, a great mane, a serpentine neck and body of great size – and the legend of the hippocamp. I say legend, because that is precisely what it is; stories, passed down by early adventurers on the Mediterranean to more land-locked listeners, who took tales of what we must assume to be whales and sharks, and turned them into what they could more easily conjure in their minds: a creature that combines features of sea-going beasts of limitless size with those they could put their own hands and eyes upon: horses and snakes.

'For centuries in antiquity, these creatures appeared in artistic representations – on vases, ceremonial bowls and the like. Yet I do not think, really, that we are supposed to put faith in their existence. Rather, we must think of them as a form of entertainment: somewhat like poetry, and not much reliant upon what might genuinely be occupying the seas that lie north of us.'

'And what of the Bible? There are sea creatures in the Bible. Powerful ones.'

Milton looked troubled. 'You refer, of course, to the leviathan.'

'Yes.'

The older man's voice became lyrical as he recited from memory: '*It makes the depths churn like a boiling cauldron, and stirs up the sea like a pot of ointment. It leaves a glistening wake behind it.*'

'Yes,' I said, again.

Milton stared into the flames. 'It is a creature that has been much in my thoughts in these topsy-turvy days. Its meaning, its message for us. I thought of it as a word-picture, a *metaphora*, if you like.'

'You suggest that it carries a symbolic meaning, rather than a literal one?'

'I thought so,' said Milton, quietly. 'A herald of Antichrist, or the end of the world. A creature of such primordial might that it can only be tamed according to the will of He that created it. Aquinas referred to it as a demon, a demon of envy.'

I was wrestling with the desire to declare such things nonsense. I wanted to argue that the beast was just a story, a vessel in which to carry the fear of Satan, or to plant hope of the Last Days in the minds of the gullible. But I hovered on the edge of certainty, and settled for shaking my head. 'Surely nothing in this can have any basis in truth?'

Suddenly, Milton looked wide awake, as hard-edged as glass. 'Everything in the Word of God has its basis in truth. We have only to comprehend it.'

After a moment's further silence, he got to his feet. We were in his library, a large, comfortable room lined with foggy bookcases, each crammed full to bursting with histories, philosophies and translations. He spent no time thinking about where in this dense forest he might find what he sought, but moved like an arrow in the direction of the north-west corner, opening the case with a key and removing a tall, leather-bound book. It had a title I could not read, in a language I had never encountered.

Milton seemed caught up in the flow of his own thoughts as he returned with the book. 'If, however, we are to think of the "leviathan" as a myth, and a myth only, there are many pre-figures, in other belief systems, that may explain how the seed of the idea came to be sown.' He opened the book, turning page after page before coming to an enormous illustration, which he passed for me to examine. 'This is from a – distant – translated version of Berossus's *History of Babylonia*, a text lost in its original form millennia ago. It concerns the defeat of Tiamat by Marduk, an event which, in their world view, established order from chaos.'

The names of writers long dead and gods from far-off lands were making my head flounder. I knew, only vaguely, of Marduk, the greatest god of the Babylonian pantheon, responsible for agriculture, magic and storms. I did not recognise the name Tiamat.

In the image, drawn on vellum in lead-point, Marduk wore a tall battle helmet and carried his arrows before him. There were crackling lines about him, as if he contained within him the power of lightning. His powerful physique spoke of strength and righteousness. He stood above churning waves, impossibly elevated against the thunderous clouds. The resemblance to the Archangel Michael was striking. Below him, writhing against the blackened water, surrounded by a low mist, lay the serpent. Tiamat. Its great mouth stood open, as if it howled in protest, and the coils of its body excited the water into towering shapes. Was it dying? Had Marduk struck its belly with his arrows already, or was its death yet to come?

'Marduk challenged Tiamat – "the glistening one" – to single combat,' Milton explained. 'He turned his own body to flame and harnessed the four winds, creating a net about her which she could not escape.'

'And he defeated her?'

'Yes, according to the beliefs of the Babylonians,' said Milton, with a shrug. 'We see something similar in Old Norse legend; the account of Thor's defeat of Jörmungandr, the Great Serpent, bears parallels to the tale of Marduk and Tiamat. And the appearance of the Great Serpent,' he said, more carefully, 'is said to herald violent upheaval in the body politic: war, famine, rebellion. The deaths of kings.'

I looked up, sharply. 'Regicide?' I thought of King Charles, sequestered in reduced splendour behind the thick walls of that other Christ's, in Oxford, like some latter-day Avignon pope. He held his royal blood to be sacred, but how long would that belief hold, if his faltering armies didn't?

Milton's answer came soft: 'Perhaps.'

I closed the book. 'We are no nearer,' I said, wearily. 'Gods and monsters, myths and legends. Even if we credit the existence of such things, it brings us no closer to explaining how, or why, my sister would find herself in its sights. Or what we – I – can do to extricate her.'

'On the contrary,' said Milton, purposefully. 'We know exactly what we must do.' He rose, went back to the bookcase, and withdrew a strip of oilskin, which he handed to me, signalling that I should wrap up Janssen's account in its waterproof folds. 'Keep that safe,' he said. 'It is the only copy.' He seemed consumed by an energy I had rarely seen in him.

As I wrapped it up, I said, 'What must we do?'

'We must go to her.'

23

April 1703

A place far from the sea

I cannot sleep. Each night, it proves impossible to drift off without nightmares; my blood rises as soon as my head lowers to the pillow and I toss feverishly, shivering in the dark, imagining the turn of the earth through each interminable hour. Mary keeps her back to me, and holds the coverlet tight. She is awake, and I could so easily touch her, this woman who has been all my colour, all my music, but there is a hurt between us. The words she wishes to speak – and will not – have built a wall I cannot scale.

'Keep still, Thomas,' she says, irritably, as I shift again on the mattress.

I lie on my back and try to comply, counting, staring at the ceiling. The moon has waxed thick, but is still low and can't be seen, and it is so dark I cannot tell whether my eyes are open or not. I squeeze my lids until it hurts.

Time elapses. For once I do not dream. I do not want to wake, but something tenacious pulls at me, as though a rope connects me to the real world and someone tugs at it. I am woken from half-sleep by a demented shrieking – it is several moments before I realise the sound is the wind, and then comes a sudden crash. I spring upright, still not fully awake. What was that? What age am I, and which house is this?

I anchor myself – *you are old* – and look above my head, but the sound came from this floor, from one of the bedrooms. It sounded like broken wood and glass. A window blown open, perhaps, and a pane shattered. Nothing to concern a person unduly. Not ordinarily. The sound comes again, just the banging now, but not so loud, dampened by the shrill wind against the walls.

Pulling on my robe, I whisper to Mary to stay in bed. 'I'm not asleep in any case,' she says. 'Who could sleep through this?' She follows me.

The window has indeed blown open. I walk over, and something bites at the ball of my foot, eliciting a yelp. Broken glass gleams on the floorboards. Hopefully, it has not cut too deep. Wrestling with the frame, I struggle to stand against the ferocious blast of air that comes through. I look out, squinting into the dark. For a moment nothing is visible at all, then the moon emerges, and I see the old barn shaking on its foundations, until clouds sweep in to obscure the light again. There are intermittent flashes, as if the moon is a great torch blown out and rekindled over and over, and as the trees in the orchard and about the low walls rock and sway, the stuttering light makes them seem alive.

Her voice is almost drowned out by the cacophony. 'What does she want, Thomas?'

'It,' I say, too curtly.

'What do you mean?'

'Not "she" – "it",' I grunt, yanking the window closed. 'That thing is not my sister.'

She cries out, a sudden, frustrated eruption. 'By God's heart, Thomas! Have I not been a proper wife to you? Not stood with you, through all these years of concealment and care?' I start as she bites down on her fist, her whole body shaking. 'Have I not… have I not given up…?' She stops, speaking almost to herself, wrapping her arms about her middle. 'No, not that, it is not fair.' Again, she looks at me. 'This must have an end. It *must*.'

'Let's go back to bed,' I say. I am pleading with her, holding her arms, trying to draw her close to me, but she pulls away.

'Will we not make an end?' she repeats.

In the half-light, I can imagine that colour remains in her cheeks, can wish away the dark smudges beneath her eyes and her dilated pupils. 'Come, wife. To bed.'

Now comes the storm.

With the gale skirling about the roof, I protect the windows, hammering in nails to secure planks over the glass. Soon, the wind has become a tempest, a shrieking fit that refuses to behave as it should, that will not build to a climax or exhaust itself in rain.

It goes on, day after day, that angry, full-throated wail, with air barrelling down the chimney to ransack the lower floor of the house. The mercury in the barometer is lower than I have ever seen it. Every morning Mary stays in the kitchen, exhausted and whey-faced, and every morning I go to the attic, filling holes in the roof where tiles have blown off. If we leave the house, we sometimes find the tiles a hundred yards away or more, but often they are not found at all, and we can only believe them carried off on the wind.

Each day, as I try to read to or feed Esther, it gazes at me, not at all stirred by the chaos outside. Her eyes, the precise cobalt shade of the absent blue sky, follow me across the attic as I beat in nail after nail. *It won't stop*, they say. *It won't stop until you concede. Until you surrender.*

'I won't do it,' I say, at last, on the fourth day. I come close to her, picking up a smell of salt-spray and seaweed so potent my breath catches in my chest. When I have air again, I lean in. 'I *won't*.'

A laugh carries down the stairs after me.

On the morning of the sixth day, I shelter in my study, reading Bunyan, or trying to. Over the previous two days the storm has climbed to a roiling fever. The old barn fell down during the night, and pieces of the frame lie strewn about the orchard. Another upstairs window went in at daybreak, and I found a long batten of wood stuck through the pane. We dare not leave the house for fear of being swept up like last year's leaves.

I am praying the roof is not torn off entirely when the familiar discomfort at my core returns. My lungs tighten and I start wheezing. A burning sensation spreads down my gullet, my chest, my arms, and when I rise, I almost fall back into my seat, but force myself to walk.

I hobble through to the kitchen, where Mary plucks a snipe for the evening meal. She is halfway through her task, surrounded by knives and mottled brown feathers. In this, the most protected room in the house, you could almost imagine yourself safe from the chaos outside, except for the turmoil in the chimney, where the wind keeps putting out the fire.

'Mary...'

She hears me, turns, and sees my face. 'What's wrong? What is it? You're grey.'

'My chest,' I say, coming down heavily in a seat at the table. I clench my fist and wrap my other hand about it, instinctively pushing on my sternum. 'There... there's nothing to be done. I must just wait.'

She comes closer, and I see she is frightened by my infirmity. She crouches, and places both hands on mine. 'Let me prepare some honeyed water and mallow. It might loosen your chest.'

I nod, grateful. As the water heats, she busies herself at the table, expertly bending the head of the snipe around and trussing its legs with the beak. She hardly looks down as she does it. Instead, she is watching me. I inhale and exhale deeply, and within minutes the pain is more localised. 'It's easing off,' I say.

The feeling of being caught in a vice subsides, and soon I can breathe normally.

Mary pours the water and gathers ingredients. She moves swiftly, selecting bottles and pots from the drawer where she stores such things. She combines her palliatives, then brings the steaming pewter beaker. 'Drink,' she says, and holds the cup to my mouth. I take in its hot sweet vapour. Beneath the balmy scent of honey is something acrid. I sip. The liquid burns me. My wife's eyes gleam with something softer than of late – a sort of pity, a gift I both crave and resent.

'I'll let it cool,' I say.

'But you will drink it?'

I agree, though it is more for her than for me. There is no remedy for a failing body. No potion or tincture that can rob Father Time of his due.

I take the tea back to my study and when it is cool, as has always been my habit, drain it quickly, to the last drop. Then I return to Bunyan.

But it is no use. For around fifteen minutes I study the same page, but can't keep my concentration. The noise outside is bad enough, but a leaden tiredness has engulfed me. I turn back to the frontispiece of the book and place a polished stone on top of the page to hold it, then cover my eyes with my palms. Deprived of one sense, I am more aware of the rest: the yowling wind, the steady pulse of blood through my fingers, and a curious sensation of drifting.

I remove my hands, blink hard, and try again to focus, but the long title undulates before me: *from this world, to that which is to come, delivered un...* I cannot read the rest. Thinking of some dust speck or flying gnat, I scrub my right eye, then my left, and look to see if any dark blot emerges on my fingers. Nothing. But my hand looks peculiar, outlandishly large. My surroundings are a blur. The room spins like a whip top. Now I am sinking,

241

clawing at the earth, going deeper and still deeper. No, it is not earth, but water, and I claw, not at soil, but at my own suffocating lungs. A phantasmagoria of light and shadow, currents and whirlpools, pulls me down, down, down.

I try to walk as the floor pivots and tilts like the deck of a ship. I grapple at the walls, trying to form Mary's name, but silence has me by the throat. Between my study and the kitchen, I fall. I look through to the kitchen, and see her, watching me out of her unreadable eyes. I reach out – *help me* – but she does not move from her table. She stands, eyes screwed closed, the knife clutched tightly in her right hand, rocking back and forth on her heels with her forearms over her ears, to exclude something, some sound or voice she cannot bear to hear.

I realise I have been drugged. But why…?

Oh, Mary, no.

She turns towards the fireplace. One, two, three steps. The wind has quieted the flames, but the hearth is still searing hot and she moves with care. Her body partly obscures her actions, but I can just about see as she uses the knife to lever out a single brick, places it to one side, and removes an object from the cavity. What is it she has there? Something that jangles in her left hand. Something ancient and rusted, red with brick dust.

A set of keys.

She walks towards the stairs with the knife by her side. Her steps are strangely agitated, as if some outside force prevails on her, or she is divided in her purpose.

You cannot – must not… My words die on my tongue. My sight goes black.

―――――――

I float back to the surface. Opening my eyes is agony, and for long moments I flounder, not knowing, not remembering. But slowly, the mist begins to thin. How much of what I have seen is real? Is this some trick, or delusion? I move like I am underwater, my senses blunted, cotton-wrapped. Yet the fear retains its edge. My limbs shudder, my heart gallops, and the distance between here and the attic might be a thousand miles.

Am I too late?

I drag myself to the door and lean against the frame. The stairs tower above me, an impossible feat. Is it my drug-clouded brain, or have the walls begun to shake?

With each step, I come closer to Mary. I hold to this thought. In my mind's eye I see her, clutching her knife, moving as if under some spell.

Panting and wheezing, I reach the top. The door to the second stairway is open. Just a little, just ajar. And despite the knowledge that bites at me, that she has opened the lock with her old skeleton keys, my mind almost rejects the sight – of course the door is locked, and of course the key is safely stowed in my pocket. But no. It is open. The candles are all out.

I push the door. It strikes the wall, and admits the ravening wind. I trip on the third stair, then stumble up the rest, until I am in the attic. Inside, the wind whips at me like a lash. Furniture rattles like old bones. And there is no sea-salt smell; instead, the air holds the coppery hint of blood. In the corner, a dim light glints off steel. Perched behind Esther on the bench, Mary holds the knife to the notch of our captive's throat. It is a wicked-looking thing, the blade whetted, the tip honed to a needlepoint. Mary's other hand is in Esther's hair, pulling back her head to expose her neck, like an animal. Above it, my wife's face is a mask of pain and indecision, her skin waxen, blue on white. But now I see her hands are crimson-splashed, like the bright, bright flowers she loves to grow.

My sister's blood pools on the floor, seeping into the wood. I skid in it, and fall, landing hard on my side. It is warm, congealing, coating my hands. 'Stop! Mary, don't!'

She does not answer. Terrible cries come from her mouth.

I can't see where the blood is coming from. Has she cut deep enough? Will it – finally – be over?

Only now do I really look at Esther. In the midst of chaos – the spilled blood, the storm, Mary's feral sobbing – she is the calm epicentre. Her face, smooth, unlined, registers no fear or shock. Her arms are in her lap, still shackled, and there is a weeping laceration from her wrist to her elbow.

I get to my feet, still sliding. Hold out my arms to my wife. 'Mary, come here. Come to me.' Her arm shakes, the knife wavers. I take a step forward. 'Don't, my love – it is what it wants.'

Doubt leaps in her wild eyes.

'It wants you to set it free. It wants you to make yourself a murderess. But I cannot let you carry this for me; it is not your responsibility, but mine. *Mine*. I must decide.' I face my sister instead, and those eyes bore into me like steel points. 'Do you hear me? *I* will decide. And this will end.'

The pause before the knife clatters to the floorboards lasts an age. Mary releases her hold on Esther's hair, and sinks back, sobbing, with her head against the wall.

––––––––––

The wind has dropped.

Now they come to me in my dreams, the dead. Joan. Goodwife Gedge. John Rutherford. Milton. My father. On Acheron's distant shore they wait, and I greet them as people I will soon see again. Yet I am nervous as a boy, lest they have not forgotten my sins.

My father extends his long arms to me. His strength is given back in death, and he is now as I remember him – tall and solemn and wise. Milton often stands beside him, but for reasons

I cannot fully grasp, in these moments, the poet remains blind, unrestored, his hair as thin and grey as mouse fur, as in his final years. His voice drifts towards me, like smoke across the water: *remember that you have free will. Remember.*

The dreams always develop in the same way. I wade into the water until the mist creeps as high as my thighs. The current is cold and strong. I try to cross, but my boots stick, and I am as heavy as if they have filled with mud. I reach for those on the other shore, but their voices rise in chorus: *go back, go back! He is not finished with you.*

Then, in the centre of the river, something ripples beneath the surface, and I wake, panting and shaking. I must decide.

24

February 1644

North Norfolk

The journey north was interminable. Milton rode a small white mare, slower than Ben, and carried side satchels crammed with books and papers, food enough to feed a regiment, and several bottles of good wine. I bit back comments about travelling fast and light. He was willing to come, that was all that mattered, and for the first time since I had encountered the mutilated remains of my father's flock, we were moving forward. Still, I was horrified by any delay. Milton, being older and no longer in the best of health, could not ride from dawn to dusk. Yet, desperate to see familiar spires and woods about me, I entreated him to eat and drink in the saddle, to go on just that little bit longer before stopping for sleep. We could not afford to squander a moment.

The intimacy of the library, the near friendliness I had experienced from my old tutor, pursuing a shared goal in the company of old books and a high fire, had evaporated. Milton appeared deep in thought, and spoke little as we rode. When I tried to talk of Esther, or the creature, he wished to talk of other things, and we did: the war, Parliament, and Milton's travels on the Continent.

'You truly met Galileo?' I said, awestruck.

'Yes. First, of course, I met his son, Vincenzo. The son introduced me to the father.'

'And Galileo was imprisoned for heresy?'

'Oh, yes. He was a very great heretic. His son was a talented lute player,' he added, in the mildest of tones.

My mind staggered at the idea of meeting such intellectual giants, the celebrated geniuses of Florence and Rome. 'It was his contention, was it not, sir, that the Earth revolves around the Sun, rather than the other way about?'

'It was,' came the answer, as though this were no very great matter.

'What do you think of that?'

Milton drew to a halt. We were at a crossroads. 'I do not know these roads,' he said. 'Which way is north-east?'

It was still early, and the sky was lit by stars and moon. Looking up, I could see the pattern of the Plough in the Great Bear, showing the way to the North Star. I pointed, quickly, north-east. 'That way,' I said.

'Then let us be about it,' said Milton, digging in his heels and picking up the pace. I shook my head as I followed, reminded of Milton's worst habit – that of not quite answering a question put to him, and expecting the listener to know what he meant anyway.

It took five days to get to Norfolk, and by the time we approached Worstead, the middle days of February were upon us. Milton showed pleasure at sights he had seen before, remarking on the prosperous old churches and weavers' hamlets that lined the way back to the farm. Here, thankfully, there were few signs of the war; it felt much as it always had – peaceful, sedate, unchanging.

Yet, as we passed St Walstan's, I grew ever more wary. I had carried my nerves close on the journey, but now we were so near home I could not dispel the thought that something had gone wrong, that I had been foolish to leave Mary and Henry for so long. I could not stop picturing Esther waking up, escaping her bonds, or – and I did not know which was worse – her body reacting badly to a dose of the dwale.

But as we approached the house, a figure stood in the doorway, tall, wearing a striped gown and apron, dark hair pinned neatly, and no cap. Mary watched quietly as we directed the horses up the path. I met her eyes as I dismounted, and was aware again of what I had been able to forget in Milton's company: the fear, the dark circles beneath her eyes, the strain in the set of her mouth. I wanted to run to her and take her in my arms, take the fear from her in any way I could. I wanted to sink to my knees and feel her long arms about my head and neck, to rest on the softness of her stomach. I wanted to sleep beside her, a deep sleep, clouded by no dreams.

Milton, dismounting, had a small smile on his face as he saw Mary, and watched me watching her.

'Mary, this is Mr Milton,' I said. 'My old tutor.'

'Sir,' Mary said. 'Thank you for coming here.'

'Good morning, Mary,' said Milton.

'Is Esther…?' I asked.

'She still sleeps,' said Mary.

'We must cease giving her the sedative at once,' frowned Milton, picking a stray hair out of the pottage in front of him and trying to wipe it on the linen without Mary seeing. 'It is the only way we shall reach the truth of what it is, of what has possessed her.'

I hesitated as Mary turned from the stove with freshly baked, black-topped bread. It thumped as it hit the table. I smiled encouragingly. She did not smile back, and looked unhappy. 'The drug has worked so far,' she said. 'She has not stirred since we began to administer it. Even Henry has been prepared to remain in the house without further fear, but that will change if she wakes.'

Henry certainly seemed more confident. He had assisted Mary in preparing a meal, gulped his own food down and now was in what seemed to be his favourite place: the stables, where he had offered to feed and brush down the horses while the adults talked.

'That is so. And yet her body will be building a tolerance to its agents,' Milton advised. 'Soon more and more will be required to achieve the same result, and then there will be no amount which will do so short of killing her.'

Their eyes came to rest on me. It was my decision. I reached for the bread, cutting a thick slice, smearing it with too much butter to compensate for the charcoal taste. As I ate, I kept my eyes on the table, thinking Mary was right; it was dangerous to wake Esther, and the drug was doing the job it had been designed for. But equally, we could not leave her under its influence forever. In the end, it would threaten her life. And what sort of life would it be anyway, caught in perpetual sleep, never to see the sun or feel the wind on her face?

I addressed Milton. 'Do you think we can make any difference by speaking with it, sir?'

Milton shook his head. 'I cannot say. I do not wish to raise any hopes.' But he could not disguise the lustre behind his eyes: here was knowledge, here was the possibility for discovery.

I turned back to Mary. 'You have given me more than I could have asked, by caring for my sister in my absence. Most would have run from this. You have earnt the right to speak your mind. What, in your opinion, should I do?'

She seemed to waver, and I saw her bite back her instinctive response. What was she thinking? That an overdose of the drug would allow Esther to slip away, painlessly? That, dead, she could present no further danger? That I was a fool to risk all our lives, and who knew how many others, just to save one young woman who was not even my sister?

She sighed. 'You must try,' she admitted, and I breathed again. She saw my relief, and a smile, very slight, appeared at the corners of her mouth. I smiled back.

Milton coughed. 'Then we are agreed? We will cease the delivery of the drug and, when she comes fully round, approach her?' I nodded. 'And which of us will be present? I would very much like it if I...'

'Yes,' I said. 'You will be there, sir. I will need you in this.' Milton looked relieved. I turned to Mary. 'But I do not want Henry here when this happens, so you cannot be here either.' She started to object. 'I know,' I interrupted. 'You have done more than any of us – so long alone with her, and caring for Henry and this house, too. But now I must insist on Henry's safety. I would ask you to take him and shelter in the church – there's said to be a priest's shelter in the tower, through the vestry, and nobody will know you are there – until we come for you. Until we know, one way or another, what we deal with, and what we must do to overcome it.'

Reluctantly, she agreed. Did she know that my fear was for her, as much as for her brother? I couldn't bear the thought of harm coming to her.

Milton rose, dabbing the unpalatable stew from the sides of his mouth with a linen square. 'I will visit the privy,' he said. 'Then we will see her, and guess how long it might be before she wakes.'

Alone with Mary, I thanked her for the meal, but didn't compliment it; she was, truly, a terrible cook. She made faces as she ate from her own bowl and, after a failed attempt to finish it, pushed it away, laughing. 'I never had much opportunity to learn,' she said. 'Henry has a better grasp of the art than I.'

'And I. He's a good boy,' I said. 'And his life has been hard.'

More soberly, Mary nodded. 'It is of great regret to me that I have not been able to give him something better.' She looked about the kitchen. 'He likes it here, even given what we face.'

I watched as she began clearing the bowls and spoons. I should have been helping, but allowed myself the brief luxury of thinking forwards, to the years ahead, perhaps, with Mary still here, moving around this table, but this being her kitchen, now, and several energetic forms crowding about her feet. She would bend down, and her dark hair would fall like a velvet curtain, caressing the cheek of a toddling child as she rose with it in her arms, kissing it. She would hand me the child and I would feel the passing touch of her fingers like lightning.

Beneath that, like a sea-siren, another image was rising. A ship, huge, and pitching on wind-roused waves. As if my mind's eye could see through the boat's hull, I peeped inside, and there we were, like a set of tiny dolls: Mary, Henry, Esther and I, the demon banished, England behind us, the prow set for the New World. From somewhere in the darkness came the sweetness of a psalm, sung as the night watch was set. Esther held her hymnal close and Henry sat on my knee, a little seasick, as his sister spoke to him of the adventures we would have, and how he would have a horse of his very own. I turned to Mary in the half-light, took her hand in my own, and kissed her...

I stopped. Foolish imaginings, I scolded myself. This was a cursed house, and if I could keep Mary in it another day, I would be lucky.

I realised she was speaking to me, that she had said my name more than once. I started, embarrassed by my fantasies. 'Forgive me. I was caught by my thoughts.' For a moment she looked curious, and I believed she would ask about them, but she did not.

———

As Mary and Henry put together their few possessions, some water and a little food, and left to seek shelter for the night in the church, Milton and I mounted the stairs.

Mary said Esther had not stirred at all since being fed the dwale, so there seemed no reason now to lock or close the door.

The liquid had been given daily, along with water. After the first attempts at feeding her, Mary feared she would choke if she tried to force porridge or even a thin gruel down her throat. As a result, Esther's body had begun to collapse in on itself. She appeared to shrink before my eyes. Her limbs, always slender, now resembled those of a newborn calf or deer – just bones and sockets. Her shoulders were tiny, like a small child's, holding up a head that seemed to have ballooned to twice its former size. I pulled the covers up to warm her, or perhaps to distract myself from what I did not want to see.

'It's hard to believe such a face could disguise evil,' Milton said, sitting in the chair by her bed.

'It doesn't,' I said, firmly. 'Esther is the sweetest of girls. A man could not wish for such a sister.'

Indeed, there was something saintly about Esther's face now. It seemed to glow in the thin rays of the winter sun that lanced the little room like spears. Her hair shone in a halo around the pale repose of her head on the pillow. Her closed lids were lined with tiny blue veins that trembled with each breath. They might have been closed in prayer. I perceived that the thread-like veins glistened, and knew, now, that I was not imagining the smell of the sea around her: salt and wind and brine.

'Do you think she dreams?' I asked Milton.

'Perhaps of Heaven,' my tutor replied, softly, leaning forward to watch her more closely. 'Or the motion of the spheres.'

While Esther dreamt, we waited. Outside, the sun had long attained its height and begun to fall before she breathed a little more lightly. Her hands stirred before the rest of her, the fingers gathering against the linen and leaping in tiny convulsions, minutes apart at first, then closer together, as if she returned to life just as something on the other side of the veil sought to keep her from us. I did not exhort her to wake. I did not know whether I truly wanted her to do so.

We had brought water and wine, and left a chamber pot just outside. I had explained to Milton what Not-Esther had done with Rutherford and the Gedge women, how the voice had twisted them to its will; we had decided neither one of us could be left in its conscious company without the other.

But Milton must have been growing bored. As the sun started to set, he stood and stretched his limbs and splashed his face with the warming water from the jug. He approached the window and peeped through the nailed planks on the outside, across the fields. 'You can see the church from here,' he commented. 'Which is it?'

'St Walstan's,' I said.

'Ah. Patron saint of farmers and labourers. Not picklocks, though.'

I had told Milton about Mary during my initial telling of the story in Chalfonte, and now regretted it, but did not rise to the bait. 'No, just farmers,' I said.

'Do you know my wife is called Mary, too?'

'I did not know you had taken a wife,' I lied.

'Oh, certainly, you did,' Milton answered, with a frown. 'Mistress Bern is the greatest gossip in three counties.'

Not wishing to lie again, I said nothing.

'And you know my Mary has left me,' Milton continued. 'Gone back to her people, at least until we see the outcome of this war.'

'Will she come back?'

'I do not know. Don't marry, Thomas,' he said, his face showing a rare flash of humour. But it was a hard humour, offering no reassurance that he did not mean it. 'Far easier to be alone.'

'My father said a good marriage is like having a constant song in one's heart,' I said, rubbing away a growing stiffness in my lower legs. How long had we been sat here? It felt like days.

'Well, your father had sound taste in music,' Milton said, dourly.

The matter that had lain silent for so long between us was surfacing. I could not help my next question. 'I have wanted to know… Do you blame me for Elizabeth, sir? I could not fault you if you did.'

Milton seemed far more interested in the view from the window. His voice was unruffled as he eventually said, 'We can blame no man for the plague. It is God's will. She died because she had always been destined to die, and nothing you or I could have done would have changed that.'

'But…'

At that moment, Esther made a small, gasping noise, like a kitten's mewl. We turned to see her arching her back, clawing at the sheets with white-tipped fingers. She was in pain. I rushed to her side. 'Esther!' I pressed her hand, too hard, to see whether I might persuade her to open her eyes. In my heart bloomed the smallest of hopes: what if, when she woke, she was Esther again? My sister, pious and gentle, and entirely herself.

I held my breath. I was afraid as I touched her clammy skin, not knowing whether I touched her or something far more ancient, and more malevolent.

Milton stood back. His face betrayed his curiosity. I remembered that I had often found my tutor cold – Milton wanted to know, to discern truth, but often it was as if he himself were unaffected by what he discovered.

Slowly, Esther stirred from the land of dreams. Her lashes fluttered. She murmured something I could not hear.

'Will she take water?' Milton held the jug and a cup, which he now half-filled, pressing it into my hand.

I lifted the cup to my sister's lips. She struggled to control her mouth and could barely hold her lips against the rim. This was how my father had concluded his days – chained in a second childhood.

But she was surfacing. She cleared her throat and accepted more water. Moment by moment, a shaky awareness returned to her expression. I could see no malice in her face. And, for a few wild, untethered beats of my heart, I wondered... Tremulously, I said, 'Sister, it's me. It's Thomas.'

But when she spoke, it was in the voice I had dreaded, the voice that had turned my sleep to torment and my hopes to ashes. 'Everything turns yellow. It is as if they look directly at the sun. Old and young burn to death, white bones are scattered over reddish rubble. The survivors cling to the earth and forget to cry. Autumn rain falls on a city of blood.' She was hoarse from sleep and her breath foul. I squeezed my eyes closed, sagging so that my forehead touched her hand.

Milton moved closer. He was close enough to smell her, not just the watery scent of her, but the essence of stale sheets and uncleansed skin. He said, 'What do you see?'

'Everything,' she – it – whispered. 'The whole life of man.' Her brow was tightened, crumpled with pain.

Milton's voice throbbed. 'You spoke of a city. Where is it?'

'Do you like cities, John Milton?'

I heard a swift intake of breath. 'Yes.' I wanted to stop them, to call out an objection, to say that this exchange was not helping us discover what we did not already know.

It said, 'I will show you a city rich with streets of trodden gold.'

'Where?'

'You would see it?' came the quick reply.

'I would see everything.'

'Here, then. A foretasting of the darkness that waits for you.'

Esther flicked her free hand and though it rose just inches from the bed, Milton recoiled, lifting his clenched fists to shield his eyes. He cried out, pressing his hands into the sockets as if they had flooded with bile.

I released Esther and ran to Milton, who had fallen back into his seat. 'What is it? John? What's happening?'

He writhed, his mouth gaping and twisting. I gripped his shoulders and tried to still his struggles. 'Speak!' I commanded. But Milton could not speak. As I exerted all my force, pulling his hands away from his eyes, I saw they were staring and open, rolling back in their sockets, clouded over and corrupted. Milton was blind.

As I called his name over and over in an effort to calm him, I glanced back at the bed to see Esther's reaction but instead saw only rumpled sheets. A half-second later, I heard the unmistakeable sound of the door closing, and a key turning in the lock.

25

My entreaties were short-lived. In those brief seconds I had tended Milton, Esther had slipped from the bed like a spirit and locked the heavy door.

For several minutes, I shouted: 'Esther!' But it was futile. Whatever could hear me, if anything could, it was not Esther. There would be no reasoning with it. And the door was made from solid New Forest oak, the lock of wrought iron. I had no hope of breaking it down. I tried anyway, bludgeoning its mass with my right side. Pain exploded across my shoulder, eight, nine, ten times, and eventually carried me through to numbness, until I fell, gasping, to my knees.

Milton had sunk into something like a trance. His eyes were open and clouded in moonlight-pale blue. I slapped his flaccid cheeks – an action, only weeks ago, that would have given me pleasure – and shook him like an errant child. All to no avail. Moments after being robbed of sight, he had collapsed, all his faculties and will cut off, as swift and dreadful as death. Now my panic was rising. Not-Esther was free. The fear of its malice swept over me. Should I, after all, have given her an excess of the drug? Should I have let her die? That whispered regret racked me – how could I call myself her brother, while countenancing such thoughts?

But what would it do? What had it done already, to Milton, and for what purpose had it imprisoned us?

My thoughts developed a chaotic momentum of their own. Not what was, but what *might be*, unfolded before me like the fall of Fortuna's great wheel. Not-Esther, escaping my reach and my protection, going inland, towards Norwich or Ipswich, heedless of winter, needless of food or shelter, that loathsome voice surging through her like an evil wind, seeking out ears in which to pour its venom, its mastery of scripture, its prophecies, its revelations… It would carry with it a hint of the divine, or the damned. And so its vision would take form, and Esther would be a temple made not by human hands – a vessel of Antichrist, a tabernacle of death and destruction.

It was foreseen in Revelation.

And I saw a beast coming out of the sea… He was given power to make war against the saints and to conquer them.

This was the time of the saints. The time of the Puritans. Was it also the time of the beast?

And eventually, when men caught her, hunted her down in the fens or forests like an animal, deaf to mercy, they would condemn her, drag her to the stake, and there, before the eyes of the faithful, burn the beast's house to the ground.

I could not let it happen.

Recovering my breath, I stumbled to the window. Dark gathered, the light through the nailed slats fading fast. Bats rustled in the eaves above my head, and, near the stables, Guppy barked for a meal. But my senses were drawn below, towards the door, as I feared to hear it close, or to see a shape, light-footed, venturing from the house. Through the gaps, I strained my sight towards the church, sending out a silent communication to Mary and Henry: *stay put and I'll come for you.*

But how? I eyed the window doubtfully. With my body fully extended, I could drop to the ground. The fall wouldn't kill me. But could I get it open? My boots were sturdy leather, but the planks were nailed from the outside with all the force of my fear. Looking around, my heart sank again: I had been too vigilant. My sword was downstairs – I had not thought to need it.

Nothing remained to use as a tool, nothing but my own body, and that was weaker than I had hoped. Even if I succeeded, this window was smaller than the one in Manyon's study. It was designed to keep in heat and keep out the wind, not for a grown man to climb through. Still, I had to try. I girded myself against the whitewashed stone, my palms pushing outwards like Samson's, as if I intended to move the walls themselves, raised my foot, braced, and kicked.

Nothing moved. I had hammered in those iron rose heads as though our lives depended on it; they held fast.

Next, I dug my fingers around the wood, forcing the tips through the cracks. Splinters broke through my skin, driving deep into the pads and beneath the nails, but I didn't stop. There was a near-savagery about that movement, yet even as I yielded to it, and cried out, I knew the planks would not shift. My nails were shredded and bleeding. My shoulder ached where I had pounded the door and my neck throbbed. I sat on the bed with my back against the headboard. A few feet away, Milton whimpered. I propped myself up again, thinking he might have regained consciousness, but whatever Milton could see that was frightening him, he and it were far away.

The sounds of evening came on. The call of a linnet, an owl hoot, then the first uneven patters of rain. These grew more rhythmic and louder as the minutes ticked by. Outside, wherever Esther was, the snow would be melting, the brooks and streams rising, the water flowing inexorably towards the sea. It was almost soothing, that picture, in its timeless monotony, and its distance from our human troubles. I let myself see it, imagined the waves carrying me, releasing me, and as the turbulence of my thoughts began to calm and my raging blood cooled, leaving me bone-weary, I allowed my eyes to close, just for a moment, just for a few seconds without grief... I slept, fitfully.

In my dream, I was five or six, and Father showed me how to build a fire. He cleared the ground of twigs, bark and foliage, then piled dirt on the bare earth. 'Gather tinder,' he said, walking me through the forest, pointing to the types of grass, leaves and funguses that would help to ignite a fire and the dried wood that would sustain it. Then he lit it using his tinderbox, and I watched, fascinated, as the yellow flames crept up the twigs, licking the outside of the larger chunks, climbing higher and higher. 'You want to get it as hot as possible or it won't catch.' Father's voice was moving away; I reached out, trying to close the distance, but found I was now a man. 'Wake up, Thomas,' said my father. 'You must wake up.'

'Fire!' This was not my father's voice. It was nearer, and full of fear.

I opened my eyes. They stung, and my vision was blurred. Evening had given way to night, but how long had I been asleep? My throat was parched and rough. I breathed through my nose and sat up, spurred to action by the smell of smoke, still thin, but pungent enough to fill my chest and make it smart. My limbs seemed affected, too. I moved like an old man, levering myself off the bed. Somewhere outside, Guppy barked an alarm. Then I saw it, coming in beneath the door: the slow drift of grey danger every man and woman feared. Smoke.

'Milton!' My exclamation fell on deaf ears; if it had been Milton's voice that had woken me, its owner had spoken unwittingly, still lost in whatever labyrinthian subconscious he explored. The man was no more aware than the chair in which he sat. He could be no help.

Now, terror drove me harder and further than I had thought possible. I thought I had kicked at those nailed boards with all my might before, but I hadn't. Of course I hadn't. With my hands over my mouth and nose, holding my breath until my chest felt like it would explode, I drove my foot at the window like a gunstone cannonball, and on the third blow, with a ringing snap, the slats broke, and I dragged my foot back through the gap. I kept kicking, coughing, not pausing for breath, and within a minute, my throat so full I thought it was on fire, I was leaning out, drinking in the drizzly air like cold, fresh water. Behind me, the room had filled with smoke.

I was about to try to squeeze through, when I turned back to Milton.

I could leave him. I knew I could do it. I had harboured my dislike for so long that it had grown in the shadows of my mind in the years since I had last seen him, and it would be easy to seize upon it, to make my excuses and go.

The smoke snaked into the room in spiralling threads that quickly became malignant ropes. I could feel no heat yet, and did not think the upper floors of the house were alight. I wanted nothing more than to jump, with the desire growing inside me like a great wave until I thought I would do it.

I looked at Milton, still and quiet in his chair, a shadowy shape, seemingly oblivious to the dark pall thickening the air around us. I went to him, placing my good shoulder against his chest and my arm behind his back. 'Come on,' I said, using every ounce of my strength to pull the smaller man up and over my shoulder. 'Move, you clever bastard,' I grunted. 'I'm not dying for you.'

'Thomas!'

I dropped Milton back into his chair. The voice had come from the other side of the door. It was real and pitched high with fright. 'Thomas, are you in there?'

Mary.

'We're here!' I called out, caught between fear for her safety and relief at her voice. Then I cursed. 'I told you not to come.'

'The key has gone!' she cried.

'Where is the fire?'

'The kitchen,' she said. 'But it's spreading. I can't stop it.'

'We're going out of the window. You need to get out.'

'Is Esther in there with you?' Her voice was muffled, and she coughed repeatedly, a horrible, hacking sound.

'No. She locked the door. She must have set the fire, and she's gone. It's just Milton and me. Go,' I said again, coughing violently. 'We can't get out and it can't be long...' Thoughts of her succumbing to the smoke, or the stairs collapsing as she attempted to flee, crowded out any hope of rescue, but even so, to me, her voice was a lodestar, gleaming out of the dark like Venus in the north-western sky.

'Hold on,' she said. 'I'll be back.'

The feeling of being alone, that terror that had been briefly settled by her presence, intensified, until it rose inside me in a feral howl.

I wavered. I could not wait long, but was torn. If I attempted the window, I would risk Milton's life, but by leaving I would abandon Mary, and that I could not do. Yet I could not get to her through a locked door.

The next sound was a quiet and unobtrusive clicking, as if a small, deft bird pecked at the lock. More smoke spiralled in, filling the room, making my eyes water. I could no longer see properly. The noise continued. I crossed to the door, choking on the smog, and leant against the wood, trying not to breathe. What must have been no more than thirty seconds felt like an age, but then the handle moved, and the door swung open.

A cloud of noxious, hot fumes rushed in, but beyond it, there was Mary, a huge bunch of keys clutched in her hand, her face covered by a tied wet cloth.

We managed between us to get Milton out of his chair. I poured what water remained in the jug on a sheet and draped it over his head. At the door, Mary went first, and I dragged Milton's senseless form behind me, holding him beneath his armpits and using my knees to keep him off the floor. As we crossed the landing, the smoke was hot and heavy. Breathing was painful, so I held my wind as we staggered down the stairs, fumbling for each step in the suffocating blackness. The fire, which had started in the kitchen, must have been slow to spread due to the heavy wood of the furnishings and flagged floor, but we could hear the flames rushing now, beginning to lick the timbers of the kitchen ceiling. From there, inevitably, they would come through the floor into the rooms above, and as the smoke heated the walls and staircase, so these would catch more easily. There was no stopping it.

The front door was open. We dashed for it, craving clean air. Mary was out first, then I blundered through with Milton, dropping his weight, falling to my knees on the cobbled flint path, gasping deep and urgent breaths. I gagged, thinking I would vomit, but nothing came. We lay in the glow and gathering roar of the fire.

After several minutes in which neither of us spoke, Mary got unsteadily to her feet. She looked down at Milton, who lay insensate with his blind eyes wide open. 'What's the matter with him?' she said, breathlessly.

'Esther – she – it – did it. Where's Henry?'

'He's still in the church. We were watching and saw the smoke. I ran. I thought...' Her face was blackened, smeared with smoke and sweat. She carried her fright in her stance, all stiff and still. I stood up and went to her, putting my arms about her, feeling the heat rising from her cloak and dress. She was shaking; so was I. For several moments we stood, not knowing what to do next, but I felt a strange comfort in our shared paralysis. It was the first time I had held her, and she seemed to fit like the unlooked-for return of some childhood treasure, something lost, but not forgotten.

'Picking locks, eh?' I said, after a minute had passed, speaking into the smoky webs of her hair. Her replying laugh was low and husky. 'You must show me how you do that.'

'I imagine she carries lots of different keys, such that each lock has its match, along with a lantern and a chisel. There is little mystery about it.' These words were uttered between hoarse coughs and splutters, by a voice as conscious and aware as my own. Mary removed her arms from where they had rested on my waist, and looked over my shoulder, to where Milton lay on the ground, meeting her eyes, wide awake.

26

'Henry is still in the tower?'

Mary nodded, looking numb. We watched for several minutes. The fire was greedy. Brave raindrops spattered the blaze, and were consumed. The timbers were alight now, and hissed and spat as they burnt. The roof caught, began to bow, and clouds of smoke belched from the windows. Furnace-like, vapours and sparks escaped in a column of orange and black against the overcast sky. The heat roasted our faces and made our eyes stream with tears.

'Come away,' I told them. 'We can't do anything. And we'll freeze without shelter.' We could not douse the flames. We could only watch, half-transfixed, as all I owned was taken, yet I was so exhausted, I could not even rouse myself to anger or pain.

We huddled in the stables. Guppy nosed my hand and the horses stomped and whinnied in fright. Milton was barely able to walk. Mary and I had supported him between us, and now released his weight into the straw. He lay with eyes wide and staring while I took several candles from the store, staggered back towards the house, and lit them from the blaze itself.

When I returned, Mary threw her arms about my neck without warning. 'I'm so sorry,' she whispered. Her embrace was tight. She, like me, was thickly coated in ash. I accepted her comfort, pulling her close, and allowing my fingers to catch in the loops of her hair, as though I could tie myself to her. For a few moments, we stood stock-still. There was something about her nearness that calmed me, as if she were the peace I had

searched for all my life. Slowly, my body realised I was alive
– I had survived the fire. Mary and Milton were safe. My limbs
stopped urging flight. I began to breathe normally, to relax the
knotted muscles of my throat, and to think: *what next?*

Then, from where he lay in the straw, Milton said, 'I saw a
terrifying horde of martialled spirits filling a great barren space;
more than the barbarian, more than the stars of Heaven's endless
plain, so many that of their true number no record could keep
account. They were mighty, each more imposing than a man,
yet all formless and as yet unbodied. Some I recognised, countless ages from their pagan dominations upon the Earth: Moloch,
lover of human sacrifice; Chemos, he that was worshipped by
Solomon in his utmost folly; Baal and Astarte, Tammuz and
Dagon. Innumerable, illimitable; monstrous in their rebellion.
They were the children of chaos, ten thousand banners strong.

'Then, the Arch-Fiend spoke. I cannot speak his words, not yet.
They were heavy with defeat, yet hot with resolve. They evoked
the crash of shields and the din of war. His minions resolved upon
building a city, atop a great hill of fire and smoke. They rifled
for their tools – metal and ore, to build their impious structure.
Driven on by this multitude, a work of which men would boast
for a thousand years rose up within an hour: a temple, of columns
and pillars high, of wrought gold, arched roof, and untold cham-
bers within, dwarfing Babylon itself. A city, just as she told me,'
he concluded. 'Raised by a demonic army.'

Milton had regained his sight, but blinked repeatedly and
rubbed his eyes, as if testing whether he could really see. He
spoke with something like awe. His speech seemed different –
trapped in some pattern of poetry and pictures, like he had not
entirely returned from whichever world in which the creature's
words had ensnared him. I realised it was important: what he
had seen during his trance could throw open this mystery.

'Why?' I asked, bewildered. 'Why would it show you that?'

Milton thought. 'I think it is showing me where it comes from. What it is.'

'There's no time for this,' snapped Mary, just as suddenly as Milton had spoken. 'Henry is alone, and she is out there.' She had released me, and stood between us, her eyes wild and conflicted. I realised, of course, that she might not know the way in the dark.

'Yes,' I said, feeling inexpressibly weary. But there was truth in her words: with Not-Esther free, Henry was in danger.

I looked at Milton. 'When I return, we will talk more upon this.' Then, at Mary, who was gathering up her cloak. 'But I will go, not you. I know the fields much better.' She moved to argue, and I held both her hands in mine. 'I'll have Guppy. Better to stay here with Mi— Mr Milton. I'll bring Henry, then in the morning we'll look for Esther.'

'All right,' she said, finally. 'But I'll look for him at first light, whether you're back or not.'

'I'll be back,' I promised, fearing it was an empty promise, for I did not know how I would find my sister, what would happen if I did, anything beyond these few black hours to come.

———

With the bristle of the hedgerow spiking my bare left hand, the glow of the fire behind, and the lantern's halo before me, I felt my way along the edge of the field. My lungs still burnt from the smoke, and the numbness after shouldering the door had receded, only to be replaced by brutal aches over my entire body.

It was six fields' walk to the church. The ground underfoot was slippery with softening snow, undulating with troughs, hillocks and low knolls. Worried about the vicious teeth of poachers' traps, or the mantraps laid by my father's men to deter them, I kept Guppy to my rear on my right-hand side; he was unsettled by the fire and my tense, silent presence, and growled often at unseen movements – more than likely just the rustlings of foxes, sheep or weasels, but I leapt each time he snarled, training the light towards the open field and my unprotected side. It was not the dark that affected the mastiff. He and I had been out here often to bring home an injured or sick sheep, or to attend a birthing ewe, and he knew the journey instinctively, padding along the surest ground, but he was uneasy.

He was not alone, there. We both felt there was something here that should not be.

I took each step gingerly, unable to afford a stumble in a chance burrow or molehill that might break an ankle or put out the light. As we came to a boggy patch, I encouraged Guppy up the soil bank, where the hedgerows grew tall and the undergrowth sat heavier. I flinched at a cracking sound, and the knowledge of having broken something. My mind was screaming as I withdrew my boot, suggesting starveling wolves, bugbears, boggarts – everything impossible, or unnatural, that a frightened man might imagine taking shape. Reaching down, my hand shaking, I retrieved something jagged at the edges, smooth and domed about the middle: a skull, picked bare long ago, rinsed by the wind and rain, belonging, once, to some unfortunate mammal. I dropped it. Everything seemed wrong and strange tonight, heightened by the dark, and my trepidation about what was out here, just beyond my reach.

As we crossed into the last field, moving west, I turned to look behind. Morning was creeping up. The sky was still ink-dark and thickly carpeted with cloud, but over the eastern horizon came the first grey hints of dawn. We were on higher ground, now, with a view of the inferno we had escaped: the blaze had reached its zenith, the roof of the house had fallen in, and my home was a fire-bright ruin, charcoal-etched against the sky.

Beside me Guppy snarled again. As I swung the light, I saw his shoulders were hunkered low, his attention on something ahead. I raised the lantern – it was only bright enough to let me see two or three steps in front – and beyond its influence, something flickered across my sight, white and uncertain.

'Esther!' My voice rent the darkness. 'Esther...!' I took a step forward, too fast, and tripped over a mound, which sent me tumbling down the bank. The candle died as I fell, leaving me blind. Between Guppy's deep barks, I heard the frantic bleating of the sheep as they ran off.

I lay in the ditch. My breath came in saw-toothed bursts and my heart drubbed in my chest like a forger's hammer.

It was just the sheep. Just the sheep.

Guppy nosed my hand, whining. I clambered to my feet and patted the stiff hair at the top of his neck. 'Come on, boy.'

The church loomed a hundred yards ahead, up a winding path. Heavy clouds, blown in from the sea by a wind picking up as the day broke, maundered about the tower. Around the chancel, hogback gravestones and simple crosses ran east to west in a low forest. Guppy and I cut through a breach in the crumbling flint wall that marked the boundaries of the graveyard. With no lantern, now, I relied on the thinning dark to find my way to the south porch. I pictured Henry as I went. Mary had said she'd left him in the priest's shelter, in the tower, so I would have to enter the vestry, climb the ladder to the first floor, then coax him out, all in the dark.

Had Esther come here? I wondered, as I pushed the door, and heard its grind against the stone flags. *Could* she even come here? Would the creature inside not prevent her from venturing on to holy ground? And yet, even the reformers admitted, the church itself had no power to keep out the wicked, or those predestined to Hell; it was only faith that could drive out evil, not bricks and mortar.

'Henry?' I whispered; then, a little louder, 'Henry?' In reply, something gave a feverish squawk – a bird, I thought – and then was silent.

Guppy whimpered behind me, but followed as I edged towards the nave. In days gone by, a candle or lamp would have burnt by night over the altar, symbolising the eternal presence of Christ, but the godly men said candles were to see by, not to shore up popish beliefs about the sacraments. The church was not used by night, and therefore it was not to be lit by night. And now that I wanted to see...

I decided Esther wasn't here; or was not here now. Guppy wouldn't have entered if he had sensed the creature, and the frigid air smelt of damp and caustic limewash, not sea-salt and shells. But I hoped... Henry was skilled at concealing himself, as he had shown me, and this crumbling spot was the monarch of hiding places, where a resourceful little boy might find any number of corners in which to lay low. As I felt my way down the aisle, I raised my voice, just slightly. 'Henry!' If he was in the tower, he might not hear me. I reached the back, and ran my hands over the wall, hunting the narrow door to the minister's private chamber. There were three steps up from the floor of the nave, through a poky archway that seemed designed for gnomes, not men, and I thumped my head on the stonework, cursing aloud as I came down into the vestry.

It was surprisingly hazardous. This unfashionable church had no permanent cleric. There was nobody to order the jumble of what, from feeling about me, I judged to be ancient pews, dirty cassocks, bowls and alms plates strewn across the floor. It was a tawdry, neglected place. And it felt empty. No warming spark of life anywhere. 'Henry?' No answer arrived but the wind's fretful moan.

I pulled Guppy back and heard him yelp in frustration. 'Stay here,' I said, firmly. He sat. I found the ladder, a rickety thing cobbled together with twine rope, and simple slats for rungs. It hung down from the ceiling and, although I could not see above, it had to go somewhere, probably to the first floor; there, I hoped I would find the old priest's storm shelter, no more than a hole, where a travelling curate or monk might outlast bad weather. I climbed as quickly as my sore body would allow and, after twenty or so steps, poked my head through a trapdoor into a loft thick with the smell of damp straw. Again, I called Henry's name. Its anxious echo reverberated around the walls.

I sweated, but not from the effort. From fear. Henry was not my blood, but I found that did not matter, and now, as I went up through the hole and came to my knees in the musty loft, something else surfaced within me, something I had repressed on the ill-omened walk from the house: the terrors of what I might find here, the crawling things I had buried deep as barrow-wights, and not allowed into existence in the presence of Mary's frightened face. *He'll be fine*, I had said. *He knows how to hide.*

Had he hidden so well I could not find him, or...?

'Henry?'

The boards creaked under my weight. Rising, I found my balance and turned in a circle, seeking a doorway, an arch, any glint of light. I had no idea of which direction I faced when I saw it: a shadow among shadows. There was a recess in the wall. Half-blind, I groped my way towards the gap. The wind, finding a path through the thin lancet windows, made a doleful whistling sound, almost drowning my voice as I called Henry's name for the last time.

I crouched, reaching into the space, hardly long enough for a man to lie flat in, or tall enough to stand. My hands met no warm flesh, no shrinking child doing as he was told and *hiding*, lest the monster should find him again. They touched instead a small pile of coarse wool, cold under my fingers: the blanket I had given him. I swept it up and held it to my face, swallowed rising grief and panic, for the cell was empty, and the little black-haired boy was gone.

I arrived back at the house, alone except for Guppy. I attempted to cover my own fears, and tried, unsuccessfully, to soothe the dread in Mary's face. No, I did not yet have Henry, but there was no cause to think the worst. Not yet. 'He'll be hiding some-where,' I reassured her. 'He hid at the house, so perhaps he would again.'

'I told him to stay in the church. *In* the storm shelter. And not to move. He wouldn't disobey me.' She was lime-white, utter-ing the same things over and over, her composure vanished, her teeth chattering with fright. 'She's taken him, I know she has. I know it. I know it.'

Abhorrent images circled my mind like buzzards, but I tried to sound hopeful. 'He might have seen the fire go out and come back to the house. We can ride the perimeter, and I suspect we'll find him—'

'No. No, Thomas. He would do as I bid him.' She was adamant. And her apprehension was spreading to me because, of course, she was right. Henry would have remained where she told him – if not in the church itself, nearby. He would not have run off into the smoky, freezing night.

That could mean only one thing: Not-Esther had him.

What for? What did it want?

Like prattling ghouls, memories pressed in against me, threat-ening to overwhelm my hope: I saw Rutherford, and the way the rope had stretched his neck, so his head lolled low on my chest as I dragged him from his house; my nostrils heaved with the sweet, deathly reek of the Gedge women's cell; I felt again the dark despair of my father's demise.

Would it harm him, or induce him to harm himself? It was true that, of the men and women it had attacked, none had been overpowered physically. The creature's voice had – I could only assume – arrested them as it had me. But it had not hurt me, or inveigled me, other than to frighten me out of my wits.

The worst possibility – the one that Milton acknowledged with a shake of his head, even as I comforted Mary – was that it was too late.

But what if not? What if it could rein in its impulses, and see that Henry was its best chance of escaping us? With him alive, we would – we would have to – negotiate with it. There was a chance it had taken him but not hurt him, and that, if we found Esther, we would find Henry alive. I veered between optimism and savage fear. And a crushing guilt. I had sent him there, and now I had to find him.

We waited for the daylight. I fed the horses. Mary had wanted to return to the church immediately, but I persuaded her that we would not see what we needed to see – footsteps, signs of a struggle – until the sun came up. Instead, we sheltered in the barn and talked of where Esther might flee and where it made the most sense to look. Whatever we talked of – she had taken the road to Norwich; she had returned to the scene of John Rutherford's death – nothing seemed more likely than anything else. Mary and Milton argued, with Mary insisting we search the local farms, suggesting they might be hiding in a barn or stable just like this one, and Milton saying, with haughty authority, that we could not predict the actions of such a creature based on our human needs for shelter, light, food and drink. Reluctantly, Mary conceded this.

Finally, doubtfully, I shared what was on my mind. 'It might seek out people. It might not be satisfied with one death, or five. Perhaps it feeds off these deaths, in some diabolical way. Perhaps it… it might not be content unless it takes hundreds, even thousands. In which case we must look to towns, cities, the more souls the better.'

Milton sat cross-legged in the straw, his hands steepled beneath his beardless chin, his eyes closed. He was deep in thought. I recalled his vision, a vision of Hell, and how I had not comprehended it, but perhaps my old tutor, with his labyrinthian mind, had understood more of it than he had told us. After a long pause, I said, 'Mr Milton, what is it? The creature.'

He opened his eyes. For a split second, he was far away from us again. Then he shook himself, sat up straighter, and spoke with conviction. 'A demon, I believe. A fallen spirit of the ancient world.'

'Like Satan?'

'Or one of his servants. One of those that, after the Fall, became the gods of the pagan pantheon.'

'It's a god?' I was reeling. How could a god possess my sister? How could we fight one?

'There is just one God,' said Milton, sombrely. 'But there are many idols, and not all of them entirely false.'

'And this one is...?'

'It's impossible to say with certainty,' said Milton, his cracked voice sounding even more weary than mine. 'But I believe that when we sat by my fire and read Janssen's account, what we were reading was a man's description of the appearance of a slumbering monster, a deity of the ancient world. And somehow, for a reason we might never know – though it is my own suspicion that it was injured, and sought refuge in the only living soul it could find – its consciousness attached itself to your sister's. And then, for a long time, it slept.'

I remembered from Janssen's story the hideous scream of the serpent as it fell against the ship. Perhaps Milton was right. Perhaps the creature had always lived inside Esther, lived with us, shared our table and known all that we knew... I felt a warmth against my fingers as Mary wrapped her hand about mine beneath the straw. I returned the squeeze, taking reassurance from her touch.

'But why has it woken now?' I asked.

'I can only speculate,' continued Milton, 'but if all you have told me is correct, then I must conclude that Esther, who had been so pure, so incorruptible, never gave the parasite any cause to dominate any part of her, until you arrived, Mary.'

'I?' Mary said, shocked. Her hand tensed in mine.

Milton nodded. 'It's possible. From what you have said, your arrival, and her father's fondness for you, particularly, triggered such a deep envy in Esther that it allowed the monster room to surface, where otherwise, perhaps, it would have remained dormant. Maybe forever.'

At this, Mary clasped her hand to her mouth. 'It's my fault?' she cried. 'For coming here?'

As always, Milton was oblivious of other people's feelings. I gripped Mary's forearm and drew closer to her. 'Of course not. None of this is your fault. You did nothing to bring this about. Do you understand?' Our faces were just inches apart. Even with everything that had happened, it knotted my stomach to be this close to her. I loved her. I had to tell her. But not now. 'Do you? This is *not* your fault.'

Without agreement, she huddled in the crook of my arm.

As soon as there was light enough to drown out the last stars, leaving Guppy to a bowl of water, but taking the horses, we followed the road towards the church. It was a longer route, and cut out the fields I had crossed in the dark, but I thought that gamble was sound. I was certain Not-Esther had not returned in the direction of the house; it might have gone south, towards Norwich, or down the coast, but not back upon itself.

The wind had got up even more in the night. A storm was on its way. We rode beneath bare branches that whipped back and forth across the path, and trunks that swayed precariously on the slope up to the church. There was no rain yet, but the air had that quality of the nascent year that told you, when the rain came, it would lash your face like a forest of frozen needles. The land around us was hard and unyielding, not yet awash with the subtle green that would say spring was around the corner.

A second search by daylight confirmed Henry was not in the church, and the animals were unfussy and obedient, so we were certain Not-Esther had travelled out of the range of their scent. Still, we scoured the immediate fields to the west, north and south, working quickly, avoiding talk of what we might discover. I dismounted and parted the hedgerows with branches, Mary went down into ditches and checked hollow trunks, and Milton waded across muddy quagmires to root through copses and coverts, and peer up into the branches of the trees. Without speaking of it, with our hearts full of boundless fear about the worst thing we might find, we searched for a sign.

By the time, finally, we turned east, and began to follow the coast road, a six-mile track straight to the sea, Mary's face was ashen. Walking his horse, Milton met my eyes often, and I was not imagining the pessimism I saw there. If the creature had taken Henry, it had done so without snapping so much as a twig or trampling on a wigeon's nest. In the absence of anything to indicate the direction it had chosen, we would have to turn south, to Norwich, and take our chance that it would seek out others. I looked in front and then behind again, at the ground we had covered. Nothing. There was not a thing to mark the passage of anything but deer and—

I very nearly missed it.

There. On the ground. A dull, metallic glint almost buried by windswept leaves. Dropping Ben's harness, I ran the ten or so yards back towards my quarry, and kicked aside the debris that had brought us so close to disaster. I picked up the object, then clenched it in my fist. It was Henry's sundial.

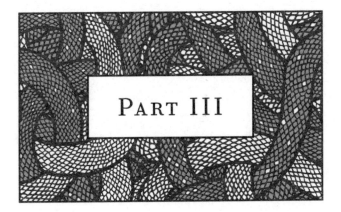

PART III

27

We followed the coast road. There was no other path, and Henry's little talisman could only have been lost, or even deliberately dropped to attract our attention, if they had come this way. It would take us to Happisburgh, a wild, wind-beaten stretch of shingled shore and crumbling sandstone looking out to the North Sea. From there, the birds flew straight and true to Denmark, with hundreds of miles between. Beyond, bigger and more unknowable than anything I could imagine, were regions of mountains and fire, lands I could not put a name to, guarded by the whale-seas, the ice fields, and, I had been told, thousands of jagged islands of bare rock and unnavigable rivers. It was a world I had never been given cause to think of, until now. Did the prospect of its freedoms draw the creature? After all our guesswork about what it would do, who it would target next, was it really so simple? That it would seek only its own return to the sea?

The wind was uncomfortable enough as we picked our way along the road to the coast. It swept in across the flat fields to shake the tops of the trees like dandelion heads, but until we reached the Happisburgh road and turned away from the land, it did not reveal its true malice. Now, unfettered by forests or hillsides, it howled around us, unsettling the horses and blowing Milton's hat into a battered coppice. He let it go, hunkering low over his mare's ears and urging her on. I, too, spurred Ben on quicker, knowing I pushed the horse harder than was fair, with two riders on his back. Mary had donned the sundial pendant, and held its wooden plate to her lips, whispering prayers I could not hear.

In the last half mile, just as the dunes rose and barricaded the water from our view, Mary leant back in the saddle, so her head touched my shoulder, and her mouth brushed my over-growing hair. I experienced a moment of acute embarrassment – misplaced, I knew – that I was not more well groomed. I doubted she had ever had a more unkempt suitor. 'I have never seen the ocean,' she said.

This was unexpected – not that she had not seen the sea, but that she wanted to talk of it. Thrown, I said, 'What, never?'

'I'm a London girl.'

I realised she wanted a distraction. I said, 'So, you have seen the Thames river? That can't be too unlike the sea.'

'I hope they are not like,' she said, emphatically. 'The Thames stinks to Heaven. And the docks. Though I think I swam in the estuary once. But no, not the real sea.'

'In happier times…' I began, intending to say I would take her swimming one day. But I stopped, feeling it was too presumptuous.

She did not move her head, so her face sat just below my jaw and ear, tickling the skin. 'What?' she said, her voice lower than the wind, just discernible.

'Perhaps you will see it in happier times,' I concluded, lamely, cursing my own cowardice.

'Perhaps I will,' she said, leaning forward again.

As we moved down a long, thin track with high hedges on either side, the mud took on a sandy texture. It was harder to hold up our heads, now, as the wind whipped the sand into our faces and made our eyes water. Ben hated it, so I rubbed his withers and encouraged him to walk on, his head carried low like ours against its blast. I lifted my sight again in search of Esther's frail form, perhaps lying in a hedgerow or tumbled down on the top of the dunes. I doubted she could stand easily in this, and her clothes had been fit for bed, only. She had not eaten a full meal in weeks. I began to seriously consider that she could collapse and freeze, or else die of exposure. But I did not know – perhaps the creature did not share the limitations of our bodies. Who could say?

In front, Mary called for Henry again, but her voice was lost on the gale as clouds continued to roll ashore, black enough to cast us back into twilight. Just before we mounted the sheer, crumbly path to the peak of the dunes, Mary seized my arm. 'There!' She pointed west, and I thought something moved over the top of the hill, but it might have been a cloud, or the shadow of a cloud, and, before I could focus my eyes against the wind and the sand, it was gone. 'No,' she said, wretchedly. 'Nothing.'

The path was even steeper than it had looked from its base. Ben was labouring, so we dismounted and set him to roam the rough slope. Milton led his mare by her halter as we crested the hill.

At the first sight of the sea, Mary gasped. Usually flat and smooth, today the pebbled beach was battered by waist-high waves, and as we turned our sight eastwards down the coast, countless small, drenched coves bit into the rising sandstone cliffs. Northwards, as the water stretched away from us, the clouds hunkered on the horizon, swept this way and that by a wind that could not seem to decide on its direction.

We considered what to do. A path, wet with spray, curved down to the sand and shale ribbon that separated us from the water. The beach extended half a mile. Towards the end a fisherman or crab-catcher had abandoned a small boat. I wondered whether the man had been intending to drag it up to safer ground, but had surrendered to the ferocity of the weather. If we went down there, the three of us agreed, the reach of our sight would be poorer, and we might have less chance of spotting her.

But what if she wasn't here at all? Could we have been wrong? Mary's eyes were on me and I felt pressure to act. We would have to search. We could split up, and Mary and I could cover the dunes to the west while Milton searched the coves to the east. If we were wrong…

It was as though she read my mind. 'They're here,' she said, raising her voice to carry over the wind. 'You can feel it, can't you?'

Yes. There was a disquiet beneath my thoughts, a vibration at the foundation of my awareness that I associated with Not-Esther, now. And Mary felt it, too. I raked my eyes across the sand, searching for twin heads: one dark and one golden. Nothing.

'Perhaps you could stay here and watch, sir,' I suggested to Milton. 'We'll go down to the water and seek her there.'

'I don't think there will be any need for that,' said Milton, calmly. He pointed straight down the path, down the beach, towards the boat, which I now saw was moving. While my inner voice had debated what to do, a tiny white figure had emerged from the shadow of the cliff and now, before our aghast eyes, began to push the little vessel across the sand. Esther was so slight, and in her weakened condition, I was certain she did not have the strength to drag the boat even a foot, let alone all the way to the water. But, impossibly, the vessel started to move, and it and its companion began their slow progress towards the sea.

I made to step forward and Milton grabbed me. 'Wait. What if the creature abandons her when it reaches the water?'

'Do you think it will?' Longing was burgeoning in my breast. Longing that this ordeal might – at last – be ending.

Milton said, 'Who can say? But we have to allow for the chance. And we could bring that chance to ruin, if we move too soon.'

Despite the incoming tide, the stretch of sand between the dunes and the water had never seemed wider. Mary framed her eyes with her hands, hunting her brother. Milton and I watched in rigid silence as the boat inched towards the waves and then into the surf. The water foamed and swelled about the hull. It was nearly afloat.

The divide inside me raged. Even if Esther's body had the strength to row against the tide into the bay, and even if the creature wanted only to be free, and left her once it found the safety of the water, it still might not save her. Who was to say she would not capsize and be drowned, or that the tide would not drag her back towards the shore, dashing the boat against the rocks further down the beach? I was caught between a desperate desire to intervene and save her body, and to let the creature leave her, and possibly save her soul.

It was only as the boat began to bob with the choppy water that I saw the obstacle, the missing piece of the puzzle that rendered my struggle meaningless.

Henry.

He was in the boat. His dark head lay unmoving, his skinny frame wedged, somehow, between the bow and the mast. Was he still alive?

As the craft took to the waves, Esther, with her white dress billowing about her waist, clambered in. She wrestled with the oars as she lowered herself to the seat, her back braced against the wind.

Mary had seen Henry a moment after I had, and now sprinted like an attacking soldier down the beach, shouting for her brother. I glanced at Milton, and we followed. I was surprised to find it so easy – my battle injury seemed like a distant memory as I passed Milton and gained ground on Mary. I caught her, then outstripped her. I was closing the distance between me and the boat, and, even knowing that I ran towards danger, it was hard not to rejoice in the return of my strength. My feet sank into the sand, but it barely slowed me. For a few moments, I might have been a boy again, exulting in the simple joy of movement.

But when level with the boat and with the water foaming cold about my feet, I saw how far away Esther was already. The keel had to be four or five feet clear of the bottom. The oars moved easily, as if the hands that wielded them could command the waves. I knew it was pointless, but I still shouted to her. My voice was drowned out by a parliament of winds, a noise going up to Heaven like a thousand voices raised in dissent.

Mary reached me and ran straight into the surf, then Milton caught up. I turned in the knee-high water, to see the older man removing his boots and cloak, preparing to come in after us.

The boat was already more than a hundred yards from shore when we waded together into the water, with the baleful shock of the cold against my thighs making me gasp. Swirling flakes of snow were just beginning to blow in from the sea as we forged deeper, pushing through the swell. When I was in up to my shoulders, I struck out with a firm stroke. The others followed, but I quickly realised that, of the three of us, I was by far the strongest swimmer. Mary was off her feet, but her face kept sinking beneath the waves. Milton was a little better, battling on, but still he was beaten back by each incoming wave.

I trod water, allowing a wave to crash over my head. In the valley between it and the next, I raised my voice. 'Go back!' I shouted to them. 'I'll get him.' Another wave crashed into my face, filling my mouth and nose with freezing salt water. I did not wait to see whether they turned back, but plunged ahead, dipping below the surface. When I breathed air again, I was alone.

Between the waves, just visible, was the stern of the little boat. I was far from sure I could do what I had promised. I kicked harder and gained on them, foot by painful foot. With a last desperate spend of energy, I came alongside; then, as the bow of the boat crested the next wave and it teetered, I grabbed the frame, gritting my teeth. Animal sounds escaped me as I clung to the slippery rib of the hull.

I fell back, nearly releasing the side as an oar struck my temple. I tasted blood. Suspended above me, outlined against the black clouds and swirling flakes, Esther's face was alien, so discoloured with the cold, it was almost purple. As she raised the oar for another strike, I hauled my weight up out of the water and into the boat. It cost me every ounce of my remaining strength, and I fell gasping against the bottom boards, my chest burning, reaching for Henry in the bow. My hand grasped a limb, a foot, but I could not tell whether or not the boy lived. I sat up, coughing water.

My assailant seemed to have given up hope of putting me off by force. She sat back, regarding me with wary hostility as I scrambled over the bench, reaching past her, and coming to my knees at Henry's side. He was glacially cold and clammy, but – thank Christ! – alive, breathing shallowly. His eyes were wide and he stared through me. I choked back a sob of sheer relief. 'It's Thomas,' I said, with no idea of whether he could hear me.

I could waste no time engaging with Esther. If I could recover her, I would, but Henry had to be taken to safety. I stood, swaying as the boat fell into the valley of another wave and the wind redoubled against my back. She stared. I waited, then feinted towards the right-hand oar but at the last moment grabbed the left from her hands; as she lost her grip on it, I snatched the other, and she fell backward into the boat. I took the helm, squatted on the bench and hauled, trying to bring us about, but the wide circle, as I fought the current, seemed to take forever to complete. All the while, Esther crouched low, wearing a strange, expectant expression.

Then, just as the nose turned towards the shore and the rowing became easier, and as the boat surged forward, we were knocked off course. It was not the current or the wind; this force was blunt and physical, and seemed to come from below, throwing the boat and all of us sideways.

When I recovered my balance, clinging to the gunwale with Esther's writhing body thrown against me, I froze at my first sight of what now disturbed the surface of the sea.

28

In spite of everything that had happened, everything I had seen, I had not really believed it. Not in my heart.

Tales of demons, of monsters that believed themselves gods, and spirits that could fly through air to possess a person's mind – they were just stories, the fruits of febrile imaginations, the natural children of the darkness before civilisation.

They were not real.

But under the boat, rising near the bow and surging beneath and past us, what I saw was real enough: a rugged peak of flesh breaking the surface. It was almost black in colour, with a curved and pitted spine, and moved like a dolphin; sleek, lithe, faster than the current. I could see only a segment of its body at a time – it did not breach the water fully – but as it poured its form back into the sea, foot after glistening, armoured foot, I began to conceive of its immensity. As I stared, dumbfounded, the waves covered it again, and it was gone.

The wind rocked the boat. I did not need to wait to see what the creature would do. I released Esther. Henry lay still in his small ball. Desperate to return to the shore, I grappled the oars again, raised my chin to the storm and began to pull. As I did, I saw where the beast was headed.

There was a ship.

The vessel bore down from the west. It had probably just left port at King's Lynn and been caught out by the unexpected maelstrom of wind and snow. It turned in an enormous circle, moving towards the shelter of the bay, and there was something valiant about its billowing sails. From so far away, I could not see the men, but there was movement on deck; rowing boats were being lowered, ready to slow the craft as she came in to harbour. And between the ship and the shore…

They don't know…

I looked towards Esther. Her gaze was fixed on the ship. For a moment I questioned whether she was aware of her surroundings, or even of time or space, because her face was so blank and resigned, reminding me, horribly, of my father's last hours, and his vacant sadness.

'Esther…?'

Before I could finish, the tension in her frame gave out, and she began to fit. Her body shook uncontrollably, her flailing hands and feet striking the side of the boat. Fearful I would lose control of the vessel entirely, I could not get to her, and screamed her name, only to have my frightened cries ripped away by the gale.

Then the snow began to fall in earnest, bucketing from the huge clouds overhead. I raised my eyes in disbelief as the sky flashed white, and I heard the rumble of thunder.

And still the ship came on. She looked small but wasn't. She was a three-decker, a great ship of the second rank, with perhaps fifty guns. I was no seaman, but knew she probably carried over two hundred men. She was sailing in a crosswind, battling the surging waves. She could not come all the way to shore – she would need to drop anchor near the limited shelter of the cliffs.

Meanwhile, Esther was fighting her own battle. The snow blanketed her shaking body, and the white foam spilling over the side soaked her blue-tinged skin. I could not release the oars to help her. We were in danger of capsizing, and my breath came harder as I struggled to keep the boat on course. I looked anxiously at my sister and the crumpled form of Henry, but before I had rowed three more strokes, my attention was wrested from them by a colossal black shape surfacing against the bow of the ship.

God or monster – it was as real as I.

They collided.

In the chaos of the wind-driven snow and with the water roiling about the hull, the captain would have seen nothing ahead. The ship staggered. There was an excruciating sound, as though something wailed in anguish. It was accompanied by a splintering crack; the craft was holed.

I could hardly watch, but could not look away.

A monstrous shadow rose further out of the water, stirring the sea like a boiling pot, and even over the cry of the wind and the melee of the waves, the dismay of the crew carried all the way to my ears. Slowly, before my unwilling eyes, the beast wrapped its snake-like body about the mainmast. It was far longer than the ship, impossibly so, and as thick as five men about its sinuous middle. Beginning with its elongated mouth, like the snouted head of an eel, with teeth as sharp as ballock daggers, it dragged itself up the rigging, tearing sails, strands and stays like dead ivy off a tree. Reaching the top, it tightened its grip, dragging its powerful tail from the water. I could see its muscular length now, plated with bony, triangular crests. The tail smashed down on the deck, port to starboard, and the vessel reeled under its weight, the masts leaning hard towards the water. The doll-like forms of men began falling from the decks like wooden soldiers. The creature seemed oblivious, its only aim, apparently, to crush, to reduce those great timbers of English oak down to firewood. Now, bearing the full weight of the monster, the ship was breaking apart down the middle. Men fell towards cruel jaws, which gaped mindlessly towards the cannons like the mouth of Hell.

Sailors are notoriously poor swimmers. Any man who fell overboard when the ship was at sea would pray for a swift death, as their pain would only be prolonged by the ability to stay afloat. The piteous cries of those still aboard went up to Heaven. It was pointless to try to turn the boat, to go back and help, but I tried anyway, calling Esther's name as she continued to shake and cough up spittle. I rowed towards the ship. If I could save just some of them...

Abruptly, Esther's body straightened. A plaintive noise escaped her, like the last cry of a trapped wild creature. Her eyes widened as though the sound had broken through her fit. Heedless of the greater battle being fought ahead of me, I dropped the oars and scrambled to her – was there a hope? – falling to my knees, no longer noticing the cold or the spray of the waves. Even the monster was, for the moment, forgotten. I gathered her close and said her name over and over. 'Esther. Return to me. Please.'

A sudden sob behind made me turn back to Henry, and I felt overwhelming relief as the boy stirred. But he did so in fear, trembling. I watched with horror as Henry, seeing Esther, shifted further back against the rear of the boat, throwing one leg over the side as it pitched in the current. He whimpered, caught between his fright of the water and his deeper terror of his captor.

'Henry!' I shouted. 'Stay where you are. It will be all right.'

'Help us!' came the child's cry. 'God, help us!' He half-hung off the back, and as the next swell broke, I let go of my sister and launched myself towards the other end of the boat, but the water took him. The boat rocked so hard we were almost vertical, and when it righted itself, and I desperately scanned the white-foamed, shadowed surface, Henry was nowhere to be seen.

On the bottom of the boat, Esther lay curled, her lips moving. The sound was barely audible, but even so, I knew the language was unknown to me and felt the same creeping terror I had experienced before. I desired only to still her tongue, or stop my ears if I could not.

The beast was moving. Its quarry remained, its timbers crushed and tortured, yet its attacker was retreating. It unwound its bulk from the shattered form of the galleon, which sagged as the monster's body fell away. As the serrated tail slipped beneath the waves, followed by the bow end of the ship, the sailors clung to the debris and to each other; but the worst was over. The behemoth was gone, the stern was still afloat, and the men in the water were now beginning to clamber on. A smaller boat was being lowered, with what seemed to be an orderly start to disembarkation.

I breathed again.

Then Esther's eyes opened wider, and the ship burst into flame.

There was a roar, and the whole hull exploded, creating a fireball that seared my eyes and made my eardrums hum like a cathedral organ. I lurched backwards with the shock, a shock that made my head spin as though the Earth had reversed its motion. Men screamed like dying cattle.

Over the noise of the fire, the thunder, the wind and the waves, I heard my father's voice in my mind: *no plan of the Lord's can be thwarted.*

I closed my eyes. The beast was of God's making – its armour, its mighty coils, every fold of its flesh – and what would be, would be as God had intended since He had conceived of it. Of that there could now be no doubt. But what would be the Lord's instrument?

Or who?

I looked to my sister. Since the explosion, she had stopped her muttering. She lay as in a trance.

As the lightning flashed nearer, so close I thought it must hit home, and thunder rolled directly overhead, I glimpsed the future.

The leviathan would never stop. It was too full of rage, too trapped, too wild. Where it saw weakness it would strike, and, striking, it would destroy. We might drug Esther's body and corral the mind within, but if we slipped in our vigilance even for an instant – and being only men and women, we would – catastrophe would follow. The creature's fury would engulf every good thing, on and on, until we stared into darkness. Hell would come after.

As we drifted back towards the shore, my sister lay on her side like a wounded animal, her mouth still now, her face so devoid of colour she seemed unreal. The thought of her suffering shredded something inside me. How could I help her? I was not strong enough.

Always, in the stories of my youth, there were signs. Spears of light would break through the clouds and doves would descend on church spires. In reality, it was not so. There were no miracles. I was quite alone with the wind and driving snow. Nobody else could do this duty – it was mine. I had never before shirked anything out of fear, yet I quailed before the choice in front of me.

Then, as I looked towards the beach, I saw two heads bobbing in the churning waves: one dark, small and still; the other fairer. Milton paddled valiantly, his left arm about Henry's neck, his efforts barely keeping them afloat. But they moved slowly towards land, and there, just visible through the billowing snow, a tall shape waded eagerly into the sea to meet them, framed by a cloud of flyaway dark hair.

I turned the boat the other way, into the storm.

29

May 1703

A place far from the sea

Henry has come.

He arrives late and brings gifts. Cutlets of veal and a quart of sugar. Potted lampreys. He knows his sister appreciates such offerings, as we can rarely afford them ourselves. He has a habit of trying to press money on us, but neither of us will hear of accepting a larger present; we have everything we need.

Henry is now the Honourable Member for the borough of Tavistock. His rivals would regard him as a Tory, but his voting record can only be described as eclectic, hardly surprising for a boy raised to manhood by that most enigmatic of thinkers, John Milton.

As it turned out, Henry was never stupid. His learning was only becalmed by poverty, his apparent foolishness a protective ploy. As he grew under the diligent tutelage of the famous poet, who offered our little family a home in those months following the wreck of the *Swiftsure* – for this was, we discovered later, the name of that unfortunate vessel – he discovered a vast appetite for knowledge, and our host found in him a careful and conscientious student.

The house that had been mine was completely destroyed by the fire and, though it was to be rebuilt in time by others, we were never again to live in it. There was too much danger of discovery. We decamped immediately to Chalfonte after the storm, where in due course I recovered from my injuries. After only a little longer, I acquired a brother, as well as a wife, the two blessings which remain with me as the most valuable of my life.

When, after a year had passed and – though we fed her no more of the drug, as we found she did not stir even without it – Esther showed no signs of regaining her wits, I sold the farm in Norfolk and we moved to our present holding, the exact location of which I still choose not to disclose. Henry remained in Chalfonte. This was partly out of loyalty to the man who had pulled him from the water, and partly, I think, because he never reconciled himself to being in the same house as Esther. It was a relief to him, I believe, when we came here, where we could more easily conceal her.

But we saw him often. There was enough money from the sale of the land to fund his time at Cambridge, and then, when the time came, to Henry's delight, Milton sponsored his ward at the Bar. And when, in later years, his adopted master became infirm and the curse of his blindness returned, Henry acted occasionally as his secretary, putting pen to paper in gratitude for the many kindnesses we had received. To make our living, I entered the book trade, buying and selling such rarities as I could find, and that took me often to Chalfonte, where I would see them keeping late hours with heads bent over raked-out embers, debating some obscure point of law or politics. It is how I remember Milton best. For myself, although I grew to like my old tutor, and to understand him much better, I never grew to love him like Henry did, like a father. Still, I was charmed by the closeness that grew up between them. I even envied it.

For I was never to become a father, or Mary a mother. A child never came. When we first married, we gave little thought to it. We took joy in one another, freely, as man and wife, and it comforted us, even in our strange circumstances. We assumed a family would follow. But when the first child failed to quicken inside her, and then the second, we began to ask ourselves whether it was meant to be. Mary went further; she thought we were punished by God, that the evil we harboured conspired to banish innocence, and that it always would. For a time, after the second of our griefs, we faced the real possibility that she would leave me. I could not have blamed her, and would have released her, had she wished it.

But we fought through it. And our love changed. It grew, even in the shade of our sadness.

Mary greets her brother today with a cry and an embrace that gives me joy. She has not seen him for several years, as he is still a busy and successful man, with children and grandchildren keeping him occupied, whereas we enter our dotage. As we settle in the parlour, she offers a glass of perry and he readily agrees. He takes his seat by the fire, shrugging off his cloak and pulling at the fingers of his gloves. He looks tired and unshaven.

'Tell me of the country,' I say.

He shakes his head and releases a hissing noise through his teeth. 'I've ridden hard to get to you, brother. But I had to wait upon the weather.' He rubs his hands together, recalling his journey. 'First a delay in Exeter, then another week in Bath. It's hard to believe the breadth of the destruction after the storm. Like the world's ending. Coast to coast, trees flattened, uprooted, whole forests thrown about like firewood. Entire villages blown down. Mills afire.' He lifts his head and, unexpectedly, laughs. It is a sound of disbelief. 'Fish, truly, Thomas, lifted from the rivers and deposited inland, miles from any waterway.' More soberly, he continues. 'Many, many dead. They're calling it the Great Storm. And out at sea...' His finger drums the arm of the chair, pattering like a light rain. 'Such wrath. The whole Navy fleet battered, and tossed to smithereens. God, but I hate to think of it; those men, less than a mile off the coast, sitting – thinking themselves safe – on top of all that iron, all that oak, all that human power, and then the sea rising around them, ship after ship dragged down with the resistance of a child's toy raft. And they see they are nothing, just dots on the skein of time.' Wearily, he removes his periwig, revealing thinning grey hair beneath, and lays it on the table beside us.

'How many dead?'

He shrugs. 'They do not know. Thousands?'

I nod. 'Thousands, indeed.'

Is the creature responsible? Our eyes meet, and the possibility lies before us like an uncovered sin. Now it has stirred it will not be buried again.

'So, she is awake,' he says, finally, his still-youthful face framed by a severe frown. 'I knew it, and I came.'

The mystery of Henry's ability to discern truths about the creature that others cannot has never been solved. Mary attributes it to the silent, watchful nature of his youth. She says it made him sensitive to that which escapes other people. As he watches me hawkishly, I wonder how much he knows of its thoughts now.

'Yes,' I answer, without elaboration.

'You must act, brother,' he says, with a similar lack of expansion.

'As I did last time?' I ask.

His eyes fall to the neck of my shirt, open at this late and more casual hour, revealing the network of branch-like scars, so like Esther's, which I have hidden for many years but which, in the privacy of our home, I have no reason to conceal.

I cannot help it; I close my eyes as my mind retreats to that far-off day, rowing into the storm with Esther at my feet. Lightning is all around us, more bolts than I suspect fell, in truth, as age and faulty memory amplify my senses. The sea still churns, so although I row with all my might, the boat makes no progress, and the waves carry us ever back to shore. But the storm moves with more purpose. Soon, the flashes are so close by they are blinding. It is still morning, but the gap between each strike is black as night, followed by shrieks of white, pulsing light. I hold Esther close and she shivers in my arms. This fire will take us both, I vow. My sister will see Heaven with her own eyes.

I am dragged back to the present moment. Henry watches me with pity, but it is a hard pity, uncompromising in its conclusions, not unlike Milton's.

'While she slept, she was no threat,' he says, grimly. 'Now…'

'You do not need to tell me,' I say, peevishly. He does not react. 'Do you think in all these years I have not thought what would happen if she came back to us? Do you think we have not lived these weeks…?' I stop, waving away my own words.

The sadness in his eyes deepens. But he does not hesitate to cut me. 'She did not. Come back to us, that is. Esther is still far away. It is the creature that has returned.'

'You don't remember her,' I say, fearful my voice has become an old man's whine. 'She would have been your sister had she lived, yes, but you never met her. Her kindness, her goodness – you have only known them through me. But I remember. I remember what she was.'

Mary, who has not spoken so far and is so close by the fire that it creates a red halo about her white head, speaks. 'Nobody could have done more for Esther,' she says, softly. 'And none could doubt your love for her.' The words are intended to soothe, but they can only bring home how I have done nothing. Nothing of use or note. Even my effort to end our lives ended in ignominy.

I shake my head. 'It is not for me to rule that her life must end. I do not hold that power. Nobody should hold that much power.'

Henry speaks slowly, steadily, iterating as though he stood before the lawmakers of our nation. '*I authorise and give up my right of governing myself, to this man or this Assembly of men.*'

My smile is humourless. 'A sovereign? You would have me be that man? Wear that cloak?'

He smiles back, with equal seriousness. 'Somebody must wear it. Or we will have chaos.'

'These are your modish beliefs talking,' I say, wearily. 'In reality there is right and there is wrong; above all, there is God, and not solely power, as your friend Mr Hobbes would have us believe. John knew that.'

Henry inclines his head in acknowledgement of his debt, hesitates, then says, 'Once, you believed it. Once, you did not fear to row into the storm.'

I watch the fire crackling and spitting. Mary is silent and Henry waits.

My memories take on a dream-like cast. In the eye of the storm, within a stone's throw of the beach, we rock on quietening waters. I hold Esther close. Prayers form on my lips, prayers for our souls. Even through closed lids, the bright flashes about me sear nightmarish shapes into my sight. The next flash engulfs everything. I remember no more before waking on the beach, with Mary holding my hand to her lips, kissing it fervently.

There was a strong stench of burning flesh, and I discovered much later that Mary, my dearest Mary, scorched her hands as she beat flames from my chest. All was slow about me. I could not move my legs. My hearing was quite gone, and Mary's words of love and concern, repeated many times in the following days and weeks, fell on deaf ears.

But my hearing recovered. The deep burns that pained my feet for months afterwards, they healed too. Yet the scars remain, mine the mirror of Esther's, like veins, like crawling ivy on the upper halves of our bodies.

And Esther never did wake. As war swept England, as sacred blood poured from the crownless head of that most unfortunate and least foresighted of kings, Charles Stuart, as a sombre peace fell upon a hollowed-out country, and men crept towards Enlightenment, she slept on. Until now.

Henry coughs, quietly. It rouses me and I realise I have been alone with my thoughts for some minutes. Henry is holding something out to me – a thin sheaf of paper. 'What's that?'

'Milton. He gave it to me. And asked me to keep it until she woke. Then I was to give it to you.'

'Have you read it?'

He shakes his head. I believe him.

It is thin, stone-smoothed, covered margin to margin in Milton's angular hand. Its corners are worn, its surface mottled. I handle it, smelling the delicate tobacco smoke from his pipe curling about the edges. Transportive. In that second, as my fingers close around the gridiron-lined paper, Milton might be beside me, eyeing me from over his beaky nose.

I find my spectacles. My hands are less certain than they used to be. It takes time to unfold the sheets.

Thomas,

I want you to consider the nature of power. Your power, and God's power. All those years ago, when you came to me a bullish and overconfident boy, a boy with such a will, but lacking the ability to take responsibility for it, you blamed me, when the choices you made went awry. Happy I was, in later years, to see you come into your own, and know yourself for the author of your actions, for good or ill.

Forgive the vanity of this parallel, but it is just as easy, I am certain you will agree, for a man to blame God for the tribulations of his own life. The Enemy expected this of Job, you will remember, and Job showed he was willing to question God, to ask why He does not punish the wicked, why the innocent must suffer in the fulfilment of His purpose. It is natural enough.

We know, though, that God does have a plan for His creation. We know that He gives us free will, the power of exercising our judgement, sometimes for the immediate better, sometimes not. That is why the first man and woman fell. Yet in God's higher Providence, even this — yes, even this — will be revealed as a blessing, when He turns all things to His good. Not without reason He asks, 'Where were you when I laid the foundation of the Earth?' He asks that we might remember that we cannot see into the womb of Time, or our knowledge encompass the parameters of His sight.

So, when you ask why I kept from you what I am about to divulge, remember all things tend to the fulfilment of God's purpose in the end, though we may not know it in the present.

During the time of my first blindness, when the creature showed me those wondrous, terrible sights, there were other things I saw. It revealed glimpses of the future, as well as the past. Its long sleep, its waking, a most mighty storm, and a choice; a choice that must be made by you, Thomas, its ultimate outcome still uncertain. I have faith that you will make it well, but there was one more thing I saw, that you must hear, that you will have to bear, though the knowledge will lie heavy on you.

I saw your sister. Her consciousness being so tightly bound to that of the creature, and I caught in the circle of both, she could speak freely. She recognised me, I know not how, and told me her purpose as she saw it.

The leviathan precedes disturbance in the natural order. Your sister described the deaths of kings and the slaughter of brother by brother. The century through which you have now lived was the most tumultuous of all, bar one that is yet to come. The fissures created by these periods of upheaval, sometimes — just sometimes — let it through. They give it power. Esther, that rare soul, realising the nature of what she held within her, saw it as her duty to bind that power to herself, trapping it. I was not to share this knowledge with you, until she woke. She said it was not the right time – that you would not hear God's true voice, until later, and I would not be there to witness it, or help.

Now, a choice lies before you that cannot be made by any other save you. Its final result can be borne by no other, but you.

I can speak no other words of use. Though I feel that inadequacy like a wound, I comfort myself that the man I grew to respect is the equal of it, that it will not stand in the way of his duty, and that even in the exercise of our wills, we remain, eternally, in the hands of God.

John Milton

Though its long confinement continues, Not-Esther no longer sleeps. Even in the dead of night, with only the caterwauling foxes for company, I hear my sister's light pacing, back and forth across the boards: pressure, creak, retort. It is a sound that keeps me awake long after Mary, who, despite the strain of these days, slumbers with the ease of one who knows what it is to sleep on the streets, her gentle snores undisturbed by the noise overhead.

So, in spite of the lateness of the hour, the eyes that greet our small band as we enter the attic are alert, as hard as glass. The room is cold, a suggestion of mist in the air just dulling the edges of my sight.

Henry shadows us into the room, and I wonder what he expects to see. I receive my answer as he steps into the glow of the new-lit lamps: a gasp. Henry stares at a woman in her eighth decade, whose hair has greyed to silver, whose skin bears the same pattern of scarring as mine but who, in all other respects, retains the appearance of a girl. We decay. We go down into the dark. Yet Esther has barely aged a day since Henry last saw her.

Mary's feelings come through the stiff set of her shoulders, the shortness of her step. It is not fear – in all these years, unlike me, she has never shown fear, but rather a brittle and unrelenting hostility to our prisoner, even while she nursed her – but there is tension there, a fierce protectiveness, as though Henry and I are the children she never had.

I had intended to speak first, yet the words wither in my throat. This leaves space for it to say something, but there is only silence, and to my surprise, Mary steps in. 'Are you thirsty?' she asks.

It nods. Mary moves forward with a cup of watered perry. She holds the drink up, and we hear a rhythmic gulping. 'More?' Mary says, and the process is repeated three times. Not-Esther lifts a shackled hand to her lips and wipes away a stray drop.

Still, my words will not come.

Henry clears his throat and a flicker of something passes over our captive's face. What? Recognition? Remembering? As he opens his mouth to speak, I press my hand upon his upper arm, stymying his words. 'What do you see, Henry? You once said… You said you saw her…'

The answer comes in hollow tones. 'I said I saw a snake.'

'And do you see it now?'

Henry pauses, and Not-Esther watches us, showing no concern, no discomfort or desire to hear our softened voices more keenly. Not a sound breaches the attic walls, not even a sliver of air through the small gaps I have not yet filled in the roof. It is as though we are cocooned together outside time.

Finally, he says, 'I don't know. There are pictures, but they shift… like candle flames. They are not a true reflection of what is in front of me. Yet it may be that my senses are deceived. My older eyes see what they expect to see. Its nature – its true nature…' He shakes his head.

'Its true nature is to be free,' I say. 'Is that not so?' I come closer, not within touching distance, but so I can smell the sharpness of rosemary where I bandaged the wound in her neck. I sink painfully to one knee. 'Is that not so?' I do not address my sister. I address the creature. I meet its eyes, those ancient windows, searching for a glimmer of agreement, or of dissent.

'Men turn from the great ones such as me,' I hear, finally, in the voice that holds, for me, so much terror. 'From fear, and the fear of fear, they offer up their will to smaller creatures, clustering together in their cities like mice. They erect new gods. They build and gather knowledge and imagine themselves to be holding off the dark, which terrifies them, when they should embrace it and shun, instead, the fire that burns forever. They doubt the fire, and trust the light of reason. But there is no reason: only chaos.'

'Do you want to be free?' I ask again, more harshly. 'And if I do free you, what will you do?' I am desperate, willing to do anything, just to know how it ends. And what I will have to live with.

Henry comes out of the shadows. 'I see it now,' he says, quietly. 'It grows. It remains hidden until the twilight, and the end of all things, when the sun's beams shine black as coal and the world becomes harsh and frigid. It rouses waves like palaces, higher than mountains, greater than continents, and it remains when the earth sinks into the sea. Then comes its death, and the deaths of the gods.' As he speaks, his words rise and fall with laboured breath, and his eyes widen in their orbits. Hearing the pitch of his voice, Mary rushes to her brother, then staggers as he collapses. I stand, or attempt to, and together we try to bear his weight, but he falls to the floor, convulsing.

30

It is almost a week after those events, and we return to Norfolk. We have travelled in secret, in a covered cart, in the early mornings and evenings, to the place where I failed, the place where I condemned Esther to be the vessel that would forever contain evil, since I was not strong enough to destroy it.

Evil. As men have done for centuries, or millennia, and as they will do, in all likelihood, until the end of time, I use words I do not understand. Words for forces that exist in places I can never tread. Perhaps we need new words, I think, as we struggle down from our horse-drawn cart, and I lead my sister over the dunes, towards the sea.

There is nobody here except us. We left Henry behind. His far-sightedness preceded a fit, and although he recovered during the night, he seems weakened. His words come slowly, and Mary fears for him, and for his sanity. He is not John Milton, and I wonder if only a mind like Milton's can stare into Hell and return to tell the tale. So we left Henry at home. But perhaps, still, we are four. Perhaps somewhere, Milton pricks up his ears, pauses in his step, and comes to stand beside us.

The red sandstone of the cliffs, which are not high, is the same stone that built the church that towers over the small village behind us. Here, the coastline is attacked by wind and rain with such constancy that it disintegrates into horseshoe-shaped harbours and tortured mounds of sand, giving way to over-grown grasses as it gets more distant from the water's edge. These cliffs I do remember. The shallow, wide bay, looking out to the North Sea, to Denmark and further, is also the same as it was then, though today it is calm and still, as if a god has reached down and smoothed its waves to glass.

But I am not the same. There are too many years between what I was and what I am now. I came here last as a man of twenty, a boy of endless doubts in a world of superstition. I return as a man of eighty, a man of faith in an age of doubt.

As we near the water, as the sights and smells begin to wash over us – salt, sea campion, speckled kale – she breaks away, and her unshod feet skip lightly over the crumbled stones and tawny sand. Mary raises her voice after her, but I say no, let her go. We follow slowly. When she reaches the shining black seaweed and the foaming water pools about her feet at the very edge of the sea, she stops.

I step forward. I hear no sound from her, just my own breath and the soft crunch of shingle beneath my feet. She – it – does not turn.

Here I am, Lord. Here is the last of my strength. I have kept it for Esther, as she kept hers for You.

The silence is disturbed only by the call of a solitary tern on its way back out to sea. I look down at my hands, their calluses, veins and purpled knuckles, and I see a life, a history, a priceless gift I have been given. How have I spent it? How have I laid better claim to that tapestry of hours, days and years, than any other man?

I am close to her, close enough, now. I reach out with those hands and pull back her head, twist her right shoulder away from me, and break her neck. She falls where she stands, and lies like a broken bird in feathered white against the sable sand. I fall too, coming to my knees to correct the unnatural angle of her neck, tidying her dress, smoothing her hair with my palms. I whisper words to her, words of comfort and sorrow, words that can never be enough.

Do I hear something in that moment? Some sigh of relief, some marker of lost liberty recaptured? I look towards the horizon, across the endless flat bay. Do I glimpse something dark in shade, finless and immense? Does it twist and turn like it swims through air? Does it glory in its own unimpeded motion as it returns to the ancient heart of the sea?

Mary comes, and holds my hand in hers. We watch.

And there, across the mudflats, between the Devil and Enlightenment, for one moment, we see it: glorious and terrible, its mighty body breaches the surface, leaving the coils of the water behind, and hangs suspended on the air, before crashing down on the waves and vanishing, as if we had not seen it at all.

I know it waits there still.

Acknowledgements

To begin with, I think the struggles of writing a novel must pale in comparison to being married to someone writing a novel. This wouldn't have happened without your unfailing love and support, Jon. You are the best husband (and dad to Jennifer) anyone could wish for. Thank you.

A huge thanks to my agent, Sam Copeland, for seeing the potential in my work and for all his sound advice. I'm in awe of Sam. I'm also grateful to Honor Spreckley and the team at RCW for everything they do.

Just as much appreciation goes to the team at Bloomsbury Raven. My editors Alison Hennessey and Katie Ellis-Brown added their insight and passion to the writing, and the book stands on the shoulders of their skills. Books don't make themselves either, so I would also like to thank Ella Harold, Kate Quarry, David Mann, Lilidh Kendrick, Sarah Bance, Phil Beresford, Emilie Chambeyron, Sarah-Jane Forder, Sarah Knight, Sarah McLean, Fabia Ma, Liffey O'Brien, and the incredible sales team at Bloomsbury. If I have left anyone off the list, it is entirely my fault.

One of the best things about writing, especially when you start, is that amazing people who love books and words often support you. Gratitude to Katherine Tansley, Joanne Rush, Gaynor Clements, Elizabeth Speller, and others who have offered their time and feedback.

Appreciation is due to Professor Quentin Skinner. I was just one more student passing through his seminars, but his passion will stay with me forever. A tiny fragment of what he knows about Hobbes and the English Civil War was borrowed for the themes of this novel.

For my family – Mum, Dad, Beth, Catherine, Alex, Annie, Mary, Emily, Lily, Susie, Louisa, Lydia and Florrie – I wrote a book and now I find myself lost for words. All families have a language no one else understands. When I say you are my strength and my treasure, I know that will be clear to you all.

Last but certainly not least, there is someone no longer with us who would have loved to hold this book. Whether he would have loved reading it is another question, but I've dedicated it to him because he gave me more than I can describe. Thanks, Grandpa.

A Note on the Type

The text of this book is set in Fournier. Fournier is derived from the *romain du roi*, which was created towards the end of the seventeenth century from designs made by a committee of the Académie of Sciences for the exclusive use of the Imprimerie Royale. The original Fournier types were cut by the famous Paris founder Pierre Simon Fournier in about 1742. These types were some of the most influential designs of the eight and are counted among the earliest examples of the 'transitional' style of typeface. This Monotype version dates from 1924. Fournier is a light, clear face whose distinctive features are capital letters that are quite tall and bold in relation to the lower-case letters, and decorative italics, which show the influence of the calligraphy of Fournier's time.